I0746484

ONE-ARMED BANDIT

ADVANCED PRAISE FOR ONE-ARMED BANDIT

"Saddle up for an absolute thrill ride!"
— *New York Times* bestselling author **Heather Graham**

"My kind of Western! Michael Knost's first foray into the Western genre is a fun read with a hero—*hero*?—Louis L'Amour never could have dreamed up—but revealing a deep love for the genre. Saddle up for a wild, unpredictable ride." — **Johnny D. Boggs**, 10-time Spur Award-winner

"*One-Armed Bandit* has more twists and turns than a snake with a bellyache. A very enjoyable tale of a rascal's attempt to stay within the law."
— **Michael Zimmer**, Wrangler and Spur Award-winning author

"You can almost smell bacon and sorghum cake in this disarming Western from Bram Stoker Award®-winner Michael Knost, where, on the run and on the take, a charming thief plays cat and mouse with the noose. With a posse of compelling characters, both nefarious and noble, and a showdown on every other page, *One Armed Bandit* is fast-paced fun. Recommended."
— **Lee Murray**, five-time Bram Stoker Award®-winning author
   of *Grotesque: Monster Stories*

"With his masterful skill to tell a complex story while making you feel deeply for the characters, Knost takes you on another wild ride. Using the perfect amount of Western ingredients, he creates a delicious tale through the eyes of an outlaw who is trying to find themselves again after a debilitating injury. Filled with wit, humor, and charm that gives so much heart, this is another hard one to put down by Knost. Western aficionados will be holding up stagecoaches to get their hands on this book. To Knost, the perfect way to show our gratitude is in the words of a particular single-handed desperado, 'I'm a thanking you, sir.'"
— **Ben Henry Bailey**, Will Rogers Medallion Award Winner

"Take a one-armed protagonist and throw him into a story with enough twists and turns to make anyone dizzy, a heap of colorful characters, stolen army horses and ten thousand buried dollars, and you have Michael Knost's first western novel. *One-Armed Bandit* is a wild and endlessly entertaining ride you won't soon forget."
— **Jeffrey J. Mariotte**, author of the Cody Cavanaugh western trilogy

"A court clerk and a bank robber become unwilling partners, as each has half the information needed to find a buried treasure. The hitch is that they refuse to trust each other. Knost reels out a fast-action adventure tale with surehanded, seamless writing . . . nimbly melding story twists and flashbacks. *One-Armed Bandit* will land on your "can't wait to finish" stack."
— **Vonn McKee**, Western Fictioneers Peacemaker Award-winner

"A riveting Western that will keep you entertained until the last page. Michael Knost captures the spirit of the Old West in a way that will have you clamoring for more—and Lawrence Thornhill, the one-armed bandit, is a likable rogue you can't help but cheer for."
— **Matthew Pizzolato**, Western author and host of *The Dusty Trails & Tall Tales* podcast

"Meet an entertaining cast of characters that will surprise and delight you, beginning with the main character Lawrence Thornhill, also known as the 'The One-Armed Bandit.' On the run astride his faithful donkey Daisy, Lawrence regales the reader with stories he lifts from his past and shares as we ride along on his adventures. I particularly enjoy the wisdom he shares and puts into action from his teachers—Charles, Ezra, and Aunt Alice. Take a deep seat in the saddle and ride along with the witty and spirited Lawrence Thornhill for an adventure you will long remember!"
— **Bobbi Jean Bell**, host *Rendezvous With A Writer* on LA Talk Radio

LAWLESS TRAILS PRESS is an imprint of

Hydra Publications
1310 Meadowridge Trail
Goshen, KY 40026

Lawless Trails Press affirms that **no** portion of this book—or any other title published under our imprint—includes AI-generated art, writing, or assistance of any kind. We are a proudly human organization, dedicated to publishing and compensating living, breathing creators: authors, artists, editors, designers, and all who contribute to the craft of storytelling.

Cover art by Julia Dreams.

ISBN: 978-1-958414-79-8

First Trade Paperback Printing: November 2025

ONE ARMED BANDIT

Bram Stoker Award-winner
Michael Knost

For my wife, Jewell
True to her name
Brighter still in my heart

Chapter One

I'd only met Ezra Tackett a month or so before I lost my arm during that second bank job in Topeka. You woulda thought we'd learned a lesson or two from the mistakes we'd made during the first one, and you woulda been flat-out wrong. But let me interject something here before I go much further: my arm ain't *really* lost, I know exactly where that useless thing's buried.

And don't go thinking I'm laying any blame on Ezra by bringing it up, neither, because that ain't the case at all. Why, truth be told, the rest of my sorry hide would more than likely be buried along with that decaying appendage had it not been for the quick thinking of Ezra Tackett.

"And yet here I am, rotting away in this miserable jailhouse."

"What?" the sheriff's voice muffled from the other side of the jailer door. Or at least that's what it sounded like he said.

"Don't mind me, I'm just quarreling at myself!"

They say I killed a man, and that's why I'm in this place. Now don't get me wrong, I'm not trying to say I didn't kill that poor Paddy—I'm just saying I don't recollect doing it if I did. But witnesses at the saloon say I was drunker than Cooter Brown when it happened and that I'd done what I'd done out of self-defense—even if it was a bit *too much* self-defense. Whatever the hell that's supposed to mean.

Sheriff Langford came in, making his way to the holding cell. "I said you've got a visitor."

"Visitor?" The heat in my chest moved to my neck and ears. "I ain't in no mood for some hellfire and brimstone preacher trying to convert my wayward soul."

Shaking his head, Langford nodded toward the door. "They finally caught up with you, Lawrence." He lifted his shoulders toward his ears. "Why didn't you tell me you were in the Army?"

My legs were a bit wobbly when I rose from the cot. "Have you been drinking?"

"I'd reckoned he had the wrong man when he first started asking about you, but he's got paperwork and everything."

"I have no idea what you're talking about. I was never in the Army—Union or Confederate."

Langford started back toward the door. "All I can say is everything he's presented is as official as you can get."

The stranger kept a hand on his campaign hat as he ducked through the doorway. The dark blue sack coat was set off impressively with five of the shiniest brass buttons I'd ever seen on a chest.

"Well, if it isn't Lawrence Thornhill," the soldier said, holding out his hands in dramatic fashion. "The One-Armed Bandit."

"Oh, that's funny right there. Makes me right sad that I can't clap my hands to show just how much I appreciate all your wit and humor."

"I'm glad you approve." A smirk lifted the man's left cheek. "After all, you're going to be exposed to all my *wit and humor* for the next three days as the two of us travel to Fort Hays."

I couldn't lay my finger on it, but the man carried a familiar scent—something like cigar smoke, clover quirlies, or something somewhere in between. "I don't understand."

"I'm Sergeant Jonathan Meade, and I'm here to escort you to stand trial for your military crimes and eventual court-martial."

"Are you not listening to me?" I stepped forward, grasping one of the bars. "I've never worn a uniform in my life. You've got the wrong man, I tell you."

The sergeant opened a document and focused on the page. "Your name *is* Lawrence Thornhill, is it not?"

"It is."

"Born to Wally and Martha Thornhill on August fourth, 1849, in Booneville, Kentucky?"

The dryness in my mouth made my tongue feel two sizes too big. "Now hold on just a doggone minute. How did you procure that information?"

Holding the document up for me to see, Sergeant Meade raised his eyebrows. "It's all right here in the paperwork you signed when you enlisted."

I eased back to the cot. "I don't know what's going on here, but I ain't going nowhere with you."

Smiling, Meade turned toward the open door. "Let's get him ready to transport, Sheriff." He glanced back my way. "You're *my* prisoner now, Thornhill." He folded the document and lowered his voice. "And if you so much as give me a thimble of trouble, so help me God, you'll end up *completely* armless by the time you finally make it to trial."

"Sheriff!"

"I'm afraid there's nothing I can do, son." Langford stuck his head back through the doorway. "The Army's authority supersedes those of us keeping law in these territories."

I wiped my hand down my leg. "I'm not lying, Sheriff. I've never been in no army," I said, gesturing toward the sergeant. "Check his paperwork again. You'll see that *ain't* my handwriting."

"I'm sorry, Lawrence, but it's out of my hands now." He jutted a thumb toward Meade. "Best thing you can do is follow that man's orders every step of the way."

The sergeant smiled. "Much obliged, Sheriff."

"I expect you brought your own shackles?" Langford started putting items into a small sack.

"I did, indeed. I'll fetch them directly."

"Here are all the belongings Thornhill was carrying when we locked him up." Langford held out the small sack. "There's also a report in there with my signature, detailing every item."

"I'll make sure it all gets properly turned in when we get there . . . including the prisoner." Meade folded down the sack's top and stole another glance at me. "I'll go fetch those shackles now."

"What do you need fetters for?" I held up my hand and gestured toward it with my head. "I ain't got but one arm, remember?"

"You still have two legs, don't you?" Meade made his way toward the door. "The chains will limit your gait—and weigh down that arm."

Once he was outside, I put my face between the bars. "Langford, I might be a lot of things, but you know I ain't no liar—and I swear to you, I've never spent a minute in the Army."

"I don't know what to tell you, son. Except all his paperwork is in order—and he has the authority to take you to be tried."

The midday glare was painful as the sergeant pushed me through the front door. "Once I get these chains on you, we'll get the donkey ready to . . ."

I turned to see what had captured his attention and found several men making their way toward the jailhouse. Lord knows I felt as though I was slipping out of the frying pan and staring straight into open flames when I recognized the two fellas from my trial.

Meade stepped in front of me, one hand grasping my empty shirtsleeve, the other resting for show on his sidearm. "Move along, boys. I'm in no mood for theatrics."

"The t'ing is this, officer. We don't have a quarrel with you," one of the leading men said. "But we ain't about to let you take that one-armed son of a bitch with you."

"You don't have a say in the matter, boy. I'm taking this prisoner to his court-martial in Fort Hays."

"That scum of a human being murdered our father," he said, gesturing between himself and the fella standing next to him. "And we don't intend on allowing him to leave before justice is served."

The silent brother stared straight ahead, his perennially gaped mouth revealing long, jutting teeth and a severely receded chin.

"Like I said, I'm taking this prisoner to Fort Hays to stand trial." Meade's fingers appeared to whiten around his Colt's handle.

"Do what's right and decent, sir. Turn that murderin' bastard over to us, and there won't be any trouble."

"Sheriff!" Meade didn't take his gaze away from the mob. "We have a situation out here."

"All you have to do is allow us to take that murderer to the nearest tree, and you won't have to worry about any paperwork or hassle or nothing."

"What has gotten into you boys?" Sheriff Langford had a shotgun pulled into the crook of his shoulder when he stepped outside. "Jarvis, you and Liam know damn well this man shot your father in self-defense. You were there and saw the whole thing yourselves."

"It don't matter a lick at all." The boy's face was gnarled with anger. "He killed our father, and we're gonna do the same to him."

"You fellas are going to be too busy stanching blood to worry about a lynching if you don't move along." Meade lifted his piece ever so slightly inside the holster. "This is my final warning."

The only thing I could do was try and make myself as small as possible behind the sergeant.

The group's spokesman stared at Meade for a moment, likely trying to read his intentions. "You don't understand." He gestured to the fella next to him. "That man *killed* our father."

"And *you* don't understand." Meade slowly removed his pistol from its holster. "I couldn't care less if the man killed the father of every one of you sons of bitches, he's heading to Fort Hays with me to stand trial. Do you hear me?"

One of the men on the far end moved as though he was going for his sidearm, and Meade fired twice, leaving that fella and another one on the opposite end of the group writhing on the ground with leg wounds.

Sheriff Langford eased a step forward, shifting his aim to each man still standing.

Screams and grunts came from those two fellas writhing on the ground as they groped at their legs, rolling and rocking in pain.

One thing I've learned while running with a pack of wolves over the past few years is just how easy it is to recognize farm dogs trying to pretend to be wolves. And there was no doubt the eyes and faces of all these fellas were yipping from just one nip.

"I will no longer waste what's left of my bullets on legs." Meade's voice was calm and composed. "Walk away now, or your stiffened corpses will have to be carted away."

"Get those two men some help before things get worse." Langford shook his head. "You don't want the Army coming after you fellas."

The spokesman's defeated gaze moved to the ground before returning to Meade. "Please, sir." He wiped at his mouth. "If that man had killed your father—"

"My condolences to you and your brother," Meade said, maintaining his bead on the boy. "But you have to realize I have orders to bring this treasonous bastard back to Fort Hays to stand trial for his crimes. And that's *exactly* what I intend to do."

The boy's gaze dropped to the ground again. "I understand." He removed his hat and wiped a grimy sleeve across his forehead before turning his attention back to Meade. "Would you at least grant me a few words with the murderer?"

The sergeant stared a moment before lowering his pistol midway. "Say what you want from where you stand, but make it quick. We need to get moving."

Craning his neck to see past Meade, the man pointed at me. "You're gonna pay for what you did, T'ornhill." His words came through gritted teeth. "If the Army lets you go, we *will* find you and deliver justice."

"You boys know damn well I didn't kill your old man." The words were out of my mouth before I could stop them. I admit it wasn't the smartest thing I've ever done, considering I was an unarmed prisoner with nowhere to hide.

"We witnessed you doing it!" the man said, leaning forward so quickly that Meade brought his Colt back into aim.

I offered a sympathetic smile. "What's your name?"

"Jarvis O'Sullivan." I'm telling you, that boy looked as though he'd literally spat the words at me.

"Like I was saying, Jarvis, I didn't kill your old man." I smirked and cocked my head. "That drunken jackass took his own life the very moment he threatened mine."

O'Sullivan's face turned as red as a beet as he lunged toward me. "You son of a—"

The sheriff's shotgun blast into the air stopped every one of them where they stood.

Grabbing my shirt, Meade pulled me away. "If you men do not disperse at once, I will have no other choice but get your names from the sheriff so that when I return with reinforcements, we'll take every one of you into custody for interfering with government procedures." He shoved me against the building while maintaining his aim on O'Sullivan. "Do I make myself clear?"

Chapter Two

Meade had to take the leg clasps off my feet in order for me to ride, so he wrapped the chains around my waist and attached all four clasps to my one arm.

The irons were rusty and bit into my skin something awful. And it didn't help none that Meade tied the blasted things to the donkey's saddle horn so tight that I had to hunch forward the whole way.

"I think it's hilarious that you have me riding an ass . . . and yet your roan there is carrying the biggest ass in these parts."

Meade's gaze never wavered from the trail in front of him—as though he hadn't even heard a word I'd spoken.

"You'd think the Army would have sent one of them tumbleweed wagons to transport such a heinous criminal like myself. Riding in a traveling cage would have to be more comfortable than being bound to the back of this lop-eared beast."

"Do you ever shut up?" Meade didn't turn toward me—didn't even slow the pace. "You've been going on now for over an hour."

Sitting up as much as I could, I stared into the back of his head. "I apologize, Sergeant. I've been told I'm an unbearable chatterbox when I get accused of crimes I did not commit—or coerced into believing I'm something I'm not."

He glared back at me. "I'd advise you to stop provoking me." His eyebrows rose so high they disappeared in the shadow of his hat's brim. "I'm in no mood for your nonsense."

"Nonsense? I'll tell you about nonsense if you'd like. Nonsense is a fella getting hauled off for a trial and a court martial that has absolutely nothing to do with him. *That's* nonsense."

Meade turned back toward the trail ahead. "We'll see about that. In the meantime, keep your mouth shut until I tell you to speak."

I'd never been to Fort Hays before, never even been near it, so I didn't know what to look for or how far away it was. But I kept my attention to the plains and hills for natives—not that I could have done much if we were attacked . . . I mean, I was unarmed, shackled, and tied to a donkey, after all.

And this whole time, I couldn't help but wonder if Ezra was still in jail. I'd heard he'd been arrested for stealing horses a little further south, and that they were aiming to hang him for it. But that was weeks prior, and I hadn't heard anything about him since.

Now you think about that—I flat out killed a fella, and they were contemplating setting me free—at least until the Army laid their claims. And yet they want to hang poor Ezra for taking an animal without paying for it. Now I ain't saying he's innocent—I'm just saying the penalty between killing a man and stealing a horse seems a bit cockeyed if you ask me. But don't get me wrong, I ain't complaining nary a bit that they didn't hang me, mind you.

Fact of the matter is I hadn't seen hide nor hair of Ezra since we went our separate ways a few years after that terrible day.

We lost James and Charles in that fiasco. And a few others were injured as well. None as bad as me or my dearly departed appendage.

We all knew the plan. After all, it was the same plan we'd used in all the other jobs we'd worked together.

Ezra and I were positioned outside the bank, making sure the fellas working inside didn't get surprised by anyone entering the building unawares.

Well, everything went sideways when some fella come running out of the bank, screaming his dang head off, and heading right towards me and Ezra. Before we even had a chance to react, James stepped out from the bank, drew his Colt, and dropped the fleeing man with one shot.

'Course, all hell broke loose at that moment. Because, as our luck would have it, the sheriff and his deputy just so happened to be strolling toward the location at that very moment and started firing.

We ducked into cover—Ezra under a stationed buckboard to the left, and me behind a pile of stacked timber to the right.

Now they were obviously shooting at James, mind you, and I don't reckon they suspicioned Ezra and me, nor any of the other citizens milling about, of having anything to do with James shooting that fella as he fled the premises.

Then Ezra started firing at the lawmen, doing what he could to give James a few moments to find cover. Well, when those fellas started aiming toward Ezra, I laid into shooting too.

I distinctly remember my elbow jerking from a bullet's impact and then not being able to hold my piece. The useless arm dropped to my side, the Colt to the ground.

The strangest thing of all was that it took several seconds before the pain came on me like a forged fire. The searing only intensified when I went to move.

Somehow, Ezra wrapped everything to cease the bleeding, got me on my horse, and led me to a doctor somewhere far away while the fighting moved inside the bank. Apparently, everyone was so focused on the gunfire, they paid us no mind as we high-tailed it out of there.

"We'll camp near those rocks just ahead," Meade said, pulling me from the memories. "Food and sleep—then get back on the trail first thing in the morning."

"Where are we?"

"Remember when I told you to keep your mouth shut until I said you could speak?" He gently kicked his roan's side. "That still applies."

The warmth of the campfire was about the only thing I was thankful for out in the middle of nowhere—especially having no idea where that *nowhere* was.

Meade somehow managed to burn the beans, and I honestly thought the hardtack was made from chunks of coal. And may the good Lord strike me dead if that scalded smell wasn't in my mouth just as much as it was in my nostrils.

"The least you could do is loosen these manacles so I can reach my mouth to make sure I haven't broken any teeth on this grub."

Meade shoveled in another spoonful without even looking at me.

"You know I'm not going to be able to escape with these blasted things back on my ankles."

"Tell me something, Thornhill." He wiped his mouth with the palm of his hand. "When you and the Johnson Bandits got split up during that last bank robbery, where did you and Ezra Tackett go while James and Charles were getting themselves shot all to pieces?"

I'm not sure how he knew those details, but I wasn't about to give any information that may or may not be used against me later. And Lord knows the fellas hated how the newspapers named us as bandits and not a gang. "What are you talking about?"

For just a moment, he put me in mind of a grinning bobcat. "You no longer have to hide anything, son. In fact, I just might be able to help you out of your mess."

The shackles jangled when I lifted my arm toward him. "I can't think too straight with this thing rubbing my wrist raw."

His grin became less threatening. "I don't have a problem with taking it off your arm, Thornhill. But I make you this promise: I will *not* hesitate to deliver a corpse to Fort Hays if I'm forced to do so."

"I won't give you any trouble." I stole a quick glance at the clasp on my chafed wrist before meeting his gaze again. "I promise."

Rising to his feet, Meade came closer and reached for my arm. "All right. Now tell me where you and Ezra went when you got shot."

A breeze washed over us, swirling campfire smoke and dust.

"I don't rightly know," I said, rubbing my freed wrist against my shirt. "I'm here to tell you, I was about out of my mind from the pain, which caused some kind of fever."

His gaze bore through me. "I'll not stand for falsities. You'd best tell me the truth."

"I'm telling you the God's honest."

"That might be the case." He moved to sit back down. "But you're not telling me *all* the truth."

I dropped the hardtack to my plate. "I was out of it when Ezra took me to the doctor. In fact—"

Meade held a hand up for me to be silent, his attention focused on the surrounding darkness. The horse and donkey made abrupt movements, spurring Meade to draw his piece.

I searched the night, trying to identify whatever spooked him. "What's—"

His gaze still roamed our surroundings when he shushed me with a forefinger over his lips.

I noticed the quiet for the first time as a sourness clenched my stomach, churning up gurgles and growls like I'd never heard.

Meade slowly rose to his feet, holding the revolver up and ready, his gaze scanning the cold blackness around us.

With a soft breeze and no sound or warning whatsoever, more than a dozen Kiowa Indians crept into the campfire light from all directions, weapons focused on the two of us.

Chapter Three

When Ezra put me on that horse and we traipsed off to find a doctor, he said it was to save both our lives. And there ain't a doubt in my mind we would have both ended up dead just like the others if we'd stuck around longer than we did.

Now I wasn't all there in the head, mind you. Lord knows I was going in and out of it like I was on some kind of peyote bender. But Ezra kept talking to me, telling me it wasn't too much further and to hang on.

I don't remember when we got to the doctor's place, and I don't exactly remember him saying much, but I do remember the old man telling me the arm was going to have to go if I wanted to live.

I found out later his father and brothers ran the local sawmill, and that he'd worked there some when he was younger. Well, I'm here to tell you that sawmill must have been where the old pill got his doctoring papers.

"Are you sure?" At least that's what I think I said . . . and if it wasn't, it's what I *should* have said. It's a thousand wonders I can remember anything after all the whiskey those two kept pouring into me.

"You can choose to save your arm," the man had said, rolling up his sleeves. "Or you can choose to save your life—unfortunately, you *cannot* choose both."

Now I don't remember making a choice, but I sure as hell remember waking up the next morning with barrel fever and pain like I'd never experienced.

It didn't take long to realize I'd lost more than just my arm during the bank altercation. To be honest, I lost my family. Those men in the gang meant more to me than any flesh and blood. I know that may sound strange and all, but when a man gets around like-minded fellas, and those men are looking out for you, it's easy to look out for them as well.

I reckon Ezra was the closest thing I ever had to a faithful brother. And it appears now that I'm about to lose him to the gallows. I ain't too proud to admit it, but if I was a praying man, I'd sure be directing my prayers toward him as hard as I could.

But I wasn't so happy with Ez at the time. No sir. Not after he started pushing for me to get out of the bed once I'd healed up enough and get back to normal—if you want to call our chosen occupation *normal*.

"I know it was your good arm—your shooting arm." Ezra's smile always made him look like he was hiding something. "But you're going to have to teach yourself to make *that* arm your good one now."

"What are you getting at?" I remember asking. "You know good and well I'm as worthless as a stack of wildcat banknotes now."

"Hush that kind of talk right this minute. You'd best get over this feeling sorry for yourself and get to moving around, learning how to make do with that one good arm."

"I just want to lay here and—"

"Absolutely not!" Ezra yanked the quilt off me and shook his head. "You're not going to just lay there and wither up. By golly, you're going to get out of that bed and make an effort to live."

He was right, of course. But I sure didn't want to admit it in the middle of my angry spell. In a way, I reckon Ezra Tackett saved my life twice.

Even the crickets ceased their rhythmic trilling when the Kiowas slinked into the firelight.

Meade dropped his piece and surrendered his hands quicker than a cat running away from a thundercrash. I can't say that I blamed him—after all, I was hoping those savages would realize I only held one hand in the air because I didn't have another one to offer.

"Let's all take a deep breath here," Meade said in a soft voice. "And see if we can simply talk this out."

A few of the savages started babbling on to one another in a language I surely didn't understand. But it appeared Meade had an idea of what they were saying, as he nodded and smiled at every gibberish utterance they made.

"No, I am only passing through." He briefly gestured toward me. "I'm taking this prisoner to Fort Hays . . . far away from here," he said, gesturing with his hands. "There are no others like me nearby."

There were a few moments where they stared at Meade, and he stared back at them before he commenced to speaking a shaky version of their gibberish.

One Indian stepped forward and spoke directly to Meade, still using his native tongue. He pointed in a particular direction at one point, and the only words I recognized out of his mouth were the awkwardly pronounced Fort Hays.

Even I could tell Meade was butchering their language, and I don't know the first thing about any of it. But it didn't seem to bother those Indians. In fact, within a few moments, they all lowered their weapons and moved closer as the sergeant pulled out a few bottles of whiskey and a handful of stringed glass beads from his saddlebags. "Here, pass these around." He must have said the same in their language as he handed the items to the one who'd spoken to him.

That same Indian said something to a few others, and they handed him a couple of furs, of which he turned and presented to Meade with a stern nod.

Meade said something to them in their tongue. And if I was a betting fella, I would have wagered everything that he'd thanked them.

The leader of those savages stepped closer to where I sat, staring down at me with that same stern countenance. At first, I thought he was addressing me when he spoke, but Meade quickly answered in their language.

"What's he saying?" I asked, turning to the sergeant.

"Keep your mouth shut if you want to live."

The savage squatted next to me, examining my empty sleeve like I was a side of beef he was interested in purchasing. He then spoke again.

I stole a glance at Meade, whose face had soured.

The Indian gestured at my empty sleeve and broke into more gibberish.

The sergeant's eyes narrowed on me. "He wants to know how you lost your arm."

"Tell him I got shot," I said, before turning toward the Indian. "By one of my own people."

Meade's glare was immediate.

"Go on. Tell him."

Taking hold of my chin with his forefinger and thumb, the savage leaned closer. "You say *white man* do this?"

Meade looked as though he'd just swallowed a tainted oyster.

"That's right," I said. "And now they're trying to—"

"You do realize this man was robbing a bank when—"

"Hold tongue!" the savage said, turning toward Meade. "Let this one speak."

I waited until the Indian turned back to me. "It was indeed a white man who did this." My voice rose in spite of my gritted teeth. "And now they're trying to send me to prison because they say I'm one of *them*," I said, pointing at the sergeant. "But I am not in their army."

Rising to his feet, the Kiowa nodded toward me. "We take."

Meade's gaze moved from the Indian to me and then back to the Indian. "Take what?"

The Indian moved toward the sergeant. "Remove chains."

As though on cue, the other Kiowas closed in without a sound.

"You better do what he wants," I said, trying not to laugh. "He don't look much like a jokester to me."

As we rode, I wasn't sure if I was a prisoner or if those Indians was riding as hard as they were in an effort to lose me. But not one of 'em made any effort to speak to me. Hell, not one of 'em even looked my way.

I swallowed more dust than a hoot owl coal miner trying to keep up. It felt good to be free, but I couldn't help but wonder what they were planning to do with me once we got wherever it was we were going. I'd heard all the atrocities and savagery about the Kiowas. I ain't going to lie about it, I worried I may have made a terrible mistake and should have just kept my foolish mouth shut.

Everything happened so fast I didn't know what exactly was going on, especially since I couldn't understand a word any of them were saying. But at least they let Meade live, telling him to go back to his people and leave theirs alone.

When the savages slowed their pace, I thought it was so me and that ambling donkey could catch up, but they appeared to be stopping. I got a little nervous about the whole thing when I realized we weren't stopping anywhere near a camp or anything. We were right in the middle of nowhere.

The one that did all the talking sidled his horse next to me and pointed toward the right. "Fort Hays that way." He then pointed in the opposite direction. "You go that way. No stop at first town."

"You . . . you're letting me go?"

He reached toward another Kiowa, who handed him a couple of items. "Since you no trust blue coats," he said, handing me my bag of personal items the sheriff packed. "You no enemy to our people."

"I'm a thanking you."

He also handed me a bladder of water and Meade's gunny sack

with what remained of the hardtack and jerked beef. "No stop at first town."

"I sure appreciate . . ."

They just rode off like I wasn't even there. I reckon they turned me loose on account of me being gimped and all, but I'd sure like to think it was because they viewed me as an enemy of their enemy.

Taking out the sack the sheriff gave Meade, I noticed everything was still there. Not that I didn't trust the sheriff or them savages, to be honest, but as for Meade, how can you trust a man who's trying to take you in for a court-martial when you ain't never served?

Bless Langford's soul if he didn't include that letter he mentioned with a list of every item accounted for—the knife, Colt, seven cartridges, gloves, and my trusty thousand-mile shirt. But I'll be right honest with you, I was surprised to find the twelve dollars still there after going through so many hands.

It was good to get to ride at a slower pace, but I'll be dogged if I hadn't felt a mite safer riding with all those cutthroat savages than I did following a dry trail all by my lonesome.

I kept checking over my shoulder to make sure Meade wasn't sneaking up behind me. I never could figure out what the U.S. Army wanted with me in the first place or why they wanted to court-martial a fella who'd never enlisted in the first place.

The trickling of the creek caught my attention before it came into view, and that donkey must have heard it as well when it perked up and broke into a trot straight for the water.

Finishing off what remained in the bladder, I swung down from the creature to refill. "Drink all you want, Daisy." I rubbed the donkey's side before digging out the gunny sack. "You deserve every drop you get."

The morning sunlight bore down on us like a wet blanket—a suffocating heat that clung to the body and soul.

The donkey showed no signs of letting up when it came to guzzling.

"You're gonna founder yourself if you don't slow down." I took hold of its harness and pulled the beast away from the water. "I didn't mean for you to drown your fool self."

Blowing water from its nostrils, the donkey stared at me as though I'd just slapped it in the head with a dead rabbit.

I took out some hardtack and did my best not to break a tooth by softening the dang things in my mouth with water. Daisy foraged for a while and drank more water that I had to again pull her away from. I don't believe for a minute that creature would have stopped on its own.

Smoke rose in the quiet distance, threatening to conceal the rising sun.

"We better get to moving." I stowed the gunny sack and bladder. "That's a town not too far off—I reckon the same one that Indian warned us about."

"That savage obviously didn't warn you about *all* the dangers out here."

I heard the pistol's hammer being pulled back before I could turn all the way toward the voice.

"I told you we'd come after you, ya son of a bitch," Jarvis O'Sullivan said with a smirk. His buck-toothed brother was next to him, mouth agape as usual. "Now get your hands up."

I shook my head as I held up my arm. "That's hilarious." My anger was more at myself for not paying better attention to my surroundings any better. "You ought to join one of them traveling shows the next time one comes into town."

"Liam, get the rope." Jarvis gave me a smile that was anything but a smile. "We thought those Indians were going to rob us of seeing you hang, T'ornhill, but I'm glad they left you for us so we could finish what we started right here and now."

"Listen, fellas." My chest tightened up like I was breathing in heated gaslight fumes. "You should know that your pa and me were too drunk to know where we were that night, much less what we were saying or doing." I shook my head. "And I'm real sorry for what happened, but to be fair, I'm told he started shooting first."

Keeping his pistol aimed at me, Jarvis took a step forward. "You slipped out of the hands of the sheriff, slipped out of the hands of that

Army sergeant, and then slipped out of the hands of those savages. But you ain't about to slip away from us this time."

"Listen—"

"I can't find the rope," the slack-jawed brother said from beside his horse.

Jarvis rolled his eyes. "It's in the saddlebag on me horse."

"I thought you said it was in *my* saddlebag."

"Liam, for the love of God, would you just listen to me for once?" He glanced back at his brother for the briefest of a moment. "Just come over here and keep an eye on him while I get it myself."

"I can get it, but I could have sworn you said you'd put it in me saddlebag."

"Just come over here." Jarvis's face reddened. "And keep your pistol trained on this bastard while I fetch the rope."

Liam O'Sullivan held his aim on me and stared without any emotion or movement. I'm not sure if his open mouth and receded chin made it seem that way or if he was just there doing what his brother told him to do.

"But I could have sworn you said you'd put the rope in me saddlebag," Liam said, looking back toward his brother.

I was so surprised that he'd turned his attention away from me that I didn't react right away. And then I realized neither one of them had taken my pistol.

Liam was just starting to turn back to me when I quickly drew my Colt, cocked the hammer, and squeezed the trigger in nearly one motion. The gun's report sent Daisy into a panic, but I was able to catch her, somehow mount in the movement, and sped off as Liam tumbled to the ground, clutching a bloody shoulder.

Jarvis fired in our direction but missed both shots as Daisy took to a gallop to get us away from the exchange.

It wasn't much of a town to speak of, but it had a couple of saloons, which were hard to pass if you want to know the truth about it.

Didn't seem like anybody paid much attention to me at all. Everybody was too busy doing one thing or another, going somewheres, or just lost in their own thoughts.

But I suspected that Indian's warning had some kind of reasoning behind it. So I kept riding, continuing to scan the area for any surprises that might lie ahead. I can still hear Charles harping on about it: "If we're going to be successful," he'd say, "we need to find all the surprises before they actually become surprises."

I reckon his lectures took hold more than I realized, as I found myself following his precautions to the letter at every moment. Every movement, every person, and every detail had to be noted. And that's what I was trying to do to the best of my abilities. Charles used to say certain details distracted me. Said I was prone to missing things because I focused too much on those that stood out.

Lord knows if I'd been paying more mind to that advice, the O'Sullivan brothers wouldn't have caught me off guard. And those fellas gave me even more reason to keep moving, but I figured James's wound would send them back home or at least slow them down a great deal.

The streets in town weren't too busy, but people was out and about, especially at the stage station.

I made sure it appeared as though I was gazing in another direction when I caught sight of a fancy stagecoach while riding by. And talk about fancy, the man and woman who were climbing inside that carryall were gussied up like they was some kind of royalty or something. Lord knows there must have been four leather-covered trunks tied to the roof.

Why, if there woulda been a strong enough wind, I bet you five dollars square you coulda smelled the money.

But I didn't let on that I even noticed there were other people anywhere near me. I just kept my pace through the town, keeping to myself as best as I could.

Coming up on another saloon, I noticed the reason I wasn't supposed to stop—what appeared to be three soldiers stood near the entrance just talking and laughing. Nary a one of 'em seemed to be aware of anything around 'em, including me. Thankfully.

I kept myself turned in the saddle in such a way that if those men looked in my direction, they wouldn't notice anything out of the ordinary—specifically that there was a one-armed fella riding by on a donkey.

I wanted to pick up the pace, but I knew that would only increase the chances of attracting attention. So I held Daisy to the same pace.

"Just be patient," I could hear Charles saying the words just as plain as day. "And don't draw any more attention than you have to."

Just quietly get out of town and find the closest place to stop on the trail.

"Hey, you!"

I acted as though I didn't hear the voice, hoping it wasn't directed toward me.

"You, on the donkey. Hold up!"

Glancing back, I could see one of the soldiers rushing toward me. I brought Daisy to a stop and rested my hand on my Colt's handle.

Chapter Four

"Just a minute," the soldier said, stepping next to Daisy and me. I was trying to calculate as to which of the men I would shoot first with this fella so close within reach and the others still at the saloon door.

"Here you go," the young private said, holding something out to me. "You dropped your gunny sack."

I eased my hand off the Colt, collected the sack, and quietly released a breath. "I'm a thanking you. Didn't even realize I'd lost it."

"No worries." His smile looked to have had more whiskey behind it than mere social graces. "I can't imagine you'd get too far without your provisions."

"That is true." I nodded and smiled. "Thank you kindly."

I had a time trying to read his expression. It was about like gambling with a few of the gang's stone-faced old-timers.

Glancing at the donkey, the private appeared as though he was about to say something else when one of his buddies called out to him about going back inside for another round. "Well," he said before staggering back toward the door, "duty calls."

The ruckus coming from the saloon sounded as though an entire platoon was having a real hog-killing time in there. The only difference between it and any other saloon I'd ever been in was there weren't nary a piano note to be heard.

I held the sack in my hand while moving on down the street—I wasn't about to waste any more time than I had to there in the open. My stomach burned, and I just wanted to be as far away from that place as I could get.

Seemed like I couldn't shake off the queasiness in my guts no matter how far away I rode. The whole thing was too much for me, just knowing I was no more than a whiskey breath away from putting bullets in those fellas. And God knows those bluebellies woulda never rested until they got their hands on me—and they sure as hell wouldn't have dawdled a bit at taking me to the nearest hanging branch. Lord knows they'd probably work together with them O'Sullivan brothers.

After half an hour or so, I couldn't hold myself any longer and stopped as far off the road as I could get to make water.

Any stops you take, be sure you are hidden from all roads or structures. I could hear that sermon-like voice Charles was known for. *Remember, you're always safer when you're completely out of sight.*

After my relief, I tied off the gunny sack and stood frozen when I heard rumbling coming down the road. I pulled Daisy closer to the cover and watched as the stagecoach I'd noticed earlier go by so fast it nearly bowed the tallgrass all the way to the ground.

While keeping watch on the road, I stumbled over some kind of small mound. It didn't appear to be fresh, but it also didn't look to have been there for a long period of time.

What caught my eye was a glinting from what looked to be gunmetal. Digging around in the dirt mass, I found the burnt remains of two rifle barrels and a Colt revolver.

I scanned the area again and brushed off more dirt. Somebody must have had some serious reasons to not want to be caught carrying them . . . that or they didn't want the firearms to show up in a courtroom for the same reasons.

Like I said, it was obvious the remains had been there for a little while, but not long enough for the metal to get all pitted or rusty. I brushed off everything as best I could and stuffed it all into the gunny sack.

"We're gonna have to make some money, Daisy." I patted the side of her neck and scanned the area again for movement. "And I've got myself an idea how to get us some."

It felt like I'd been in that saddle for days before we finally reached the next town. If you care to call it a town. I reckon it was more of a trading post with several structures around it. I'll say this about it: I don't recollect ever seeing a muddier place in all my life. And I've been to Deadwood, mind you.

I tied Daisy to the nearest post and rubbed her belly. "You sure are a fine one, girl." She looked a mite content with no more walking. Rubbing her nose, I tried to walk through the mud in such a manner as to not stumble or fall.

As if it wasn't muddy enough, storm clouds hovered over the buildings like vigilant turkey buzzards.

Inside the trading post, a big fella with the bushiest beard I ever laid eyes on stood near the back of the room. "Come on in," he said with a cough. "Get out of that god-awful muck."

"I'm a thanking you." I removed my hat just long enough to wipe my forehead with a sleeve. "And I promise I didn't bring them clouds with me."

A grin cut across his face just before a coughing fit took him over. "I can assure you," he said after catching his breath, "those damned clouds have been here for more than a week now, they have."

"Well, if you've got any luck at all, they'll probably follow me wherever I go."

The man's laughter broke into another coughing fit. "You and me must be kin of some kind." He wiped his mouth and inspected the bandana. "You looking for something in particular?"

Scanning the shelves to the left, I cleared my throat. "I'm in need of suspenders."

"I can help you with that." He made his way toward a shelf to the right. "In fact, I've a few different ones to choose from."

"Yeah?"

Holding up several pairs, he stepped closer. "Which of these do you like best?"

"Don't matter. What's the cheapest you got?"

"I reckon it would be these," he said, holding out a dark pair. "They're pretty sturdy. And I'll sell them to you for a dollar."

"I'll take 'em. And I'll be needing a spool of twine as well."

Moving toward another shelf, the man chuckled and fought off another coughing fit. "If the suspenders don't hold, you'll have a backup for your britches, I expect."

"Something like that." I glanced back at the door. "Any place to eat around here?"

"Oh yeah, just next door." He jabbed a thumb behind him. "Nothing fancy, mind you, but you won't go hungry."

The man's hands were big and rough-looking, as if the grime had somehow grown into the prints of his stony skin.

"Well, it's got to be better than old hardtack and jerked beef."

"Not a doubt," he said, accepting my money. His gaze wandered toward my missing limb before moving quickly back to my face. "What brings you to these parts?"

I've seen that expression a thousand times. The person notices the arm is gone, and then they snap their gaze back to see if I caught their prying eyes. "Just passing through," I said.

"Where are you heading?"

I studied his face a little longer, picked up the suspenders and twine, and turned to leave. "Next door to get me something to eat."

Thank the good Lord they had wooden planks stretched out to walk on, so you didn't have to slop through all that muck to get to the grub.

I caught a whiff of cooked bacon as soon as I walked inside that shack of a building. A man and a woman sat at a makeshift table, laughing and smiling until they turned to see who'd walked in.

Why you'd a thought I was packing a hornet's nest in there with an ill-tempered swarm about my head. The fella elbowed the woman next to him so she'd ungape her mouth.

"Be with you shortly," the proprietor said as he carried empty dishes out of the room.

"I'm a thanking you." I eased myself into a wobbly chair at a table as far away as I could get from the gawking couple.

Nobody left anything on their plates for me to get an idea of what was being served. I reckon that was a good sign, not to mention them aromas liked to have starved me to death they was so good. Either that or my smeller was dumbfounded after all the hardtack and jerked beef I'd been eating.

"I hope you're hungry," the proprietor said upon his return. He was wiping his hands on a towel and grinning.

I turned a bit to the side as to not show my empty sleeve. "I'm so hungry my stomach thinks my throat's cut."

He laughed so hard I worried he would break into a coughing fit like the fella at the trading post. "What can I get you?"

"You got pancakes?"

Swinging the towel over his shoulder, the man nodded. "Sure do."

"I'll get me a stack of them pancakes and some of that bacon I was sniffing when I came in."

"I can do that. How about some coffee?"

I nodded and smiled. "That'll do me just fine."

The couple glanced my way a few more times before making their way out the door, leaving me the sole patron.

"I ain't never seen a muddier place in all my life," I said to the proprietor's back as he cooked. "Is it always like this?"

Chuckling, the man moved a pan on the stove. "Only when it rains."

"Well, it must have rained forty days and forty nights." I leaned back in the chair. "Why, I'll bet there's somebody nearby building an ark just as we speak."

The rattling of pans reminded me of Ma cooking breakfast back in Kentucky. We was so poor we had beans and whatever else we could scrounge up in the woods for damn near every meal.

You'd think I wouldn't even be able to look at a mess of whistle berries after all I've had in my life, but I reckon the years of constant consumption has made me quite fond of 'em.

Ma would always put extra bacon and molasses in the beans when me and my brother Virgil would get scared at the dark of night. She called 'em gumption beans. Said they would ward off any haints and such.

"You passing through?" the proprietor asked, glancing over his shoulder. "Or maybe planning to settle here in the valley?"

"Mister, I don't even know the name of this place. For all I know, it's called Soggy Fork."

The man turned back to me and smiled. "Warren's Gap."

"Come again?"

"That's the name of our settlement." His eyebrows rose to join his smile. "Warren's Gap."

I near chuckled. "Who is Warren?"

"Ain't no Warren." He turned back to his labor. "That's just the name we came up with."

Them pancakes were better than I expected, but then again, I didn't expect much out in the middle of nowhere. The syrup was a little thick for my liking, but it sure was sweet.

"This bacon is delicious," I said, stuffing another slice into my yap. "What do you cook your bacon in to give it that flavor?"

He grinned. "Bacon grease."

"I reckon I asked for that." My stomach was making gurgling noises, but I wasn't about to let up on putting those vittles away. "I ain't sure if it's just been a while since having real food, or if this is the best I've had in a month of Sundays."

"Well, I'm sure glad it is to your liking."

Sunlight filled the room through unadorned windows, warming the skin to the point of grimy perspiration. I reckon the rain and mud intensified the heat like a kettle of boiling water.

A man caught my attention in the haze as he made his way across the planked walkway.

My stomach felt like I'd been kicked by a mule. "Can't be," I said, dropping my fork and scooting away from the window.

"Something ailing you?" The proprietor stepped closer as he followed my gaze out the window.

"Is that man coming this way?"

"Are you talking about Jonathan Meade?" the man said, gesturing beyond the window. "No, it appears he's making his way to his place out back. Do you know Jonathan?"

"He ain't wearing his uniform, but I recognize him."

"Uniform?" The man's eyebrows met at the bridge of his nose. "I don't think I follow your meaning."

Peeking out the window, I found Meade and his roan heading toward the back walkways. "How much do I owe you, mister?"

Going back the way I came seemed the reasonable course of action, considering everything that had taken place over the past few days.

I couldn't overlook the fact that Meade hadn't followed me into that settlement. But him showing up out of uniform, and that restaurant fellow saying the sergeant lived there, was a little more brain-addling than I was comfortable with. *Did he not notice Daisy when he came in?*

Knowing he more than likely wouldn't be heading back the way he'd just traveled gave me a morsel of relief, but I knew he very well could be following from a distance, setting me up for a trap.

After an hour or so of riding, the sun started setting, and I knew we were not too far from the place I'd gone through earlier—the very town that Indian warned me about. But I needed to get more money if I was going to find a decent place to sleep.

When I came upon the site where I'd found the rifle barrels, I guided Daisy around the brush and tied her to a sturdy sapling, making sure she was out of sight from the roadway.

I gawked about where the mound had been and kicked around for anything else that could be there. Checking out the bushes and tallgrass near the road, I realized there was a concealed embankment under it all, which helped create the perfect cover.

A distant rumbling carried a concentrated dust storm down the roadway as what must have been an approaching stagecoach. Moving back behind the cover, I pulled Daisy's bridle toward me to make sure she remained out of sight.

The stage drove by at a slower pace than I'd expected, with its team of horses barely at a relaxed canter. And the driver didn't seem to pay much attention or be on the lookout for possible problems.

Daisy bobbed her head at the noise, trying to pull away, but I managed to hold her steady, keeping her close and calm.

"Easy, girl," I whispered. "It's just a stagecoach going by. Nothing to worry about."

Once the noise faded into the distance, I released Daisy's harness and pushed back against the trees and shrubbery. That's when I noticed a hidden path that seemed just barely wide enough to ride through. The ground in front of the hidden entrance was an enormous rock slab, preventing tracks of any kind.

"Let's see where this leads us, girl," I said, untying the reins. "If the thicket gets too dense, we'll turn back."

I led her through at first, where the path was narrow with branches and foliage brushing up against us on both sides. Then it opened up a bit wider after a while, giving me room to climb into the saddle and press through.

My biggest concern was stumbling upon a rattler—or worse, bear cubs. The younger they are, the scarier they can be because bears are usually frightened off fairly easy—but a momma bear won't hesitate to maul your brains out if she thinks her babies are in danger.

The scent of fir came and went the further we drove, mixed with the smells of richer soil than what was normally found in the scorching sun.

After what felt like an hour or so, the path narrowed again and ended near the town that Indian warned me about.

"Well, how do you like that, Daisy?" I rubbed her neck and gawked around to see if anyone would see us come out from the brush. "This could pan out to be a mite easier than expected."

Chapter Five

I was still feeling right poorly when Ez and I finally left the doctor's residence. The pain wasn't all gone by any means at all, but soreness slowly replaced one kind of pang with another. And riding under those conditions made it nearly unbearable. I'll tell you this much, a fella sure doesn't realize just how important a limb is until it's gone. It was all I could do to just stay in the saddle.

We still had a bit of money from the job we'd done before the last one, but we knew we were going to have to do something soon if we were going to make it. We headed a little further west and stayed with one of Ezra's kin.

"Aunt Alice has some empty cans lying around out back," Ezra said a few days after we arrived. "Let's go set them up on the fence and practice some shooting."

I gave him the best angry face I could muster. "You trying to be funny?"

"Don't you start with your horse shit." He was shaking his head without even looking me in the eye. "I don't want to hear none of it."

"You know—"

"Or we could sit in the shade and chat with Aunt Alice all day if that's what you'd rather do," he said, lifting an eyebrow.

Now Ez knew what he was doing—don't think for a minute he didn't. Because although his aunt was a welcoming host, I swear to you that old woman could talk the ears off a billy goat. She was a kindly soul, no doubt about that, and a wonderful cook, but upon my honor to God, she'd ask you a question and then let into talking again 'fore you even had time to open your mouth.

I shook my head. "Let's set up the cans."

Lord knows everything I tried doing with my left arm felt like I was doing it for the very first time. Things that for years were just second nature, if you will.

"Try again," Ez said after my efforts missed the mark a dozen or more times.

"It ain't no use, I'm worse than a woman shooting with this arm."

Shrugging, Ezra glanced back at the house. "You want me to get Aunt Alice out here to show you how it's done?"

"You go right on ahead and keep provoking me."

His smile stretched further across his face. "Shut up and try again."

I knew there wasn't any use trying to argue with him. He'd just keep on until I either relented or stormed off. And even if I stormed off, he'd follow me with more of his needling.

Aiming the revolver out in front of me, I released a frustrated breath as my arm started trembling again from the weight. "I can't do this," I said, lowering the piece.

"Christ almighty, if you don't sound like a wailing infant." He pointed toward the cans on the fence. "Just fire the thing!"

My jaw ached something awful from clenching my teeth. "Damn you," I said, bringing the piece back up and aiming.

The pistol's discharge, along with the clank of metal down at the fence, seemed to come almost before I even squeezed the trigger, causing me to nearly drop the dad-blasted thing as a can flew up before crashing to the ground.

"That's it," Ez said with a better grin. "It's just going to take practice and patience."

"Lucky me," I said, getting the Colt back into its holster.

Ezra gave me a gentle smile. "Come with me. I wanna show you something."

An enormous rock jutted from the ground near the corner of the fence line. It was smooth and slanted toward the house.

"Apparently my grandfather squared off with Kiowas on this very rock when he and my family first settled here. As Pa tells it, the old man put several bottles of whiskey on this rock, and the next morning they were all gone. My family never had problems with the Indians after that."

"Sounds like your grandfather was a strong man."

"Pa said Grandad admitted he was scared, but he did what he thought was best and never gave up." There was pride in Ezra's smile. "He put whiskey bottles out on the rock every year with the same result."

"Smart man," I said.

"After Pa passed, I buried coins he'd given me next to the rock, right there in the front." It was obvious his smile wasn't meant for me. "And I've buried coins and items from Aunt Alice there as well."

I didn't know what to say, didn't know what to do. "It's a sacred place."

Ezra stared at the rock without moving. "It is," he whispered. "It's a sacred place indeed."

I checked in at the hotel just across from the stage station for a few nights and damn near spent all the money I had left. It wasn't nothing fancy or anything, but the food wasn't bad in the small restaurant.

I'd take my plate at the front window table every chance I got and watched the movement on the street, especially the activity with the station across the way.

It appeared they had two coaches on different schedules, so their customers didn't have to wait too awful long at any given time to get where they needed to get.

One of the drivers was a lanky fella wearing a dusty Bowler and clamping down on a cigar butt that looked as though it hadn't been lit in years.

The other driver was a portly fella with a coat that had to be at least two sizes too small for him. It usually took him a while to get up into the seat, and many times he'd just sit there waiting until everything was loaded and the horses swapped for the next trip.

Both reinsmen had rifles secured in their scabbards as well as revolvers on their sides. And both of them rode alone on the bench.

The fat man drove at a much more relaxed pace than the other fella, and he never seemed to rush or stress the horses. One thing I couldn't help but notice was that instead of using his neck to turn his head, this fella moved his whole body in the direction he wanted to view.

"Are you sure you don't want more coffee?" The woman's voice pulled me back inside the hotel's eatery.

"No ma'am, I reckon I've had my fill." Noticing I was the only customer in the room, I cleared my throat and moved to rise. "But thank you kindly."

"Sit as long as you like," she said, picking up the empty plate. "And if you want more coffee, just let me know."

Her smile seemed gentle, but there was something underneath it that told me she could stand up for herself should the need arise.

"That's an odd brooch you got there," I said, gesturing toward what looked to be a silver beetle on her collar flap.

"Oh, that belonged to my momma." She put the dish on the table and opened the two back wings to reveal a painted rose. "She gave it to me before she passed." Her eyes suddenly matched the sadness of her mouth. "My name is Rose."

Not knowing what to say or do, I just nodded. "Well, it's right pretty, ma'am. That much is for sure."

She seemed to realize she was getting emotional and closed the wings. "Thank you. It obviously reminds me of her," she said, reclaiming the plate and fork. It was her turn to clear her throat. "Will you be staying with us another night?"

I shook my head. "I'm afraid I have some business to tend to, but I just might be back in a day or so," I said with a forced smile. "I don't reckon I can stay away too long now after tasting the sorghum cake here."

She laughed while collecting the dishes and utensils. "We'll be sure to set aside a healthy slab for you when you come back."

Pushing my hat into place, I smiled again as I made my way toward the door. "Looking forward to it, ma'am. Thank you again for all the hospitality."

My thousand-mile shirt was a mite stiff after all that drying in the sun from the last rain. The dad-blasted thing smelled mostly like crusted cowhide . . . and was damn near as coarse.

I'm here to tell you, no matter how many handfuls of tallgrass I crammed into that right sleeve, there never seemed to be enough. I tied off the cuff and secured a stuffed leather gauntlet to the end to make it look like a real hand, filling the rest of the sleeve to the shoulder, where I tied that off as well.

I figured the middle of that hidden path would be ideal for setting everything up. After all, there'd be no one around to witness anything. But that don't mean I wasn't vigilant, listening for noises or scanning for movement around us.

We'd camped about a mile away for a few days to get everything prepared. I sure didn't want to draw any more attention to the hidden path than I had to with fire or anything. And it's hard to tell if the trail was made by someone or if it was just a well-traveled deer path.

"There we go," I said, pulling the shirt on over the one I was already wearing and then donning the overcoat over both. "What do you think, Daisy? Reckon it'll fool anyone?"

That cantankerous gal didn't even bother looking up from her foraging.

My favorite part of the whole ordeal was tying the gauntlet fingers around the grip of the burned revolver I found, making it appear as though the fake hand was actually holding the piece. The metal made the rig heavy, so I used the suspenders I'd recently purchased as a makeshift arm sling to hold everything in place.

Tying Daisy to a strong sapling just inside the hidden pathway, all I could do now was wait. Everything was in place—every detail had been studied over and over. Everything was settled except for my nerves. Lord knows I always got myself in an awful shape before a job, no matter how much planning and practice.

I reckon Charles would be right proud of me for all my preparation. Oh, who am I kidding? He would no doubt find something to quarrel about. But I reckon that's what made us better with each job.

Sweat started forming from all the shirts and that heavy overcoat I was wearing in the heat of the day, but according to my estimation, the fat man's team would be coming through just any minute.

Keep in mind, I ain't never done a job solo, so I had to do all the figuring for myself. That made me uneasy, that's for sure. It wasn't worry, just uneasiness. Charlie always said being uneasy is healthy—it means you're not overconfident or unprepared.

"Worry is another thing altogether," he'd say. "Worry never takes away tomorrow's troubles. It only takes away today's peace."

At first, I thought I heard a thunderstorm in the distance, and then I could see the dust cloud rolling toward me from far away. I took hold of the flour sacks I'd acquired from the hotel and wiped my forehead.

The closer the stagecoach got to me, the more I realized I should have made water beforehand. You'd think I'd know better by now. You'd think.

And just as I'd predicted, the team came in at barely a canter, slow and easy, just as this driver has kept them every time I'd watched. Just before the horses came into view, I placed the flour sack over my head and adjusted it to make sure I could see clearly through the holes I'd cut out for my eyes.

I finally stepped out into the road and fired a round into the air. "Hold it right there," I yelled in a growling voice while leveling my piece toward the driver.

The horses clustered together, trying to avoid what was in front of them as the fat man finally brought them to a halt.

"Hold your fire, boys," I yelled toward the barrels sticking out of the brush. "This fella knows he's surrounded!"

Putting his hands in the air, the driver looked as though he'd just swallowed a hunk of tobacco. "Ain't gonna have no trouble outta me," he said as his gaze moved toward the planted barrels. "No trouble at all."

"You keep your hands away from your revolvers and rifle, and you'll live to drive another day."

The man's face looked whiter than the flour sack I had over my head. "Like I said, you ain't gonna have no trouble outta me."

"Passengers, step out of the coach!" I glanced back at the driver. "How many are in there?"

"Five," he replied in a near whisper.

"Passengers, step out with your hands where we can see 'em." I bounced my gaze between the cabin door and the driver. "As long as you do as you're told, we promise no one will get hurt."

I continued using that deeper growl when I spoke so that no one would be able to recognize me by my voice later. I'll never forget the first time I heard Charles do it. It took me a spell 'fore I understood what he was doing, but I couldn't help but grin like a simpleton every time he did it.

A tall dandy with a thick mustache was the first to exit. He held onto his pristine derby as he descended the steps.

"That's it," I said, making sure my phony arm was pointing the burned revolver toward him while keeping the good one trained on the fat man. "Just keep them hands where we can see 'em."

"I have every intention to comply," the dandy said, turning without looking into my eyes. "But, if possible, I pray you grant me the courtesy of assisting our lady passengers as they disembark the coach."

I could have sworn I saw the driver roll his eyes. "Granted," I said. "But hurry it up."

Three women in all clumsily eased down from the door and started adjusting their hats and dresses. The last passenger was an older man who seemed to require the dandy's help far more than the women.

"Here," I said, kicking the other flour sack toward them. "Put all your money and valuables in that. And no dillydallying."

The dandy picked up the bag and finally gazed in my direction. "We will most certainly comply, sir."

The passengers were handing over items without protest, just not fast enough to satisfy me.

"You, too, fat man," I told the driver. "But I promise you this: if you so much as make one wrong move, the boys here will not hesitate to blow your fool head off 'fore you can even finish that move."

"Hand me the sack," he said to the dandy. The old fella did this without lowering his hands . . . and without taking his eyes off me. He wasn't going to do anything foolish, but I kinda enjoyed putting him through the stress to make sure of it.

"Empty the strongbox into that while you're at it," I said before turning toward the dandy. "Get the rest of 'em into the coach."

Once the passengers were back inside and the fattened sack was on the ground next to me, I aimed my revolver at the driver. "Get going now."

He didn't move his hands, just stared at me with a bewildered look on his face.

"Go on," I yelled. "Move!"

I waited until the team was nearly out of sight before heading back toward the hidden path. The flour sack was heavy, and that fact alone made me happy. But I didn't have no time to go through it to see what was there. I had to do some moving myself.

I was shucking the overcoat as I went, which is a right difficult thing to do for a man with one arm carrying such a load. I had to stop a moment and drop the sack in order to get the blam-jammed thing off. Then commenced to removing the thousand-mile shirt with the fake arm. Lord knows I was sweating like a worn-out racehorse.

When I got to Daisy, I hid the overcoat, rigged shirt, rifle barrels, and flour sacks in the middle of the thicket, as far off the path as I could get. The last thing I needed was to be caught with any of those items or for someone to happen upon them out here. 'Course I transferred the valuables into my own gunny sack so as to not attract any unwanted attention.

"We did it, girl," I said, rubbing her neck. "We actually did it." My belly had that queer movement it always got when we'd finished up a job and everything had went as planned. "Let's get into town and lay low for a spell."

I took out a room back at the same hotel I'd stayed at before, thinking it would be the last place anyone would consider searching for the road agents that robbed the stagecoach company just across the street.

And they would be looking for a gang after all, not a fella out and about all on his lonesome. Especially someone with a missing arm, since the robber who led the gang had all his limbs and barked orders from a growly voice.

Quietly pouring the valuables onto the bed, it was all I could do to keep my excitement from getting the best of me. I started separating the money from the jewelry and valuables and immediately began working out a plan in my head as to how to sell the items without exposing myself as a thief.

A few rings, necklaces, and even an intricate watch were among the items in the pile. Beautiful things that would likely fetch more money than was actually collected in the job.

A noise from the hallway caused me to sit quietly and pull the quilt's edge to cover the stolen items. My stomach rumbled as I rose to my feet and crept to the doorway, where I stood listening. After a moment, I opened the door and peeked out.

The empty hallway eased my stomach a bit, so I returned to the bed and began raking my fingers through the abundant haul.

My stomach took a turn for the worse when I noticed the silver beetle brooch.

"Well hell."

Picking up the decorative pin, I briefly glanced at the door. I didn't have to pull back the wings—I just knew. Sure enough, the painted rose was there when I finally checked. I closed my eyes and shook my head.

Slipping the beetle into a pocket, I slowly started dropping all the valuables back into the gunny sack, leaving only the money on the bed to count.

I tallied a little more than three hundred dollars in all. Hell, this was a better yield than a few of the jobs we'd done as a gang.

But the trick was most certainly going to be how I would be able to get money out of the valuables without giving myself away. More than likely, I'd need to travel a far piece so there's no chance of someone recognizing something from someone they know.

Lord knows my neck gets right itchy just thinking about the whole thing.

But that beetle in my pocket. I didn't even want to take it out to look at it again. The thing that really kicks me in the gut is the fact that I didn't even recognize the woman while it was all happening. I don't know if it was my nervous nature while doing the job, especially doing it all alone, or if it had more to do with trying to see through the flour sack, but I didn't recognize her at any moment.

Well, that's not important now, I reckon. But I'm gonna have to study about this a bit, that's a certainty. I'm gonna have to study on this one long and hard.

Chapter Six

For all of Aunt Alice's faults and quirky ways, that old lady sure knew how to cook. And I mean every meal was as delicious as you'd find in the finest eateries about. Now don't get me wrong, her faults weren't any worse than anyone else's, but she sure could hold her own. She was a robust woman, there's no doubt about that . . . both in size and spirit. I reckon that's why she talked so much. Lord knows she was always laughing and cavorting and cutting up like one of the boys. She sure knew how to make people feel welcome, that much is true.

I took a liking to her biscuits. She called 'em cat-head biscuits because they were so big and fluffy. Lord knows I'd eat 'em right out of the oven if she'd let me, but they was just as good cold later on in the day . . . that is, if they lasted that long.

Upon my honor to God, may He strike me dead if I ain't telling the truth. I ate more biscuits during that little bit of time we spent at her house than I had in my life prior to meeting her. Now that's the truth. But she also made sure the two of us was working for our keep, mind you.

"Ezra Dale, I need you to go into town for supplies." She leaned back in her chair and cut off a small hunk of tobacco. The front porch was dusty, but it seemed to always be dusty. Even right after sweeping the blasted thing.

"I can do that."

She plopped the hunk into her mouth and worked it with exaggerated movements that drew attention to what resembled the sparse whiskers of a teenage boy on her upper lip. "Go fetch the list I left on the table."

"Yes ma'am," he said, rising to his feet. At the door, he turned toward me. "You wanna go into town with me, Lefty?"

"You go on without him, son," she said to Ezra. "I need Lawrence to help with something else." She leaned forward and spat. "And stop calling him that God-awful name!"

She handed me the tobacco plug as Ezra rode off down the way. "Ezra's a good boy," she said with a concentrated smile. "He don't mean any ill will when he calls you . . ." She gazed down at her hands.

"I know that, ma'am." I cut off a piece of tobacco and handed the plug back to her. "To be honest, though, Ezra's done more for me than my own family has." I moved the chaw from one side of my mouth to the other. "Why, I wouldn't be sitting here today if it weren't for him."

"He gets that from his daddy, my brother, God rest his soul." She smiled more genuinely at this. "Gerald wanted to be a preacher but struggled with his letters." Her smile left her abruptly. "I reckon that wife of his drove him to struggle with a lot of things."

"Ezra's mother?"

Her eyebrows came down together over her nose. "Bottom feeder."

"Come again?"

"You heard me," she said, lifting her head. "That woman was nothing but a worthless bottom feeder." She leaned forward and spat again. "And for as bad as she was to Gerald, that woman was far worse to Ezra Dale."

"I had no idea."

"By the time the poor boy was six years of age, she'd run off with some businessman heading east." She nodded sharply. "Never said goodbye, never let on that she was leaving, and never once tried to check on her boy."

Wildflowers fragranced a slight breeze as the sun lingered overhead.

"That young'un cried himself to sleep near every night, wondering where his momma was. Wondering why she didn't want to be with him and his daddy." She gazed out into the field, but I could tell she wasn't looking at anything out there. "I blame that woman for what Gerald did."

I needed to spit but didn't want to move. "What happened?"

"He said he was going to shoe a neighbor's horse." She pursed her lips like someone does when they're trying to hold back tears. "I found him the next morning down past the hog pen with a bullet in his head." She closed her eyes. "Gun still in his hand."

"Jesus." The word came out before I could even stop it. "I'm sorry for your loss."

She finally looked up. "The worst part of the whole thing is that little boy grew up to be a man, knowing his momma didn't want him, and his daddy didn't have a reason to live."

"He's never mentioned any of this to me." I sat forward and cleared my throat. "That's an awful lot for a man to face, much less a young'un."

"Indeed," she said. "It is indeed."

"You'd think he'd be bitter or angry or something. But he don't let on that it bothers him none at all."

"I'll tell you, same as I told Ezra Dale," she said, placing a hand on my forearm. "The best revenge is to heal, move on, and refuse to be like those who hurt you."

I searched her gaze to see if she was reading deeper. "Those are fine words, ma'am."

"Lord knows they are easier to say than to live." She winked at me. "Cause that woman is still a lowdown bottom feeder if you ask me."

I welcomed the laughter and slapped my knee.

"Now," she said, moving to rise from the chair. "About that chore I needed you for."

"Yes ma'am?"

"I need some wood chopped for supper."

"I'll get right on it."

"Good." She gave me a sneaky grin. "I'll need a few cords, as I'm making a fresh pan of biscuits."

The hotel's restaurant was so busy I had to wait a spell to get a table. And even then, it wasn't the front window table I'd been observing from. Now that was just fine by me, as I hadn't planned on sitting there any longer. I didn't want to raise any eyebrows, if you know what I mean.

It smelled like a fat man's heaven in there with all the cooking going on. Reminded me of something my grandpa used to say after we'd devour supper, filling our bellies.

"Can you smell that?" he'd say with a grin.

"What?" us young'uns would answer.

"I can smell bacon even though the bacon is all gone. We done ate all the bacon, did we not?"

We'd laugh and nod.

"Ghosts," he'd say, widening his eyes. "It's the ghost of bacon!"

I was looking around for Rose, wondering if she was here today. And I didn't even know what I'd say to her if she was.

Reaching into my pocket, I held the silver beetle in my hand without bringing it out. It was cold and seemingly heavier than I remembered.

"Here you go."

I'm not sure what startled me more: Rose's voice breaking the silence or the motion of a plate sliding across the table in front of me.

"What's this?" I said, leaning back to inspect the dish.

"Sorghum cake." Her smile was a downright thing of beauty. "I did tell you I'd save you a slab for the next time you came in, didn't I?"

"That's right," I said, letting go of the beetle and retrieving my hand to tip my hat. "Thank you, ma'am."

"I'm sure you're gonna want more than cake for supper, but I couldn't resist bringing that out to you right away." She put a hand on my shoulder, and I'll be dogged if it didn't feel like my shoulder warmed at her touch. "How about some coffee first?"

"That'd be great."

The room started thinning out, and after eating the sorghum cake and a mess of beef stew, I stuck my hand back into my pocket and took hold of that beetle.

"Did you hear about the stagecoach getting robbed?" Rose said, collecting empty plates.

"Robbed?" I let go of the beetle again but left my hand in the pocket.

She nodded. "I was on the coach when it happened. I was terrified. There must have been five or six armed men."

"When was this? And why haven't I heard about it?"

"Yesterday," she said, reaching toward her lapel. "Took my silver brooch. You remember the beetle I showed you?"

"I do remember."

Tears welled in her eyes. "It was the only thing I had to remind me of Momma."

"Lord have mercy," I said, rubbing the back of my neck. "It's getting right dangerous out there."

Dabbing her eyes with a handkerchief, Rose released a noisy breath. "I'm so sorry. I'm just feeling poorly about the whole thing." She forced a smile. "I've tried to be strong about it all day, but it's just been the worst feeling in the world."

"I might it would." I didn't know whether to stand up, take her hand, or reach back into my pocket. "Hopefully tomorrow will be a better day."

The morning heat was dry yet somehow sticky. My shirt was already clinging to me, making my breathing something of an effort. It'd been two days since I'd done the job, and I hadn't been back to check on the items I'd left there in the hidden path. Lord knows I didn't want to get caught in the act of messing about in the area or with the items.

So I kept vigilant for anyone who might be watching or following travelers getting near the area. I stopped at a few places and went back the other way once just to appear as though I was out doing other things.

Once I was confident that nobody paid any mind to me and Daisy, we made our way to the path's closest entrance. Nothing looked disturbed or as though anyone had been sniffing around.

Stopping near the hidden entrance, I dismounted and acted as though I was trying to find a place to make water. I glanced in all directions, and when I was finally satisfied that no one was around, I pulled Daisy into the entrance.

"There we go, girl," I whispered. "Everything is fine. You know where we are."

A breeze rustled the foliage on both sides of us as we made our way toward the items I'd hidden away on the day of the job.

I didn't depart the path for the hiding spot right away, just in case someone was watching and waiting for the guilty party to return to get the materials. My stomach was burning something awful. But then again, satisfied that we were alone, I tied Daisy at the path and traipsed back to the spot.

My stomach settled a bit when I laid my eyes on the items, especially when I was able to confirm they'd been left alone, unmolested.

Taking hold of the thousand-mile shirt, I removed the gauntlet and burnt revolver before cutting the twine from the shoulder area. I started pulling out the wadded tallgrass, allowing it all to pile at my feet. The vegetation was warm and gave off a sour smell that lingered in my nostrils.

I wrapped the shirt around the overcoat, hiding it so it wouldn't draw attention if recognized by anyone who may have been on the stagecoach during the job. Then I loaded everything into the gunny sack and headed back to Daisy. Lord knows that donkey would have cleared another path with her foraging if I'd let her. I swear to you, she was worse than any goat I ever knowed.

I took a notion to head on out and exit the path from the end where I did the stagecoach job, watching and listening the whole way. That damned sour smell was still clinging to me something awful. For the life of me, I don't recollect it stinking like that when I first stuffed the sleeve.

Just before closing in on the mouth of the path, I stopped and listened. I coulda sworn I heard a rider coming down the road at a slow pace. I held Daisy's head and stroked the side of her face, which usually made her stop moving. It kinda reminded me of how a kitten will seize up and become downright lifeless if you pick it up by the nape of its neck, just like it does when its mother carries it from one place to another.

There was no doubt I was hearing a rider heading toward us, slowing down as if searching the area for something . . . or someone. Sweat threatened to run into my eyes, and that burning returned in my gut. Lord knows my mind went straight to them O'Sullivan boys.

Through the foliage, I could see a fella on his horse, but the dad-blasted sun was positioned in such a way that the man was just a shadow figure. But he'd stopped in the road and was, it sure as hell looked to me like, staring in my direction.

Dismounting, the fella searched the road toward where he was traveling and then scanned the way he'd just came from. He was quiet and calm, downright deliberate in nearly every motion. I still couldn't make out his face or features, but I had a suspicion I was about to meet the bastard if he kept coming this way.

My stomach really started burning when he took to kicking around the area where I'd found the buried rifle barrels and revolver. Then he gazed right towards me. I let go of Daisy and put my hand on my piece. If I didn't know any better, I would have sworn he was able to see me through all the foliage. *Shit*.

Easing toward the hidden entrance, the man glanced at the ground and reached up to pull back the vegetation.

"I'm gonna need you to put them hands up," I said, pressing my pistol's muzzle against the fella's forehead. "You so much as *squint* the wrong way, and I'll make it look like a grizzly mauled you to death."

I could hear Daisy back to her foraging like nothing was going on.

"Back up real slow," I said to the man, moving with him while maintaining the muzzle against his head. "That's far enough."

"Well I'll be damned," the man said, his face coming into view. "If it ain't Lawrence Thornhill, the—"

"Don't say it," I said, pressing the muzzle harder against his head. "Don't you say it, you son of a bitch." His smile vanished quickly. "Is your name even Jonathan Meade?"

"I was sure those Indians had taken you out somewhere and left you for dead."

"Them Indians saved my life, the way I see it." I lifted my chin. "You were taking me to my damnation under falsities and you know it."

"That's not entirely true." A trickle of sweat moved down his nose and hung there a moment before dropping.

"The hell it ain't. You know good and well I wasn't in no army." I glanced at his shirt. "And where's your damned uniform anyway, you chickenshit?"

Meade smiled. "When Parnell said there was a one-armed man asking about me, I couldn't believe it."

"Parnell?"

"The man who owns the eatery you were at," he said, slowly lowering his arms.

I cocked the revolver's hammer, shocked that I hadn't done so already. "Ain't nobody said nothing about dropping them hands, now did they?"

"Look, can we sit down and talk this over?" His arms looked to have gotten a mite shaky from holding 'em up for so long. "I swear I'll tell you the whole story. I was going to tell you everything that night anyway, but the Indians took my chance before I could do it."

"I ain't interested in your sob story." I spat off to the side, hoping to get that sourness out of my mouth. "I just want to go my way without having to worry about you following me."

A breeze washed over us, but it was so warm it didn't do us a bit of good.

"Tell you what, if you hear me out about why I came for you, I swear to you I will never seek you out again." His eyebrows lifted.

"And if we happen to meet somewhere by coincidence, I'll move along right away."

"You know I can't trust you."

"I know that. And you have every right to feel that way, but I promise if you'd just listen to what I have to say, you'd see the situation much different."

"I tell you what." I glanced at his belt for a moment. "You drop them pistols to the ground, without giving me a reason to shoot you, and I'll study on it."

"Sure. I can do that."

His gaze never left mine, but he wasn't staring at me in a cocksure manner. No sir, his stare was there in hopes of studying my face out of fear. He wanted to see if he could discern any fatal intentions on my part.

"I'm gonna do one at a time," he said in a calm voice. "That way you don't get unwarranted suspicions."

"Just drop 'em, you jackass."

He brought down his right hand as slow as molasses poured in winter. Using just his pointing finger and thumb, he pulled the first pistol out of the holster and dropped it. He done all of this while still maintaining his gaze on mine.

"Good boy," I said with a nod. "Now the other one."

Lifting his hand back up, Meade started lowering his other one. With the same motions, he dropped the second revolver and returned that hand back in the air.

"All right, Meade. What is it that's pressing on your mind so much that you want to air out?"

"Can I put my arms down?"

"No. Just start talking."

"What if I told you it's about Ezra Tackett?"

Coldness moved into my chest and shoulders. "What the hell are you talking about?"

Nodding, he offered a pained expression. "Just let me put my hands down, and I'll tell you the whole story."

Chapter Seven

"Go on," I said, maintaining the muzzle against his head. "Tell me how you know Ezra Tackett."

"It's a long story." He nodded toward his upheld hands. "And my arms are getting downright shaky."

His face seemed a mite whiter than usual, and beads of sweat spread everywhere. "You can put 'em down," I said, pulling the muzzle from his forehead but keeping the aim there. "Just back away from the pistols. Slow."

He didn't drop his arms right away, but when he did, he lowered them easy and slow while stepping back from the revolvers at his feet. "I appreciate that." He worked his shoulders around a few times. "I didn't know how much longer I could keep them up like that."

"You just remember this one thing: you try anything foolish, and I'll make sure I have more arms than you." I lifted my eyebrows with a quick nod. "Do we have an understanding?"

"We do."

"Good." I lowered my piece but kept it in my hand. "Now tell me how you know Ezra."

"I met him at the Coopertown jail. He'd been caught stealing horses, and they were going to transfer him somewhere to be tried."

"You mean to be *hanged*." I chastised the word "hanged" as best I could.

"Well, they said he was going to be tried, but you're not wrong—more than likely, he was heading for the gallows."

"You were in the cell with Ezra?"

"Not exactly." He mopped his face with a sleeve.

"Well, where *exactly* was you?"

"I worked at the courthouse when he was incarcerated." He was now avoiding my gaze. "And I had interactions with each prisoner, as I had to handle all the paperwork."

"Why does the Army have someone working for a courthouse?"

"That's the thing." He offered a nervous grin while studying my reaction. "I really don't serve in the Army." He lingered there like he was trying to work the words in his head.

"Go on."

"My father's brother was a judge for the Ninth Circuit a number of years back, and he hired me as a clerk for the county." He dabbed at his forehead again. "So I had access to every document that came through the courthouse, as well as materials and anything else, to say the least."

"I don't follow."

"When I'd read about Ezra's ordeal, I visited his cell to process the paperwork in person," he said, making eye contact.

"Hold on a second. What do you mean by *Ezra's ordeal*? I thought they got him for horse thievery."

"That's true, but he was also involved with a bank robbery in Sandy Bluff."

For the life of me, I couldn't remember that job. "Are you sure about that?"

"Oh, he admitted it to me. Did the whole thing by himself, if you want to know." He grinned. "And that's where this story begins. You see, they caught him, but they didn't find a trace of that money." He lifted his eyebrows. "Over *ten thousand* dollars."

"Jesus."

"Apparently there was some kind of event in the area, which meant the bank was deserted except for a few employees and was full of money."

"Lord have mercy. Ten thousand dollars." That cold spot returned to my stomach. "That's gotta make a job take on a far more dangerous nature than usual."

"Especially when they can't find the money."

I tried to rustle up some spit in my dry mouth. "So they're holding Ezra at the courthouse jail?"

"I don't believe so," he said, shaking his head. "They were getting ready to extradite him somewhere else the last I heard, and that was related to the horse thievery convictions."

"Where did they take him?"

"I honestly have no idea."

"Stop your lying, Meade. You just told me you have access to all documents and information."

"Had," he said, holding up a single finger. "I'd *had* access. I no longer hold that position." What appeared to be a genuine smile crossed his face. "But I got to know Ezra in the little time he was there. I took him food occasionally, and he talked quite a bit about you and the boys. But he knew his fate. He knew he was going to hang. So he told me where he hid the money."

I studied his face. "From the bank job?"

"That's right." He angled his face downward while keeping his gaze to mine. "And he wanted me to share it with you."

"You mean to tell me that you've had my share of the money this whole time with intentions of just handing it over when you was good and ready? That's a bunch of horseshit, and you know it."

"I didn't say I *had* the money." He lifted his eyebrows again. "I said he told me where he hid it."

Returning the pistol to my holster, I smiled and nodded. "Now we're getting somewhere. Now we're getting to some truth. Because if you really *knew* where the money was, you wouldn't have searched me out so we could share it."

"Ezra told me where he hid the haul, but I do not know the location."

I couldn't help but chuckle. "Ezra always had a way of confusing the hell out of everything. But there again, there was always a reason for how he did things."

"The truth of the matter is that *you* know where the money is, Lawrence. Ezra made sure I'd need you to be able to get it."

"Me? I don't have the foggiest as to what you're talking about."

"I'm saying Ezra hid the money in a location where only you and him would know. When I tell you what he told me, apparently you will know exactly where that is."

"And that's why you even bothered with me. It all makes sense."

"So when they extradited Ezra, I took the information he'd given me and searched for you. It didn't take long to learn you were in a cell yourself." He shrugged. "So I took a confiscated uniform from the courthouse we were holding for the Army to pick up and drew up the documents to convince the sheriff that I was to take you to Fort Hays for a court-martial."

I chuckled again. "Son of a bitch. That's right smart. You even had *me* fooled."

"And then the Indians came and messed everything up before I could tell you the story."

"You had *plenty* of time, you sneaky bastard. You had plenty of time, yet you kept me chained up and at your will."

His face turned as red as a cooked beet. "I had to make sure you wouldn't turn tail and head out on your own without me." He pointed a finger at my face. "And then I'd never see a cent of that money. I had to protect myself."

"So what did he tell you? Where is the money?"

He shifted his gaze to the ground and cleared his throat. "Now we're gonna need to come to an agreement about that. I mean, you don't trust me, and I don't trust you. I have part of the answer, but you have the other." He smiled. "The way I see it, we need each other."

That warming sensation was back in my belly, spreading into my chest. "So you're saying Ezra is dead?"

"I'm sorry about your friend, Lawrence, but I think you and I both know what they do to horse thieves." He shook his head. "And Ezra knew it as well. Why else would he have told me what he told me?"

I could just see Ezra's face, smiling like an idiot every time I made a good shot or accomplished something that helped build my arm's strength or agility. I'd never see that stupid smile again. "You know what," I said in a low voice. "That was Ezra's money. Not mine or yours."

"He wanted us to have it. Me and you."

That burning spread to my face and ears. "He wanted to live, too, Meade. But we don't always get what we want."

"Now hold on just—"

"You said if I just listened to your story, you'd walk away and leave me be. Now that's what you said to me when we started this." I kicked his revolvers toward him. "I've listened to your story."

"Lawrence, I need you to think about this. Five thousand dollars for each of us. That can change our lives forever. Are you willing to just throw away five thousand dollars?"

"I've made my decision. Now get your pistols and head out."

A warm breeze came through again as he picked up his revolvers, holstered them, and then stood there staring at me for what seemed like minutes. "You won't be able to find it without me."

I nodded. "And *you* won't be able to find it without *me*."

I left Meade and headed back into town, taking the main road this time. I was feeling right poorly, to be honest. I reckon all the activity had upset my stomach something awful. But I realized it likely had more to do with not eating anything as of yet in the day, and here it was, well past noon. I had a bit of unfinished business to see to with Rose, so I decided I needed to get some food in me at the same time.

Hearing the news about Ezra was hard—far worse than when I'd received word that my own brother had succumbed to consumption a few years back. Hell, Ezra was more of a brother to me than Virgil ever was. Virgil—or any of my blood kin for that matter—never would have stuck with me like Ez did. None of 'em would have made sure my wound was cleaned properly and healing good. And not a damn one of 'em would have pushed me to live day after day. Now I might be wrong about all that, but I sure as hell don't believe so.

But there's one thing about it: I should have been there for Ezra. I sure didn't think he'd get himself into a mess like the one that did him in. But I should have been there for him, just like he was there for me at my lowest. And it don't make things any better knowing it was his idea to go separate ways, saying the law would be looking for us together.

The place wasn't busy, but there was a smattering of people at a few of the tables. I smelled beef stew as soon as I made it through the door. Sitting myself at a table next to a fella that gave me the assumption he was traveling through the territory peddling his wares, I did my best to keep from making eye contact with the drummer, as I didn't want to invite his patter.

"You're turning out to be a regular here," Rose said, stepping up to the table.

I offered what I thought was a friendly smile. "Well, the food is good, and the hospitality is even better."

"We're all out of sorghum cake," she said with a laugh. "But we've got some roasted beef if you'd like."

Nodding, I leaned back in the chair. "Now that sounds downright appetizing for sure."

"Coffee?"

I slipped my hand into my pocket. "Yes ma'am."

'Fore I could say another word, she took off toward the kitchen. The salesman next to me sat up straighter every time I looked up, hoping to strike up a sales spiel, I'm sure. He put me to mind of a dog getting excited at the chance to fetch a stick. But I quickly turned away every time I noticed the man's movements.

"Here you go," Rose said, placing the plate in front of me. "I'll be right back with your coffee."

I reckon I'd swallowed about half the beef and potatoes by the time she'd returned. "Mighty good," I said, nodding.

Chuckling, she put the coffee on the table. "You must have been famished."

A breeze swept through the place when the front door opened, and a tall fellow wearing an Army uniform stepped inside.

My gut tightened as he made his way toward us.

"I'm told you were on the stagecoach that was robbed," he said, stepping next to Rose and removing his hat. "Ma'am."

The look of surprise crossed Rose's face. "Why, yes, I was . . ." She let her words linger there a bit.

"Reginald Collins," he said. "Lieutenant Reginald Collins." He raked lanky fingers through his hair. "Can you tell me about the road agents involved?"

"Oh my, what do you want to know?"

Shrugging, the lieutenant placed his hat under his arm. "Anything you can remember about them. What they wore, how many there were, any noticeable things that may have stuck out?"

Rose put a finger to her chin. "There were several of them, but I only got to see one of the men up close." She shook her head. "But he was disguised with something over his head, and to be honest with you, I was too frightened to stare."

"If I may," the salesman said, leaning forward. "Why would the Army be interested in a stagecoach robbery?"

Lieutenant Collins looked as though the man had tried to cut him with a razor. "And who might you be?"

"The name's Clarence McDonald," the drummer said, rising to his feet with an extended hand. "I'm in the territory selling home goods."

Without shaking the man's hand, the lieutenant offered a stern look. "It's my understanding there may have been Army funds on that run." He turned back toward Rose. "Can you tell me anything else about the men?"

"Why would the Army have money on a stagecoach?" The salesman was nearly laughing his words. "Is that a normal practice for the U.S. Army?"

Lieutenant Collins returned his hat to his head. "If you think of anything else, please let me know," he said to Rose. "I'll be staying here at our camp for the time being."

I realized I was holding that silver beetle inside my pocket again. I let it go and took another mouthful of beef.

"I will let you know if I think of anything," Rose said before turning to the salesman. "Can I get you anything else?"

"No," he said, plopping back into his chair. They both watched as the lieutenant walked out the door. "Stolid fellow, isn't he?"

I didn't get a chance to say to Rose what I'd hoped to after the lieutenant came in. It was everything I could do to keep my peace . . . and my seat. All I wanted to do was just get outta there as soon as possible, but I knew that would have drawn attention to myself. Thank the Good Lord that salesman was there to distract everything. I'd sure buy a pot or a pan from him right now if I saw him out.

But as soon as I settled my bill, I took to the road. I didn't know which way to go at first, and I don't reckon it really mattered, but I knew I needed to get myself as far away from that place as possible.

The evening sun was still burning by the time I found the streets and buildings. It was a bustle of activity with people and critters moving in all directions. The whole thing kinda reminded me of Deadwood without all the mud and mining gear. As it turned out, Sanderson was a much bigger town than I'd first thought. In fact, it was right close to being a full-fledged city.

I followed a quiet alley to find a place to make water and dismounted near the back end, where it was darker and quieter. As I was relieving myself, I heard the thudding footfalls of someone coming down the alley at a right swift pace. Fearing someone was trying to catch me by surprise in hopes of robbing me, I finished in time to draw my Colt and turn toward the approaching figure. "You better think about this," I said, laying a bead on the man. "You better think long and hard about this."

The man stopped and stared right at me. "Is that you, Lefty?"

"Ez?" I said, focusing on the man's face.

Ezra Tackett stepped forward, grinning like a possum eating sand briars. "Ain't you a sight for sore eyes!"

We met halfway and embraced. "I feared you was dead," I said, thudding his chest with the back of my hand. "And how many times do I have to tell you not to call me that!"

His grin stretched even further. "They wanted to hang me for horse thievery, but I busted out."

"I told you, stealing horses ain't worth the trouble. The law ain't near as sympathetic for a horse thief as they are with a murderer."

"Ain't that the truth? But I can't wait to tell you about . . ." He quickly stepped back and studied me and Daisy. "Where'd you get the donkey?"

"Long story," I said, shaking my head. "We can talk more about it directly, but we'd best get to moving along. They'll be searching for you, and I've got my own troubles. Army troubles, in fact."

Ezra's face soured up like he'd just gotten a mouthful of rotted eggs. "Army?"

"I did a stagecoach job not far from here, and as it turns out, they think some of the cash I stole was money belonging to the Army." I smiled. "And you're really gonna soil your britches when I tell you about who busted me outta jail for killing a fella." I bit off a small hunk of tobacco and worked it around in my mouth. "And how Kiowas grabbed me before turning me loose right out in the middle of nowhere."

"Kiowas? Good God, are you all right?"

I handed him the plug and spat toward the street. "They gave me food and water before pointing me in this here direction."

"Well, Lady Luck seems to still be riding with you."

"Well, they warned me about stopping in this town for some reason." I glanced back down the street. "I ain't got no idea why, but they was adamant about it."

A commotion from down the alley got louder as a group of men moved toward us.

"I know exactly why they warned you," Ezra said, pulling me to the side.

My legs wobbled a bit when I noticed the blue uniforms.

Chapter Eight

Ezra pushed me behind him as the soldiers closed in with rifles aimed on us. "Don't do anything stupid, Lefty."

Heat rose in my chest. "I reckon anything I do in this situation is bound to be considered stupid," I said, pulling away from his grasp. "And I told you not to call me that!"

A corporal stepped forward with his chin set upwardly. "Did you *really* think you could get away without us finding you?"

Lord knows I should have listened to that Indian and stayed out of this place. "I don't know what to think anymore," I said through gritted teeth.

The corporal squinted into my face. "And just who the hell are *you*?" He ridiculed the word "you" with his tone.

I leaned to the side and spat. "Are you—"

"He's here for me, Lefty," Ezra said, pushing me back.

"What are you talking about?" The burning in my belly threatened to expose the roasted beef from earlier.

Putting his wrists together, Ezra stretched out his arms. "Lefty here was just passing by when I stopped him."

"Hold on a minute." I grabbed Ezra by the shoulder. "Them horses you stole—"

"That's right," the corporal said, pulling Ezra from my grasp. "U.S. Army property."

Stepping closer, I slapped at Ezra's arm. "Army horses, Ezra? *Army* horses?" It took everything in me to hold back from punching him in the face. "Sometimes I wonder how God fit all that stupid in your dang head. You beat everything, you know that?"

"How was I to know they belonged to the Army? It ain't like I could just ask the critters."

I took notice of the corporal's bewildered expression before refocusing on Ezra. "Are you drunk?"

"Let's go, Tackett," the corporal said, pulling Ezra toward the other soldiers. "Even your friend here thinks you're spooney."

A few soldiers took Ezra by the arms, shackled him, and led the poor fool back down the street as the corporal lingered back with me.

"How do you know Ezra Tackett?" he asked, lighting a pipe.

"Well, it weren't from no horse thieving, I'll tell you that much."

A plume of grayish smoke drifted about his head. "I don't suspicion you, son. I'm sure it would be a burdensome task for someone in your state."

I turned to the side and spat. "Where are you taking him?"

Getting another draw of the pipe, the corporal nodded in the direction his men were leading Ezra. "Courthouse. And then back to the jailhouse, just down the street, to await trial."

A tightness came over my chest. "What do you reckon they'll do with him?"

The man tapped his pipe against the meat of his palm to clean out the residue. "I'm sure you know what his fate will be." He trousered his pipe and brushed at his coat. "Because of this little excursion, he's now going to be facing more than just stealing government property."

"They're going to hang him, aren't they?"

The corporal pulled off his hat and wiped his forehead with a folded handkerchief. "I would say that is a fair assessment."

My stomach started rumbling. "You reckon I could visit him a spell?"

"Son, my advice to you is to move along." He slapped me on the back. "You and Tackett are both going to be better off if you do."

I started to say something, but the corporal turned in the direction his soldiers took Ezra without another word.

I tried my damnedest to get past that saloon without stopping. Lord knows I really tried. I know that sounds like I'm kicking some fun, but I truly wanted nothing more than to make myself just move on past and keep riding until I found a location far enough away that I wouldn't have to worry about anything. But I also needed a whiskey worser than I reckon I've ever needed one. Oh hell, who am I kidding? I needed more than just *one* whiskey.

A few of them soldiers was milling about at the front when I walked in. I didn't care how much my stomach protested, I was bound and determined to get my hands on a much-needed drink. I took in the crowd before I moved on toward the bar, scanning faces and studying sidearms as I went.

It looked to me like three of the tables was filled with poker players, and most of those gambling were not soldiers. I reckon, as usual, the other four tables were set aside for conversations and tall tales. I was here for one thing. I was here for the whiskey.

"Evening," the barkeep said when I stepped closer. "What can I get you?"

"Whiskey." As he was moving, I added, "Just give me a bottle."

Reaching under the bar top, he glanced at my empty sleeve. "Here you go," he said, sliding a bottle and glass in front of me. "Two bits."

"I'm a thanking you," I said, placing the coins next to the bottle.

A ruckus of laughter came from the door where a few younger men in uniform walked in. Noticing an abandoned table toward the side, I placed the empty glass over the top of the bottle and made my way to take a seat. Nobody paid me any mind as I walked by, and that's just how I like it.

I took the stool against the wall so I could keep an eye on everything going on in the room. The glass was cold when I placed it on the table, but I had full intentions of warming up that blasted thing before the night was over. I bit the cork and pulled the bottle away to separate the two, then poured.

Horse thievery. I shook my head and stared at my hand. *Army horse thievery at that.* I drained the glass and poured another. It felt like I'd swallowed a campfire ember as the alcohol burned its way down my chest. *I can't believe he'd do such a thing.*

Tobacco smoke settled near the rafter beams like an early morning mist, settling there just as pretty as you please.

"Mind if we sit at your table? All the other chairs are taken."

I looked up at the familiar face of the private from the night I first came through town. His two friends were with him as well. "Please," I said, gesturing to the empty chairs. "Sit down."

"Hey, aren't you the fella that lost his gunny sack a while back?" The private sat across from me and his friends on each side. "You were on that donkey. If my memory serves me correctly."

Nodding, I raised my glass and drank. "That is me, and I can't tell you how much I appreciate you letting me know I'd dropped that blasted thing."

"I reckon we're trained to watch out for things like that." His smile was huge, revealing a smattering of yellowed teeth. "I'm Private Daniel Rogers." He nodded toward the others. "That's Carter and Baker."

"My name's Lawrence Thornhill." I studied their faces for any reaction. "Tell you what, Private Rogers. In order to show my appreciation, slide your glasses near, and I'll fill 'em for you fellas."

"Thank you, sir," the boy to my left said, moving his glass first.

I poured for the three glasses and then my own. "Where are you men stationed?"

"Fort Hays," Rogers said. "But we have a camp set up nearby."

"Have been for a while," one of the other boys said. "Only God knows for how much longer."

I raised my glass over the table. "To Fort Hays and the finest fighting men in the U.S. Army."

"Here, here," the men said, holding their glasses near mine before downing the whiskey.

I gestured toward their glasses. "Come on," I said with a chuckle. "We can't stop with just one."

We drank a few more rounds before I noticed their eyes getting red and watery.

"How'd you lose your arm?" Rogers asked while rolling a quirly."

I glanced at my shoulder. "Jesus!" I said, widening my eyes. "What the hell has happened to my danged arm?"

The men broke into laughter as I poured more whiskey.

"Gunshot shattered the bone." I studied their faces more. "But truth be known, I reckon the doctor just wanted to use his new saw."

Laughter again, and again we drank.

"I bet that was painful."

"You would be correct in that assumption," I said, holding up the near-empty bottle. "And I'm still *medicating* the best I can."

This time while they laughed, I rose to my feet. "Stay where you are, I'm getting another bottle."

When I returned, the soldiers were talking about a particular detail they were assigned to and that they only had a few days before leaving.

Rogers blew smoke upward. "That's the extradition I'm looking forward to. We'll get to be at Fort Hays for a few days before coming back here."

"Extradition?" I placed the bottle on the table and took my seat. "What are you talking about?"

Rogers grabbed the bottle and pulled out the cork. "That's why we're here. We escort prisoners to and from Fort Hays."

A coldness gripped at my belly. "I didn't know that's what you fellas were doing here."

"Yes sir," he said, pouring whiskey into the glasses. "Hard to believe how many trips we make. People getting court-martialed, serving prison sentences, and a few executions." He drained his glass. "Unfortunately, that's what's in store for the poor fella we're taking next."

"It's still a few weeks away," one of the others said.

I feared I was about to expose the roasted beef from earlier. "Do you know who your prisoner is?"

"Not personally, no."

I picked up my glass. "I mean, do you know the *name* of the person you're extraditing?"

"Let's see." Shrugging, Rogers started rummaging through his pockets. "I've got the order here somewhere."

Sweat beaded my forehead in spite of the growing coldness in my chest. "I didn't know that's what you fellas did."

"That's what we've been doing for several months now," one of the other soldiers said as Rogers continued searching his pockets. "It's surprising how many of these we have to do each week."

"We have several small units, so the same group doesn't have to do every run." The boy lifted his eyebrows. "Our units alternate, or we'd never get a chance to catch our breath."

"Here we go." Rogers unfolded the paper. "His name is . . ." He paused a moment, searching the document. "Reginald Bailey."

Lord knows I came within an ace of casting up my accounts. "Thank God."

Rogers looked up at me with a queer expression. "What?"

I refilled our glasses and held mine over the table. "What I meant to say was thank God it's not one of *our* names on that document."

The men laughed again and drained their glasses.

The coldness began to fade, and my stomach settled somewhat as the crowd started leaving little by little. "Well, fellas, I better get back on the trail. I've enjoyed the company."

"Thank you for the whiskey," Rogers said, and the other two agreed.

Rising from my chair, I brushed at the front of my shirt. "You fellas take good caution while out on your run." I held my hand out to the boy closest to me. "And thank you for your service."

All three stood, each taking a turn to awkwardly shake my left hand.

"By the way, does that order tell you what the guilty fella did?"

Rogers studied the document again. "No sir. It's just an order explaining to us when and who. It doesn't go into any detail as to his charges."

I couldn't pull my gaze from the paper in his hand. *That's it.* "Would you mind if I got a peek at that letter?" I offered a smile. "I don't reckon I've ever seen an official order from the U.S. Army."

Shrugging, Rogers handed the document to me. "I don't see any harm."

It looked almost exactly like the document that Meade carried when he broke me out of jail. *That's it.* "Them officers sure have some fancy handwriting, don't they?" I took note of the name and date before handing the document back to Rogers. "Reckon that's why they act all snooty?"

The men laughed again as I started for the door. "Take care of yourselves, fellas."

The longer I rode, the more I realized that I'd drunk a far more piece than I'd reckoned I had. And it was decidedly more than I'd intentioned, that's for sure. Lord knows it was everything I could do just to stay in that dad-blasted saddle.

And all that jostling from Daisy's gait pert near had me airing the paunch a few times, I'll tell you that much. Lord knows I would be finding myself ailing something terrible come morning.

Darkness was still a good half hour away, and I needed to get to wherever it was I was getting. I just didn't know exactly where that was just yet.

That damned Ezra and his horse thieving. And of all horses to steal, U.S. Army critters. Lord have mercy, I wish he'd paid more attention to Charlie's harping like I did. But the problem with Ezra was he was far too busy focusing his attention on fancy women and California widows. Tainted his thinking, if you ask me.

In the distance, I could see two riders approaching from the opposite direction, a dust cloud rising behind them. They weren't riding hard or fast, just at an easy pace as if they'd been at it a while. My first thought was the O'Sullivan boys, but I shook my head when I noticed them uniforms. *They're turning up everywhere I go.* I kept my pace, not wanting to show excitement or worry.

"You boys look as though you've been riding saddle sore a while," I said, hoping to stir a laugh. They were mere boys, neither with insignia on their sleeves.

"That about says it all," one of 'em said with a smile.

"Can I offer you water?"

Halting just in front of me, the two soldiers were pushing themselves off their saddles, stretching their legs. "Appreciate the offer," the same one said. "But we have plenty."

"I reckon you fellas are on extradition duty?"

Cocking his head, the man said, "We are." He stole a quick glance at his partner. "How would you know that?"

I offered a smile. "I've been drinking with some of the fellas from your company back in Sanderson." I shrugged. "Daniel Rogers, private, I believe I recollect him saying, and two others."

The soldiers chuckled. "I'm willing to wager those fools talked your head off," one said. "I'm Private James McKinney, and this is Private George Smith."

I nodded. "Nice to meet you men. My name is Lawrence Thornhill. But I got to admit, those friends of yours made right good company as I shared a few bottles of my whiskey with 'em."

McKinney glanced at his partner again. "He's met Rogers for certain," he said with a laugh. "That guy sure has a knack for finding free whiskey."

I joined in their laughter. "So are you fellas just gettin' back from Fort Hays?"

"Yes sir," McKinney said. "It's been one hell of a ride this time."

"Oh? Anything ahead of me I should pay mind to?"

"We didn't see anything, mind you, but there's word out that a gang of road agents are in the area," McKinney said with disgust in his mouth. "Said they robbed a stagecoach a few days back and took off without a trace."

"Lord have mercy." I shook my head. "It's downright dangerous in these parts nowadays." I grit my teeth like I was angry. "What'd they steal, the robbing bastards?"

McKinney rubbed his neck. "Money and valuables is what we heard told."

"One of the items was a surprise gift for our company commander," the other soldier said.

"Gift?" I studied the boy's face. "Wait, I heard about this. But I thought it was Army funds that was stolen."

"From what we know, it was some kind of keepsake for the commander," McKinney said. "Bought with money all of us in the company put in together for his upcoming retirement."

The second fella leaned forward. "Where did you hear it was Army funds?"

"Some lieutenant came into a hotel eatery posing questions toward a woman who had been on the stage when it was robbed." I shrugged. "He told that it was Army funds when a salesman asked, not a valuable of any sort."

The soldiers looked at one another. "Sounds like Lieutenant Collins," McKinney said. "He's the second in command."

The other soldier nodded. "That's just what I was thinking."

"He's probably saying that so word don't get back to the commander," McKinney said to his partner.

"Makes sense. After all, seeing how the gift is supposed to be a surprise and all."

I cleared my throat and searched a pocket for what remained of the tobacco plug. "What kind of gift did you fellas pitch in for?"

"We never heard for sure," McKinney said. "Lieutenant Collins took care of choosing and securing the gift. And he probably didn't mention what it was just to knock down any chances someone would spoil it for the commander beforehand."

I cut a piece off the plug and put it in my mouth. "Any word as to the whereabouts of them road agents?"

McKinney stretched again. "Haven't heard a word." He removed a picket spike and lifted his horse's front leg. "But it's said there are several in their gang." He commenced to cleaning packed dirt from the hoof. "I'd just be on the lookout if I were you."

"Say," the other fella said, lifting his chin. "You wouldn't happen to have any of that whiskey left, would you?"

McKinney let the horse's leg drop. "We're still on duty, Smith."

"I know that." The boy's eyebrows dropped. "But that's never stopped us before."

"I wish I did," I said with a laugh. "But I reckon the Good Lord is looking out for me, 'cause I sure as hell don't need any more of that stuff tonight."

The men laughed.

"We'll get back in time to have a few." McKinney put the picket spike back in its sheath. "And make no mistake about it, we are going to have a few as soon as we get there."

"Well, tell Rogers and the boys I said thanks again for the company and laughter." I leaned to the side and spat. "Mighty good fellas you have in your platoon."

Climbing back into his saddle, McKinney grunted. "Will do."

I got Daisy to moving and turned back to the two. "Safe travels to you fellas."

Chapter Nine

Darkness came slowly as Daisy and I made our way back. And the longer we rode, the harder it was to keep my eyes open. When I barely caught myself from falling out of the saddle, I decided to stop for a spell and do some figuring about what to do next. Luckily, there wasn't as much tallgrass on the side of the road, so I went off to the side as far as I saw fit, tied Daisy in place, and cleared a place for my bedroll.

I contemplated a fire but chose instead to stretch out and stare into the dark sky. I just needed a brief spell to let the whiskey settle and then get back on my way.

If they hang Ezra, I'm gonna have to be the one who breaks the news to Aunt Alice. My stomach started burning again. I couldn't stand the thoughts of her hearing the news from somebody else. Lord knows she'll be just as angry over him stealing Army horses. There's no doubt about that. *Ain't no way in hell I can tell her the truth.*

A chill came over me from the evening air, and I damn near worked up a campfire after all. I sure didn't want to take any chances of a snake or some other critter getting too close here in the night. But I decided against it after all, as I just didn't have the gumption to rise and get the damned thing started.

I reckon the Almighty was looking out for me again, as it was a good thing I didn't have a fire going when I heard the horse approaching on the road. I sat up and put my hand on the Colt. I thought about getting to Daisy to make sure she didn't move or make a noise, but I feared my own movement would give away our cover. The rider was still a distance away, but I wasn't taking any chances. From where I sat, I could see the dark figure of a man on a horse, slowly making his way in the same direction the two Army privates were riding.

I wondered if it was Jarvis O'Sullivan now riding on his own since his brother's shoulder was injured. Whoever it was, he went by us without even peering in our direction, as best I could tell. I wasn't able to make out any details of the man or the horse because of the darkness. I waited until I could no longer hear the horse's hooves before rising to my feet.

The burning in my stomach had spread to my bladder as I found myself in desperate need to make water. The good part about the whole thing was I was no longer about to fall asleep.

The damned place was as muddy as it had been when I'd left it. Hell, it might have been even muddier, if that was possible. Why you couldn't see the sky for the clouds—and the curious thing about it was those clouds didn't threaten storms or anything—I reckon they just kept the sun from drying everything out. Now don't get me wrong, I usually find the smell of mud right agreeable, or at least the smell of what the rains leave behind. But this was like a soured bog or a hog pen of some sort.

I tied Daisy and made my way toward the eatery, just past the trading post. I don't know how they kept the muck off them stretched-out boards going from one place to the next. You'd think everybody woulda been tracking everything with each dad-blasted step. The only thing I could figure was the rain kept 'em washed off.

There wasn't a soul at the tables when I entered the eatery, but the proprietor was busy kneading a big glob of sticky dough like he was expecting customers to walk through the door at any moment. "Be right with you," he said, looking up from his task.

I had intentioned to just get the information I was seeking and move right along, but I got to studying about how it'd been a right smart spell since I'd had anything in my belly. "I'm a thanking you," I said, moving toward the same table as before.

Wiping his hands with a towel, the man finally made his way to the table with a curious smile. "Aren't you that fella that was in here not long ago, asking about Jonathan Meade?"

"You are correct." I pushed my hat to the back of my head. "And might I presume you to be Parnell?"

It was more than his smile that was curious now. "I am," he said, cocking his head. "I don't recollect saying that the last time you were here."

"No sir. You didn't," I said, shaking my head. "Jonathan mentioned your name in the middle of a recent conversation."

Seemingly satisfied with that, Parnell placed his hands on his hips. "So what can I get for you?"

"I was just telling Meade that I reckon those pancakes I had here were the best I'd ever put in my mouth." I nodded, laying it on as thick as I could. "Told him I was bound and determined to get back here and get me another stack as soon as I was able."

Parnell's smile lit up his entire face. "That's right generous of you saying so." He smiled again. "Care for bacon and coffee as you'd had before?"

"Wouldn't have it any other way," I said with a nod.

Parnell gave a little nod himself and headed back toward the cook stove.

"'Course, Meade told me to drop by and see him anytime I was back in the township." I gazed out the window into the grayness of the day. "I reckon I'll do that after the meal."

It didn't take long for the bacon to smell up the place, and I mean that in a good way, mind you. Just about the time a couple of men entered the establishment without a word, seated themselves at a table near the door, and started mumbling to each other. Looked like farmers to me—men with hands as rough as tree bark, sturdy backs, and leathered faces.

"Give me just a moment, fellas," Parnell said without looking up. "I'll be right there."

The men just kept their mumbling conversation going as though Parnell hadn't said a word.

I glanced out the window again when I heard the steady drumming on the roof. And just as sudden as it came, it was gone just like that.

"If that don't beat everything I've ever laid my eyes on," I said, jutting a thumb toward the window. "Upon my honor to God, you can't blink around here or you'll miss a downpour. I ain't never seen anything like it."

One of the farmers looked in my direction. "Good for the crops." And just like that, them farmers went back to their conversation.

"You want your usual, boys?" I reckon Parnell just recognized the man's voice without looking up.

"That'll do," one of the two said.

Parnell brought the plate and coffee, sliding them right in front of me. "Mind your tongue, that bacon just came out of the pan."

"I'm a thanking you for the warning," I said, picking up my fork. "You make this syrup yourself?"

"I get it with the other supplies." He turned to the farmers. "I'll have yours out in just a jiffy."

I was sure glad I'd decided on getting the food. It was like medicine to my quarreling stomach. And I'm not sure if it is possible, but Lord have mercy, I believe it was tastier than the last time.

After the two men finished their meals and left, I sat there drinking my coffee and watching the sparse movement outside the window. "How long have you been here, Parnell?"

"Right about six years, I imagine." He collected the plates from the farmers' table. "I was one of the first folks who settled here."

"What about Jonathan Meade?" I asked, studying his face. "How long has he lived in this settlement?"

Wiping his hands on the towel again, Parnell turned his gaze toward the ceiling. "Oh, I reckon he's been here a little over a year or so."

I gazed back out the window so I wouldn't appear to be pressing too hard. "I can see why he settled here." I smiled at him. "I mean, in spite of all the rain and mud, it sure is peaceful."

"Peaceful is a right good way of describing Warren's Gap," he said with a prideful grin.

"Yes sir, I was just saying the same thing to Meade the other day about how peaceful it was here." I forced a chuckle. "He said that's the very reason he's planted his roots here."

"He's been an asset to the community."

"Well, now that don't surprise me nary a bit," I said, exaggerating my eyebrows upward. "He has always been a giving fella—one you can count on in times of need and such."

"I like the sound of your voice," Parnell said. "Just where do you hail from exactly?"

"Kentucky." The word damn near left a bad taste in my mouth, but I didn't let it show. "Born and raised in Booneville, Kentucky."

"That makes sense. I had a friend from Kentucky, and he talked a lot like you do."

"Well, you'd better not trust that son of a bitch," I said with a laugh, and was relieved when he laughed at it as well. "Especially when it comes to your tobacco and whiskey."

Parnell's face reddened from his laughter. "I'm going to have to remember that next time I see the old cuss."

I rose to my feet and stretched. "I reckon I'll go pay my old buddy Meade a visit now," I said, handing Parnell payment for the meal. "I don't want to hear him sworping and complaining if he finds out I came by here and didn't stop for a visit."

"He would be right disappointed, I'm sure," Parnell said, collecting my plate and items. "Do you know where he lives?"

I donned a confused look on my face. "Lord have mercy, I know he mentioned it, but for the life of me, I can't remember what he said." I shook my head and laughed. "'Course we had been drinking a mite heavily at the time."

We both laughed again.

"Keep following the planked lumber toward the back." He pointed in the direction I remember Meade walking when I'd spotted him through the window. "You'll find several homes in a row back there, including a two-story boarding house." His gaze went to the ceiling again. "It's the third house in the row, painted blue with white trim. You can't miss it—it has a white picket fence."

"Board house, huh?"

Nodding, Parnell lifted his eyebrows. "Bernice Appleton owns the place. Her husband worked himself to death getting the home built just the way she wanted it." He rolled his eyes back. "And I do mean he worked himself to death. The poor man died before he could finish all the painting."

"Lord have mercy."

"So she turned it into a board house in order to make a living as a mournful widow." He smiled. "But don't think for a moment that old woman is weak or helpless. Bernice Appleton runs as strict a household as you will find anywhere, clean and orderly."

I tugged my hat back to the front of my head. "I'm a thanking you for the directions and information." I opened the door and turned back toward Parnell. "And I sure look forward to coming back for more of your cooking the next time I'm through here."

"You're more than welcome anytime."

Them pancakes was sagging in my belly like a wet sack of feed when I left the eatery. I decided to fetch Daisy before heading out in search of the board house. The last thing I needed was for Meade to be tipped off by the sight of his own critter out there.

I'd no more noticed the horses tied right next to Daisy at the hitching post when I felt the cold steel of a muzzle pressed to the back of my neck.

"Do not make me shoot you here in the open." It was a hoarse voice, but no doubt that of Jarvis O'Sullivan. "You t'ought you'd get away, didn't you?" He yanked my Colt from its holster. "T'ought you'd outright killed Liam as well, didn't you?"

I held my arm in the air without movement. "Had I been aiming to kill your brother, I assure you he would not be with us at this very moment."

"Let's go for a ride," Jarvis said, pushing me forward. "Get on that donkey of yours so Liam can tie you down."

I couldn't see another soul out and about, other than Jarvis's open-mouthed brother. "I'm awful sorry about your shoulder, Liam." I offered the makings of a smile. "But I'm curious to know, did you ever find that rope?"

"Shut your mouth, T'ornhill." Jarvis pressed the muzzle further into my neck. "You ain't nearly as funny as you t'ink you are."

"Don't you worry about that rope none," Liam said without a trace of emotion or tone. "You're gonna get to see it soon enough."

"And you'll get to feel it for a short period of time as well," Jarvis added. "A *very* short period of time."

We rode out into a remote wooded area about a mile or two away. I didn't need to see the shape of the trees to know what was going on—those fellas had been promising to hang me since I laid eyes on them for the very first time at the courthouse.

Climbing down from his Morgan, Jarvis scanned the canopy of branches overhead. "This will do just fine, Liam."

"Want me to loosen his bindings?" Liam said, dismounting.

"Not just yet."

Now, I ain't about to act like I wasn't worried or scared. I was pretty much terrified, if I'm being right honest. But I couldn't let them boys recognize it on my face or in my voice. Fact is, it was all I could do to keep myself together by just grinning as much as my mouth would let me.

Liam stood staring at me with eyes nearly as wide as his open gob.

"Something wrong, Liam?" Jarvis moved closer to his brother. "Are you taking ill?"

Liam nodded in my direction. "Why's he smiling like that, Jarvis? Don't he know what's about to happen?"

"Pay him nary a mind." Jarvis glared at me. "He won't be grinning like that for too much longer."

A breeze rustled the branches and leaves around us, promising heavy rains that the sunlight sorely contradicted.

"I can't hardly believe you fellas are so hellbent on avenging your pa after hearing him talk to the two of you the way he did the night of the incident." I didn't know what else to do but talk. "I mean, the drunker the man got that night, the nastier he became with the two of you."

"Do not speak ill of our father, you murdering bastard!" Jarvis pointed a grimy finger at me. "Do you understand?"

"Or what? You'll kill me?" I forced a laugh. "I took up for you boys that night, and you know it. I got so sick and tired of that old man treating the two of you like piles of horse manure." I shook my head, knowing damn well I couldn't remember a thing from that fateful evening. "Hell, I'd never have even guessed that man was your pa the way he was letting on."

"I told you to shut your mouth." Jarvis cleared his revolver from its holster and took a step in my direction. "I've heard about enough from you."

I'm fairly certain I saw more pain than anger in Jarvis's eyes and reaction. "I'll be honest with you fellas, I reckon the reason I took such offense to your pa's abuse toward the two of you was because he reminded me of my old man and how that bastard always mistreated me in the same fashion."

"Our father never treated us any different than how he dealt with anyone else." Liam said this with that same frozen look on his face. Lord knows you could never tell what that boy was thinking or feeling. I'd sure hate to play a game of poker with that odd fella.

"That's my point," I said, nodding. "A man ought to treat his blood kin better than he does anyone else."

"Knock it off, T'ornhill." Jarvis put his revolver back into its holster and turned to his brother. "Leave him on the donkey, Liam, we'll hang him from right where he sits. Just be sure to hobble the creature or tie it to something so the damned thing doesn't take off until we're ready."

"If you boys thought your old man was abusive, let me tell you how mine taught me to stay alert and at the ready for anything." I moved my gaze back and forth from each brother. "In the middle of the night, while sleeping in my bed, the old man would just start beating me out of my sleep with whatever his drunken hands could find." I ran my tongue through my mouth, reliving the taste of blood. "Belts, boots, and even wood for the fire."

Both men just stared at me as though they understood exactly what I was talking about. Even Liam's eyes showed pain or some other emotion for the first time.

"Problem is, he wouldn't stop his thrashings. I had to run away from him time after time, or I swear I believe he woulda killed me." I dropped my gaze to the ground. "I'm sure you can imagine how I learned to sleep with one eye open, if you know what I mean. In fact, there were a number of times I slept so lightly I'd break into running out the door when I thought I heard him approaching, but he wasn't even in the house."

"Sounds like something our father would have done," Liam said, stealing a glance at his brother.

"He only did what he could to make us strong men." Jarvis put a hand on Liam's good shoulder. "Men who could work out situations and issues without hesitation."

"Rattlesnakes never do what they do to try and teach anyone a damned thing, fellas." I tried to keep the turmoil inside my chest from getting into my voice. "They just strike at whatever is close."

Jarvis stared into the trees without moving. "I reckon rattlesnakes beget rattlesnakes." He turned to me with a strange countenance I couldn't quite read. "You . . . me." He gestured toward his brother.

"And even Liam here. We're all just rattlesnakes who learned our slithering ways from our fathers." He patted Liam on the shoulder again. "And our way of life is to either strike first or be killed."

"Just because our fathers took the low ground doesn't mean we have to live there." I stared into Jarvis's eyes, searching for something I knew I wouldn't find.

"It don't matter none at all about that, T'ornhill." He wiped his mouth with the back of his wrist. "We still wear the scales . . . we still have the fangs." He nudged his brother toward his horse. "Go on and fetch the rope, Liam. We need to move on so we can go get that bullet out of your shoulder."

Chapter Ten

Aunt Alice's voice rang out from the house as she sang that old hymn again. I swear I believe she only knew the one: "Rock of Ages." And I reckon she felt like she had to make up for that fact by singing it as much as she did. Now she didn't have much of what I would have called a singing voice, mind you. But I'll be dogged if it wasn't right comforting every time I heard it.

"Let's go," Ezra said, kicking my foot. I wasn't asleep, but I was stretched out on the front porch with my hat over my eyes. "We need to do some more shooting."

"Can't I just lay here and enjoy the caterwauling in peace?"

"If she hears you call her singing *caterwauling*, she'll wring your neck." He kicked my foot again. "Go on now and get up."

Rising to my feet, I brushed the dust from my shirt. "Don't you think we've wasted enough cartridges already?"

"The cartridges are not wasted if you're improving."

He collected our revolvers and headed toward the back fence. "I gotta say, Lefty, you're improving every day." He stopped and turned back to me. "I know, I know, don't call you that."

I gave him a shove and chuckled. "You think you're funny, don't you, jackass?"

He smiled. "Gather the cans and let's go."

"Not much left of them cans," I said, holding one up. "We've shot the hell out of 'em already."

"There's still enough left to shoot." He pointed toward the fence. "It's your turn to set them up."

There wasn't a lot of wind to worry about, and the skies were about as blue as I reckon I'd ever seen 'em. Fall would be on us before long, and that meant Aunt Alice would be working the guts out of us to get the house and everything prepared for winter.

"Ready?" Ez handed over my Colt once I returned from placing the cans. "Let's see what you've got."

I lifted the pistol with ease, pulled back the hammer, and aimed. "Do I have to show you up again today?" The pistol's report came a second before the first tin can fell.

"I do get a little jealous at your accuracy now," he said with a laugh. "That's no joke. But it does me good to know just how far you've come."

"I never would have dreamed it," I said, taking aim again and firing as another tin fell to the ground. "I didn't think I would ever get used to having one arm—especially since it was the one I'd hardly ever used."

"You've come a long way, that's for sure."

I lowered the Colt. "I couldn't have done it without you, Ez."

"Now you know—"

"No, I mean it. I really couldn't have done this without your help."

He smiled again and shook his head. "All you needed was somebody with enough gall to get you off your ass and make you do the work."

Lifting my piece again, I took aim. "Well, if that's the case, I had the best to do it." The report came as the next can went down.

Ezra lifted his pistol and took aim. "You know what my worry is?" He fired, missing his mark. "My worry is knowing the law is still searching for you and me." He glanced back toward the house.

"And because of that, we're going to bring a lot of trouble to Aunt Alice's doorstep."

"What do you mean?"

"You know exactly what I mean." He briefly glanced at the ground before refocusing on me. "They could get her for aiding and abetting, harboring thieves and murderers. They could take her just the same as they would take you and me." He shook his head. "If nothing else, she could lose everything. And I don't think either of us want that."

"Of course not."

"She deserves better," he said with reddening eyes. "She doesn't deserve to be dragged into our problems."

"I am in agreement. She's been better to me than my own kinfolk."

"I'm glad you agree. We'll leave in the morning."

I glanced back at the house. "Does she know?"

"She does," he said, aiming toward the cans again. "I told her earlier." He fired, hitting a can. "She's not happy about it, but she knows it's for the best."

My stomach felt like I'd had too much sweet syrup. "Where should we go?"

He stepped close and laid a hand on my shoulder. "You do know they are looking for us together, right?" He shrugged. "I think we should split up for a while."

"What do you mean, split up?"

"Look, the reason I brought you here was to get you mended and ready to get out on your own." He shrugged again. "For the time being, at least. They're going to be looking for us as a pair."

"I understand."

"It's only for a while," he said with a smile. "And then we can meet up somewhere down the road when they lose interest in us."

The door at the back of the house rattled, revealing Aunt Alice making her way toward us with a scattergun in one hand and a rifle in the other.

"Something wrong?" Ezra called out to her.

"Other than the two of you leaving me here all on my own?" She shook her head in an exaggerated motion. "Oh no. Why would you even ask?"

"Aunt Alice, I told you—"

"Oh, I know what you told me, Ezra Dale." She handed him the scattergun. "I know *exactly* what you told me."

She dropped to a knee, placed the butt of the Winchester on the ground beside her, and with only her left hand, cocked the lever action. She looked me right in the eye. "Did you see how I did that?" And with just her left hand, she brought the rifle up and into her shoulder, took aim, and fired. One of the cans instantly flew into the air. "The thing you need to keep in mind is knowing where the balance is when you lift the rifle to fire."

Ezra and I briefly glanced at each other.

"Here," Aunt Alice said, rising to her feet while holding out the rifle toward me. "Hand me your Colt, and let's see you do it, Lawrence."

I glanced at Ezra again. "I don't reckon I've ever seen anything like that in my life," I said without moving.

"How?" Ezra looked as though a bank mule had just stepped on his foot. "How did you learn to do that?"

"You find a way to do a lot of things when Kiowas are attacking your cabin," she said, nodding. "I wasn't even ten years old when we were under attack. Your granny and pappy were shooting at the Indians through the windows while I was on the floor holding the baby—your daddy." She closed her eyes. "When Pa got himself shot, I had no choice but to pick up his rifle and start shooting at those savages while holding Gerald the whole time."

Ezra stepped closer. "You've never told me this before."

"Well, it's not exactly the type of bedtime story you share with a young'un, now is it?"

"Is that how Pappy died?"

"Lord no," she said, rolling her eyes. "That old buzzard drank himself to death."

"Show me how you did that one more time." I handed Ez my Colt. "I ain't never seen anything like that in all my life."

"You can drop to one knee," she said, doing just that. "And either do like I did and place the rifle butt on the ground or remain standing and hold the stock between your knees. You see my meaning?"

"Yes ma'am."

"Then you're going to cock the lever, right here," she said, touching it. "And then, finding the rifle's balance point, bring it to your shoulder like this."

"All right."

"Then you just take aim and fire." She rose to her feet and handed me the rifle. "Now you do it."

I took it and dropped to a knee, glancing up at her to make sure I was following her instructions.

"That's it," she said with a smile.

It was the most awkward thing I ever did, but I was able to cock the Winchester, raise it to my shoulder, and fire. "Missed," I said.

"You'll get the hang of it." She turned to Ezra and lifted her chin. "I know you're leaving in the morning, and since the two of you are splitting up, I'd like for Lawrence to stay here a while longer until he is comfortable with the rifle and scattergun."

"Well, I don't have a problem with that," Ezra said. "But don't you think you should ask Lef . . ." He shook his head. "Don't you think you should ask Lawrence?"

She turned right toward me. "You are staying here with me until you are comfortable with the rifle and scattergun." She lifted her eyebrows. "Do you have a problem with that, Lawrence?"

"No ma'am."

Charlie always said it takes a great deal of talent to be able to tie a decent hangman's knot, and I'm here to tell you Jarvis O'Sullivan had that talent and then some. But him intentionally sitting in my direct field of vision throughout the entire process turned the whole thing into an intimidation arrangement.

"I hate to tell you boys, but when the fellas from my gang hear about this, they will not stop until they hunt the two of you down." Neither of the brothers glanced my way. "They'll do unto you as you have done unto me."

"We're not worried about that." Jarvis finally looked up from his handiwork. "After all, dead men aren't too adept at hanging people. You know damn well you're on your own, T'ornhill."

"That's right," Liam said, rubbing his bandaged shoulder. "We heard all about the incident in Kansas."

"Ah, so you think we had *all* our men at that one specific job?" I forced a laugh. "Is that what you're telling me?"

Liam glanced at Jarvis without a word.

"If what you're saying is true, then why have you been out on your own all this time?" Jarvis shrugged. "Seems to me your friends would have been protecting you or busting you out of your cell or even here right now fighting to keep you from swinging on this rope."

"We don't believe that, do we, Jarvis?" Liam said, leaning toward his brother.

"No sir, we most assuredly do not. But if you are telling the truth, T'ornhill, then the only other explanation is you either left the Johnson Bandits, or they no longer wanted you in their ranks."

I blew a fly away from my face. "I would think it obvious that we had to split up for a while, as we feared the law would find us far easier if we were all collected together in one place. And it's the Johnson *Gang*, by the way, not bandits."

"Well, it don't matter none at all to us at this moment." Jarvis climbed to his feet. "We'll deal with those men when the time comes." He held the noose up so I could see it dangling from his hand. "Because as of right now, *your* time has come to an end."

Liam grunted as he rose from the ground. "Want me to loosen his bindings from the donkey?"

"It's time for you to do just that," Jarvis said, searching the thick branches overhead. "Get on your horse and sidle up next to him. Loosen everything so he's no longer tied to the saddle horn, but make sure his arm remains firmly secured."

"All right then."

I can't say whether or not the temperature had actually turned warmer at that moment, but I can sure tell you with no uncertainty I was sweating like an expecting nun in the middle of confession.

"That looks like the perfect branch," Jarvis said, peering into the trees before turning back to meet my gaze. "What do you t'ink, T'ornhill? You reckon that branch will hold you?"

"I sure hope so." I forced that same stupid grin from earlier. "I swear to goodness if I ain't about sick and tired of gawking at your ugly faces."

Jarvis smiled as he tossed the noose-end of the rope over the branch while Liam mounted his horse. The whole time I was moving my arm, shoving it as far as I could, trying to loosen the bindings to get free. I figured while Liam untied me from the saddle, I would push my limb as far as I could so it wouldn't tighten too much during his efforts.

"I t'ink that's a little too low," Liam said, moving his horse next to Daisy.

Briefly glancing toward us, Jarvis tied off the rope's other end to the base of another tree. "That won't be the case when his donkey leaves him."

I could feel my arm moving a little more. But when Liam began untying the bindings while I pushed my arm away, I knew I was dang near free.

"Put the noose around his neck and I'll remove the donkey's hobble," Jarvis said, moving to the front of Daisy.

Liam grunted as he guided the rope over my head and around my neck while leaning against me. "It's hard to do that with all this pain in me shoulder," he said to his brother.

"Just take your time and get it on good." Jarvis didn't come back into my field of vision right away.

I knew this was the only chance I would have, so I worked my hand out of the bindings and quietly took Liam's revolver from its holster before placing the muzzle against the underside of his chin.

"Get this damned thing off me," I whispered into his ear. "Get it off me now, or I swear I'll blow your head clean off right where you sit."

The old boy sounded like he was about to say something, so I pressed the muzzle a little more firmly.

"We'll get someone to get that bullet out of your shoulder as soon as we get back to town," Jarvis replied.

Liam barely got the noose away from my head when I heard the sudden movement from Jarvis below. "Liam, are you all right?"

Liam's eyes were wide and pleading.

"I've got your brother's pistol under his chin," I said, keeping track of Jarvis's location. "You so much as act like you're gonna do something, and I swear I'll spew his brains all through these trees!"

"Don't move, Liam." Jarvis's voice was thin and shaky. "Just ride away, T'ornhill. All I ask is that you let me brother live."

"Drop your revolvers." My chest tightened as I stretched to keep Jarvis within sight. "Slow and easy. Slow and easy like."

"Don't do it, Jarvis!" Liam groped at my arm and pistol before the words could even leave his mouth. I swear there was a split second where I was honestly trying to grab hold of something with my missing arm to keep from being pulled to the ground.

But as the two of us tumbled between his horse and Daisy, I heard the revolver go off at the same time that I felt the kick in my hand. I landed on top of Liam and scrambled to pull back the pistol's hammer, but he didn't move.

"Liam!"

I could see Jarvis's legs moving to get around our critters and knew I had to take cover before he realized the top of his brother's head was gone.

"Liam! Are you all right?"

I rolled and scrambled toward a large tree with a dense growth of brush around it, trying to listen for movement over the pounding of my heart in my ears.

"You killed him, you son of a bitch!" Liam was obviously near his brother's body. "I told you to just ride off, and you killed him anyway."

I wasn't about to give away my cover, so I sat as quietly as I could, listening and waiting for whatever was to come next.

"You just murdered him for no reason!" The words came amid sobs and screams. "You could have just ridden off like I said."

That's when I realized this was never going to be over. I'd killed his pa, and now I'd just killed his brother, possibly his only brother. Lord knows the boy's grief had never allowed him to listen to reason, and he was sure as hell going to be worse now with his brother's death. "You heard him defy your words," I called out to him. "The fool attacked me while I had the pistol to his head."

Expecting an argument from him, I pressed closer to the trunk of the bristlecone when a bullet whizzed my way. "You just murdered him for no reason!"

"The two of you were trying to murder *me*!" I yelled back. "And I woulda done like you said and just rode away if he hadn't attacked me."

His answer was another bullet flying over my head.

I heard his careful footsteps coming closer, as well as the cocking of his revolver's hammer. Then I could see him studying the brush further to the right of where I hid.

He fired a round into that general area and took a step with the revolver's report, and I smiled. He was trying to hide his noisy movements with the shots, as though his gunshots weren't giving away his location.

He aimed further to the right of his first attempt, and I waited until he pulled the trigger before firing at him at the same time, so he wouldn't be able to distinguish where I hid. His shot went off into the empty thicket—mine found the meat of his left thigh.

He grunted and growled like a bear as he retreated toward the critters. "Damn you, T'ornhill!" He clambered onto his horse and glanced toward his dead brother. "I swear to you, Liam, I'll make that son of a bitch pay."

He rode off, and I honestly thought about following him to put an end to the whole thing right then and there but decided to let him go, as he would need quite a bit of time with that leg. And hopefully during that time, he'd realize he wasn't messing with a farm dog.

Chapter Eleven

The planked lumber going out back was a mite slippery at Warren's Gap, forcing me to take my time and sure my footing. What little sunlight that made it through the stubborn clouds did very little in drying out the wood. Something I took notice of almost right away was the fact that the buildings toward the front of the settlement appeared to have been built in rough, shack-like structures in order to hide the fancier homes in the back. If that was the plan, it was a right smart one for sure. And I'll be dogged if the planked lumber didn't turn into fully constructed sidewalks by the time I'd reached that back row.

The houses there reminded me of some I'd seen back east. Not in Kentucky, mind you, but mainly in a few gaudy sections throughout the country we'd traveled while heading west when I was younger. And for some reason, this part of the settlement didn't have that swampy smell like it did out front. I reckon it may have had something to do with all the flowers planted in front of the homes, or maybe the sidewalks was simply keeping everyone from tracking through and stirring the muck.

It was easy to figure out which was the boarding house—it was the only one with a white picket fence around it, just as Parnell mentioned. The blue paint looked to be fresh and clean, immediately reminding me of the poor bastard of a husband who gave his life in service of his burdensome bride.

A woman was sweeping the front porch as if she was trying to fight varmints back, keeping 'em from getting inside. And for the life of me, I didn't see a speck of dust or dirt she was cleaning. She wore a high-collar dress with puffed-out sleeves and a thick waist belt that matched her round-toed shoes.

"Excuse me, ma'am," I said, removing my hat. "I hear tell this is a boarding house?"

Stepping forward, she studied me right good without allowing her gaze to linger on my empty shirt sleeve but a second. "It is. May I help you?"

"I'd like to inquire about letting a room if you have the space."

She leaned forward and lifted her eyebrows. "And where, exactly, did you hear that this was a boarding house?"

Clearing my throat, I tried to smile but was too busy trying to figure out if she was gazing or glaring at me. "Parnell," I said, gesturing back toward the way I'd come. "From the eatery here in the settlement."

She didn't react to that, just stared blankly.

"And a friend of mine boards here." None of that seemed to reach her softer nature—if she even had a softer nature. "Jonathan Meade is his name."

"How do you know Jonathan?"

"Well, ma'am, you could say we traveled a bit together." All I wanted to do was look down at my feet or somewhere else and stop gazing into those eyes, but I knew I couldn't look away. "He's a fine fella, that Jonathan. Right smart as well."

"Uh huh." I swear to you that old woman squinted as though she was peering right into my soul. "What did you say your name was?"

"Well, I didn't, ma'am. And I do apologize." I tried again to smile. "But it's Lawrence Thornhill. That's my name."

Shaking her head, the woman scrunched her nose without a word.

"Parnell told me the owner of the boarding house was Bernice Appleton. Would that be you, ma'am?"

"It would be," she said matter-of-factly. "Tell me, Mister Thornhill, just where are you from?"

Nodding, I finally worked up what I felt was a genuine smile. "It's because of the way I talk," I said with a forced laugh. "I get that all the time. I'm from Booneville, Kentucky."

"I might have known," she said before taking a deep breath. "My late husband, God rest his soul, was from somewhere near Kentucky."

I figured this was a perfect opportunity to finally look away. "I'm sorry for your loss, ma'am."

"You have better manners than he did, I'll say that much for you." She opened the gate and stepped aside. "Come in and take a look if you like."

I moved past her to give her plenty of room to close the gate back. "I'm a thanking you, ma'am."

"Come along," she said, ascending the porch steps. "Do you have any other impediments that would hinder you from a room upstairs?"

The word "other" was obviously in regard to my missing arm. "No ma'am. I can walk or climb just fine."

Everything was clean and orderly, with no clutter to be found anywhere. And there was a lingering smell of pine throughout the whole place. And I'm gonna be right honest with you, I couldn't help but notice there was a different wallpaper pattern in each room we passed.

"A few things you need to know that I will not tolerate." Her no-nonsense disposition returned. "Absolutely *no* alcohol," she said, emphasizing her point with a raised forefinger. "No visitors," she added with a second finger. "And *no* blackguardish talk whatsoever." She waved her three fingers in front of my face to drive home her point.

"Yes ma'am."

"The boarding includes breakfast and dinner every single day." She said this as a prideful smirk lifted one side of her upper lip. "If you are not present while the food is on the table, I shall hold back nothing for you."

"Yes ma'am."

"Each room gets a fresh washbasin and towels every day."

I damn near laughed at the thought that Mrs. Appleton and Charlie would have gotten along just fine. "Yes ma'am."

"Come along," she said, leading me through a doorway. "This is the dining room." A long table with what must have been a dozen chairs centered the room. "This is where all the meals will be served." Turning to me, she lifted her eyebrows. "I prepare meals as I see fit. There are no special orders or requests."

Before I could say a word, she marched out the doorway and headed through another hallway.

"This," she said, gesturing toward a large room, "is the parlor." Sofas and chairs lined each wall except for the back one, where an ornate fireplace stood. "This is where most of the boarders gather in the evenings."

The next thing I know'd, we was climbing the stairway, heading for the second floor. And Lord have mercy if it didn't take no time 'fore that old woman had me winded something terrible. I like to have keeled over from her pace.

"This is what the beds look like," she said, gesturing toward a small wooden frame with clean bedding. "There are two boarders to a room, except small families get a room to themselves."

"It's a right handsome house you have here, ma'am. Right handsome."

"I feel as though I am forgetting something," she said, rubbing her chin. "Well, there's a privy out back . . . I suppose that's everything." Her eyes widened as she snapped her fingers. "Oh, curfew is nine o'clock each night."

"You sure keep everything in order, ma'am. I sure do appreciate that, I do." I caught myself curling my hat's brim in my hand. "So how much are you asking? And is it weekly or monthly?"

"Oh dear," she said, her face reddening. "We don't discuss costs aloud." She started for the staircase, and I was just thankful to be going *down* it this time.

She retrieved a slip of paper from a rolltop desk in the study and began scribbling with a pencil. "Here you go," she said with her first warm smile of the visit. "Now that does *not* include laundry service. Should you require laundry service," she said, scribbling again. "*This* will be the overall price."

Taking the slip of paper and reading her numbers, I smiled and nodded. "This is quite agreeable," I said, paying her right then.

"Since you and Jonathan are friends, I suppose you would be fine rooming with him?"

"That would be perfect." I tried my damnedest to keep the smile as small as possible. "I haven't seen him around, is he here?"

"No," she said, making her way back to the stairs. "I'm afraid he is away on business for a few days. He paid me in advance and said he should be back in a day or so."

We made our way back upstairs and into a particular room with a bed on each side. "That one is Jonathan's," she said, nodding toward the bed on the right. "So that one"—she gestured to the other—"is yours."

"Looks right comfortable."

"Oh, and one more thing, the stable at the back of the house is for the horses of the boarders." Her stern face returned. "You just supply your own feed for your animals." She turned toward the doorway. "The shelter and water are both complimentary."

"Oh, might I ask one favor, Mrs. Appleton?"

She turned toward me, lifting her chin. "Yes?"

"Would you be so kind as to not inform Jonathan I'm here? I would love to surprise him myself."

I'll be right honest here: the boarding house bed was more comfortable than it appeared. I reckon the reason for that is anyone with any sense at all could tell right away it wasn't bought—it was built. And somebody had put a great deal of time and effort on scraping and rubbing that lumber into a fine finish. And if I was guessing,

I'd wager that that *somebody* had been Appleton's dearly departed plow-horse of a husband. But I'll say this for the old woman: the bedding was clean and smelled right pleasant.

Both beds in the room had sheets and blankets spread, smoothed, and tucked just as pretty as you please, every detail attended to. I knew good and well that wasn't the handiwork of Meade—that was the attention of an orderly woman like Bernice Appleton.

I'd searched around the room and couldn't find any of Meade's possessions, which worried me that the conniving bastard might not be coming back to the board house. But there again, he'd have better sense than to leave anything behind that a prying landlord could easily find and question, especially when it came to forged Army documents and such.

Not that the old woman would have been able to discern that those documents were faked. Now I'm not saying she was stupid, mind you, because Bernice Appleton most certainly was not a stupid woman, but it was because Meade's skill was that good. I mean, the jackass nearly had even *me* second-guessing my own past and wits.

I'm telling you, the document he'd presented to Sheriff Langford regarding me looked identical to the papers that the private in the saloon was carrying. For the life of me, I couldn't figure out how Meade did it. Why, I'd wager everything in my gunny sack that those boys in Sanderson wouldn't even give his forged documents a second look.

I glanced at my sack and thought about the fellas I met on the road. I listened for movement in the hallway. I was fairly certain I was the only person on the second floor at the moment, but some folks could be light on their feet.

Dumping the sack's contents onto the bed, I watched for shadows at the doorway. I still didn't have a clue as to what I was going to do with all these valuables. It was better to use caution than to give yourself away by approaching the wrong people about selling any of it.

I brushed my hand over the goods, thinking about what the boys on the road said about their company commander. Nothing looked as though it could be a gift for a retiring Army officer.

Wait just a doggone minute.

I picked up the watch and flipped it over in my hand. Although the face cover was decorated with intricate carvings of a hound pursuing a large stag, the backside was plain with no scratches or marks. It was obviously gold, but it seemed to have had more heft to it than similar watches I'd held in the past.

I opened the cover, and my stomach soured at the inscription. MAJOR J.B. MARTIN.

Shit.

I snapped the lid shut and started returning everything back into the gunny sack when I heard footsteps coming up the stairwell. It wasn't Appleton, as her footsteps were quick and choppy. So I sat back and watched the doorway.

I smiled when Jonathan Meade stepped inside the room. "My roommate has returned after all."

Staring at me for a moment, Meade lifted his hands in surrender. "What are you doing here?" His face was flushed. "I'm not following you, I swear."

"Oh, I believe you, Meade," I said, standing. "You can put your hands down. I'm not here to bring you harm."

Slowly lowering his hands, Meade moved closer to his bed. "How did you know I lived here?" His expression changed. "And this explains the donkey in the stable."

"Well," I said with a playful shrug, "the same person who tipped you off about me gave me some information about *you* as well."

"Parnell."

Nodding, I sank back to the bedding. "He really does make the finest pancakes I've ever put in my mouth."

Meade briefly glanced at the floor before returning his gaze to mine. "What do you want?"

"Well, I need your help if I'm gonna be right honest."

He sat back on his bed. "So you changed your mind."

"I wouldn't go that far," I said, dragging out the words. "But what I have to say, I think you will find far more agreeable."

He stared at me a moment. "And what is that?"

"I was in one of the dark alleys of Sanderson a few nights ago. I was to the side making water when this fella come running toward me. I reckon I thought I was about to be robbed . . . or even worse. I pulled my Colt before the son of a bitch was on me and realized I knew this fella." I couldn't help but grin.

"Mrs. Appleton obviously did not give you the rules for this boarding house." He folded his arms over his chest. "Profanity is not tolerated."

"She only mentioned blackguardish talk. She didn't say nary a thing about profanity."

Meade closed his eyes for just a moment. "That's what she means."

"Well, she's not here, Meade." I stepped forward to peer out the doorway. "She obviously can't hear me."

He just shook his head.

"It was Ezra, Meade. Ezra Tackett had escaped the jail."

He sat forward, squinting. "So why exactly would I find this news more agreeable, pray tell? He's going to claim his buried money now, knocking you and me both right out of the picture."

Buried? I tried not to allow the acknowledgment of this information to alter my face. "The problem is, while he and I stood there talking, they captured him and took him back." I lifted my eyebrows and shook my head. "And you never once told me it was the Army that was holding him."

His brow came down over his nose. "Army? What was the Army doing picking him up?"

"Well, that's who holds a fella when the horses he steals belong to the U.S. Army."

"Dear God."

"Now you see my plight, don't you?"

Meade shrugged. "I still don't see what any of this has to do with me. Unless, of course, you've changed your mind."

I stepped toward him and leaned in. "I want you to bust him out of jail like you did me."

"Have you been kicked in the head by that donkey? *My* donkey, by the way!"

"Hear me out. If you do this, you get it all."

"What do you mean *all*?"

"The ten thousand dollars. You get it all." I wiped at my forehead. "I just want my friend to live. And I will freely tell you what you need to know once it's done so you can claim the ten thousand dollars."

Closing his eyes, he chuckled. "Look, I appreciate your offer, and I do believe you are completely sincere with this, but it's too big of a risk."

"Too big a risk? Hell, you busted *me* out of jail for half that amount! What do you mean it's too big a risk?"

"Just what I said, it's too big of a risk. When I came to get you, I was dealing with an ignorant territory sheriff who probably has never seen an Army document in his entire life." His face reddened. "It's completely different from going into a jail dressed as an Army sergeant with counterfeit Army documents when that jail is run by the Army. They will know the difference."

"Listen to me. Just a few days ago, I spent some time with a number of the privates who had extradition orders that they were getting ready to follow. They showed me the document. I saw it with my own two eyes. It was *identical* to the order you made to bust me out. Identical."

"You're not in the Army, Thornhill. My forgeries will look authentic to you or any other person." He shook his head again. "But these fellas work with those documents every day. They will be able to spot the difference. I assure you, they will spot the difference."

I stared at the floor. "They're gonna hang him, Meade. They're gonna hang my friend. Over stealing a few lousy critters."

"I understand," he said in a near whisper. "But if I get caught, they're gonna hang me right alongside him."

"Ten thousand dollars, Meade. Hell, Ez and I would even dig it up for you." I studied his reaction. "That money could change your life."

Meade held a hand up for silence when the quick and choppy footsteps grew louder from the staircase.

Chapter Twelve

Bernice Appleton stepped into the doorway with her usual dour expression. "Why, Jonathan," she said, turning toward him. "I did not hear you come in."

Jonathan and I rose to our feet.

"Yes ma'am. Fortunately, my business did not last as long as I had anticipated."

"Well, I am certainly glad I did not engage with you earlier, as I am quite terrible with secrets, and Mr. Thornhill specifically asked me not to spoil his surprise."

"I apologize for putting you in such an awkward position, ma'am." Heat collected at my neck and ears. "And it's my hope that I didn't put you through too much stress."

She stared at my face for a moment. "Yes, well, I came to inform you that dinner is on the table." With that, she turned to leave.

"I'm a thanking you, ma'am."

"Oh, one detail I failed to mention earlier," she said, turning back to me. "Our gentlemen residents do not wear their hats at the dinner table."

"Yes ma'am," I said, removing my hat. But before she could witness the gesture, she was out of the room and moving down the stairs.

Meade's smile looked to be holding back laughter.

"What's so funny?"

"You," he said with a chuckle. "A ruthless gang member, someone who has faced all sorts of danger in his life, and has even stared death right in the face." He chuckled again. "And here you are, afraid of a little old woman who runs a board house."

The heat moved into my chest. "Why don't you—"

"Watch yourself," he said with another chuckle. "I'll be forced to report your blackguarding ways to Mrs. Appleton if you're not careful."

"You keep up with your funning," I said, making my way toward the door. "And there's something you need to know," I said, tugging at his arm. "I told Appleton that you and I were old friends."

"That's fine." His smile widened. "Watching you squirm is going to be quite enjoyable."

I don't reckon I've ever witnessed a finer spread than what was on that dinner table. Before we could even get downstairs, I recognized the pot roast and potatoes speaking directly to my nose. Lord have mercy, there was so many dishes set out, and I couldn't recognize but maybe half of 'em. But I was damn sure gonna try 'em all. That's for sure.

"Come in and take your seats, gentlemen," Appleton said, removing a pristine apron.

I followed Meade as he made his way to two empty chairs. "This looks mighty appetizing, ma'am," I said, still looking over the bounty.

"Everyone, I would like to introduce our newest resident to you all." Appleton motioned in my direction. "Mr. Lawrence Thornhill is a friend of Jonathan's, and I'm sure we are all excited to get to know him better."

"Thank you, ma'am." I scanned the faces of the folks seated around the table. "I look forward to meeting all of you."

There was only one young'un at the table, a right mannerly girl, no older than eight, if I was to have to guess, the rest were men and women of varying ages.

Appleton turned her attention to the elderly gentleman at the end of the table. "Would you mind offering the blessing, Mr. Hamblen?"

"Certainly," the man said, bowing his head while interlocking his fingers in front of him. "Our most gracious heavenly Father, we approach thy glorious throne room with thanksgiving in our hearts. We thank thee for thine daily blessings and constant hand upon our lives. We give thanks for this wonderful meal set before us, and we ask that you bless it so that it will be nourishment to our bodies. Just as we also beseech thee to bless the hands that prepared it for us. In Jesus' name, amen."

A chorus of amens followed around the table.

Now I ain't gonna lie about it, I worried the old man was about to pass a collection plate after that long-winded prayer.

"Thank you, Mr. Hamblen," Appleton said as she took her seat. "I hope you all enjoy the meal."

Except for a few folks asking others to pass something they couldn't reach, there was no conversations at the table. I felt right queer during the whole thing, to be honest. But Lord have mercy, the food was good.

As soon as Jonathan finished his meal, he cleared his throat. "Mrs. Appleton, as always, this meal was delightful. Thank you for being so gracious."

She merely nodded.

"And if you will excuse us, Lawrence and I will convene in the garden to catch up."

I moved to speak, and Jonathan placed a hand on my arm.

"Certainly," Appleton said with another nod. "And I am delighted that you found the meal enjoyable."

I rose with Jonathan and found myself almost bowing toward the old woman. "I'm a thanking you, ma'am."

When Jonathan mentioned the garden to Bernice Appleton, I'd reckoned he meant the board house's flower garden out front, but instead, he led me to the edge of a cornfield where a fenced chicken coop stood nearby. And considering the number of hens clucking about, I'd have to say it wasn't nowhere near as noisy as I would have guessed.

"It's a right peaceful place here," I said, staring out at what seemed to be a thousand rows of cornstalk. "And it sure doesn't appear to be so from the front side of the settlement."

"I hope you know that I'm truly sorry about your friend." He wiped his mouth and gazed off into the distance. "In the meager time I spent with Ezra, I'd always found him to be a fine man."

"I'm alive today because of Ezra Tackett."

His gaze moved to his feet as he kicked at a few clods. "And I hate like hell that he's in the predicament he's in."

"Then would you please help me get him out of that predicament?"

"I told you, Lawrence, the risk is too great." He turned to me. "I know you think I'm just being difficult, but *I* would be the one putting my neck on the line, not you."

"Then I'll do it. The uniform will fit me just as well."

Shaking his head, Jonathan offered a weak smile. "That would be worse. Think about it, they have already met you. And how do you think those who hadn't met you would react to a one-armed sergeant?" He placed a hand on my shoulder. "You know what I am saying to be the truth. They would hang *you* right after they hung Ezra."

"We have to do something."

"Like I said, the risk is too great."

My mind went back to the soldiers in the saloon and the document Private Rogers carried. "What if we removed the risk?"

"How's that?"

"I said, what if we removed the risk?" I rubbed the back of my neck. "What if I told you we could bust him out without risking either of our necks?"

"I'd say you were out of your mind, but I think we already know that to be true."

I tried my darndest to keep a grin off my face. "I'm serious."

"All right," he said with a shrug. "How would we be able to do that?"

"The document I told you about, the one from the private in the saloon?"

"Yes?"

"The date on it is about a week and a half away. I know the exact date and the exact name that was on that document."

His face scrunched up. "So?"

"So," I said with building excitement. "What if I was to give you the name and the date from that document so you could create an exact copy of it?"

"I don't follow." His brow came down. "What good would that do?"

"I could take your forged document and swap it with the one Private Rogers has to see if any of those soldiers can tell the difference." I chuckled as the plan came to me. "I can get them to drinking as we'd done before and find the perfect time to make the switch. And the best part of the whole deal is *your* neck is not on the line if they suspect anything."

He lifted one eyebrow. "And if the forged document doesn't raise suspicion?"

"Then we move forward with our original plan."

"I don't think so," he said, shaking his head. "I don't want to risk pretending to be an Army sergeant, in uniform mind you, while being around real soldiers and trying to pass a forged document to them. Again, the risk is too great."

I had a headache coming on and rubbed my forehead. "It'll work. I just know it."

"Again, I'm sorry as hell about Ezra, but the risk is just too much."

Putting my hand in my pocket, I found the beetle. "Hold on a second," I said with my smile returning. "What if I told you there's another way we could do it?"

Daisy was damn near purring like a kitten while I brushed her in the stable. She'd just ate a big bait of carrots and grain before guzzling enough water to drown a tall dog. I was satisfied that the stable was hidden away to the point that Jarvis O'Sullivan wouldn't find it if he came back this way searching for me.

"You didn't think I'd forget about you, did you, girl?"

She especially loved having her neck brushed, but Lord have mercy, her backside must have been the sweet spot.

"You seem to be enjoying the nice shade in here," I said, brushing just under her chin. "I don't blame you nary a bit, it sure beats that heavy sun any day of the week."

She nudged my chest with the side of her face.

"Why, you ain't nothing but a big old puppy, you know that?" I couldn't help but chuckle. "Just a long-eared, stubborn puppy."

I turned toward a noise at the open door and found Bernice Appleton with a surprised look on her face. "Please forgive my intrusiveness," she said, craning her neck to see Daisy better. "I did not know you were grooming."

"Come on in and let me introduce you to my girl," I said, brushing Daisy's neck again. "Daisy, this here is Bernice Appleton, the owner of the accommodations we are currently enjoying."

"This looks like the beast Jonathan had."

"Yes ma'am, Jonathan is how I got her." I rubbed the side of Daisy's face and smiled. "Isn't that right, girl?"

Appleton watched us in silence, and for just a brief second, I could have sworn I spotted a smile on her face before it quickly disappeared.

"Well, I won't hold you any longer," she said, lifting her head. "I came out here in hopes of speaking with Jonathan."

"I'm afraid he's away at the moment. Said he had a few errands to run today, but he should be back within a few hours or so."

"I see," she said, turning to leave. "Then I shall speak with him when he returns."

"Yes ma'am."

"Oh, one thing, Mr. Thornhill," she said, glancing back toward Daisy. "I want you to know how much I truly appreciate your caring nature toward your beast." This time she didn't attempt to hide her smile. "It is quite refreshing, I must say."

"I'm a thanking you, ma'am."

By the time Jonathan made it back to the board house, I was stretched out on the bed, fighting off sleep even though it was only a little past midday. The cool air from the open windows didn't help matters, as I'd removed my boots and socks.

"You turning in early?" Jonathan said, placing his saddlebag next to his window.

I raised myself onto my elbow. "Lord knows I'm trying my best not to," I said with a grin. "And I'm afraid once I get that big meal in me with the upcoming dinner, I won't be able to fight it off any longer."

"One thing about it," Jonathan said as he plopped onto his bed, "Mrs. Appleton sure knows how to heavy up the stomach, that's for sure."

I swung my feet to the floor and sat up. "So how's the document coming?"

"It's coming along nicely. In fact, it should be finished tomorrow by my estimation."

Pulling my socks on, I glanced at the doorway. "So where is it that you go to do this work?"

"I still have access to my old courthouse office." He closed his eyes and tilted his head. "They don't know this, of course, but I have to be very cautious."

"Let me ask you something. Since you know more folks than I do in these parts, maybe you can help me with something." I stuck a foot into one of my boots and pulled it on. "I'm getting a mite low on money, but I have a number of items that are . . ." I shrugged and smiled. "How shall I put it? Ill-gotten?"

"Stolen."

"Well, yes. That is another way of stating it." I pulled on the second boot. "I need to sell the items, but a fella can't be too cautious when it comes to approaching someone under these circumstances, as I'm sure you understand."

"I'm not interested in purchasing your stolen goods, Lawrence."

"No, no. I fear you misunderstand what I am asking. I was just wondering, as a man who plays a similar fiddle as I do, so to speak, you just might have an idea where a fella could sell an instrument or two?"

"I see." His gaze moved to the floor. "But I'm sure you fully appreciate the position this puts me in. You're asking that I disclose the identity of an individual who has put confidence in me to keep our identities and activities secret." He lifted his gaze to mine. "You understand the risk this puts all of us in, right?"

"I do," I said with a nod. "But I'm certain you know beyond a shadow of a doubt that the secrecy of you and your *business partner* would be safe with me. Think about it, if I were to reveal either of you, I would bring indictment upon myself in the process, now would I not?"

He studied my face for a moment. "What matters most is that I trust you. And although I have no reason to actually trust you whatsoever, I suppose I do." He sat forward with his forearms on his knees. "About ten miles south of here, you'll find a town called Tall Junction. Jeremiah York runs a trading post there, and if you tell him that I sent you, he should be able to help you."

"So I can trust him?"

Jonathan chuckled. "As much as you or I can be trusted."

Tall Junction sounded as though it would have been a large city where its railroad stop brought in thousands of people and goods by the hour. At least that's what I expected. But the truth of the matter is although it was not a small town, it wasn't exactly a major city.

Now don't get me wrong, there were more people on the streets here than I've seen in many of the big towns I've been through, but I reckon I expected more.

I also found it right odd that for a town just ten miles south of Warren's Gap, it was as dry and dusty as could be. Not even a hint of mud anywhere. They should have named the place Tall Desert if you ask me.

The trading post was a massive structure and quite a bit fancier than any other I had ever laid eyes on. The front of the building had large windows with gilded lettering that stood out, adorned with decorations of flags and bunting all around. Jeremiah York had obviously done well for himself, that's for sure. And who am I to question just how he accomplished that?

Tying Daisy out front, I took in the other structures and surroundings. The bank just down the street was a small brick building with large wooden doors, slate roofing, and a small porch with ornate columns. Most of the other businesses were brightly painted wooden structures, all clean and bustling with activity. One thing stood out more than anything else: I couldn't help but notice the sidewalks appeared freshly constructed and heavily treated with creosote, and they weren't tacky to walk on like I'd figured.

I couldn't see it from where I stood, but my nose kept telling me there was also a bakery somewhere nearby. I thought about searching it out before my visit to the trading post, but Charlie's voice kept coming to mind, reminding me to stay focused on the job and that there would be time to go there when the job was finished. And I couldn't help but reckon Bernice Appleton would be right impressed if I brought a few loaves back for dinner.

Stepping up to the trading post's door, I couldn't get over just how clean all the windows and siding was in spite of Tall Junction's swirling dust. Jeremiah York may have kept his hands dirty on the inner workings of the trading post, but he truly kept everything speckless on the outside.

Just inward of the door, there was items hanging everywhere. Anything you could think of or ask for they was right there within reach: pots and pans, towels and tools, clothing and furs, all hanging or stacked and neatly folded on shelves. The place downright smelled like a freshly built cabin—the headiness of new wood and the staleness of drying hides. And somewhere among all of that was coffee.

I heard voices on the other side of the mountain of merchandise, but I could not make out the conversation. I was able to determine it was two men—that much I knew, but that was about it. It must have been York and a customer coming to some agreement as to price.

I followed toward the end of the displayed goods to get to where the proprietor's counter would be. I realized that had I gone the opposite direction at the door, it would have been a clear path to the front. But I could better hear the voices the closer I got to the side.

I started to make the turn at the end but quietly stopped when I saw the man behind the counter conversing with Lieutenant Collins.

Chapter Thirteen

I'm sure I don't have to tell you that a one-armed fella stands out in a person's memories far more so than someone with all their limbs. I mean, think about it: if someone asked you to describe what I looked like as a witness to a crime, you wouldn't tell them that I had brown eyes, or that I had a thick beard, or that I was tall and skinny or short and fat—you'd mention right away that I was missing an arm. And that's the reason I couldn't let the lieutenant see me there in the trading post.

After all, he just may have noticed the one-armed man eating at the hotel when he was talking with Rose as she stood right there at my table. And even though I hoped that the loudmouthed salesman distracted him enough from taking note of me at all, I had to move forward with the assumption that he'd laid eyes on me. And you need to remember, the Army trains men like Collins to always be aware of their surroundings and to take notice of the smallest details. And for that very reason, I could ill afford for this man to see me in another location of his investigation.

"So if someone brings the watch in to sell or pawn, please let me know," I overheard Lieutenant Collins say as he returned his hat to his head. "And I assure you that the U.S. Army will reward you quite handsomely."

"I would be more than happy to do so," the man behind the counter said. "And just where might I send word should the watch in question make its way here?"

"We have a camp set up in Sanderson for the time being." He pulled the hat further down above his eyes. "If I'm not there, leave word with one of the men, and I will come immediately. Just don't mention it in front of Major Martin, as again, the watch is a surprise gift for his retirement."

"Understood."

I ducked back further when the lieutenant turned to leave.

"The U.S. Army thanks you for your time and trouble," he said, moving toward the door.

Once Collins was outside and walking away, I continued to search the items on the wall as though I'd not heard the conversation.

"I did not see you come in," the proprietor said, moving out from behind the counter.

"You sure have the selection." I pushed my hat back and grinned. "Lord have mercy if you ain't got everything a body would need, no matter what the need would be."

"I do try," the man said, holding out a hand, then turning a mite pinkish when he realized my shaking-hand arm was gone. "My apologies."

"I'm used to it by now, I reckon." I held out my left hand. "My name's Lawrence Thornhill."

"Jeremiah York," he said, awkwardly shaking left-handed. "Welcome to my establishment."

I searched the room for other individuals milling about but couldn't find another soul. "I have something I'd like to discuss in private, if you don't mind."

"I don't suppose it gets any more private than this," he said, looking the place over. "Come and rest your legs."

The scent of coffee was stronger at the counter, mixed with a hint of tobacco. Not tobacco smoke, mind you, but tobacco ready to be purchased.

York reached under the counter and retrieved a bottle of whiskey and two glasses. "I hope you like bourbon," he said, filling each glass. "Because unless I'm mistaken, I recognize a Kentucky accent when I hear one." He slid a glass toward me and winked. "And us Kentucky fellas are truly fond of our bourbon."

Picking up the glass, I held it out to clink against his. "We do indeed." I drank it back and smiled. "What part of the Commonwealth are you from?"

"Maysville," York said, placing his glass on the counter. "Moved here nearly fifteen years ago." He lifted his eyebrows. "What about you?"

"Booneville."

"Is that right? You know, you're the first person I've ever met from Booneville."

"I highly doubt that," I said with a laugh. "I'm probably just the only one dumb enough to actually admit it to you."

York broke into hearty laughter as he refilled our glasses. "You just might be correct on that fact." He motioned toward the stool in front of the counter. "Have a seat."

I drank back the whiskey and wiped my lips. "That's some good stuff right there."

"Now," York said, settling onto his own stool behind the counter. I couldn't help but notice the scattergun he had within reach. "What was it that you wanted to talk about in private?"

"Well, first of all," I said, sliding my glass onto the counter, "I reckon the best way to commence this conversation would be to let you know we have a mutual friend and confidant."

"Oh? And who might that be?"

Leaning forward, I studied his face. "Jonathan Meade."

A twitch of a smile was all he offered, and it appeared to be more of a reaction than anything. "Ah," he said, leaning back against the wall. "I haven't seen Jonathan in quite some time now. I hope he's in good health."

"He's doing fine." I nodded. "He's doing just fine."

"That's good. I have always thought of Jonathan as a fine, upstanding individual."

I lifted my eyebrows and moved my head just slightly to the right. "Jonathan and I have been working on a few jobs together." I smiled. "And after a discussion as to how we can sell a number of *items* that, I should say, require a bit of discretion, he mentioned you."

"Did he now?" York said, sitting forward. "And exactly what kind of items are we discussing here?"

"First, let me tell you that Jonathan wanted me to make sure to let you know that he'd sent me and to make sure you know that he and I were working together." I glanced at his fidgeting hands before returning my gaze to his face. "But he told me you could be trusted."

"I see," he said with a blank expression. "Stolen goods."

"Stolen is a mite strong word." I cocked my head and squinted toward the rafters. "Perhaps *acquired* would be a more suitable word in this case."

"Am I to assume his uncle is still protecting him?"

"From what I gather, his uncle is out of a job, and so is he."

This caused York to give in to a smile. "And that explains why the two of you are working together."

I nodded and grinned. "He told me you were smart."

"So what *acquired* items do you have?" he asked. "And please don't tell me you have a gold watch."

"No watches." I placed the gunny sack on the counter. "Take a look for yourself."

Lifting the bag, he bounced it lightly in front of him. "It's got a bit of heft to it, I'll tell you that much." He gazed up at me before looking inside. "I don't want to know where any of it came from. Understood?"

"I didn't want to tell you anyways."

"Give me a few minutes," he said, making his way to the doorway just off to the left. "Should anyone come in, let them know I will be out directly."

"Certainly."

"You do trust me to examine everything in the back, right?"

"Jonathan assured me that you could be trusted. And that's good enough for me."

"The fact that both of us put our trust in that old buzzard speaks volumes about you and me," he said with a laugh. "Volumes."

"You truly *do* know him," I said, laughing along with him.

A few moments after York left the room, a tall woman came through the front door, pulling a young'un by the hand. The woman looked weary with age and stress, no more than forty years of age, and the boy was dressed right smartly for a toddler.

"Is Mr. York available?" the woman asked in a breathy voice. "Alvin broke my pot today, and I'm in desperate need of a new one if I'm to have supper ready before his father comes home."

"He's just in the back room, ma'am," I said, nodding toward the door. "I'm sure he will be back in just a few minutes."

"Thank you," she said, pulling the boy away from the shelves.

"Mrs. Hamilton," York said, stepping from the back room. "And to what do I owe this pleasure?"

"I'm afraid Alvin has broken my good pot, and I need a new one for supper."

"Well, Alvin is just a growing boy," he said, moving toward a shelf and retrieving a pot. "Is this the size you need?"

"Yes, thank you."

Handing her the pot, York offered an exaggerated smile. "Shall I just put this on your account?"

"Would you please?" she said, pulling the boy toward the door. "I need to get supper started." And with that, she made her way outside, still tugging the poor boy along the sidewalk.

"I declare, if that little Alvin doesn't keep me in business," York said with a laugh. "Now," he said, turning toward me, "you have a number of expensive items here, that's for certain, but the rest are typical."

"Is that good or bad?"

"I'll give you four hundred dollars for the lot of it."

"We have a deal," I said with a smile. "But I want my gunny sack back."

I'm not sure which of us was happier about making it back to the boarding house, me or Daisy. Lord, I ain't never looked forward to traipsing in mud in all my live-long days. And Daisy downright acted like she was about to commence into clog dancing when we got her in the stable. But the old gal was too tuckered to even feed or take water, so she went right to her side on the ground with her legs sticking straight out. It had been a long and dry ride, that much is for certain, and we came within an ace of depleting the water bladder on the way back.

I feared we wouldn't make it in time for dinner, but as luck would have it, we got back nearly half an hour beforehand. And I'll be dogged if I didn't need every minute of that time to make it up them stairs to the room. It was right quiet, as I'd expected Jonathan to already be there, since he usually made it back well before that time.

I'd no more sat on the edge of the bed when Bernice Appleton showed up, wiping her hands on a towel.

"Dinner is ready," she said as her gaze swept the room. "Oh, is Mr. Meade still out and about?"

"I reckon so, ma'am. I just got here myself and ain't seen hide nor hair of him. Come to think of it, his roan wasn't in the stable when I put Daisy up."

"That isn't like him," she said, twisting the towel in her hands. "Jonathan is always punctual."

"Yes ma'am. I was studying about that myself." I offered a smile to comfort her, but it didn't do a dad-blasted thing for me. "I'm sure he'll be along shortly."

Nodding, she took a small step backward. "Yes, I'm certain you are correct." She took another step back. "Nevertheless, wash up and join us in the dining room."

"Yes ma'am."

Residents sat patiently at the table, offering smiles, nods, and welcoming gestures, yet somehow managing to refrain from conversations. After all, it was Bernice Appleton's belief that discussions prior to the blessing was not of God. It was also her belief that friendly discourse after the fact would not bring reproach upon the home. But introductions and announcements was about the extent of what was permissible before the praying ensued.

"Everyone," Appleton said, stepping into the room. "I would like you to join me in welcoming my niece to the home. Rose will be staying with us for a few days."

Well, I'll be damned. The woman from the hotel stepped into the room and offered a nervous smile.

"Let's take our seats," Appleton said to the girl.

Lord knows I got a mite fluttery in my gut when the young lady offered a recognizing grin as she sat next to me.

"And Mr. Hamblen, would you please offer the blessing for this meal?"

Nodding, the old man raised his face toward the rafters and then back down as he interlocked his fingers in front of himself. "Our most gracious heavenly Father, we come before thee today with thanksgiving in our hearts and humbleness in our souls . . ."

I ain't gonna lie about it, I had an awful time trying to pay mind to the prayer with that floral scent that kept sneaking over my way.

". . . Thou hast shown thy glory upon us again this day, oh Lord, as thou doest every day of our lives. We ask that thou bless this wonderful bounty set before us and also bless the hands that so graciously prepared it. In Jesus' name, amen."

As the amens echoed around the table, I leaned toward Rose and whispered, "Somebody sure needs to tell the parson that this ain't no time to get caught up on his prayer life."

Rose's hand may have concealed the smile on her lips, but it did very little in the way of hiding the laughter in her eyes. "You're going to get me in trouble with Aunt Bernie."

"I had no idea the two of you were related."

She reached for a platter and smiled again. "She and my mother are sisters." Her smile dimmed a bit. "*Were* sisters."

"And you call her *Aunt Bernie*?" I said with a laugh.

"What's so funny about that?"

"I don't know." I quickly glanced at Bernice Appleton. "Your aunt just doesn't strike me as someone who would appreciate being called Bernie."

Scooping cut potatoes onto her plate, she nodded. "Ever since I was just a little girl." She motioned toward the platter she held. "Potatoes?"

"Yes ma'am. But I can get them myself."

"Don't be silly," she said with a laugh. "I have them already in my hands." She didn't check with me as to how much I wanted—she scooped what she felt was appropriate and handed the platter to the woman waiting to her right.

"So what brings you here?"

"I like to check on Aunt Bernie from time to time." She used a fork to place chicken on my plate and then into hers. "I have to make sure she is taking care of herself." She gave me that smile again. "She takes pride in caring for everyone else and for everyone else's needs. And sometimes all that attention to others can blind her from caring for herself."

"I could see that with her."

"Well, my goodness, we were beginning to worry about you," Appleton said when Jonathan stepped through the doorway.

"My apologies, ma'am. I lost track of time while finishing some work in town."

"Thank God evil had not beset you, Mr. Meade," Hamblen said, reverently. "We're living in the end times when men will rob and kill for mere silver and gold."

Jonathan took a chair across from us and started filling his plate.

"Why Rose," Appleton said, leaning forward to inspect the young woman's lapel. "What has happened to your beetle brooch?"

Rose's hand went to the spot where the pin normally rested. "Road agents took it," she said, shaking her head. "They robbed the stagecoach I was on. Took all the money and valuables we all had in our possession at gunpoint."

Jonathan's gaze met mine without offering a reaction.

"Come quickly, Lord Jesus!" Hamblen said toward the rafters. "Just as it was in the days of Noah."

Appleton moved behind Rose and embraced her. "I am so sorry this happened, my dear. I know what that brooch meant to you, seeing how your momma was the one who gave it to you."

"It's been hard," Rose said, her voice breaking. "I've shed more tears over the past few days than I have over the rest of my life."

I cleared my throat. "I'm right sorry for your loss."

Jonathan raised his eyebrows, maintaining his gaze on mine.

"Thank you," Rose said, dabbing at her eyes with a handkerchief. "Thank you all. I guess I needed to be with you, Aunt Bernie. Seeing how you and Momma were so much alike and all." She dabbed at her eyes again. "It kind of feels like being near Momma."

"Well, you are welcome to stay as long as you like," Appleton said, moving back to her chair. "And we'll pray that the Lord brings nothing but shame and guilt upon the hearts of those evil men."

"Amen!" Hamblen said with vigor. "As well as eternal damnation!"

"Amen," I echoed with the others and then realized my hand was in my pocket holding the cold beetle.

"You seemed a mite distracted at dinner," Jonathan said, plopping onto his bed. "And you sure couldn't hide your interest in that young lady."

Rubbing my leg, I eased onto the edge of my own bed. "I've known her for a while." I kept my gaze on my feet as I removed a boot. "She works at the hotel I frequent."

Jonathan lay back on the bed and crossed his legs. "Were you able to sell the items to York?"

"I was," I said flatly. "I'm a thanking you."

He placed his hands behind his head. "Tell me. Was there a silver beetle in the items you sold to York?"

"There was not."

"And you have nothing to do with that young woman's brooch?"

I reclined into my own bed and released a deep breath. "I wouldn't go *that* far."

"That's what I figured."

My stomach commenced to cramping to the point I thought I was going to have to make a trip to the privy at this late hour.

"So you still have the beetle?"

"Keep your voice down," I said, glancing toward the door. "And yes, I still have it."

His chuckles seemed to be more for me than himself. "You sure beat everything, you know that?"

"It appears so."

"Tell me, what are your plans for the beetle?" He rose to an elbow. "You must have a plan since you didn't sell it, and you can ill afford to be caught with it." His smile was deliberate. "And through it all, you appear to be smitten with this young lady."

"Just shut the hell up, would you?"

"And you're still using that blackguardish talk. I'm just waiting for shame and guilt to weigh on your evil heart."

Chapter Fourteen

If we're speaking truthfully here, I ain't ashamed to say I learned just as much from Aunt Alice when it came to hard things as I did from Charlie or anyone else for that matter. And she never once made me feel as though she was looking down her nose at me when she did it.

She taught me to pay close mind to preparation and that behind every exciting action, there was real work to be done—duties that nobody wanted to do. It was Aunt Alice who taught me to spend more time, more than double in fact, cleaning and oiling pistols and long guns than actually firing them.

So with all the practice shooting she had me doing, I found myself on the front porch more often than not, scrubbing and oiling.

"Well, I want you to look at that," she said with her hands on her hips. "I do believe you're getting the hang of it."

"I could be practicing right now."

She gave me that stern glare that seems to be in every momma. "You *are* practicing."

"I don't—"

"It's just as much practice to keep your firearms prepared and maintained." She pointed a crooked finger my way. "And don't you sass me."

"I don't mean to, ma'am." I tried to soothe the aching from my fingers. "I just don't know why this water has to be scalding like you've got it. It sure burns something awful."

"Heated water dries faster on the metal," she said, taking the Colt from my hand. "That way it won't take to rusting so quickly." She looked the pistol over and handed it back to me. "Yes sir, I do believe you're starting to get the hang of it."

"That does make sense, but it sure don't make the burning go away."

"This is true," she said with a laugh. "Now come inside, breakfast is on the table."

The hearty aroma of pork shoulder filled the house, and when I laid my eyes on them cathead biscuits, I came mighty close to doing a jig right there.

"I won't know how to act when I have to leave here," I said, taking a seat. "But I'll tell you this much, I sure won't be eating this good wherever it is I end up."

"I appreciate you saying so, but I have no doubt that you'll forget about my cooking within a few weeks once you settle in at your next stop."

She placed a dark, amber-filled Mason jar beside my plate. "I know how you like sorghum syrup."

"Yes ma'am," I said, dribbling a puddle onto my plate. "Perfect for biscuit sopping."

Aunt Alice eased into her usual chair next to the window and smiled. "It sure does my heart good to see someone enjoying my cooking."

"Are you feeling poorly?" I asked before taking another bite.

"No, I'm fine. Why do you ask?"

"Just curious is all," I said in between chewing. "Seeing how you're not eating."

"Like I said, it does my heart good just watching someone enjoy my cooking."

"Then keep watching," I said with a laugh. "'Cause I'm fixing to make you even happier when I dig into seconds!"

She threw her head back and laughed harder than I reckon I'd ever witnessed.

"Tell me about growing up in Kentucky, Lawrence." She leaned back in the chair and rubbed her neck. "You don't talk much about it, or your ma and pa for that matter."

"Not much to say, really." The back of my legs tingled. "We was the poorest family on the hollow, and that's saying something right there because the whole place was poor." I scooted the plate back a smidge. "Didn't help nary at all that Pa was a drunkard." I steadied my breathing to avoid the looming hitch in my chest.

The tingling spread to my back. "Mean drunk," I was finally able to get out.

Aunt Alice remained silent, even when she placed a hand over mine.

Shaking my head, I dropped my gaze to the table. "I reckon Ma got the worst of it, but the son of a bitch beat Virgil and me nearly every evening." I tried to swallow back a sob. "He'd use his mining belt, fists, and sometimes even tree limbs. Our backs and legs would be striped with blood and cuts and welts."

I looked away, cleared my throat, and breathed as slow as I could.

She squeezed my hand. "You don't have to say any more if you don't want to, Lawrence. I'm so sorry for dredging up those memories. I had no idea."

I tried to smile the tears away, and it almost worked. "But if you want to know the truth of it all, I reckon the part that hurts the most was him telling us that we'd never amount to anything." A single sob broke through, and tears warmed my face. "Said we was worthless, and he'd wished we'd never been born."

"Oh, Lawrence," she said, moving to put her arms around me. "I am so sorry."

I wiped at the tears that I'd sworn for years I'd never let return.

"Listen to me." Her whispers were right at my ear. "There will always be someone in your life who doesn't see your worth. Whatever you do, Lawrence, don't ever let that someone be you."

I sat up in the bed. "Well, tell me, did you get the document finished?"

"Not completely." Jonathan rose to his feet and shut the window. "Had some delays while trying to get into the office."

"Delays?"

"It seems there are a few new workers in the courthouse." He closed his eyes and lifted his brow. "And they have been moving things around, even into other offices and storage areas."

The cramping returned. "So no problems with the workers, right?"

"No problems, just delays. It takes longer when I have to search for the things I need.'"

"When do you think it will be completed?"

"I had to wait for the ink to set well in particular areas before I can place signatures and final touches." He shrugged. "I'm certain I will be able to bring it here tomorrow."

We stared into the hallway when footsteps echoed from the stairwell. Hamblen appeared at the top and shuffled forward in the hallway.

"Mr. Meade," he said with a wheezing breath. "How joyous it is to know you have made it home safe and sound. Glory be unto our heavenly Father for keeping His hand upon you as you traveled through this modern-day Sodom and Gomorrah."

"Thank you. You have a good evening."

"And to you," he said with a nod. "And you as well, Mr. Thornhill."

"God bless you, Mr. Hamblen," I said as he moved on down the hallway.

Jonathan gave me an unimpressed gaze. I wouldn't have called it a glare, but it damn sure appeared to be warming up to one. "Will you stop it?" he whispered.

"What? I can't say 'God bless you' to Mr. Hamblen?"

He moved back to his bed and climbed in. "Don't play senseless with me."

"What makes you reckon I'm *playing*?"

He released a long yawn. "How much did you reveal to York?"

"Nothing much," I said, rising to my elbow. "I told him you and I were friends and have worked some together. You know, just to build his confidence."

"I hope this doesn't put a strain on the working relationship he and I have."

"Why would you fear such a thing?"

"Oh come on," he said, nearly laughing. "How would you feel if I pointed someone in your direction, revealing your illegal past?"

"Well . . ."

"That's right. You'd probably feel betrayed."

"If he had a problem with the situation, he didn't show it." I smiled. "And he went through the process and made the deal."

"He had no choice, Lawrence." There was real anger in his voice now. "And I can't help but feel as though I defiled his trust."

"I apologize for putting you in that position. And I do see your point. I'm just used to working in gangs where there are many associates in many areas."

"I'm sure he is fine." Jonathan's voice became calmer, quieter. "I reckon I will just need to pay him a visit as soon as I can manage it to thank him for his help and to apologize for putting *him* in that position."

"Understood," I said, laying back on the bed again. "But what I don't understand is why I am not allowed to tell Mr. Hamblen, 'God bless you.'"

"I tell you what," Jonathan said, rolling over onto his side, turning away from me. "Why don't you just go to hell? All right? Why don't you just put on your Sunday best and go straight to hell?"

"Be careful there," I said, chuckling. "I'll be forced to report your blackguardish talk to Mrs. Appleton."

Daisy was up and at 'em when I got to the stable the next morning. She was obviously happy to see me, but she was also a bit standoffish, as if worried we were about to make another burdensome trip.

"Don't you worry, girl," I said, holding out an apple. "I ain't in no shape to make another trip like that either."

She took to the apple after eyeing me for a brief moment. Her ears twitched, and her tail shooed flies away as she chewed.

"How's that for a special treat?"

That apple was gone lickety-split, and the old gal went to nosing my hand and pockets for another.

"That's all I got," I said, patting her side. "But I'll see about getting you another one this evening. Lord knows you've earned it."

"I heard talking when I came up on the door," Rose said, entering the stable with a bucket of water. "I thought for sure you were having a conversation with someone in here."

"I am." I rushed over to relieve her of the load. "Been talking to my best gal there, Daisy."

Rose laughed. "Well, she sure is a pretty girl," she said, rubbing both sides of Daisy's face.

Placing the bucket next to the stall, I leaned against the railing. "She and I are recuperating from a long, dry ride yesterday."

"I see," Rose said with a smile. "Well, I think it's wonderful that you have each other to care for."

"I reckon Mrs. Appleton has a long list of chores for you today, but I sure hate to see you packing water like that."

"Oh no, that's not the case at all." Rose looked at me with those beautiful eyes. "I just knew the water needed brought out here, so I did it."

"So you don't have any other chores waiting then?"

Shaking her head, she smiled. "Nope. Aunt Bernie treats me like I'm a resident. But I want to help as much as she'll let me."

I poured some of the water into Daisy's trough. "You're gonna keep saying that, and one of these days I'll end up embarrassing myself by calling her that."

She laughed and looked back toward the doorway. "Have you been to the chicken coop?"

"Seen it," I said. "Is it your aunt's?"

"Oh no, Parnell owns it. I'm not sure if you've met him, but he owns the restaurant in front."

"I have met him." I nodded. "Now that's a fella who knows his way around the cookstove, I'll tell you that much."

"He sure does. His pancakes are delightful."

"Well, I reckon it makes sense for him to have the coop," I said. "Seeing how he owns the eatery and all."

"Of course. But he also sells eggs to Aunt Bernie and the other residents as well."

"I see what you're doing." I gave her a sneaky grin. "You keep saying her name like that just to get it in my head. I know what you're doing—you're trying to set me up."

She laughed and took my arm. "Come with me, and I'll show you the hens."

The chicken coop was larger than I'd remembered from when Jonathan and I stood by the cornfield. And it was also louder the closer we got to it.

"Mind the rooster," Rose said, opening the gate. "He's a testy cuss who is a bit overprotective of the hens."

"How can you tell the difference?"

"Tell the difference in what?"

"The rooster and the hens."

She stopped at the coop door. "I thought you were from Kentucky."

"I *am* from Kentucky, but we'd never been around chickens."

"You're telling me they didn't have chickens in Kentucky?"

"That's not what I meant. I'm just saying we were too poor to have any livestock or critters. And our neighbors were all the same."

"Well, the rooster has a much larger and brighter comb and wattles," she said, gesturing around her head. "Longer tail feathers, and they have spurs on their feet." She gave me a pointed look. "And you do *not* want anything to do with those spurs. Trust me."

"Right, no spurs. This sounds like a lot of fun."

She laughed. "If you don't get too close to the rooster or challenge him, you'll be fine."

"Why in God's name would I challenge the rooster?" I followed her as she made her way around to the side of the structure. "And what would the rooster consider a challenge?"

She laughed again. "Just do as I do, and you'll be fine. Oh, and don't stare the rooster in the eye."

I had a burning sensation go through my stomach. "Lord knows the things I'll do for a pretty girl."

She turned to me with a playful smile. "What was that?"

"I said I'm gonna have a new appreciation for eggs after this is all over with."

Laughing, Rose reached down and picked up a reddish hen. "This is Loretta."

"Howdy, ma'am," I said, tipping my hat to the chicken. "Right nice to meet you."

The hen's head twitched from this way to that without appearing to look at anything.

"Would you like to go inside and take a look at the nests where they lay the eggs?"

I gave her a confused look. "Are you talking to me or Loretta?"

She placed the hen back to the ground and made her way to the door. "This coop is much larger than most I've seen. But Parnell wanted to make sure he always had plenty of eggs." She turned to me again before opening the door. "Remember what I said about the rooster."

"You have nothing to worry about, I ain't about to challenge the dad-blasted thing," I said with a laugh.

I was surprised at how much quieter it was inside the structure and that it wasn't as stuffy as I'd imagined. There weren't many chickens in there, but it appeared there was room enough for dozens of them.

"Those are the nesting boxes," Rose said, pointing toward a row of segregated spaces lined with chopped straw. "That's where you find the eggs." She motioned toward the other wall where boards stretched from end to end over an empty space. "And those are the roosting perches."

"Where's the rooster?"

"He's around here somewhere," she said, searching in all directions. "I'm sure he's been watching us since we came in."

"Well, that's exactly the news I wanted to hear."

"It's no big deal," she said with a laugh. "He flogged me the last time I was in here." She shook her head. "But he didn't spur none. He just wanted to warn me."

"What did you do?"

"I left."

"You're smarter than I thought you to be."

One of the chickens, bigger than the others now that I recollect upon it, dropped from a perch, lowered its head, and stomped its way toward us.

"That's him," Rose said in a whisper.

The rooster pretended to charge a few times with its neck feathers all hackled up like an old angry dog, and I swear to you that damned thing growled. At least, that's what I thought I heard.

"Let's go," Rose said, pulling me slowly toward the door. "Just don't make any sudden movements."

That little bastard hounded us all the way to the door. "I don't think he cares how fast or slow we move," I said, keeping my gaze on him.

"Just keep moving."

Right about the time we were getting ready to get out the door, the rooster launched at us, flapping its wings against me while feathers were flying everywhere. But the moment we stepped outside, it turned back to where it came from.

"Are you okay?" Rose asked, inspecting my pant legs. "You're not cut, are you?"

"I don't reckon." I closed the door and felt at my shins and calves.

"I think he was just trying to scare you."

I laughed. "He didn't *try*, ma'am. He succeeded."

We both laughed.

Once outside the fence, I inspected myself more closely. There weren't any cuts or holes in the material, and thankfully, I didn't feel any pain.

"Are you sure you're okay?"

"I'm fine," I said with a smile. "He didn't get you, did he?"

"He couldn't get to me with you between us." She took my arm and led me toward the board house. "Thank you for protecting me."

"I reckon *protecting* is a might strong word for *getting in the way*."

She stopped and turned toward me. "The truth is, I felt safe with you, that's what I mean."

Now I ain't gonna lie to you, that caught me a little off guard. "Oh," I said, trying desperately to find words. "That is mighty kind of you to say." I nodded. "I'm a thanking you."

She turned back toward the board house. "I sure wish I'd had you with me when those road agents attacked the stagecoach."

Lord have mercy if my stomach didn't sour up like I was sweaty from barrel fever. "And I sure wish I'd been there for you, ma'am."

Chapter Fifteen

It was everything I could do to keep myself busy in order to get my mind off watching and waiting for Jonathan's return. But I reckon the more I worked at it, the more it laid on my mind something awful.

Why, I even offered to chop wood for Mrs. Appleton, but she put up such a fight, saying she worried I'd hurt myself seeing as I only had the one arm. But when she saw I could do it, she left me be and went on about her other chores. Thank the good Lord Aunt Alice put an axe in my hand and set me to practicing while I was at her place.

I ended up in the stable cleaning Daisy's hooves. The dirt was really packed in there with dried mud—putting me to mind of plaster, making it hard to scrape out. I studied about taking her to a nearby creek to help wash it all out easier but didn't want to leave.

"I'm gonna have to get you to a blacksmith, girl." I ran my fingers over the metal shoes and determined it wasn't a dire need just yet.

But Lord knows she was getting a mite nervous with all the scraping and picking, and the last thing I wanted was to get myself kicked.

"All right, just calm down," I said, easing her leg to the ground and rubbing her belly. "I'll stop." I cautioned myself as to just where to stand and for how long.

The old gal's side took to a few shivers when I finally commenced to brushing. Lord knows she enjoyed it so much she ended up talking to me, I reckon letting me know just how much she appreciated it all. And one of the things that always got me to laughing was how she'd show her teeth when I'd brush under her chin.

Now Jonathan could claim that donkey was his all he wanted, but I reckon Daisy and I both had something to say about that.

I'm not sure how Bernice Appleton did it, but there wasn't nary a smell you'd find in any other stable. She'd obviously tidied up quite a bit since I'd been here, but it was just downright odd that a body could make a stable smell like . . . well, anything but a stable.

My knees got a mite queasy when I heard a rider coming up on the door. Jonathan looked as though he was downright surprised.

Dismounting, he grasped the roan's reins and led the beast inside. "What are you doing in here?"

I put the brush away and opened a stall for him. "Just piddling around."

"I see." His grin was aimed right at me. "You've been waiting on me to get back."

Well, I couldn't exactly deny it, but I sure didn't want to admit to it either. "Daisy needed brushing."

"Uh huh." His grin dug a little deeper. "I can see that."

I shook my head. "Don't start with me."

"You're worse than any fretting mother I've ever met, you know that?"

"Don't give me no guff," I said, dipping my head. "Did you get the document finished or not?"

Turning quickly toward the door, Jonathan shushed me with a dour look. "Will you keep it down? My God, why don't we discuss this at the dinner table so we know everyone can hear it?"

He was right, of course. And damn it all to hell if I don't hate nothing more than being wrong in an argument. But I'd been cooped up all day trying to be patient while he was gone, not knowing when he'd be back and whether he was having problems or not. Hell, for all I knowed he coulda been laying by the roadside somewhere, scalped. But there is no doubt about this: he was absolutely right.

"Need help with the saddle?"

He shook his head. "Sorry for being so disagreeable. I've had a time today trying to get things done and not getting myself into any predicaments that would endanger my freedoms."

"Oh?"

Nodding, Jonathan removed the roan's saddle and set it aside. "We'll talk about it in the room."

Making our way through the back door, we'd no more made it inside the hallway when Bernice Appleton stepped from the kitchen. "Mr. Thornhill?" Her tone had a request attached to it. "Would you mind helping me with something?"

"Yes ma'am," I said, removing my hat.

"Oh hello, Jonathan, I didn't know you were back already." She brushed something from his shoulder. "If you don't mind me keeping Lawrence for a moment, I need his help with something before dinner."

"I do not mind at all," Jonathan said, his gaze shifting to mine. "Will you need my assistance as well? I can put my things away and be right back."

"No, that will not be necessary. I'm certain Lawrence can handle it."

He nodded at me and smiled. "I will leave the two of you to your tasks then."

Either his footsteps faded as he made his way toward the stairwell, or the aromas coming from the kitchen captured my full attention.

"Thank you for your assistance," Appleton said. "I am grateful."

"My pleasure, ma'am." I nodded. "I don't know how much you will be able to get out of me with these tempting smells coming from the cookstove, but I'll do my best. What is that I smell?"

Her smile was a mix somewhere between distraction and appreciation. "I'm preparing a saddle and leg of venison, served with currant jelly."

"My mouth is watering just thinking about it."

"I'm glad you approve," she said, heading back into the kitchen.

Lord have mercy if those smells didn't get stronger and better while standing in the same room where all the cooking was commencing.

"I have a serving dish that is stored on the third shelf," she said, pointing upward inside the pantry. "Would you be so kind as to retrieve it for me? I'm afraid I'm not quite tall enough."

"Yes ma'am," I said, stepping forward and reaching for the dish. "Anything I can do to help get these vittles in my belly faster, I'm more than happy to help."

"Thank you," she said, accepting the plate when I handed it to her. "I'm not sure how it was placed so far out of my reach."

"Anytime, ma'am."

Placing the dish on the table, Appleton wiped her hands on a towel. "While I have you, Mr. Thornhill, I'd like to ask you something."

My stomach got heavy and warm as I suddenly had the urge to make a trip to the privy. "Yes ma'am."

She stared up at me with the best gambler eyes I'd ever witnessed. "What are your intentions?"

Lord knows it was all I could do to hold my water. "Ma'am?"

Placing the towel next to the dish, Appleton lifted her eyebrows. "Your intentions. I've noticed you have taken an interest in my niece, Rose." She cocked her head. "What are your intentions?"

I shuffled my feet, hoping to distract my bladder. "I don't have any intentions, ma'am. We're not courting or anything, we just know each other."

"Mm hmm." I'm not sure how her eyebrows could reach further up her forehead, but they sure did. "I've seen how you take notice of her."

"Well, ma'am, she is a right pretty girl, I ain't gonna lie about that, but that don't mean that I have intentions of any kind."

"I understand that, and I do appreciate your candor," she said with her gaze still fixed to mine. "But I suppose I'm more worried about how she looks at *you*."

"Aw, she ain't interested in me none. She's just a mannerly young lady who is nice to everyone."

"Ha!" A smile broke across the old woman's face. "You don't even recognize it, do you?"

"Recognize what? I'm—"

She held up a hand for silence when the back door opened. We stood waiting for something, waiting for someone, anything.

"Well hello," Rose said, stepping into the kitchen carrying something.

"Here," I said, reaching for the bucket. "Let me get that for you."

"Thank you." Her smile removed the heaviness in my stomach. "I didn't expect to find you here in the kitchen."

Appleton gave me a smirk.

"I'm sorry, did I interrupt anything?" She was moving her gaze back and forth from me and her aunt.

"Oh no," Appleton said, taking the dish from the table. "I just needed someone tall enough to retrieve this from the pantry's top shelf." She smiled at me. "Thank you, Mr. Thornhill."

I stood there a moment, dumbfounded. "Yes ma'am." My legs felt heavy as though I was wading hip-deep waters in the winter. "If you will excuse me, I'm going to check on Jonathan in the room."

"Yes, you and Jonathan better get washed up for supper," Appleton said with that same sneaky grin. "Make sure you get down here in time to get a good seat." Her gaze moved to Rose and then almost immediately back to me.

"Yes ma'am."

My legs were still heavy after I got back from the privy. Lord knows I didn't think I was going to make it there for a moment. But I did. And then trying to climb them stairs was right difficult. And the conversation with Bernice Appleton kept coming back to me as I stepped. *She's only looking to protect her niece.* But the way the old woman let on, Rose was interested in me and gawking at me with sweetheart's eyes or something. *And yet she acted as though she was happy about the whole thing.*

By the time I made it to the room, I was worn slap out.

"Well, what chore did Mrs. Appleton have you doing?" Jonathan was stretched out on his bed with his boots still on.

I shook my head. "She couldn't reach a dish on the top shelf of the pantry."

"She couldn't use a stool or a chair?"

"I reckon not." I eased onto my bed. "Come to find out, fetching the dish was just an excuse for her to ask about me and Rose."

Swinging his legs around, Jonathan sat up. "You and Rose? What happened?"

"Nothing happened—she's just nosing around, thinking we have eyes for each other."

"Well, she's right about that," he said, straightening his shirt. "That's as plain as it gets when the two of you are in the same room together."

"That's not true."

Jonathan gave his goading grin. "So what is Appleton saying about it?"

"Oh, she's asking what my intentions were."

"And?"

"And what?"

"What did you tell her?" He shrugged. "And what *are* your intentions?"

I let out a loud breath. "I ain't got no intentions. And that's what I told her."

His grin seemed to be trying to pry more out of me.

"So what's this about your troubles at the courthouse?"

Pulling his saddlebag closer, Jonathan grunted. "Almost got caught while in my old office." He opened the bag and sat up. "New worker was looking for something and walked right in on me. Like to have scared the wits out of me."

"What'd you do?"

He briefly dipped his head to the side. "I told him I was delivering ink."

"Ink?"

"I was so surprised I didn't know what to say. I saw the ink on the desk, and that's what came out of my mouth."

"What'd he do?"

Jonathan closed his eyes and shook his head. "He asked if I could bring some new pencils the next time I delivered."

I laughed. "So he didn't suspect a thing?"

"I don't think so, but the whole time after he left, I kept thinking he'd said that so he could safely leave and get someone else to help apprehend me." He grinned. "But that obviously never happened."

"Were you able to get the document finished?"

Nodding, he dug into his saddlebag. "I was afraid to leave anything there after the incident. That's why I finished everything up and brought it with me."

"I'm glad. I don't reckon I could have waited another day."

He handed the folded paper to me and smiled. "Which is why I wish I could have delayed the whole process much longer."

"You're an evil man," I said, unfolding the document. "Pure evil."

"Well, coming from you, that is saying something."

The document's heading looked as official as the original order Private Rogers was carrying. "Jonathan," I said, still studying everything. "Each detail is just as perfect as it can be. This is amazing."

"I think it looks good, taking into consideration the little time I had working on it."

"It's perfect, I tell you." I finally looked up at him. "I'm taking this tomorrow to find the private and see if I can't get it into his hands somehow."

"Just be careful. Like I said, it may look perfect to you, but those soldiers see the real thing every day and could spot a fake much easier than anyone."

"They're not going to catch on to anything with this document, I guarantee it." I stepped toward him. "Hey, why don't you go with me? You can see their reactions for yourself. Then you will be able to see just how good your skills are."

"That's not a good idea. Remember, I don't want to risk my neck. That's why we did this as we did."

"I know," I said with excitement. "But you wouldn't have to sit with us or even be there with me. You could drink alone at another table and pretend you're not watching and still get to see the whole thing."

"It's too risky," he said, shaking his head. "If we move forward with a document for Ezra, and I am dressed in a uniform for that exchange, the last thing I want is for someone to remember me sitting there out of uniform a few nights prior and not interacting with my fellow soldiers."

"That's a very good point."

"However," he said, taking the document, "if you are able to swap this with the original the private has, I'd like you to bring that original back to me."

"Why would you want the original?"

"For one thing, you don't want to accidentally leave it where anyone could find it and then give yourself away." He shrugged. "But the biggest reason is I can go over the original to make adjustments and changes that may be more recent. New signatures or the way they are dating the orders now. You never know with the U.S. Army."

"That's smart." I was damn sure impressed with the way he thought.

"Once I'm finished with it, we have to burn it," he said, handing it back to me.

"I thought the same thing." I folded the document and placed it in my pocket. "Well then, I will make the trip to Sanderson tomorrow."

"In the meantime, we'd better get to dinner. We don't want your date missing you too badly."

"Lord have mercy."

Spooning beans onto my plate, Rose leaned closer and whispered, "Is it just me, or is Mr. Hamblen's prayers getting longer at every meal?"

I stifled a smile. "You know good and well the Lord himself is up there rolling his eyes at Hamblen's gaudy words."

"You two seem to be in your own world over there," Mrs. Appleton said, placing venison on her plate. "Anything you would like to share with the rest of us?"

Jonathan glanced at me with a shit-eating grin.

"My apologies, Aunt Bernie." Rose passed the beans to the woman next to her. "We were just talking about our little adventure earlier today."

I turned my head toward Rose, hoping my face wasn't as red as it felt.

"Adventure?" Mrs. Appleton handed Jonathan the venison platter without glancing at him. "Pray tell what you mean by *adventure*."

I could have sworn I heard Mr. Hamblen whispering scriptures.

"Well, earlier today, Lawrence and I visited the chicken coop. He'd never seen one." Rose turned to all the other residents. "Can you believe a fella as old as he is, and growing up in Kentucky, has never seen a chicken coop?"

A few mumbles and chuckles came from this.

"To be honest," I said, "I've seen chicken coops. I've just never—"

"He's never been inside one," Rose said with a laugh. "He didn't even know the difference between hens and roosters."

Hamblen choked on his coffee, spurring his wife to slap him on the back a few times.

"I know the difference between hens and roosters," I said.

"So I showed him the nests and the roosting perches and what everything looks like on the inside." She glanced over at me. "And I was telling him that we needed to be mindful of the rooster and that he may take a notion to attack if he feels we are endangering the hens."

Jonathan was quietly laughing, covering his mouth as his shoulders shook.

"And as sure as the world, while we were in there looking things over, the rooster dropped from his perch and stomped over to us with his hackle feathers all riled up and acted like he was going to charge two or three times."

Mr. Hamblen coughed and cleared his throat.

"And then, all of a sudden, that rooster went into a full assault." She rested her hand on my shoulder. "And Mr. Thornhill protected me from the attack. He put himself between me and that creature while it flogged him until we made it safely outside."

Mrs. Appleton stared at me with a hidden smile that I could tell was meant only for me. "Well, Mr. Thornhill, I suppose I owe you a debt of gratitude for protecting Rose in such a heroic fashion."

"Like I told your niece, ma'am, I was merely in the rooster's way. I ain't no hero or nothing."

"There's no need in being modest about it," Jonathan said with that grin I was beginning to hate. "You saved that girl."

"Jonathan is right," Mrs. Appleton said, allowing her smile to finally show. "Thank you for being there when Rose needed you, Mister Thornhill."

I know it's crazy, but at that moment, I swear I could feel the weight of that silver beetle inside my pocket. "Yes ma'am."

Chapter Sixteen

Daisy wasn't all that excited about making the trip to Sanderson. I can't say that I blame her after that recent haul to Tall Junction. Lord knows the old gal was probably worried that's where we were headed again.

"Simmer down," I said, getting the saddle on her. "We ain't going far. I promise you that."

She was trying to back away while I tied the saddlebag onto her, but she couldn't go too far. I took out the gunny sack to transfer the cash to my pocket and noticed the watch. *Shit*. It'd be a bad idea to have that anywhere on me or Daisy. I took the watch and studied the stable for a place to hide the dad-blasted thing until I returned. Getting caught with a forged Army document is one thing, I reckon, but getting caught with the company commander's stolen watch would be a right difficult thing to explain. A right difficult thing for my neck, for certain.

The hiding spot needed to be somewhere Mrs. Appleton wouldn't be able to find during her daily chores. Or a place where Jonathan, Rose, or anyone else, for that matter, couldn't just happen upon.

Nothing seemed like the right place no matter where I looked. The problem seemed to be that everything was too close or within reach.

I gazed toward the rafters and found the spot. Someone would have to be searching for the watch 'fore they'd find it up there. *That's it.* I gazed out the door to make sure nobody was nearby and then started climbing the stall's half-wall. It was easy to do from where the saddle rest stood, so I made my start there. Balancing myself on the half-wall's top railing, I was able to reach the rafter beam above it.

From there, I slid the watch onto the wide rafter, pushing it toward the middle so it wouldn't be seen from below on either side, and then climbed back down. I checked again to make sure no one was around and dusted myself off as best I could. "There we go, girl. Not too shoddy for a man with just one arm, don't you think?"

I patted my pocket one more time to make sure the document was there. The last thing I needed was to ride all that way and then discover I'd left the damned thing here in Warren's Gap. Especially if I'd left it out in the open here in the stable. That'd be a tough one to explain, as much as the watch, that's for sure.

I was leading Daisy out of the stable when the board house back door opened. I was never more thankful to see Rose instead of Bernice Appleton in all my life. I reckon for more reasons than one, if you want to know the truth about it.

"Are you leaving us today?" Her voice was soft and riddled with disappointment.

"Yes ma'am," I said, tipping my hat. "I have some things to take care of, but I fully intend to be back. Hopefully 'fore dinner, but more than likely a little later than that, I'd expect."

She walked closer, bringing that perfume she wore with her. "I hope I didn't embarrass you too much last night at the dinner table."

"No ma'am, I'm fine." My cheeks tingled with warmth. "I just wasn't expecting that conversation, is all."

She laughed. "Would you like to know how I could tell you're a good man, Lawrence Thornhill?"

Lord knows the heat in my cheeks spread to my neck and ears. "Now I wouldn't claim to be a good one, ma'am." I tried my best to not shuffle my feet but couldn't help it at all. "I'm just a regular fella, I guess."

Her smile just about did me in right there. "I know better than that. And you know how I know?"

"I wouldn't have the foggiest, ma'am."

She stepped closer and touched my arm. And I'm here to tell you every bit of that heat in my face and neck went straight to where her hand rested.

"While we were inside the chicken coop where nobody could see us, where we were all alone, you remained a gentleman." She shook her head. "You didn't try to kiss me or anything."

I cleared my throat. "Well, no ma'am. Why that would—"

"You didn't even let on that you thought about it." She cocked her head. "And I gave it some thought."

"You gave what some thought?"

"I was thinking that either you were truly being a gentleman by not trying to kiss me, or you didn't have any interest in me whatsoever."

"Oh, now I wouldn't go—"

"*But* I came to the conclusion that you were being a perfect gentleman the whole time." She lifted both arms into the air. "And do you want to know how I came to that conclusion?"

I ain't gonna lie about it, I kinda felt like I'd been drinking a mite too much. "Like I said, I ain't got the foggiest, ma'am."

"It's because you made me feel safe."

I stood there in front of her smiling face, not knowing what to say or do. "I keep telling you, I ain't no hero. I was merely in between you and that rooster."

She folded her arms over her chest. "That's not what I mean, Lawrence Thornhill." She cocked her head. "It wasn't anything you *did* that made me feel safe. It was something deep inside me that knew I could trust you."

All I could do was just stare at her. "Well, ma'am. I just want you to know that I will always do my best to remain a gentleman around you."

"Rose?" The voice of Bernice Appleton rang from somewhere just outside.

"We're not finished with this talk," Rose said, turning toward the door. "In here, Aunt Bernie!"

"There you are," Appleton said, stepping to the doorway and noticing me. "Oh, Mr. Thornhill, are you leaving?"

"Yes ma'am," I said and cleared my throat. "Got some business to tend to."

"Oh my, will you be back for dinner?"

I briefly glanced at Rose. "I'm hoping to, ma'am, but I wouldn't count on it if I was you." I gave her a saddened expression. "But I plan to be back before curfew at the least."

"Well, if you're not back in time for supper, we'll hold something back for you," she said with a smile.

Rose lifted her eyebrows and grinned.

"I'm a thanking you, ma'am."

"Now," she said, turning to Rose. "I need to get you to boil some eggs and peel some potatoes if you don't mind." She glanced back at me and smiled. "I seem to have lost track of time and need to get caught up with everything."

"I will get right on it," Rose said.

"Well, go ahead and get to it." Appleton gazed back at me. "I need to speak with Mr. Thornhill before he leaves."

Rose gave me a wide-eyed stare before turning to leave. "I'll get started right away."

Waiting until the boarding house back door clattered shut, Mrs. Appleton lifted her chin and smiled. "Rose is quite smitten with you, Mr. Thornhill."

"Well, like I said before, ma'am, she's just being nice and friendly, that's all."

"Oh, I think we both know better than that."

The burning returned, but this time it was in my stomach. "Ma'am, I can assure you I have never done anything to sway her or . . ." Lord knows my stomach felt as though there was hot grease in there now. "I mean . . ."

Mrs. Appleton laughed. "I can see why Rose fancies you," she said, nodding. "You're a good talker. Always seem to have the right things to say. You're courteous and mannerly." She lifted her eyebrows. "Which is a rarity in this day and age."

I waited, knowing she wasn't finished.

"And," she said with a smile, "in spite of having just the one arm, you're as strong as any other young man I know."

That heat was moving up into my chest and face now.

"But the most impressive thing about you is that you haven't disappointed her in any of your behaviors or actions." She nodded again. "And I want you to know that I am very much appreciative of that."

I tried my best to think of something to say without sounding queer or scared. "When I told you I had no intentions, ma'am, I truly meant that." I stared at Daisy's reins. "That don't mean I don't fancy your niece. But I don't reckon that means I don't hope for intentions after a proper period of time." I tried to swallow a dry spell in my throat. "But I promise you I would never do anything to bring reproach upon her, you, or the family."

Bernice Appleton reached up and placed a warm hand to my cheek. "I do believe that, Mr. Thornhill. I truly believe that." She gently patted my cheek. "And that is all that I will ever ask or expect of you."

Upon my honor to God, if it wasn't downright impossible to get Rose off my mind the whole time Daisy and I were on the road back to Sanderson. Rose's playful recounting of our chicken coop incident at the dinner table made me think she just might be taking a shine to me after all. Lord knows why.

And I wasn't exactly sure how Mrs. Appleton felt about her niece and me cavorting about as we'd been doing. I mean, we wasn't officially sparking or anything, but Appleton sure didn't seem to mind the two of us spending time together as it was.

Daisy snorted and bobbed her head, which got me minding the road closer as well as taking in my surroundings better. Lord knows Rose's smile consumed my mind to the point that I didn't have the foggiest as to how far along we'd traveled already.

Slowing Daisy's pace, I turned in the saddle to examine the road behind us but didn't notice anything out of the ordinary. I was surprised there wasn't even a kick-up of dust from our movement, so it seemed to me we hadn't traipsed too far away from the ever-present rain clouds of Warren's Gap.

I spotted a rocky area with small hillocks just ahead and decided I would take the opportunity to make water while adequate cover could be found. A man has to take every precaution when he's at his most vulnerable—at least that's what Charlie loved to say. And I don't reckon a fella can get any more vulnerable than while he's out in the open trying to do just that.

I dismounted and led Daisy to the right as far back as we could go to get behind some of those larger rocks so we wouldn't be seen from the road. Looping the reins around my arm so she wouldn't wander off, I commenced to relieving myself.

It's a strange feeling when you don't have the terrible pangs of overfullness but immediately recognize just how badly you needed to go when you finally do.

"I can ride for days now, girl," I said with a laugh. "But I'm just as happy as you are that we are most certainly *not* going to be riding for days." I decided we would just wait there for a spell so Daisy could get a little more rest and do her business if she took mind to it. The rest would be done safely out of sight until we took back to the road.

There wasn't much of a breeze to speak of, especially among those formations and hillocks, but the wildlife sure was active with unseen chattering and so forth.

Daisy bobbed her head and turned her ears. That's when I noticed the sound of something near the road. Taking hold of her bridle, I peeked around the cover and noticed a lone horseman heading in the same direction we'd been traveling.

"Easy, girl," I whispered without taking my gaze away from the figure. "Let's remain steady and quiet."

The fella sat tall in the saddle and had a rhythmic bounce that matched the horse's gait. He never glanced in our direction, but there was something oddly familiar. I recognized the Morgan before I identified the rider as Jarvis O'Sullivan.

This is all I need right now.

It was everything in me to resist rushing out and shooting that fella down while he wasn't prepared for an exchange. I resisted because I knew it was safer for me and Daisy to just let the boy ride by. At least I knew he'd be ahead and not behind us, and to be watching for him at every turn without him knowing we were there. But I declare if I didn't have the feeling that by doing that, I would just be putting off the ruckus for another day.

Just as he was about to pass on by us, Jarvis veered toward the rock formations where we were hidden. He didn't appear to suspicion we was there, or that he was studying anything in particular. He merely dismounted, hobbled his critter, and limped closer toward the rocks with his bandaged leg I'd shot. My stomach felt as though somebody was wringing it out like a wet towel. I was ready to draw my Colt when the bastard finally unbuttoned his trousers to make water himself, oblivious to anything around him.

Look at him right out in the open. I shook my head. *That's a farm hound for sure. Not the wolf he thinks he is.*

I rubbed Daisy's neck to keep her calm and quiet. The last thing I needed was for her to pick up on my nervousness and get antsy.

Jarvis finished his business but stared toward the rocks for a moment. Craning his neck, he quietly leaned to the side, then moved his head forward. I couldn't tell if he was gazing in my direction or in some other general area, but I'll tell you this much: that knot in my gut sure got a good wringing again.

He slowly removed his revolver from its holster and took a quieted step forward, keeping his gaze fixed in our direction. I rubbed Daisy's neck again before resting my hand on the Colt's grip.

Jarvis froze in his tracks, eased that pistol into an aim toward our direction, and fired. The noise caused Daisy to flinch, but thankfully, she didn't make nary a sound.

Returning his revolver to its holster, Jarvis smiled as he limped forward and finally lifted a bloodied rabbit. "That'll be good for the empty gut, it will," I heard him say as he turned back toward his horse.

My stomach kept telling me to step out there and shoot the son of a bitch once and for all and then take his varmint for supper. But my mind kept telling me that the best way to avoid danger was to not take unnecessary chances. But I ain't going to lie to you, I feared my growling belly was going to give away our position 'fore Jarvis could even mount up and ride off.

Daisy and me waited there for a long stretch after the boy was back on the road just to be sure he was completely out of sight and earshot.

I knew we couldn't wait too long, though, as I didn't want to be on the road once darkness came. But I sure wanted to give that boy a healthy head start.

As I led the old gal back to the road, I searched to make sure no one else was coming our way from either direction. "Let's go, Daisy," I said, climbing back into the saddle. "Me and you are going to have to keep an eye out for that fella from here on out." I chuckled. "And that means I'm going to have to keep my mind off that girl back at the board house."

If I hadn't known any better, I'd have sworn on a stack of Bibles that I was pulling into Sanderson on the very same night that I'd left it last. I mean to tell you, it looked as though it was the same people out on the town, wearing the same clothing, and coming and going around the same places.

But by the time I made it inside the saloon, I could tell this was a whole new crowd from my last stop. Of course, there were a few individuals who were there from the other night, but I didn't recognize the majority of the people gambling or drinking.

"Bottle of whiskey," I said to the barkeep as I stepped forward. "And a glass, if you don't mind."

"Certainly."

Sliding the money across the bar top, I scanned the room for an empty table. "Last time I was in here, I was drinking with a few soldiers. Private Rogers, I believe, was the one fella's name, and two others." I turned back to the man. "Have you seen them today?"

He pulled a soggy cigar butt from his lips and shrugged. "Don't know their names, son. Just their faces."

"Understood." I placed the drinking glass upside down over the bottle top and carried it all to a table. "Much obliged."

I reckon the thing that concerned me the most was that there wasn't a uniform one in the place. But it was still early, and those boys could have been coming off duty at any moment. That was my hope at least.

I poured myself a drink and watched everything from the side. The poker players was as quiet as any gamblers I've ever seen, mostly watching everyone else, studying their cards, and speaking softly when they did speak. It looked to me like there was more bluffing going on than anything.

A few soldiers finally came through the door, but they weren't any of the fellas I was waiting for. They looked to be a couple of privates, though, just getting off duty and ready to commence their elbow drills for the evening.

"Excuse me," I said to them when they took the table next to mine. "Last time I was in here, I got to drink with a few of your fellow soldiers. I was hoping to see them again tonight before heading back home." I offered a smile. "Private Rogers is the one fella and two others."

"I reckon Rogers has drank with every person in the territory at one time or another," one of them said with a laugh.

"That's right," the other one said. "He's never met a bottle he didn't like."

I joined them in their laughter. "Well, that sure sounds like the fellas I was with for sure. Do you know if they'll be in this evening?"

"I wouldn't bet on it." The first soldier took a drink and turned toward his friend. "Aren't they on guard duty?"

"I believe you're right," the other said, nodding. "If I'm not mistaken, they get off soon, but they're probably going to get some sleep, as they've been up for nearly sixteen hours."

"Lord have mercy," I said, shaking my head. "They work you fellas too hard if you ask me."

"You've got that right." The soldier drained his glass and sighed loudly. "And you don't know the half of it."

I held up the whiskey bottle. "Care to join me? You fellas look as though you need more thirst quenching."

"Sure," the first fella said as the two made their way to my table. "But we don't have a lot of money to buy rounds or anything."

"Bring your glasses," I said, refilling my own. "That's all you'll need at my table. It's the least I can do to show my appreciation for your service."

"Thank you kindly," the other fella said, placing his glass on the table to be filled.

"Here," I said, sliding the bottle toward them. "Pour for yourselves."

As we were drinking, I took notice of the time and figured that since Rogers and his friends were not coming, I could more than likely make it back to the board house in time for dinner. *Maybe come back tomorrow.* "Well, gentlemen, I reckon I will be on my way, but I'd like to say thank you for spending time with me over a good drink or two."

"Wait a minute," one of the soldiers said, pointing toward the door. "Look who just made it here."

I found my hand in my pocket, holding the folded document.

"We didn't think you fellas would make it tonight," one of the soldiers at the table said. "Thought you would have got some much-needed sleep."

"You know me," Rogers said, making his way to the table. "I can't sleep a wink if I don't get some whiskey in my blood."

We all laughed. "Good to see you fellas again," I said, rising to my feet. "Give me a second, and I'll get us another bottle. You boys best get some glasses."

Rogers looked into my face. "Lawrence, right?"

"You are correct. I was beginning to worry that I wouldn't get to see you fellas tonight."

We drank a few rounds, and I bought another bottle when the first two soldiers left to go on duty. Rogers and his friends did not act as though they'd been on duty for sixteen hours. Why, unless I knew, I would have guessed they'd been up for only a few hours. The fellas may not have been tired, but they sure as hell were feeling the whiskey.

"You know that man you fellas are going to extradite in a few days, Reginald Barley. Yes, that's his name. His uncle lives in my town," I said, pouring more whiskey for us all. "He said that the fella was a pretty tough character, so you boys need to take precautions with him."

"Who did you say?" Rogers said with a slur.

"Reginald Barley. You know, the fella you boys are going to take to Fort Hays."

"That's not his name." Rogers shook his head.

I gave him an exaggerated look of confusion. "I'm fairly certain it's the same fella."

"No, that's not his name at all," Rogers said before draining his glass again. "His name is . . ." He stared off into nothingness.

"Reginald Barley," I said again. "I distinctly remember that was the name on the document you showed me."

"Are you sure about that?" one of the other fellas said.

"I'm telling you, that is not the man's name." Rogers commenced to digging into his sack. "I can't remember what his name was, but I know it wasn't Barley."

"Anyway, his uncle told me he was a mean old son of a bitch." I poured more drinks as I kept my gaze on the boy's actions.

"I'm telling you that's not his name." Finally retrieving the document, Rogers unfolded it and studied the words. "See," he said, pointing at the paper. "His name is Reginald *Bailey*. Not Barley."

"Are you sure?" I craned my neck theatrically to see. "Can I have a look?"

Sliding the document toward me, Rogers grinned. "Right there. *Bailey* is his name."

"Let me see," I said, picking up the document. "Where is that again?"

"There," Rogers said, touching the name, at which time I pretended that the gesture knocked the document out of my hand and onto the floor.

"I got it," I said, going under the table. "I believe you're right." I quickly folded the original and switched it with the one I'd brought with me, unfolding the fake as I got back into my chair. "Well, I'll be damned," I said, handing the forgery to Rogers. "I could have sworn it said Barley and not Bailey."

"I told you," he said, pouring more whiskey.

"Now the signatures at the bottom there." I gestured toward the table. "Whose signatures are they?"

Rogers glanced at the document and pointed to the first name. "This one is the company commander, Major J.B. Martin." He then pointed at the second one. "And this one is the executive officer, Lieutenant Collins."

I studied his face and couldn't find a reaction one way or another as to the signatures or the document in general. "Well, they sure have some pretty fancy handwriting." I poured another round and laughed. "Maybe if you fellas could write fancier, you'd move up in the ranks faster."

We all laughed and drank.

"I'm going to have to get back to the homeplace," I said, rising to my feet. "But I'd like to buy you fellas another bottle 'fore I go."

"You don't have to do that," Rogers said as his grin widened. "But we sure won't stand in your way of doing it."

I put the bottle on the table and turned to leave. "You fellas be mighty careful out on your runs, you hear?"

"You be safe as well," Rogers said.

As I got to the entrance, I reached for the document in my pocket to make sure it was secured, and I'm here to tell you I damn near dropped the dad-blasted thing. *Jesus*. At that very moment, the door swung open and hit me right in the face.

"Oh, excuse me," Lieutenant Collins said, reaching for me as he stepped inside. "I had no idea anyone was in front of the door."

I touched my nose and realized the document was no longer in my hand.

"Let me get that for you," Collins said, picking up the folded paper. As he was handing it to me, his eyebrows came down over his nose. "Hold on there."

"I'm a thanking you, sir," I said, groping for the document.

Pulling away, Collins unfolded the thing and looked back at me. "Now why would you be carrying an official order from the U.S. Army?"

Chapter Seventeen

"Your arm strength is fine," Aunt Alice said from behind me. "But your problem is you're pulling the trigger instead of squeezing it." She took the Colt and removed the cartridges. "See, when you *pull* the trigger, it's jerking your aim to the side as well."

"I don't think I'm—"

"But if you *squeeze* the trigger like this." She gently brought the trigger straight back. "It doesn't nudge your aim to one side or the other. Don't use the very tip of your finger or the crook of the joint. Squeeze with the cushion of skin between." She handed me the Colt and cartridges. "Try it."

"You could have at least put the cartridges back."

"You need the practice doing it with the one hand." She made sure I noticed her exaggerated squint. "And don't you sass me."

"Yes ma'am."

I took aim and paid mind to the trigger. I squeezed off a round, and the tin can flew into the air.

"See?" she said, nodding toward the fence. "That was dead center."

I retrieved the casing and holstered the Colt. "Did you teach Ezra to shoot?"

"Lord no," she said, gazing at the ground and shaking her head. "His daddy taught him." She glanced at me with a raised eyebrow. "That's why the poor boy can't hit a hillside in full bloom."

I laughed. "I've often wondered about that, but it sure does make sense."

"That's why I'm counting on you to take care of him, Lawrence." She wasn't laughing or smiling at all.

I tried to un-grin my own face. "Yes ma'am. You know I'll protect him as best I can."

"You're all each other's got, you know." She finally offered a soft smile. "And you know he'll do the same for you."

"He's already proven that."

Nodding, Aunt Alice turned toward the house. "Just don't expect the poor boy to shoot straight."

I laughed a little too hard at this. "Yes ma'am."

"I hope you've worked up an appetite," she said, turning back to me as she walked. "I've made us a stew from the rabbit you killed yesterday."

"I've been studying about what your plans would be for that rabbit."

"I'm not sure if I told you or not, but that back part of the house is the original cabin Pa built." She put her hands on her hips as though to rest. "If you remember me telling you about the time I was shooting Indians with one hand while holding my baby brother in the other, that's the very window I was firing from," she said, gesturing toward the back. "Pa built the rest of the house as he could."

"Ezra told me about him putting whiskey out on that rock," I said, pointing to the enormous slab near the corner post.

Her smile looked like that of a little girl's. "Did he tell you what happened?"

"He said the attacks stopped."

She nodded and chuckled. "Now, we never made friends with the natives, but we never had problems with them again." She shook her head. "Pa put out whiskey every year on that rock, and every year it disappeared without a sound."

"Do you still put whiskey out there?"

Her smile waned. "I do. But none's been touched for several years now." She shrugged. "You know how the natives are—they never stay put in one place for very long—they're always moving with the wind, as they say."

"More whiskey for you."

She smiled. "Oh no. I put those bottles out every year, right there in the same place, just the same as Pa did. I don't ever drink it."

I glanced at the slab and then back to her. "You think any of those Indians today will remember the pact?"

"It doesn't matter," she said, staring into the wind. "I remember. And that's all that counts."

I cleared my throat. "Ezra talked quite a bit about the rock."

"I might he did," she said, finally looking to me. "It is his sacred place, after all. And you should be honored that he shared it with you."

"Oh, I am indeed."

"Has he told you what he's buried there in the front of it?"

"Well." I studied her face for a moment. "He mentioned a few things, like coins and items his Pa gave him, and some items from you as well."

"It's hard to tell what you would find buried there," she said with a laugh. "And not just from him."

"I don't reckon I understand."

She motioned for me to follow her back to the house. "His pa did the same thing."

"He buried things there as well?"

"He did. When he was younger." She smiled to herself. "He hinted to Ezra that there was buried treasure there somewhere, and Ezra started digging holes everywhere until he found his pa's things." Her smile became something else, but I couldn't figure out just what. "I reckon that was the only thing Gerald gave that boy. Not the items in the ground, mind you, but a sense of wonder."

"He said the place was sacred before you said it."

She turned toward me as her smile returned. "And isn't it, though?" She slapped her hips and turned back again toward the house. "Let's get into that rabbit stew."

"Yes ma'am."

The stew was so good, all I could think about was getting outside and finding another rabbit as soon as I could. It didn't matter to me that the kick from the scattergun was still burning in my shoulder. I had to get more of this.

"You best slow down," Aunt Alice said with a grin. "You're about to end up with some of that stew in your lungs if you're not careful, sucking it down so fast."

"I can't help it. It's good. I feel like a biting sal with this stuff."

"Just slow down," she said, motioning toward the cookstove. "There's plenty more."

I broke open a biscuit from breakfast and sopped up what was left on my plate. "You ever bury anything at the rock?"

"I'm afraid not." She didn't look up from her plate—just kept eating. "I reckon I ain't never had that sense of wonder that Gerald had." She put her spoon down but never looked up. "But there again, look what that wonder did for him."

"I'm sorry for bringing up those memories again."

She picked up her plate and moved to the cookstove. "It's not you, Lawrence." She plopped a few more spoonfuls of stew onto her plate. "Here." She nodded at the stovetop. "Bring me your plate."

"I think I'm getting a mite full, to be honest."

Shrugging, she put her plate back on the table and sat. "You see, the thing is this, Lawrence." She pointed her spoon at me and squinted. "All memories are tied together. Every good one will almost always lead to a bad one." She scooped a spoonful of stew into her mouth. "And every bad one will eventually bring you back to a good one."

I stuck the rest of the biscuit into my mouth.

"The key," she said, pointing the spoon at me again, "is to make as many of the good ones as you can." She took another bite and lowered her gaze. "Because you're surely going to need them."

"Mighty good advice, ma'am."

She stared out the window and chewed. "But to answer your question, the only treasures I buried were not trinkets or coins. And none there at the rock." She rose from the table and moved to the window. "Come here."

When I stood next to her, she pointed toward the field's edge. "See those three white crosses?"

"Yes ma'am."

"Those are the only treasures I've buried out here." Her eyes reddened. "Ma and Pa and Gerald." She turned back to me and smiled. "Ezra Dale is all I have now." She softly placed her hand against my cheek. "Him and you are all I have now."

I don't know what got into me, but I ain't never fought off tears like I did at that very moment. I feared that if I tried to say something, I would bawl like a little young'un. Ain't nobody ever made me feel like I was part of a real family. It's hard to explain, and I ain't ashamed to say I was right confused. But it was almost like sadness and happiness and fear and joy. And the whole time, I didn't understand why I wanted to weep.

"I hope I didn't embarrass you." She smiled and went back to the table. "I hope you know that that was not my intention."

"I'm fine, ma'am," I managed to whisper. "And I sure do appreciate you including me in your family and the people you care about."

She stared right at me with a smile that I will never forget. "Just remember, Lawrence," she finally said. "We never bury our memories to hide them—we bury those memories so we will always know exactly where to find them when we need them most."

Drawing his revolver, Lieutenant Collins put a bead on me 'fore I had a chance to even move. "Get that arm up where I can see it," he said, stepping closer.

I reckon I was so stunned and angry at my own stupidity that I just stood there gawking.

"You men at the table back there," he yelled across the room. "Come apprehend this individual."

The soldiers scrambled forward and did as they were told.

"Take his sidearm." Collins nodded toward my belt. "And be sure to check for other weapons."

"Yes sir," Rogers said, taking the Colt from my holster. Other hands checked my pockets and waistband. "What'd he do, Lieutenant?"

"This." Collins held up the order for the others to see. "He was walking out the door with an official U.S. Army document."

"Want us to take him to the jail, sir?" one of the other privates asked.

"No. One of you men come stand guard at the door. Nobody leaves until I say they can leave."

I ain't gonna lie about it, my neck started itching like a son of a bitch. "I can explain everything."

"Oh, you're going to do some explaining." Collins placed the barrel of his revolver against my chest. "You're going to do a *lot* of explaining."

"Wait just a doggone minute," Rogers said, stepping forward. "Whose name is on that order, Lieutenant?"

Collins held the document up to his eyes. "Reginald Bailey. Why do you ask?"

"I knew it! That son of a bitch stole the document from me."

"Now why would you steal an extradition order from a U.S. soldier?" His eyes hardened. "Especially for Reginald Bailey?"

I shook my head. "Rogers is wrong. I ain't stole nothing."

"That's a bunch of horse shit," Rogers said to me. "And you know it."

"How did this man steal the order from you, Private?"

"I have no idea, sir. I did show it to him, but I remember distinctly putting it back in my sack." He shrugged. "I don't know how he was able to get it out without me knowing."

"I'm telling you, I ain't stole nothing."

Collins moved his gaze back to Rogers. "Show me where you had it stowed away."

Upon my honor to God, that itching in my neck turned into a genuine burning sensation.

"I didn't have it in any special place," Rogers said, digging through his sack. "I just had it here among . . ." His mouth dropped open as he retrieved the forged document. "What in the hell?"

"What's the problem?" Collins said, craning his neck to see.

Rogers unfolded the paper and stared blankly at it before turning it toward the lieutenant. "The order is here."

Collins stole a glance at me before focusing on Rogers again. "What's the name on that document?"

"Same as the name on the one you're holding. Reginald Bailey."

"What?" He stared into me. "Do you want to tell me what the hell is going on here?"

"I told you I ain't stole nothing."

Collins folded the order and put it in his jacket pocket. "Hand me that one, Private."

"Yes sir."

Collins folded the second order and placed it in his other trouser pocket. "Take him to the camp detaining cell." He holstered his revolver. "I don't want anyone else near him, and I don't want word to get out about this at all. If he has someone in camp helping him, I do not want to alert them of his capture."

"I don't have anyone—"

"You will get your chance to talk. I assure you of that."

The detaining cell they put me in was a tumbleweed wagon just out behind the lieutenant's tent. He wasn't fooling me none—I knew what his plans was. He didn't want me in the Sanderson jail or for anyone to know about the incident so he could string me up when he was good and ready. And it was all because I was too foolhardy to not secure the document better.

Darkness was already upon us, and bugs and moths swarmed the lamp the men had posted to keep an eye on me by.

Lieutenant Collins sat in a chair, smoking a pipe, and comparing the two documents. "I have to be honest," he said, squinting. "I truly can't tell which one is the original and which is the forgery." He glanced up at me. "Very detailed work you've done here."

"Not my work."

"First of all, what is your name?"

"I've got to make water."

Shrugging, he took another pull on his pipe. "You need no permission from me."

"You're not going to let me out?"

"No need. Do your business through the bars on the other side." He blew smoke into the sky. "I will ask again, what is your name?"

"What exactly are you holding me for?" I said, turning toward the back bars. "You know good and well I ain't stole nothing."

"So you think forgery is not a crime? Especially when the document being forged is an official U.S. Army order?"

"All I'm saying is this," I said, trying not to talk queerly while I pissed. "I found that document and was looking for someone to turn it in to."

Collins chuckled. "You had been sitting at a table filled with soldiers the entire evening. You had chance after chance to turn it over to them and didn't."

I finished up and turned back to the lieutenant. "I reckon I worried they weren't high enough in rank."

Collins laughed. "I hope you understand how ridiculous that sounds," he said, shaking his head. "You're worse than a fox trying everything possible to get its paw out of a trap." He rose to his feet and stretched. "Until it finally comes to terms with its plight."

"I reckon you fellas made the same order twice by mistake. It's plain to see you made a mistake."

He laughed again. "See what I mean?" He turned to go back inside his tent. "Let me know when you have come to terms with your plight and when you're ready to stop wasting our time, both yours and mine."

I put my face between the bars when he stepped into his tent. "My name is Lawrence Thornhill."

He came back outside holding up the two documents. "Well, tell me, Mr. Thornhill. Why am I holding two orders that look exactly the same?" He pointed at me. "And I want the truth."

My stomach went to warbling and cutting up something awful. "I'll tell you everything you want to know. But can I at least get me something to eat first?"

Cocking his head, Collins lifted an eyebrow. "Son, the stalling needs to end right here."

"I ain't stalling none at all, I promise. I done made it known that I'd tell you everything." I rubbed my belly. "It's just hard to think on an empty stomach."

He just stared at me. No smile, no glare, nothing. "Franklin!"

I just about jumped through my skin when he yelled that. I feared my ghost was moving on without me.

"Yes sir," a corporal said, stepping out of the tent before standing rigid still.

"Get our guest here something to eat."

"Yes sir," the corporal said, still at attention. "Anything in particular, sir?"

"I don't care what you get, as long as it's ready for him to eat now."

"Yes sir." And he went back the way he'd come.

"Now that we have that out of the way, Mr. Thornhill." He moved his head slightly to the right and lifted his eyebrows. "Tell me *everything,* as you put it."

"First of all, I wasn't the one that made the forgery." I could see he was going to say something. "But I did have it with me."

"Well, that much I could have told you."

"My goal was to see if your soldiers would be able to tell the difference between the real one and the fake one."

"As a test of some sort?"

"That's right," I said, shaking my head. "There was no plan of changing the course of action for the poor soul who is listed on the documents."

"So you just wanted to make sure you could fool us with this incident."

"That's right."

"I see," he said, moving closer to the cage. "And had you fooled us with this forgery—and let me be quite honest with you, you did in fact succeed in fooling us—what was the test for? What would you have done next had we not caught you in the act?"

"Here is the food, sir," Franklin said, returning in a rush.

"Good." Collins nodded toward me. "Just give it to him."

"I'm a thanking you," I said to the corporal.

"Thank you, Franklin. That is all for now."

The beans looked like they'd been cooking since I was a boy and smelled like they'd been burned a number of times along the way.

"You do know we could take you out right now and hang you for your actions, right?"

"I told you—"

"And the only thing that will prevent that from happening is for you to stop your stalling and talk." He offered a gruff chuckle. "Because I won't hesitate to string you up with those beans still in your mouth."

It seemed like everyone was wanting to hang me. "Now listen—"

"Franklin, bring me the lynching rope!"

Chapter Eighteen

"I'm not finished talking," I said, placing the tin plate on the floor of the cell. "I said I'd tell you everything, and that's what I intend to do."

"Here's the rope, sir," the corporal said, stepping from the tent.

"Thank you, Franklin. Put it beside my chair there." Collins didn't even look at the soldier. "Hopefully we won't have need of it tonight after all." He finally glanced at the man. "That's all for now."

"Yes sir."

"All right, Thornhill. Now, tell me why you were testing to see if we would be fooled by your forged document."

Lord knows the burning in my neck had gotten to the point where it was damn near impossible to swallow through it. "You're holding a very close friend of mine." I nodded. "You're about to extradite him to Fort Hays."

"Who's your friend?"

"Before I tell you that, I want you to understand that he don't know nothing about any of this. So, no matter what happens, I don't want him getting any trouble over it because he was totally unaware of it."

"What's his name?"

My gut felt like something was boiling in it. "Ezra Tackett."

The lieutenant's gaze shifted up into a thought somewhere. "Ezra Tackett," he repeated.

"Like I said, he doesn't have nary a clue about any of this."

"All right, what about your friend, Ezra Tackett?"

"Well, sir, the danged fool got himself caught thieving horses, and I reckon those horses wound up belonging to the U.S. Army." I shook my head. "I've told him time and again he was going to find himself at the wrong end of a rope if he didn't stop."

"That's right," Collins said. "He broke out of jail not long ago and was caught before he could leave town. So what does any of this have to do with forged documents?"

"The test was to see if you fellas would recognize a forged document of your very own. If we decided to fake an order with Ezra's name on it, and someone dressed in an army uniform showed up for him with that order, we'd save him from the gallows."

"We?"

"How's that?"

Collins shrugged. "You said 'we.' Who is the other person involved?"

"He's the reason we did the test. He made the forgery but didn't think that you fellas would be fooled. So he was totally against the whole thing."

"What's his name?"

"Jonathan Meade. His uncle was a circuit judge nearby and got him a job working in the courthouse."

"And that was your plan? Produce a forged document and send someone in a forged Army uniform to extradite your friend?"

"The uniform isn't a fake." Now as soon as I said it, I knowed that was something I should have kept to myself.

"I see."

Heat was building in my face and ears. "It was just horses," I said. "And you fellas got 'em all back from what I'm told."

"We did." He took out his pipe and packed tobacco into its chamber. "But that does not take away from his crime." He lit the pipe and puffed. "If we just let him go, what's to keep him from doing it again?"

"I promise to keep him on the straight and narrow."

"You?" His laughter sent dribbles of smoke into the air. "What makes you think you will be free to keep him in line?"

"I promise you this: if you let Ezra and me go, you will never have to worry about us giving you any problems again. None."

"I can hang you both and never have to worry again."

Lord have mercy, that boiling was in my stomach again. "That's true. That's true, but . . ."

"You see? You're reverting back to that fox with his paw in the trap, yipping in every direction to get loose and run as fast as you can."

There had to be something I could say, something I could do.

"In fact, if I hang you both, I'll scare other foxes away from giving us trouble as well."

"Again, that's true, but . . ." I stepped closer to the bars. "But if you did that, I promise you'd never see that watch again."

Now that got his attention. He pulled the pipe from his lips and squinted. "Watch?"

"You know damn well what I'm talking about. I'm talking about that gold watch you and the other men pitched in to buy for the company commander's retirement."

Collins stepped closer, cleaning the ashes from his pipe. "What do you know about the watch?"

"I know where the damned thing is, for one." Lord knows I ain't never wanted my arm back so badly just so I could cross both over my chest at this point. "Ain't nobody else knows where it is but me."

"Is that right?" He tapped the pipe's bowl against the root of his thumb. "How do I know you're telling the truth?"

"I reckon you're just going to have to trust me, aren't you?"

"I reckon the man who was in possession of that watch wouldn't have any trouble describing it, would he?"

I smiled. "I reckon not."

"Tell me, Thornhill, what does the watch look like?"

"Well, it's gold, a right handsome piece, to be honest."

A smirk of unbelief tugged at his upper lip. "Is that all?"

"And if I was a betting man, I'd be willing to bet that your company commander enjoys running hounds on stag hunts."

The smirk disappeared. "Is that all?"

"Other than the inscription inside the cover?"

"All right, it sounds like you've seen it."

I did a little smirking myself. "Major J.B. Martin."

"You've made your point. So where is it?"

I laughed. "Slow down there, Lieutenant. I think we've got ourselves some renegotiating to do now that some new information has been revealed, wouldn't you agree?"

He smiled. "Why would you think I would negotiate with you?"

"To be honest, I ain't got the foggiest. But I do know that watch means a whole heap more to you than you're letting on."

Collins lowered himself into his chair. "What do you want?"

"Oh, we *are* negotiating now?"

"Don't push it, Thornhill. Just tell me what you want."

I sank to the floor and crossed my legs. "I want Ezra, Jonathan, and me all freed and for no one to pursue us after everything is over." I shook my head. "I give you my word that not one of us three will ever give the U.S. Army further trouble of any kind."

"That's asking quite a bit." He lifted his chin. "For so little."

"You reckon getting the watch back is something to consider as *so little*?" I smiled. "And what's so important about that watch and the commander's retirement?"

Collins just stared. "It's just a watch for retirement. But it is important nonetheless."

"I don't reckon you're telling me the whole truth, Lieutenant. I just can't help but wonder what else is behind this watch."

"What if I require terms to include in our . . . negotiations?"

"That's what we are doing here. What other terms do you have?"

"Jonathan Meade. Is he the one behind the forgeries?"

"I told you he goes free the same as Ezra and me."

Nodding, Collins smiled. "I understand, but this pertains to my additional terms in the negotiations."

"Yes, Meade is behind the forgeries. Why?"

"Because part of the terms may be that he agrees to produce a document for me. Under secrecy, of course."

"I see. What kind of document?"

"That would be determined at a later date. And between Meade and myself."

The soft breeze came over us with just a hint of a cooler temperature in the air.

"I'm sure Meade would be agreeable to that, seeing how he wouldn't be in trouble with the U.S. Army."

"Now these terms say nothing as to protecting you from future offenses, you understand. If any of you steal a horse that belongs to the Army, for instance, you'll face the charges."

"Understood."

"It's settled. You will stay in the cell until we leave in the morning to retrieve the watch."

"Come on, don't make me sleep in this cramped thing—we have come to our terms."

"That we have. And allowing you out of that cell before we leave was never part of the negotiations."

"Come on, Lieutenant, don't you trust me?"

"Absolutely not," he said, rising to his feet. "After all you have told me, there is no way I could trust you to stay put until we left."

"Well, then can I at least get something decent to eat?"

Sleeping in the tumbleweed wagon was as bad as it sounds. It was my first time doing it, and hopefully my last. I was stiff all over, and my neck felt like I'd been lynched in the middle of the night.

Collins put me and Daisy in front so he could keep an eye on me.

"I had concerns that you would try to flee while we are on this trip," he said with a chuckle. "But all my concerns were put to ease when I saw your donkey."

"I have no reason to flee." I glanced back at him for a moment. "Our agreement gives me all that I want. And don't tease Daisy— she's my best girl."

"This Jonathan Meade you mentioned, will he be at the location we are heading toward?"

"Should be. He and I share a room at the boarding house." I shifted in the saddle and slowed Daisy's gait. "I've been thinking about something that's been gnawing at me all night."

"What's that?"

"It's this whole gold watch thing."

"What about it?"

I scrunched up my nose. "It just seems there's something more behind the watch, that's all."

"The men and I purchased a very expensive watch for our retiring leader, and it was stolen." He cocked his head. "What more could there be?"

"You tell me."

Collins released a deep breath. "I am hoping to make an indelible impression so the major will promote me to captain and recommend me for the commander position upon his retirement."

I shrugged. "It just seems queer to me that you're worried too much over your commanding officer retiring and that you may not be moving into that position."

"Why do you find that peculiar?"

"I don't know, I reckon it just seems . . . *peculiar*, as you say, that you are serving as the executive officer in a small unit with specific duties." I dug out a tobacco plug and cut off a hunk. "Seems to me that when the commanding officer retires from a unit like that, the second in command knows the job better than anyone else. I just find it queer. Or as you say, peculiar."

"I think the major just doesn't care too much for me personally. Let's just leave it at that."

I plopped the tobacco into my mouth and started working it. "So you don't reckon it has anything to do with how good or bad you do your job? Is that what you're saying?"

Collins didn't answer right away, so I turned to look at him.

"My concerns have nothing to do with my performance as executive officer."

"I see." I leaned to the side and spat. "So why do you reckon he doesn't care for you personally?"

"Mr. Thornhill, I appreciate your concern for my status and advancement, I truly do, but I would be grateful if we ended this particular conversation."

"Yes sir," I said, smiling. "I ain't trying to get your dander up. Honest, I'm not. Like I said, it's been something on my mind." I leaned to the side and spat again. "I'll tell you this, though. I sure am thankful you didn't bring me all this way in that tumbleweed wagon. Lord have mercy. I reckon that thing would have jarred the ever-loving guts right out of me."

"I gave it consideration."

"I might you did, but I sure am glad you decided to trust me a little more."

I heard him chuckle. "Mr. Thornhill, I have a number of considerations when it comes to you, and I can assure you *trust* is most certainly not one of them."

I couldn't help but do a little chuckling myself at that. "You're right smarter than I'd originally given you credit for, Lieutenant." I pulled Daisy to a halt and turned back to him. "But there is one thing I'd like to ask of you."

"What's that?" he said, bringing his own horse to a stop.

I rubbed at the back of my still-aching neck. "When we get to the boarding house, I would hope we could refrain from mentioning any of the issues we've talked about as it pertains to Jonathan and myself?"

He smiled. "Oh, I see, the boarders and landlord aren't aware of your criminal pasts. Is that it?"

I cleared my throat. "Well, that's not exactly how I would have put it, but to be honest with you, I reckon that about sums it up perfectly." I leaned again to the side and spat. "Let's just tell them you're an old friend who is stopping by for a moment as you're passing through the territory."

His smile turned downright smug. "All I'm hearing is the fox yipping again to get his paw out of the trap."

Lord knows I was beginning to hate him and that damned fox. "We agree to this now, or the deal is off." I leaned forward. "I don't want to see nary one of these fine folks hurt in any way. Understood?"

"What's this?" Collins said, lifting his eyebrows. "If I didn't know any better, I would suspect you of having a great deal of love and loyalty to a group of individuals other than those in your band of thieves and criminals."

I held my gaze to his. "I said we agree now, or the deal is off."

"It was a compliment, Mr. Thornhill." His original smile returned. "And you should know that this is the same feeling I have about my men and the company I serve under."

My gaze did not move. "I didn't hear an agreement."

"Yes," he said, nodding. "We have an agreement."

Upon my honor to God, if there seemed to be more mud at Warren's Gap when we arrived than there had been when I'd left the day before.

"Hold your judgment until we get around back," I said as we led our critters by the planking.

"This is worse than any hog pen I have ever witnessed."

"You're going to be as surprised as I was the first time I saw everything out back." I found myself smiling. "Just you wait and see."

When we made the turn at the corner and started down the broad sidewalks, sunshine poked through the clouds to brighten our path.

"I must say, you are not wrong." Collins was looking over the homes and flowers as we walked. "I never would have guessed this was back here."

Nodding, I tried to contain my grin. "I said the same thing the first time I saw it myself."

I was relieved to find no one in front of the board house, particularly Mrs. Appleton, who would need to be introduced and would surely have questions and more than likely would invite the lieutenant to dinner. The quicker and quieter we could get the watch and move on, the better, as far as I was concerned.

"This is the boarding house," I said, nodding toward it.

"It is a grand structure, that is for certain."

"It is indeed. The inside is as handsome as what you see out here."

"It is a peaceful place."

"I said the same thing." I gestured toward the field. "It's a small township, but we've got farmers growing crops, as you can see, we have a chicken coop, and so many things you just wouldn't expect out this way."

It sure appeared to be appreciation on the lieutenant's face. "Very nice indeed."

"We're going this way to the back of the board house."

When we got inside the stable, I put Daisy in her stall. "The watch is out here. I just want to make sure nobody is watching or approaching." I removed her saddle and placed it to the side. "The landlord and her niece come out here frequently, delivering water and tidying up with no set schedules."

Collins scanned the vicinity. "Maybe I should move my horse to the doorway to block the view of anyone outside."

"That is smart," I said, removing the halter from Daisy's head. "I just hope the strange beast doesn't rouse curiosity if seen from the house."

"I will keep watch and let you know if someone approaches."

"Then I should get moving as quickly as possible," I said, shutting the stall door and locking it. I climbed onto the saddle rest and slowly worked my way up the half-wall, listening for any noises outside that might bring a surprise. "Just a little further."

I slid on the first try but made my way to the top of the structure, squatting at first to get my balance and then slowly rising to an unsteady stand.

"That's quite impressive for a one-armed man," Collins said.

My arm trembled from the exertion. "That's what all the ladies say."

"Good Lord."

Still balancing myself, I stretched as far as I could, reaching toward the rafter. "Almost there," I whispered. I touched the beam for a second to get a better balance and then gently moved my hand to its top. "Well shit," I said, feeling in all directions.

"What do you mean?"

"It's not here," I said, searching further. "The watch is gone."

Chapter Nineteen

"**I** should have known better than to have put my trust in you." I heard the lieutenant's revolver coming out of its holster. "This has all been nothing more than fox yipping, hasn't it?"

"No, I swear to you this is where I hid it 'fore heading toward Sanderson. Check on the ground on both sides of this stall barrier. Maybe some varmint got up here and knocked the danged thing to the ground."

I knowed that wasn't the case, and my mind went to working on figuring out who got it and how they could have knowed it was there. *Jonathan*? Whoever it was probably saw me put it up there in the first place.

"Just come down from there," Collins said, his voice coming through gritted teeth.

"Take it easy now." I continued to feel around the top of the rafter, knowing damn well it wasn't there. "It's got to be here somewhere."

"I said come down. Or I'm going to hang you from that very rafter."

"All right, just take it easy," I said, working my way back to the ground. "I'm just trying to figure out what is going on here."

I couldn't come to any conclusions that made sense. It could have been a cat or another critter that knocked it off, making it possible for Mrs. Appleton or Rose to find while fetching water.

When I finally got into Daisy's stall, Collins put the barrel of his revolver to my forehead. "This is your last chance, Thornhill. I'm giving you one more opportunity to tell me where the watch is."

"I know this looks bad," I said, trying not to sound like I was about to soil my britches. "But listen to me, I swear to you that was where I put the watch before leaving. No one else even knowed I had it."

His face changed to something as close to a smile as you could get without actually smiling. "Or maybe it's up there," he said with the near smile turning into one. "Maybe you were pretending it wasn't there so you could sell it later, thinking that I'd just let you go."

"Check for yourself," I said, shaking my head. "But the longer we sit here arguing about it, the longer it will take for us to find the dad-blasted thing."

"Mr. Thornhill?" Appleton's voice rang from behind the boarding house. "Is that you?"

"It's the landlord," I said in a hushed tone. "Put your revolver away and follow along."

"If you try anything—"

"Just do it," I said, turning toward the doorway. "In here, Mrs. Appleton."

Collins pulled his horse inside as Appleton made her way to the door.

"There you are," she said, stepping inside. "I've been worried sick about you and Jonathan." She studied the stalls. "Is Jonathan not with you?"

Collins and I shared a quick glance. "No ma'am," I said, tipping my hat. "Jonathan didn't go with me. Is he not here?"

"Oh, forgive me," Mrs. Appleton said when she finally noticed Lieutenant Collins. "I didn't know you had someone with you."

"This is an old friend, Lieutenant Collins. He's with the U.S. Army." I smiled. "Obviously."

Collins removed his hat and kissed Appleton's outstretched hand. "The pleasure is all mine, my lady."

Lord help me if that old woman's face didn't turn three shades of pink 'fore she could even speak. "Oh, I hope nothing is wrong," she said, never taking her eyes off Collins. "We rarely see distinguished officers in these parts."

"No ma'am," he said, playing the part perfectly. "Thornhill and I just happened upon each other yesterday, and I invited him to stay at camp so we could catch up on things."

It was everything I could do to keep the stupid grin from growing. "That's right, ma'am. That's the reason I didn't make it back last night."

"Oh my," she said, "I just assumed Jonathan was going with you. He didn't say anything before he left, and that's not like him at all." She shook her head. "And he left no more than a minute or so after you departed. That's why I assumed he was trying to catch up with you."

"No ma'am," I said. "I haven't laid eyes on him since packing to leave." I shared another glance with Collins. "And you say he left right after I took off, is that right?"

"That is correct." She wiped her hands down her apron. "He came running inside right after you left and then back to the stable like something was on fire." She shrugged. "It was just minutes later I noticed him leading his horse out of the stable and toward the street."

"And he didn't say anything as to where he was going?" I reckon I said that more for myself than I did to Mrs. Appleton. But I said it out loud.

"I'm afraid not." She turned her gaze back to the lieutenant. "Is something wrong? Is Jonathan in some sort of trouble?"

"Oh, no ma'am," Collins said, giving her a diplomatic smile. "But if you will excuse us, Mr. Thornhill and I must be off again."

"That's right," I said with a nod. "We just stopped by to water the critters."

"Nonsense," Appleton said, placing a hand on the lieutenant's arm. "You'll stay for supper." She looked to me. "The both of you. You need to eat before you get back in those saddles."

Collins offered a charming smile. "We would love nothing more to do that, ma'am, but I'm afraid we truly must get back on the road."

"No sir," she said, shaking her head. "I will not allow the two of you to leave without the hospitality you deserve." She looked to me again. "I shall refuse to take no for an answer."

"Yes ma'am," I said, turning toward Collins. "Looks like you've been outranked on this, old friend." I smiled. "We can do some thinking and planning in my room until dinner is ready. And besides," I added, nodding toward her, "you will not be disappointed in Mrs. Appleton's spread. That much I guarantee."

"All right, ma'am," Collins said. "But I regret that I will not be able to stay long, as Lawrence and I are working on a special project that we need to get back to."

My neck started itching again.

"Then it's settled." Appleton smiled. "Now let me get back to the kitchen and check on everything."

Collins placed his hat back on his head as she walked out the door. He waited until the back door closed. "You think Jonathan has the watch?"

Along with the itching neck, my stomach commenced to gurgling again. "It appears so." I searched the ground around the stall. "I reckon he was watching me 'fore I left and witnessed me hiding the watch on the rafter top. But I assure you, he did not even know I had the watch." I glanced back at the lieutenant. "And I'm a thanking you, by the way."

His eyebrows came together. "For what?"

"For keeping your word as to what we discussed with Mrs. Appleton and the residents here at the boarding house." I nodded. "I appreciate your word. And your patience as we figure this thing out."

"You may not be the straightest arrow I know," Collins said with a laugh. "But I don't believe you to be the stupidest. And because of that, I have to say I believe you in this." He lifted his eyebrows and chin. "Don't make me regret it. Or you will regret it far more, I promise."

"I don't reckon we should jump to the judgment that it was Jonathan who took the watch, though." I poured water into Daisy's trough. "I still think we should consider all possibilities. Although I have to admit, everything seems to point back in his direction."

"Do you think Mrs. Appleton found it? Or her niece, as you mentioned earlier?"

"Mrs. Appleton would have mentioned it if she'd found it, thinking it may have belonged to me." I gestured toward the next stall. "Take your horse in there for the time being, and we'll put out some water and hay." I took off my hat and wiped my forehead. "And I reckon if Rose would have found the thing, she would have told Appleton, who again would have mentioned it while here."

Collins removed the saddle from his horse and placed it on the nearby stand. "Anyone else come in here other than those two women and Jonathan?"

"Some of the others from time to time, but most of them do not have need for the stable, so I cannot think of another soul."

Pouring water into the trough for his horse, Collins shook his head. "If it was Jonathan who took it, where do you think he's gone off with it? What do you think his intentions are?"

"Well," I said, staring at my boots. "I reckon if it was Jonathan, he's trying to find a way to turn it into money."

I'm here to tell you my brain was just about spent. And when a fella's head gets tired like that, it just brings on a weariness to his whole being like nothing else. It'll tucker a fella out quicker than lumbering trees for a straight month. I ought to know, I had to do it back in Kentucky when I was younger. But this here kind of tired just pulls you down bit by bit, weighing on you something awful.

And the warmth and smells of the boarding house didn't help none, I'll tell you that much. All it did was make me want to crawl into that bed and forget about everything that was going on. I reckon that's what makes it so wearisome—your head is telling you two different things at the same time because I knowed I couldn't just curl up and sleep.

"Where would you think Jonathan is taking the watch?" Lieutenant Collins sat on the edge of Jonathan's bed, brushing dust from his hat. "I'm sure you have some idea."

"I ain't knowed Jonathan long at all," I said, staring at the floor. "So I don't reckon I know much of his background or places he's been." I met his gaze. "But he did mention a place in Tall Junction where a fella there by the name of Jeremiah York runs a trading post."

"I know the place."

"He let on that York is open to taking ill-gotten items," I said with a little smile. "And I reckon I can attest to that."

"You've been there?"

Nodding, I scratched at my ear. "I was there the day you were talking to York about the watch. Of course, I avoided being seen by you for obvious reasons."

"I see."

My stomach gurgled. "I reckon that's going to be his first stop."

"Then it shall be our first stop as well."

I motioned my eyes toward the doorway when footsteps echoed from the stairwell.

"I'm sorry to interrupt," Appleton said as she stepped to the room's threshold. "But I wanted to let you both know that dinner is ready."

Collins and I got to our feet.

"Thank you, ma'am," I said with a smile. "We'll wash up and be there directly."

"Now what was your name again?" Appleton asked Collins. "I want to make sure I introduce you properly to our other residents."

"Lieutenant Reginald Collins, ma'am." He nodded with this. "And let me say, I am very grateful for your hospitality in the service of the United States Army."

Lord have mercy, if that woman's smile didn't light up the room at that. "You are welcome here anytime, Lieutenant."

She made her way back down the stairwell, and I stood grinning at Collins.

"Why are you looking at me like that?"

"It's just that you high-ranking Army fellas ain't much different from folks like me, Ezra, and Jonathan, are you?" I chuckled. "Why, every one of us would make fine stage actors, I reckon."

His face reddened a bit, and then he smiled. "Unfortunately, I believe your assessment is quite accurate if you want to know the truth about it, Mr. Thornhill." His smile widened. "Quite accurate."

The dining room's air was sure easy to breathe, filled with all the wonderful smells it held. Lord help me, it seemed as though every dinner smelled the same to me—always wonderful—but Mrs. Appleton surprised me every evening with something different.

Residents were already gathered at the table, and as usual, they were quiet and patient while Mrs. Appleton and Rose placed the platters and plates where they belonged.

"Ah, there you are," Appleton said when she spotted us. "Everyone, your attention, please." She held out a hand toward Collins and smiled. "I hope you will join me in welcoming our distinguished guest this evening, Lieutenant Reginald Collins of the United States Army." She motioned to the chairs she wanted us to sit in. "Lieutenant Collins is a friend of Mr. Thornhill's, and we are delighted to have someone of his stature in this home."

We took our seats, and I couldn't help but notice the puzzled look on Rose's face.

Appleton removed her apron and smiled. "Tonight's meal is gravy-smothered lamb, roasted potatoes, asparagus, and rice pudding with raisins and a special butter nutmeg sauce." She bowed her head. "Mr. Hamblen, would you please offer the blessing?"

The old man lifted his face toward the rafters a moment before closing his eyes. "Our most gracious heavenly Father, we come before thee with gladdened hearts and thankful spirits. We thank thee for the protection and diligence of the brave men in uniform you have ordained. Keep thy hand upon them as they continue to serve their fellow man as they serve thou each and every day.

Bless this food, we pray, and the wonderful hands that have prepared it. In Jesus' name, amen."

"Make yourself at home, Lieutenant Collins," Appleton said as she reached for the potatoes.

"I was unaware that the two of you were friends," Rose said with a curious look on her face.

"Ah," I said, smiling. "Collins and I go back several years."

"Really?" She reached for the asparagus. "I was standing at your table while you were at the hotel eatery, and the lieutenant came in asking questions regarding the stagecoach robbery." Her eyebrows rose. "And neither of you so much as acknowledged that you were in the same room."

Lord, my stomach went to burning something fierce. "Well, it was—"

"It's true, ma'am," Collins said, offering his charming smile. "We did not speak or acknowledge that the other was present. But I'm afraid we had to do this in order to maintain our secrecy as we were working together on our investigation."

Rose's eyes widened nearly as much as her smile. "Oh, so the two of you deliberately ignored each other."

"That is correct, ma'am," Collins said, then turned to the rest of the residents. "And I do hope we can trust you all to keep this to yourselves, as our investigations are not just yet finished."

Everyone nodded in agreement.

"I wanted to tell you everything," I finally said to Rose. "But we had to maintain secrecy. I hope you understand."

"I do," she said, turning her gaze to Collins. "And I certainly hope you capture those responsible." Her hand reached for the empty lapel. "I still have hopes to regain the brooch my mother gave me."

Collins stole a quick glance at me. "I'm sure it will turn up, ma'am."

After finishing the rice pudding with that special butter nutmeg sauce that made my mouth all watery, the lieutenant and I thanked

Mrs. Appleton and Rose for a wonderful meal and bid them, along with the other residents, our farewell.

"I'm riding heavier now than I was when I came into this place," Collins said as we left the muddy side of Warren's Gap.

"Mrs. Appleton sure knows how to lay a meal on a fella, that's for sure."

"Indeed." Collins took out his pipe and began packing tobacco into its chamber. "I cannot stop wondering about something, Mister Thornhill."

I glanced over at him. "Oh? And what would that be?"

"I'm wondering if you were a part of the gang that robbed the stage at gunpoint?"

I chuckled. "You think a gang of road agents would have a one-armed man in their company?"

"I don't know," he said, puffing at his pipe. "Would they?"

"I worry that I may get myself in trouble with you and the law over this one."

Collins smiled as he blew smoke upwards. "I have no jurisdiction when it comes to those things, so you have no worries about me or the U.S. Army. And I suspect we've worked close enough now that I very well couldn't turn you in."

"Well," I said, trying to put the words in the right order. "First of all, I ain't part of the gang of road agents that robbed the stagecoach."

"Really? This surprises me."

"But the reason for that is there ain't no such thing as a gang that robbed that danged thing in the first place."

He took another puff from his pipe and blew again. "I don't think I follow your meaning here. All the eyewitnesses have testified that there were multiple individuals involved."

I shook my head. "Only one person." I gave him the biggest grin I could muster.

"I don't understand."

I told him about the whole plan regarding the fake arm and the planted gun barrels and flour sacks, as well as how the whole thing went down and how I escaped.

He brought his horse to a stop at some point and just stared at me. "That is the most brilliant thing I have ever heard," he said with a smile stretching across his face. "Absolutely brilliant."

"I'm a thanking you."

"So you sold the items you gained from the robbery to the fella in Tall Junction?"

"That is correct."

He lifted one eyebrow. "Including the young woman's brooch?"

I pulled the beetle from my pocket and held it up for him. "I'm trying to find the right moment to return it to her."

His smile returned. "Absolutely brilliant."

Chapter Twenty

The setting sun stretched blotting shadows across the land as we rode. The evening was cool and quiet, and the stillness always made me nervous, as wild critters stopped making noises when they sensed predators nearby and didn't want to give away their location. Now maybe it was the noises from our horses that spooked 'em, but it just seemed a mite queer to me compared to most other times on the road. Or, hell, maybe I was just studying too much on the whole thing.

Lord knows I wasn't looking forward to the trip back to Tall Junction, and I'm sure Daisy wasn't happy about it either, but it just seemed to be where Jonathan would have headed first. Or maybe that's what he was hoping I'd think, and he'd decided to head toward another direction altogether, just to throw me off his trail. My head started aching from all the thinking.

"I don't want to get you too excited," Collins said, his gaze straight ahead as we moved. "But we are being watched. Followed."

I scanned the small hills and rocks. "Where?"

"Just keep your pace and follow my lead."

Several mounted Kiowas stared down at us without moving from the top of a small hillock to the left of the road. "I see them."

"That's because they want to be seen."

I scanned the other side of the road but didn't see anything unusual. "What do you reckon they want?"

"Those are Kiowas," he said, turning his gaze toward me. "All they want is death."

Lord have mercy, if my stomach didn't go to burning and aching worse than my head. "I thought you didn't want to get me excited none?"

"Just keep your pace and don't do anything to make them think they are being threatened."

"Threatened?" All I wanted to do was stop and make water at this point. "Why in the name of the good Lord would I want to threaten a band of Kiowas?"

"Just continue riding as normal."

Daisy and the lieutenant's horse seemed to be spooked worse than me I reckon, shaking their heads and making all kinds of noises.

"Be prepared," Collins said softly. "It appears they are coming around to engage us just ahead."

"Well hell, let's just turn back the way we came."

Collins shook his head. "They're going to engage us one way or another, and we don't want them to see fear."

"Well, you better leave me right where we are because if not, those Indians are bound to see fear the moment they lay eyes on me."

The Kiowas slowly moved onto the road ahead, watching us without moving. A few others were visible from the hillock, staring down at us as well. Lord, if my gut didn't set in on me again, and it was bad enough that I needed to make water.

"One arm!" an Indian called out. "You captive?" I couldn't tell from the distance, but I was fairly certain it was the same native who freed me from Meade.

Collins glanced at me with confusion.

"No," I yelled back. "This bluecoat is a friend. He's not like the other bluecoats."

Collins didn't move, keeping his gaze straight ahead. "You know these savages?"

"Let's hope."

My legs had a wave of coldness come through 'em, not painful or numb, mind you, just a simple coldness. I ain't sure if it was because the natives started toward us at an eased pace, weapons drawn and aimed in our direction, but it all happened around the exact moment just the same.

"One arm, step to ground," the Kiowa said again. "Come behind our people."

"Better do as he says," Collins said.

I moved to dismount. "You ain't got to tell me twice."

Taking hold of Daisy's bridle, I slowly walked her around the side of the Kiowas and behind them.

"Now that safe. One arm, you bluecoat captive?"

"No, that man is not holding me captive." I exaggerated my head shake. "He is not like the one before. He is helping me with a friend."

"What is this about, Thornhill?" The lieutenant's voice came across loud and angry.

"It's all right, Lieutenant, just take it easy. Everything will be fine."

"That's easy for you to say." His voice was a near growl. "When you're not staring down a bunch of drawn arrows."

"Just take it easy," I said, trying to keep my tone normal. "They just want to make sure you're not holding me captive."

"Did you set me up?" The lieutenant's face reddened. "Brought me out this way to get me killed?"

"Calm down, Collins! You're making the Kiowas restless."

"Stop telling me to calm down," he yelled, gesturing an arm in anger.

Now I'm here to tell you I was scared out of my wits, but truth be known, my fear wasn't for my life—my fear was for Lieutenant Collins. But when he moved his arm the way he did, I reckon one of them Indians took it as a sign of aggression or that they thought he was trying to draw a weapon. No matter what the savage thought, that Indian let his arrow go into the lieutenant's shoulder, knocking him clean off his horse.

"No!" I yelled, running toward Collins as the other Indians got excited and was aiming to finish him off. "No, please," I said, shielding the lieutenant's body with mine. "He's not trying to shoot you. He's just confused and scared."

"One arm." The one who spoke earlier sat up taller. "You no captive? You no danger?"

"No, this man is a friend." I could feel the lieutenant's warm blood on my hand. "He is a friend."

The same Kiowa nodded and then said something in his tongue. At first, I thought he was speaking to me, but the other natives started mounting up and leaving the area. "One arm safe."

"Help me get this out of him," I said as they rode off.

"Let them go." Collins tried to sit up and winced. "Just let them go."

The arrow protruded from his shoulder, just below his collarbone and closer to the arm. Blood had pooled around the shaft, darkening the blue of his coat.

"Hold on," I said, trying to keep him from moving around too much. "I don't think it's hit any of your organs."

"Help me up."

"Just sit there a minute, and let's not rush things," I said, studying the location of the arrow. "I've never had to deal with an arrow wound before."

"Get me to my feet," he said through grunts.

My stomach was on fire. "Do I need to pull it out and use something to stop the bleeding? I told you I've never had to deal with this before."

"Dammit, Thornhill, just get me to my feet." His face was red and sweaty.

I wiped my hand down my trouser leg to eliminate the slickness. "All right, are you ready?"

"Let's go," he said and released a low scream when I pulled him to his feet.

"Now what?"

"I need to get to a doctor." His face seemed calm and in charge. "If you try to pull it out, it could potentially leave the arrowhead, which would make things much more difficult for the doctor when trying to locate and remove the damned thing."

"Do you need help getting into the saddle?"

"I'm afraid so," he said with another wince. "I fear I will be limited with what I can do with this arm until I get the damned thing removed."

Helping him get a foot in his stirrup, I pushed him after a bounce to get him high enough to swing his leg over and into the seat. "Where do you want me to take you?"

"We're closer to Tall Junction than anywhere else," he said through gritted teeth. "There's a doctor there who can do the job."

"All right, so keep going in the direction we've been traveling."

"Before we go, I need you to get in my bag from behind the saddle."

"Yes sir," I said, opening the thing. "What am I looking for?"

"The flask of whiskey." He coughed and winced. "I think we both could use it right about now."

I kept watch on the lieutenant as we rode, hoping he was able to steady himself in the saddle. The last thing I needed was for him to fall off and do more damage, especially after taking to that whiskey the way he did. But Lord knows I ain't about to disparage a man trying to numb his pain.

"Are you doing all right, Lieutenant?"

He coughed again and winced almost immediately. "I'll be fine. Hell, this isn't my first arrow, Thornhill." He took another gulp. "And I'm fairly certain this will not be my last either."

"Just hang in there," I said with a chuckle. "We want to make sure to get you there in one piece."

Either the whiskey was doing its job, or Lieutenant Collins was one tough son of a bitch. I'm here to tell you, the longer we rode, the less he let on that he was feeling any pain at all. And that suited me just fine if I'm being right honest. Lord knows I wouldn't have knowed what to do if he'd gotten any worse.

The evening skies brought a darkened chill, with nary a trace of moon or stars. Crickets joined the frogs in a chorus of chirps, ribbits, and trills on both sides of the road, along with the occasional whinnying of an owl. And I'll be dogged if it all wasn't downright soothing enough to force a fella to closely mind himself from nodding off and leaving the saddle unawares.

"I apologize for accusing you back there with the Indians," Collins said in a groggy voice. "Looking back on my actions, I can see where I'd made conclusions that were completely inaccurate."

"No need to apologize. Hell, I woulda done the same had I been in your position."

"Those redskins were protecting you." His face was contorted in some kind of odd grin. "I've never seen them do that with a white man before."

"I reckon it's because I'm gimped or something, but they sure don't like you army fellas, I can tell you that much."

His smile softened. "I guess I have plenty of scars to prove that." He leaned forward and let go of a heavy sigh. "I want you to know that I appreciate what you did back there."

"Oh, I didn't do any more than what anyone else would have done."

"That's not true," he said, shaking his head. "You didn't hesitate to put yourself between me and those savages. And let's be honest, had you not spoken up when you did, I wouldn't be alive right now."

I'll be real honest, I didn't know what to say to that, so I just grinned and nodded like I was some kind of simpleton or something. We rode like that for a while. No speaking. Just keeping pace with a critter chorus in the middle of nowhere.

"You raised questions about the watch," he said, as though our conversation had never stopped. "And about my personal relationship with Major Martin."

"What's that?"

"You were curious as to why the watch is so important to me. And why I said the major just didn't care much for me personally."

I didn't speak, just lifted my eyebrows.

"Did I mention the major has a daughter?" Collins gave me a pie-eating grin.

"Aha," I said with a chuckle. "Now we're getting somewhere."

"Don't get ahead of me." He was obviously fighting off a chuckle himself. And I reckon that would have hurt something awful in his condition. "Nothing happened between the two of us, mind you." He shook his head. "But thinking I was doing the right thing, before even approaching the girl, I asked the major for his permission to just speak to her." Collins rolled his eyes and wagged his head. "Why, you would have thought I'd requested to defile the young lady right there in front of him."

"Lord have mercy," I said with a laugh. "What'd you do?"

"I apologized, of course." He began nodding. "And I told him I would not seek to speak with her unless he decided to give his permission." His gaze dropped to his hands. "I told him that I hoped to be able to prove myself worthy of his acceptance someday."

I waited as long as I could when he didn't go on. "Well? What did he say to that?"

"He just grunted and left the room."

"So you're hoping the watch will put you in a better light with the old man?" I nodded. "Especially after he's had some *time* to consider everything."

I reckon I found that far more clever than the lieutenant did.

"I should have known better."

"Well, it all makes sense now," I said, trying to be more serious. "And I promise to do everything in my power to get that watch back for you."

"Thank you. But first, let's concentrate on getting this arrow out of my shoulder."

"Agreed. The Indian's arrow first," I said with another grin. "Then Cupid's arrow later."

"I should have hung you when I had the chance."

Tall Junction didn't seem as dry and dusty at night, but it sure was far from muddy, I'll tell you that much. There was more people out and about than I'd figured, and the saloon was just getting started, it seemed.

"Thornhill, go inside and ask the barkeep where we can locate the doctor." The lieutenant's face was sweaty and pale. "Don't make a big fuss getting the whole place up in arms. Just ask quietly."

The fella behind the bar gave me a proprietor's smile when I stepped up. "What can I get you?"

I leaned toward him. "Can you tell me where I might find the doctor?"

The man pointed toward a poker table. "Fella in the derby."

"I'm a thanking you."

The doctor didn't seem too agreeable as I approached. "I'd just like to win one hand," he said to the others at the table. "Is that too much to ask?"

"Excuse me, sir, I hear tell you're the doctor in town?"

"Not at the moment," the man said, never taking his eyes off his cards. "At this very moment, I'm the loser."

"I'm right sorry to hear that, sir." I offered a smile that he never bothered to notice. "Do you think I could speak to you privately?"

"Young man, can't you see I'm enjoying myself right now? Can't you see I am relaxing with a nice losing game of poker?"

"I sure do apologize for the inconvenience, sir, but it's sort of an emergency."

The doctor finally looked at me, his gaze shifting to my empty sleeve and then back to his cards. "It looks like I'm too late, son."

The men at the table broke into laughter.

I smiled and faked a chuckle. "That's a good one." I leaned close to his ear. "But I have a friend outside with an arrow in his shoulder."

He turned his gaze back to me as his face sterned.

I leaned in closer. "Army lieutenant."

"Kiowa arrow?"

"He doesn't want to stir anything up. Wants to keep this as quiet as possible."

The doctor lifted his eyebrows and tossed his cards to the center of the table. "Sorry, fellas. Duty calls. That's all the money you'll be getting from me tonight."

Groans came from the table as he rose, and we made our way to the door. "Where did this happen?"

"On the road here from Warren's Gap."

By the time we'd got outside, the lieutenant was slumped forward a mite and sweating terribly.

"Collins, are you all right?"

"What the hell kind of question is that?" he said, sitting up. "What could possibly be wrong?"

The doctor moved next to the lieutenant. "We're going to take you to my place and see what damage you've got." He turned his gaze to me. "Do you think he can ride to my house?"

Nodding, I offered a smile. "He's rode all this way. I reckon he can make it a bit more."

"Lead the way, Doc," Collins said as though he didn't have a concern in the world.

Collins wouldn't let us help him inside the doctor's house, although he was forced to accept our assistance in dismounting the horse.

"Let's get this jacket off," the doctor said, bringing a knife toward the blue coat.

"Hold on just a minute," Collins said, his face reddening. "You're not cutting my sack coat!"

"Lieutenant," the doctor said in a pleading tone. "It's the only way to keep from doing more damage to your wound."

Warmth filled my neck and face. "Jesus, Collins. The damned coat is already ruined." I shook my head. "Let's not do any more damage to your shoulder."

"I'm afraid he's quite right." The doctor didn't wait for permission as he began cutting the coat away. "You can get another sack coat without a problem. Let's make sure you'll be able to wear it, shall we?"

"Wait a minute, were you in the saloon?" Panic crossed the lieutenant's face. "Have you been drinking?"

"I was in the saloon," the doctor said, still continuing to cut away clothing. "Of course I've been drinking."

"Well, that just puts me right at ease." Collins shook his head. "I have a doctor about ready to hack an arrowhead out of my shoulder, and he's probably drunker than I am."

"Didn't say I was drunk." The doctor finally peeled the coat away. "Just said I'd been drinking. And you should be glad about that since it steadies my hands."

Collins glanced at me. "Is he serious?"

The doctor pointed toward the corner of the room. "There's a bottle of whiskey on my desk over there," he said to me. "Please give it to the lieutenant so he'll shut the hell up."

Chapter Twenty-One

Aunt Alice came out on the porch with her hands on her hips, which usually meant I was in for a long day of hard work. "It's due time I teach you the most important thing you'll need to know while out on your own."

My stomach cramped at the news. "Upon my honor to God, if you don't say that every single time you show me something."

"Don't you sass me, boy," she said, raising her eyebrows. "Now come on inside."

"Yes ma'am."

I was surprised when she led me to the kitchen table. "Are we fixing to eat first?"

"Oh, we're going to eat, all right, but just not yet." She wiped her hands on a towel. "It's high time you learned to fend for yourself when there's nobody around to cook."

"I can't cook."

"That's why we're doing this." She took a pan and placed it on the table. "I was about to teach you how to prepare pemmican but thought better of it, as you wouldn't have survived."

"That ain't something I would want to eat noways."

"Sometimes it's not about what you *want*," she said, placing a sack of flour on the table. "Sometimes it's more about what will sustain you in times of hardship." She smiled. "But I figured you'd pay closer attention if I taught you how to make my biscuits."

"Now that's something I'd want, *and* I am certain they would sustain me in times of hardship."

She chuckled. "These can be made on a cookstove, like we're going to make, or even in a Dutch oven if you're outdoors. You just need to mind how to trivet your fire and bank it on the lid."

"Lord knows I love your cathead biscuits."

"Ezra's pa fancied them almost as much as you," she said, chuckling again. "He liked to call them dough gods."

"To be right honest, I don't know anybody who wouldn't take a liking to your biscuits."

She tried to hide her smile. "You're going to need flour, baking powder, salt, butter, and sugar." She stared up at me. "You can use water if you have no other choice, but milk is what is going to make the best biscuits."

"If I'm going to learn to cook 'em, I want to make 'em just as you do, that's for sure."

She pulled a bowl in front of her. "The key is making sure your mixture has the right balance according to what each ingredient does." She slid a piece of paper in front of me. "This is the recipe with the measurements that will give you the best results." She pointed at the top of the paper. "Always start with the dry ingredients first."

"Lord have mercy," I said, staring at the handwriting. "I ain't never seen so many details in all my days."

"Mind your fussing and get to work."

"Yes ma'am."

Once I got all the ingredients together and mixed, I started having doubts that what I had in the bowl would hardly be close to anything resembling Aunt Alice's cathead biscuits.

"Now get some flour on your hand," she said, doing just that herself. "And start kneading the dough like this." She was pushing the dough away with the heel of her left palm, folding it over itself and then pulling it back again. "The flour on your hand will keep everything from sticking to your fingers."

She stepped back so I could work it myself.

"There you go, you're getting the hang of it."

I ain't gonna lie to you, I sure didn't have an idea that making a batch of biscuits would tire a fella out so fast.

"Now this is the most important part, so pay close attention." She put a hand on mine to get me to stop. "If you knead the dough too much, the biscuits will be tough and nowhere near as good as you like them."

"So how do I know when to stop?"

Her smile was apologetic. "Well, that, I'm afraid, is just going to have to come with time."

"Does it look good now? 'Cause I can't tell the difference."

"Yes," she said with a chuckle. "Now we're going to spread some flour on the table so the dough doesn't stick to it." She then took the big glob and placed it right in the middle of the flour. "And we're going to press it flat, but not too flat, because you love a thick biscuit."

Now what was on that table didn't look nary a thing like what I love, but I'll be dogged if my mouth wasn't watering.

"Then you take a wide-rimmed coffee tin," she said, holding one up for me to see. "And turn it upside down and press its mouth into the dough to make the circles like this."

And just like that, there was unbaked biscuits on the table.

"Now we're going to rub some lard into the pan," she said, pointing for me to do it. "That way they don't stick when they're done."

"I want 'em sticking to my ribs, not the pan."

She laughed. "Now go ahead and put them in the pan, and keep in mind they will swell up when they bake, so make sure you give those rascals a little room between them."

"It's starting to look like something now."

"Do you see this bit of butter I've had on the stove? I did this so we could drizzle it on top before we put the pan in the oven." She smiled. "And we put them in the oven and wait."

She closed the stove door and wiped her hands on a towel. "And while we wait," she said, handing me the towel, "you get to clean up this mess."

Later that evening, we sat on the porch, Aunt Alice sewing something while I was enjoying myself a fresh chaw of tobacco. The sun was setting with a reddish tint, bringing with it a peaceful quietness and cool breeze.

"What'd you think of your first batch of biscuits, Lawrence?" She didn't even look up from her needle.

"They was good," I said, crossing my feet at the ankles. "But I reckon they still weren't as good as when you make 'em without me."

A smile reached her lips as she briefly glanced up. "I figure that's all in your head. The important thing is you now know how to make them. And you can always add a little of this or take away a little dab of that to get everything to your taste."

I leaned to the side and spat off the porch. "I don't reckon they'd be the same as yours no matter what I did."

"Tell me, Lawrence, what are your plans now?"

She had a different tone in her voice, one I wasn't used to hearing from her. "I reckon I'll get out and try to make a living once you're done with me here. Maybe try and catch up with Ezra sometime down the road."

She stopped her sewing and looked up. "When I'm done with *you*?" She cocked her head. "You think all this has been for *me*?" She laughed a bit and shook her head. "This has all been for you, Lawrence. To make sure you were ready to make it on your own without being held back by the loss of your strong arm and all."

"Yes ma'am. I didn't mean to—"

"It has nothing to do with me." Her face reddened a bit. "And just so you know, I'll never be *done* with you." Her gaze dropped back to her hands, but she didn't go back to her sewing. "But I figure you are ready." She looked up and gave me the saddest excuse for a smile I reckon I ever did see. "I don't have to like it any more than watching Ezra Dale leave, but I am happy knowing you are ready."

I didn't know what to say. I had those confusing feelings clawing around in my gut again. "Yes ma'am. I'll leave when you tell me to go."

She laughed, and it sounded like it was to hide something. "That isn't my decision to make," she said, shaking her head. "That decision is yours and yours alone."

"Yes ma'am." I was afraid to say more, as I couldn't trust myself to hold back tears right there in front of her.

She rose to her feet and put her sewing kit to the side. "Come here." I could see the redness in her eyes.

"Yes ma'am," I said, getting to my feet. "But I want you to know how grateful I am for all you've done in helping me get prepared."

She put a soft hand to the side of my face. "I just want you to know this one thing before you traipse off to God knows where." She lifted her eyebrows and nodded. "This is your home. Just as much as it is Ezra Dale's. It's your home." She pulled me close for an embrace. "And you're mine just the same as Ezra Dale is mine. Don't you ever forget that."

I reckon I was shook up far more than the doctor and the lieutenant at the time, and keep in mind, one of them was getting an arrow removed from his shoulder while the other was doing the removing. The lieutenant's face was as white as I reckon a being can be and still hold breath.

"How bad is it?" Collins took another drink.

"We'll see once we get all the way in." He turned his head and coughed. "But I've seen worse if that makes you feel better."

"Well, it doesn't," Collins said with a laugh. "But thank you for the consideration."

I didn't know what to do or say. I just stood there watching, I reckon waiting for the doctor to tell me to fetch something or do something important. But to be right honest, I just felt like I was in the way. "At least it's not a bullet," I said 'fore I could stop the words. "That would have to be far worse."

"I don't know why folks think that," the doctor said with his focus still on the wound. "But nothing could be further from the truth."

"Tell him, Doc," Collins said before taking another drink.

"The thing is, if the lieutenant here had been shot in the very same place, away from vital organs and so forth, and if he chose to just leave the slug where it was, more than likely it wouldn't cause any issues later on. Everything would heal and grow around it." He took a towel and wiped the blood at the site. "That is not the case for an arrowhead. It will continue to do damage as long as it is still inside. No healing around it, just creates infections and more damage."

I was squinting and realized it was because of a smell that hung in the room that hadn't been there when we came in. It made me think back on the incident with my arm and losing so much blood. It was a dirty copper smell, if that makes any sense at all.

"How long do you think this will take?" the lieutenant said, his speech thick and slurred.

"Why?" the doctor asked, still working on the wound. "Do you have to be somewhere in the next twenty minutes or so?"

Collins laughed and then winced. "Stop making me laugh, you bastard."

"Well, stop asking stupid questions while I'm working on you."

Lord have mercy, if the two of them didn't have me nearly wringing wet with sweat from my nerves. "Why don't the both of you shut the hell up?"

Collins and the doctor laughed like it was a joke only they understood. I wanted to say more, but a knock at the door stole my gumption.

"Go see who that is," the doctor said, not looking up from his work.

I was never so happy to walk away from something in all my natural-born days. My head was light and swimmy, and I had that greasy feeling squeezing its way back into every crevice of my stomach.

"I'm Sheriff Walters," the man said when I opened the door. "Where's Doc Stevens?"

"He's patching up a fella right now."

"Come in, Walters," the doctor called out. "I'm a little busy at the moment."

I stepped aside for the sheriff to enter.

"Is it the Army lieutenant with an arrow in his shoulder?" he asked, walking past me.

"The one and the same." The doctor never took his eyes off the lieutenant's wound. "Just getting started on removing the damned thing."

"Hey, how did you know I was an Army lieutenant with an arrow stuck in me?" Collins sounded as though his tongue was too thick for his mouth.

"I was playing poker with Doc when this fella came in," the sheriff said, gesturing toward me. "I heard him tell the details."

"I told you to keep it quiet, Thornhill," Collins said.

"Listen, all I said—"

"He was very discreet," the sheriff replied. "I was next to the doc when he spoke, and given my occupation, I tend to listen and hear a bit better than most."

Collins seemed to accept this and took another drink of whiskey.

The sheriff stepped closer to get a better look at the lieutenant's wound. "Where did the attack take place?"

"Now listen," the doctor said, finally looking up at the sheriff. "I don't mind you asking questions or examining anything, but you know my policy." He pointed a bloody finger at the man. "If you get in my way or you distract my patient to the point that it impedes my process, I'll make you leave."

"You know I don't have a problem with that."

"Good, now stand over to the other side because you're getting in my light." With this, the doctor focused his attention back on the lieutenant's shoulder.

"So," the sheriff said, drawing out the word. "Where did the attack take place?"

"There was no attack," Collins said, wincing.

The sheriff glanced at me for a moment before turning back to Collins. "If there was no attack, then how did you get an arrow in your shoulder?"

Collins wiped his lips. "I'll tell you this, Sheriff, it was the damnedest thing I've ever witnessed." He glanced at his wound for a second before setting his focus back on the man. "Thornhill and I were riding this way from Warren's Gap when I detected Kiowas stalking us from the ridgelines and distance." He winced again, grunting as he turned his attention to the arrow. "Easy, Doc. You act like you're pulling a branch out of a pile of mud!"

"Take another drink and shut up."

Collins chuckled again. "Well, those savages stopped us in the road, and one of them started calling out to Thornhill, calling him One Arm." He nodded toward me. "On account of the fact that he only has the one arm."

"Thank you for pointing that out," I said, shaking my head. "Lord knows no one would have noticed had you not mentioned it."

Collins laughed and winced. "Stop making me laugh, damn you!"

"Are you sure these were Kiowas?"

"I know Kiowas," Collins said. "And these savages had Thornhill dismount and move around behind them to ask him if I had him in custody."

The sheriff's left eye squinted as he briefly glanced at me. "Why would they think that?"

"Hell if I know," Collins said before taking another drink. "But those savages were protecting him for some reason. It was the damnedest thing I'd ever witnessed."

"I reckon they thought because I was gimped or something," I said, shrugging. "Or they thought I was an enemy of their enemy. Hell, I'm as confused about it as the rest of you."

"So I get myself worked up in agitation thinking Thornhill had set me up," the lieutenant said, as though he'd not been interrupted. "And I made a sudden movement with my arm . . ." He moved his arm at this and grunted.

"Hold still!"

"Well," Collins continued, "one of those savages thought I was reaching for a pistol or something, I guess, and shot me. There's no way around it, this arrow was my own damn fault." He nodded toward me again. "But had Thornhill not jumped in and calmed them all down, I'd be a dead man right now."

"Is that right?" The sheriff stared at me with a little more attention. "Sounds like you have a hero riding with you."

"I ain't no hero," I said. I could feel the warmth rising in my chest. "Like I told the lieutenant, I didn't do anything more than anyone else would have under the same circumstances."

"I keep telling him he's full of shit," Collins said with a grin. "Most men would have done whatever they could to save their own neck in that situation."

"I agree," the sheriff said. "Is there anything I can do to help?"

"Are you volunteering to remove this thing?" The doctor's voice was sharp.

"I wasn't talking to your cheerful ass." The sheriff grinned. "Anything I can do for you, lieutenant? I can send word to your company about the incident or something along those lines."

"I appreciate your willingness to help, Sheriff," Collins said. "But as soon as the doctor gets this thing cut out of me, we're going to hit the road and get back to camp."

"The hell you say." The doctor looked up at the lieutenant. "You're going to need a day or two of rest before you're going anywhere."

"Doc, I—"

"Now you can say what you want to say and act like you can do what you please because you're a big fancy officer in the U.S. Army, but if you want my help getting this thing out of your shoulder, you'll do as I say!"

"I'm really beginning to like you, Doc," I said with a laugh. "It's about time someone put that son of a bitch in his place."

Collins laughed again and winced. "Dammit, Thornhill, stop making me laugh!"

Chapter Twenty-Two

In spite of a freshly sewn hole in his shoulder, Lieutenant Collins slept like a lazy porch hound, with only the occasional murmur or snore. You sure wouldn't think it by just looking at him, but that fella was the toughest son of a bitch I'd ever met.

"Let him sleep," the doctor said, washing his hands again. "No matter how tough of a fellow he thinks he is, it is still a lot of trauma for anyone to endure."

"Lord knows I've had my fair share of trauma just watching your procedure."

The doctor laughed. "Did he leave any whiskey for us?"

I picked up the empty bottle. "I don't reckon so. Between what you poured into his wound and what he poured into himself, it's gone."

"Good. That means he's heavily sedated." He laughed at this a little more than was appropriate, in my estimation.

"How long do you reckon he'll be out?"

"Depends." The old man dug through his desk drawers. "Seems to me like he has a high tolerance for pain, but I figure we can expect the pain to rouse him before the sunlight does."

"But he'll be fine, right?"

"He'll be in pain for a while," the doctor said, removing a half-filled bottle from the drawer. "And he'll be sore for a long while after that." He pulled the cork and took a drink. "Other than that, unless there are any complications, he should be fine."

"How long before we can travel?"

"It doesn't matter." He took another drink and handed me the bottle. "He's the type of fella who will leave when he's ready." He shrugged. "All I can do is threaten and advise, but in the end, he'll do whatever he wants."

"You know him better than I thought you did."

He pursed his lips. "I just know the type. That's all."

The old man reached for the bottle and stared at me right peculiar like. "What I don't understand is why the two of you are traveling together." He took a big drink and damn near closed one eye. "An Army officer and a one-armed man whose appearance gives hints of being part of a gang of road agents."

"Now what in my appearance would cause you to think that of me?"

He reached the bottle back to me. "In my line of work, we tend to see more of those folks than any other, for obvious reasons."

I smiled. "I reckon the company I've kept over the years has been of a questionable nature."

"I guess I can say the same," he said with a laugh. "And more than likely we've kept the same company."

As though to discredit the doctor's predictions, Collins was still sleeping when the sun came up the next morning. I couldn't get over how the doctor's place appeared a mite different in the daylight—I reckon the stress of the night may have had more to do with that than visibility.

"I'm going to check on something," I said to the man. "If the lieutenant awakens 'fore I get back, let him know I ain't left him. Let him know I just stepped out for a while."

"If you get hungry, the bakery down the street has some of the finest pumpernickel you'll ever taste."

"I'm a thanking you."

The streets were busy with people rushing to wherever it was they were going. They took time to speak and acknowledge one another, but they didn't seem to have time for conversation on the way. I tipped my hat and smiled at the ladies as I passed, taking in all the businesses and signs along the way.

The heady scent of the bakery seemed to pull me along like I was on the barbed end of its fishing line. That's not where I intended to go, mind you, but I'll be gibbered if that ain't where my boots ended up taking me.

The women behind the counter gave the appearance of individuals who enjoyed their wares as much as their customers did. *Big-boned*, as Charlie would have said.

"Good morning," one of the women said with a thick German accent.

I removed my hat and nodded. "Morning." Lord knows I hadn't been in a bakery in so long I damn near forgot how to act. "What and all kind of bread do you have here?"

Now I'm here to tell you that her accent had her sounding like she was reciting a poem or something while she gave the list, and I couldn't hardly understand a word she was saying. But I felt like I was just grinning like a simpleton at her the whole time.

"I reckon I'll get me a loaf of that pumpernickel."

She nodded and went to wrapping a loaf for me.

"What are those?" I said, pointing toward some frilly bread concoction.

The woman followed my gaze. "Franzbrötchen," she said, as though that meant a damned thing to me. I reckon she noticed the confusion on my face and smiled. "Very sweet pastry."

"I'll take three of them."

The trading post had a few customers perusing the shelves when I walked in. York was at the back wall talking to some fella about a

Dutch oven they had on the countertop. I walked closer, and York looked in my direction for a moment before returning his attention to the customer.

"Feel how heavy that lid is," he said, putting the thing into the man's hands. "That's how you know you have a good Dutch oven. It's solid and thick. That, my friend, will serve your children and grandchildren after you're dead and gone."

Once the man made his purchase and left, York moved behind the counter and studied the room for other customers. "I didn't expect to ever see you again," he said, putting the money into the cash register. "I figured you would have hit the road and gotten as far away from here as possible by now."

I glanced around the room myself before turning back to him. "I reckon I have a few things to tidy up 'fore I move along."

He closed the register door and smiled. "So what brings you back to me?"

"It's not a *what*," I said, stepping closer. "It's a who."

His eyebrows came down over his nose. "This is about Jonathan, isn't it?" He nodded 'fore I could reply. "And that blasted watch he brought in here."

I reckon my face told him the answer. "You have it?"

"Hell no. I told him I didn't want any part of the damned thing. Told him if he knew what was good for him, he'd take it to the U.S. Army and be rid of the problems it would cause." He shook his head. "He got himself in a huff, saying my decision to turn him down was because I was angry over him sending you my way. He said I probably felt like he'd broken my trust."

"When was he in here?"

"It was about this time yesterday." He brushed something from the countertop. "He seemed in a rush, agitated. And when a fella acts like that, more than likely he's in something too deep."

"Did he say where he was going?"

"Not a word. He left here cussing and sworping like I've never seen before." He shrugged. "Just so you know, the U.S. Army is looking for that watch. And they will not stop until they find it."

I studied the shelves behind York just in case he wasn't telling the truth. "So you don't have any idea where he might be heading?" I shook my head like I was worried. "I want to make sure he is all right."

"It's hard to tell with Jonathan." His gaze softened. "You know as well as I do that he knows a lot of people and moves around quite a bit."

I studied York's eyes, trying to see if he was hiding anything. The last thing I wanted was for Jonathan to have told him he'd stolen the watch from me and needed to get away. "That is true."

"There's an Army lieutenant that is hell-bent on getting that watch," he said, raising his eyebrows. "And I fear Jonathan may be getting himself into a heap of trouble he won't be able to worm himself out of. I really do."

"I feel the same way," I said, shifting the bakery bag in my arm. "But Lord knows I don't have an idea of where to start searching. You were the only place I could think of."

"He didn't seem right while he was here. Seemed agitated like I've never seen." He shook his head again. "Who knows, he just might take my advice and take the damned thing back to the Army, claiming he found it somewhere and heard they were looking for it."

"That might just be his plan now, especially if he thinks he can get some kind of reward for finding the dad-blasted thing."

"But then again," York said with a frown, "it's hard to say what's going through his head right now."

I ain't gonna lie about it. It's true, I fully expected to find Lieutenant Collins awake and conversating when I got back to the doctor's house, but what I didn't expect was for the son of a bitch to be up and about, walking around like he hadn't just had an arrowhead cut out of him just hours before. But there he was, just as big as life, acting like nothing had ever happened.

"There you are," he said when I walked in. "Have you seen what this man did to my sack coat?" His face was reddened but didn't carry a trace of the sweatiness he'd had during the night. "My damn sack coat."

"I reckon the Kiowa who shot you with that arrow is the one who ruined your coat," I said, placing the bag on the doctor's desk. "If you're gonna blame somebody for it, you should put the blame where it belongs."

"He didn't have to cut it off me like he did."

The doctor just smiled. "It's true. I could have left the damned thing on you and went back to my poker game."

"Just get another sack coat." Heat was moving into my neck and ears. "Good Lord, the man just saved your life."

"But he didn't have to—"

"Oh, sit down and shut the hell up," I said, retrieving the loaf of bread. "Doc, do you have a knife to cut this with?"

"Is that pumpernickel?" the doctor asked, handing me a knife. "I told you their pumpernickel is wonderful."

"It was damn near the only thing I could understand the woman saying," I said, cutting into the loaf. "How big of a piece do you want, Collins?"

The lieutenant's gaze went to the bread. "Hey, is that the knife used during my procedure?"

The doctor's face was scrunched up. "I washed it."

"Jesus!" Collins lifted both arms and winced from the movement. "Damn it all to hell."

"Just shut up and eat," I said, handing Collins a piece of the bread.

The doctor started laughing hard. "You two act like an old married couple."

"Same goes for you, Doc," I said, handing him a piece of bread. "Sit down, shut up, and eat. Upon my honor to God, if I haven't had my fill of the both of you over the past several hours."

I ain't gonna pretend to know how, but I'll be dogged if the quietness didn't help the aromas of the bread to come alive. And that bread was still warm when you broke into it.

"That is good," Collins said, tearing another piece from his portion. "You say this is pumpernickel?"

"It is." The doctor's smile revealed a certain amount of pride. "The German family who runs the bakery came here from Hamburg. We're lucky to have them here in Tall Gap."

"Well, they sure know what they're doing," I said, chewing the hearty sweetness. "It's like this just came out of the oven."

"You're going to need to keep from using your arm as much as possible," the doctor said to Collins. "You need to give the wound a chance to heal for as long as you can."

"This isn't my first arrow wound." Collins didn't even look up from his bread.

"I understand," the doctor said with a little bite to his words. "But this is the first one in your shoulder. The others were in locations that arm movement wouldn't hinder the healing process."

"Just listen to the man," I said to Collins.

"And you're going to need to keep it clean." The doctor turned his attention to me. "He will need the wound cleaned often and the bandages changed."

"What are those?" Collins said, pointing toward the three pastries I'd put on the desk.

"That woman told me what they are," I said, shaking my head. "But I wouldn't be able to say the name even if I knew it."

"Franzbrötchen," the doctor said.

"That doesn't sound appetizing at all," Collins said, finally looking up.

"Ah, but they are quite delicious." The doctor picked one up. "It is a variant of the croissant. From what the family has told me, while the French occupied Germany, the soldiers asked the local bakers to make croissants for them, and Franzbrötchen is what came from those efforts."

Leaning closer, I studied the frilly things. "So it's a bread?"

"Pastry," the doctor said with a smile. "Much sweeter than just bread."

"Well, I've survived an arrow—I might as well give one a try."

"I bought one for each of us. They sure caught my eye when I saw them, that's for sure." I took a bite, and the sweetness damn near overwhelmed me. "There's a taste there that I don't reckon

I've ever had before—it's good, but I don't know what it is." I took another bite. "Kind of spicy in a sweet way."

"Cinnamon," the doctor said with a grin. "I had the same response when I first tried one."

"Puts me in mind of bear signs for some reason." Collins pulled his apart. "But in a different way somehow."

Collins popped the rest of his in his mouth just as there was a knock at the door, as though he was worried someone was going to try to take it from him.

"Sorry to bother you," a younger man said when the doctor opened the door. "But you need to come check on Clarence again." Worry was on the fella's face. "He's having a real hard time collecting his breath."

"Is he still coughing?" The doctor put a few things in his satchel. "Wheezing?"

"No sir, just struggling to catch his wind."

Taking the bag with him, the doctor turned toward the two of us. "I'll be back directly. Don't leave until I return."

Collins licked his fingers. "Were you able to find out anything while you were out?"

"I have confirmation that Jonathan did, in fact, take the watch." I rubbed my fingers down my trouser leg. "And our assumptions that he would bring it here to York were correct."

"So the watch is at the trading post?"

"No. York said he told Jonathan he didn't want anything to do with the thing." I moved to sit at the desk. "He said Jonathan was highly agitated over the whole situation."

"I guess so," Collins said, rising to his feet. "Especially after coming all this way and not being able to get what he wanted." He gently touched the bandages on his shoulder. "Did he have any idea as to where the bastard's run off to?"

"He said he warned Jonathan about the watch and told him he should take it straight to the Army and not get himself into any deeper waters."

"So that means he'll end up heading back to our camp in Sanderson."

I nodded. "More than likely."

"That is if he actually pays heed to York's advice." His smile wasn't a happy one. "And it's pretty obvious that the man doesn't take advice well."

"I will agree that Jonathan is a mite unpredictable." I glanced up at the lieutenant. "So what do you think we should do?"

Collins studied the room for something. "First of all, I need you to go back to the trading post and get me a shirt."

"The doctor said—"

"I don't care a whit what the doctor said." His face darkened with reddish tones. "We don't have a lot of time to find him. Just get me a shirt to travel in and see if York will give you any more details that he may have been keeping from you."

"All right," I said, reaching for my hat. "Anything else?"

"You might as well pick up some bandaging supplies if he has any. I don't want to give the doctor any reason to try and hold us back." He smiled. "If he sees we intend to follow his instructions, he won't be as much of a yapping dog when we take our leave."

"Now what?" York said when I stepped through the trading post door. "I told you everything I know."

"Calm down," I said in a low manner. "I just need to pick up a few items 'fore I head out of town." I searched the shelves as I walked. "I need a new shirt and some bandaging supplies."

His face took on a new look at that. "Bandaging? You injured?"

"Do you have any or not?"

"You're running with that Army lieutenant who took the arrow in his shoulder, ain't you?"

Heat grew in my chest. "All I want—"

"Listen to me, Lawrence," he said, stepping closer. "I'm going to give you the shirt and bandaging, and I want you out of here." He started piling things onto the counter in a huff. "You have no idea what you're getting yourself into." He pushed the items toward me. "Here. Now go."

"I'm aiming to pay you for these things."

"I don't want your money," he said with what I swear looked to be fear in his eyes. "I just want you gone."

"Fine by me."

As I was trying to pick up the items, he touched my arm, his countenance softening. "Watch your back with that lieutenant. You hear me?"

"Is there something you want to tell me, York?"

He pulled his hand away and dropped his gaze to the floor. "Just watch your back. That's all I'll say."

Chapter Twenty-Three

The ride back to Sanderson was quiet except for the occasional grunt from Collins when he'd forget about his wounded shoulder and move his arm. We didn't figure on trouble with Kiowas after that first incident, but that sure as hell didn't stop us from keeping an eye out for them. Lord knows you could better predict where a lightning strike was going to land far better than you could guess when and where the Kiowas would show up next.

"Once again, I want you to know that I owe you a great debt of gratitude," Collins said, holding his gaze to the road ahead. "And I'm sure you think I'm just saying it, but there's no doubt in my mind I would have died right there without your help."

"You know, we're not too much different, men like you and men like me." I took out a plug of tobacco and bit a piece from the end. "You and your fellow soldiers ain't too much different from fellas like me and my gang members."

He finally glanced over at me. "How so?"

"Well, we have something deep down in us, a bond I reckon you could call it, that makes us think more about the others we run with than we do about our very own hides." I shrugged. "I reckon it's a matter of taking care of our own."

Collins smiled. "You know, I believe you're onto something there." He nodded. "You can't train or teach honor or sacrifice. But it can be passed on with honor and respect shown to you by fellow members."

"And I reckon while you and I were on our excursion, I looked to you as one of my own." I leaned to the side and spat. "And I ain't about to leave one of mine to die with an arrow in his shoulder."

The lieutenant's smile broadened. "That's mighty kind of you to say, Thornhill. I wish many of my soldiers could learn this very thing."

"Now don't get me wrong," I said with a grin. "That don't mean I'm aiming to enlist, mind you."

His laughter ended with a wince. "I can't say that I blame you." He returned his gaze to the road ahead. "I told you a little about my personal relationship with the commanding officer and how the details have created a rift between the two of us."

I just waited for him to continue.

"There's a little more to the story that I failed to mention." He scratched behind his ear with the arm that didn't affect his shoulder wound. "The major has fallen ill, and the doctor doesn't seem to think he's going to make it. That's why the old man is retiring." Collins shook his head. "The men don't know anything about this, and those of us who do don't even know what's put him in this condition."

I wanted to say something, offer condolences or something, but I decided to just wait.

"So, that's why I want to get the watch in his hands as soon as possible." He lifted his eyebrows and shrugged. "It's also the reason I was interested in your friend's skills in creating false documents."

Lord knows I was trying to figure out what kind of document he wanted Jonathan to create in this situation, and I reckon the confusion was on my face when Collins glanced at me and laughed. "The documents would show the old man's signature for my promotion to captain and formally recommend me as the next company commander."

Heat moved into my gut. "I see. And when the major dies, you would have everything in place, with no one to dispute any of it."

The lieutenant's nod seemed to carry as much shame as it did acknowledgment. "It's funny how far self-preservation will push a man."

"So true. Everything I've done has been to save my friend, Ezra Tackett."

The lieutenant's smile softened. "At least you were doing the things you did for someone else."

I studied the road ahead. "I sure wish I could say that was true, Lieutenant."

We rode in silence for a while after that, and I reckon we were both thankful for the break in conversation. The heat of the day just drained us anyway, taking out just about any gumption we had for anything extra.

"I reckon we should probably stop at the board house since we'll be riding past Warren's Gap," I said, stretching my back. "You never know, Jonathan may have stopped there on his way back himself. Hell, he may even still be there."

"That's a smart plan," Collins said, trying to stretch but wincing. "It would be nice to rest before heading on to Sanderson, and knowing if Meade stopped there or not will help us in decisions to come."

"Wouldn't be a bad idea to change your bandage."

Collins rolled his eyes at this. "You're not going to turn into a mothering hen, are you?"

I shrugged. "You can do what you want, it was just a suggestion."

I'll be damned if the mud in front of Warren's Gap wasn't dried up a mite. It was the first time I'd ever seen it like that. Now I ain't saying it was dried up completely or normal, mind you. I'm just saying it wasn't as muddy as usual for some reason.

Jonathan's roan wasn't in the stable when we arrived, and I wasn't expecting it to be there if I'm right honest about it.

I dismounted and led Daisy into her stall. "Do you need help getting down?"

The lieutenant studied on that a moment. "I suppose it would be best if you did."

"Oh my! What happened?" Rose stepped inside the stable with her mouth agape. "Have you been shot?"

"He took an arrow to the shoulder," I said, moving to the lieutenant's side and reaching up toward him.

"I can do it myself," Collins said, kicking at me. "Just move."

I damn near laughed at him. "He had the arrowhead removed in Tall Junction."

"You should help him down," Rose said, gesturing to me.

"I just tried, and he didn't want nary help." Lord knows the heat in my face and neck must have been three shades of red. "He's more stubborn than that donkey in the stall."

"Has the lieutenant been injured?" Mrs. Appleton said as she stepped inside the stable.

"Yes ma'am." I found myself desperately trying to hold back a smile.

Collins grunted and growled his way down from his mount. "I shall be fine," he said through a bit of heavy breathing. "The soreness is expected."

"Please, come inside," Mrs. Appleton said. "Rose, go boil some water while I prepare a comfortable place for the lieutenant to rest."

"Of course," Rose said as she headed for the back door.

"There's no need for all this fuss." Collins stretched his back. "We are only—"

"You can talk once you're inside and resting," Mrs. Appleton said, gesturing toward the door. "Come along, the both of you."

I couldn't help but give Collins a playful grin as he walked past me. "I'll stall your horse and be in directly."

He didn't say anything as he stared at me while making his way toward the door, where a wide-eyed Appleton awaited.

After putting the horse away and removing the saddle, I did the same for Daisy and patted her neck. "I know, girl. It's been another long ride. You're probably thirsting to death."

After getting water for both critters, I glanced toward the rafter where I'd hidden the watch. Nothing appeared any different from the moment we'd left. In fact, the brush was exactly where I'd left it. I looked up toward the rafter again and started the climb at the saddle stand, working my way up the half wall that divided Daisy's stall from the next one. Lord have mercy, if I wasn't worn slap out from the ride, but I figured this would be the best time to check again.

I got my feet on top of the half wall and slowly rose to a stand. The exhaustion from the ride shook my legs in the effort, and for just a brief moment, I worried I wouldn't make it. But I pushed through and found myself stretching my arm toward the rafter and steadying myself with it at first. Sweat threatened to run into my eyes, and all I wanted to do was jump down and rest for a while. But I continued.

Once I was able to steady myself better, I stretched further and moved my hand to the rafter top, feeling around for anything. The stretch was so far, I couldn't look up as I did it, but I wouldn't have seen anything even if it had been there. I gently patted my hand around the top and found no watch. So I quickly made my way back down and headed toward the house. "Where has that son of a bitch run off to?"

Mrs. Appleton had the lieutenant in a parlor chair by the time I'd made it inside. Collins offered a get-me-the-hell-out-of-here look when I stepped closer. I couldn't help but grin, which only made his expression worse.

"Would you like some coffee?" Appleton asked as she leaned closer to him.

Collins never took his gaze off mine. His glare was probably a better word if I'm honest, as if I was to blame for all the attention. "No ma'am," he answered.

"Rose? Is that water coming to a boil yet?" Appleton looked toward me. "Will you go and check on it, Lawrence?"

"Yes ma'am."

Rose looked as scattered as I've ever seen her in front of the stove. The water was not yet at a full boil but was slowly working its way in that direction. Her face was pale, and I thought she'd taken ill while we were gone to Tall Junction.

"You look a mite peaked," I said, stepping closer.

"I'm sorry. I'm not very good with these sorts of things." She placed both hands on her cheeks. "I get to feeling dizzy, and my stomach threatens with all sorts of actions."

"Come on over here and sit down a spell," I said, touching her elbow. "Lord knows the last thing we need is for you to fall out into that hot water."

She shook her head. "Aunt Bernie said—"

"I'll take care of the water." I gestured for her to move. "Go on now and sit down."

She finally plopped into the only chair in the kitchen and put her face into her hands.

"He's going to be just fine," I said with a nod. "Don't you worry yourself none about that."

The water finally came to a boil, and I moved the kettle to the table. I made my way to the parlor door and cleared my throat. "Water is done, Mrs. Appleton. I'm letting it cool now."

"Very good." She quickly glanced at me. "Is Rose helping?"

"I reckon she's not feeling up to it right now," I said with as much compassion as I could muster. "Poor soul is struggling something awful with it all."

"She's never had to deal with anything like this," Appleton said. "Now you come and help me, Lawrence."

Collins grunted as Mrs. Appleton pulled his shirt away from his bandage—his gaze briefly met mine before he turned back to Appleton's hands. "There's no need for this—"

"I'm certain this is not your first injury, Lieutenant." Appleton didn't take her gaze off her handiwork. "So I'm sure you know better than any of us that keeping the wound clean and changing the bandages is the most important thing at this moment." She turned to me. "And you will need to know how to do this on your own."

"Yes ma'am."

"We'll let the water cool some, but in the meantime, let's get this bandage removed." Appleton was surprisingly gentle yet thorough.

"Forgive me for saying so, but this doesn't seem to be the first time you've done this, Mrs. Appleton," Collins said as he watched her every movement.

"My father was a doctor in Texas," she said, keeping her attention on her working hands. "My sisters and I often had to help him, and these types of wounds were common, it seemed."

"I have some bandaging in my saddlebag," I said. "I'll go fetch it."

"Leave it be. I have bandaging we can use." She gave me a quick nod. "You'll need the supplies you have for later." She rose to her feet. "I'll get what I have and return directly."

I waited until she was gone and sat down. "I took the opportunity to check the rafter again just to make sure Jonathan hadn't put the watch back for some reason." I shook my head. "Nothing."

"We don't have time for all this," he said, sitting up straighter. "We need to get back on the road."

"I'm working on it."

"Here we go," Appleton said, returning with bandaging. "That water should be cool enough for us to use, Lawrence." She nodded toward the doorway. "If you don't mind."

"Yes ma'am."

Rose came back into the parlor with me when I returned with the kettle. She carried a bowl and towels. "I apologize for not being as helpful as I should," she said to the room.

"Thank you, Rose," Appleton said, taking the bowl and towels. "Now pour some of the water into this, Lawrence."

The lieutenant's wound was in better shape than before and didn't have that odd smell to it either. Mrs. Appleton put a towel in the water and told Collins to hold the dry one under the wound.

"Oh, this looks better than I expected," she said, squeezing water from the soaked towel over the wound. "It appears you had a knowledgeable doctor tend to this." She smiled. "And the bandaging did not seep into your shirt, so he was very good at stanching the blood."

"If you will excuse me," Rose said as she hurried out of the room.

"If you let the water do the cleaning, Lawrence, you don't have to touch the wound, which is far more favorable to the lieutenant, I'm sure."

"Yes ma'am." I leaned closer. "I was wondering if Jonathan ever made it back while we were gone."

"I'm afraid not," Appleton said, dabbing the towel around the wound's edges. "And I have to tell you, I am quite worried about him."

"Do you recall if he mentioned where he may have gone off to?" The lieutenant's voice sounded just a mite shaky if I'm being honest. "Or where you think he may be?"

Appleton stopped her work with the towel, gazed at me, and then at the lieutenant. "Oh my. Is Jonathan in some sort of trouble?" She looked back at me. "Is that why you are asking these questions?"

"No ma'am, he ain't in no trouble, but we just want to make sure he's safe, is all."

She started putting the bandages in place. "He didn't mention anything before he left," she said. "And he left in such a rush, it surprised me, as he's never acted like that before."

"Well, Lieutenant," I said, taking a step back, "we'll need to get back on the road as soon as she's got you patched up."

"He will need to rest—"

"I'm afraid he's right, ma'am. And trust me, I will have the doctors at camp look at this just as soon as we get there."

"If you will excuse me, I'm going to get our critters saddled and ready for the trip." I nodded. "But the lieutenant and I sure can't thank you enough, ma'am."

I could read the *thank you* in the lieutenant's smile. "Yes, I would like to thank you for all your hospitality and service, Mrs. Appleton."

Rose was in the stable when I got there. She'd brought water for our critters and was just standing there as though she didn't know what else to do. "You look as though you're doing better," I said, stepping inside.

"Some." She smiled up at me. "I don't know what got into me." She put her fingertips to her neck. "I just felt overwhelmed."

"You'll be fine."

The redness in her eyes took me back to her conversations about her ma, and I couldn't resist slipping my hand into my pocket where the silver beetle was hidden.

"Thank you for stepping in and helping."

I smiled. "I've got something for you," I said before I could stop myself.

"Oh?"

"Something I reckon will make you feel a whole heap better." I retrieved the brooch in my closed hand. "Shut your eyes."

"Shut my eyes?" A gentle smile eased across her face. "Lawrence Thornhill, you wouldn't be trying to kiss me, would you?"

"No ma'am!"

Her eyes widened. "Well, don't act like that would be a bad thing."

"No ma'am, I don't reckon that would be a bad thing at all." Lord knows my stomach went to clenching on me something awful. "Just shut your eyes, please."

"All right." She did as I asked, and upon my honor to God, if she didn't pooch her face out a little as if she was expecting my lips.

I held my hand out, palm up, with the silver beetle revealed. "All right, open them."

At first, she looked to be disappointed, then confused, and then she burst into tears when she laid her eyes on that brooch. She snatched it from my hand as the tears flowed. "My beetle! You found my beetle! I didn't think I would ever see it again."

"I told you it would make you feel better."

The rest of her face caught up with her smile, and she wrapped her arms around my neck. "Thank you, Lawrence." And I'll be dogged if she didn't haul off and kiss me right square on the mouth.

I'm here to tell you her warm tears were on my face, and when she let me go, I felt a little overwhelmed myself.

She opened the wings and smiled again at the painted rose. "Where did you find it?"

"Well," I said, wiping my face. "That's a longer story than I have time for at the moment. But I'll make you this promise: I'll tell you the whole thing later on when we have more time."

"There you are," Parnell said, rushing into the stable and grabbing my shoulders. "You've got to come quick—it's Jonathan!"

Lord knows my stomach started burning like I'd swallowed an ember. "What's going on? Where is he?"

"Come on," Parnell said, pulling me toward the door. "He's at the restaurant, and he's in pretty bad shape."

Chapter Twenty-Four

I found Jonathan's blood trail well before I found him sprawled out on the floor of the eatery, struggling to catch his breath. Lord knows my stomach felt like it was stuffed with a knotted rope. I'm here to tell you there was so much blood I wasn't able to see where it was coming from or even what kind of wounds had brought it about so freely. But it was as bad as I reckon I've ever witnessed.

It was a good thing I told Rose to stay at the boarding house to inform Collins as to what had happened. If she had been that squeamish at the lieutenant's wound, Lord knows she would have given up the ghost at the sight of Jonathan's state.

"Jonathan," I said, dropping next to him. "What happened?"

His eyes searched for me as he coughed. "Lawrence? Is that you?" He coughed again, and blood sprayed from his lips.

"Jesus, where are you injured?" I studied him closer and found a few areas that seemed to be soggy with blood. "Have you been shot?"

Coughing wracked his body as he groped for me. "Lawrence . . ."

"Can you hear me, Jonathan?" I grasped one of his hands. "I'm right here."

His cough came again, sounding like an old man hacking up years of phlegm, but it sure didn't take long to realize it was blood he was coughing up.

I leaned closer. "What happened, Jonathan? Who did this to you?"

His empty gaze kept searching for me. And Lord have mercy if he wasn't mumbling something over and over again, but I'll be damned if I could understand a word of it.

"Go tell Mrs. Appleton she's needed," I said to Parnell. "Tell her to bring as much bandaging as she can muster. And tell her to hurry!"

The door clapped shut, and I leaned as close as I could get. "Jonathan, where is the watch?" I put my ear to his mouth but only heard mumbling whispers. "I need you to tell me where the watch is." I started checking his pockets and opened his shirt where blood was seeping heavily. I grabbed a tablecloth and pressed it against him before pulling it back to find what must have been a close-range scattergun wound. "Jesus, who did this, Jonathan?"

Hoping to stop the bleeding, I held the tablecloth against the wounds as his breathing became a wet, whispering rattle. The smell brought me back to the night of the lieutenant's wound, only this was stronger. This was in my mouth. This was in my throat.

The door banged open with Parnell, the lieutenant, and Mrs. Appleton rushing inside. "What's happened?" Collins said, stepping closer. He barely had his shirt back on.

"Looks like it was a scattergun to the chest," I said, glancing up at them. "And *close* to the chest, if you ask me."

"So much blood," Appleton said, getting down next to me. "Let me try."

I moved back and rose to my feet as she applied pressure. "This is about as bad as I've seen it," I said to the lieutenant. "And I've seen more than I've ever cared to."

Collins leaned toward me. "Did he say anything?"

I shook my head, meeting his gaze. "Nothing." I leaned closer so only he could hear. "And he doesn't have it on him," I whispered and nodded toward the door. "Go check his saddlebags while everyone's attention is in here."

Nodding, Collins made his way outside.

I turned back toward the urgency. "Can I get you anything, Mrs. Appleton?"

She sat motionless with her hands on the tablecloth until she slowly pulled them away and gazed up at me with tears streaming down her face.

"No," I said, shocked by her reaction. "He can't be." I knelt beside her, and before I could do anything, I knew it was too late. "I don't . . ."

She leaned into me, pressing her face against my chest and sobbed. "Who would do this, Lawrence? Who could do such a heinous thing?"

I just wrapped my arm around her and closed my eyes. "I don't rightly know, ma'am. I don't rightly know."

Collins came back inside and slowed his pace when he took notice of our grief. I met his gaze and lifted my eyebrows. He shook his head.

"Let's get you back to the boarding house, Mrs. Appleton," I said softly. "The lieutenant and I will take care of everything here."

I was never so happy to take in the smells of a stable in all my life, just getting that god-awful wound sourness out of my nose. And this was in Appleton's stable, mind you, where it was clean like none other.

"Hold still," Rose said, wiping my face with a wet towel.

"What is it?"

She looked as though she was going to be sick. "You have blood specks on your face," she said, closing her eyes.

"Here." I took the towel from her hands. "You should go inside and check on your aunt." I scrubbed my face. "Trust me, she's not as strong as she lets on right now."

"How do you mean?"

"She just had someone die in her care, Rose. Someone she truly cared about. She needs you right now."

"Lawrence?" Her face was pleading. "Who could have done something like this?"

I shook my head. "I don't rightly know, Rose." I started wiping my arms. "But we are going to find out." I nodded toward the door. "Now go on and get inside."

My stomach burned as she slowly made her way to the house. I couldn't make myself go inside just yet. I needed time to breathe. I took out the last of my tobacco and plopped it into my mouth. "Do you need water, Daisy?" I said, entering her stall. "I know you've got to be as tuckered as I am."

I glanced back toward the board house when I heard the back door close. I was never so thankful to see Collins making his way toward me. God knows I don't think I could have continued consoling either of the womenfolk at that moment. My head was tired.

"Well, this has been an unexpected turn of events," Collins said, stepping inside the stable.

"That is a fact." I nodded toward the house. "How is Mrs. Appleton?"

"She'll make it." He stepped closer. "How about you?"

I stared at Daisy's twitching ears. "You know, for someone I barely knew, I reckon I got myself too close to him." I smiled. "I tried not to do that, and even though he turned around and betrayed me, I still can't help but feel sad that I lost a friend." I looked into his eyes. "It's a strange feeling, that's for sure."

"I understand far more than you think." He moved into his horse's stall and poured water. "Any idea who did this to Jonathan? Or where the watch may be?"

"I don't reckon I have an idea. How about you?"

"Unfortunately, all I know about him is through you." He stepped out of the stall and shrugged. "I wouldn't know where to even begin."

"I'll be right honest with you." I leaned to the side and spat. "I don't know why, but I just cannot stop thinking about that Jeremiah York fella in Tall Junction."

He cocked his head. "You said you visited him, and he told you that Jonathan left with the watch." He shrugged. "What makes you think of him?"

"I don't rightly know." I dropped my gaze to my boots. "But I can't figure out why he wouldn't have taken the watch and made sure to get it in your hands." I looked up at him. "You offered him a reward."

"That's true."

"But I reckon the thing that keeps gnawing at the back of my head is recalling that scattergun he had behind his counter." I nodded. "I don't know why that sticks in my head the way it does, but I'll be damned if I can't get it out."

"Well," he said, stretching and wincing almost immediately. "We don't have anything else to go on. Do you think we should go back and check on it?"

"I reckon it's the only option we have at the moment." I leaned to the side and spat again. "But first, we need to assist Mrs. Appleton in getting Jonathan buried."

"That is a good plan, but we need to be swift with doing so." His eyebrows were high on his forehead. "We will need to get on the road back to Tall Junction as soon as we can get away."

"Yes, but we do not want Mrs. Appleton to feel we are rushing off." I rubbed the back of my head. "And when we do leave, we need to let her know we are going to search for Jonathan's killer. At least this way, she will not feel as though we are leaving in a careless manner."

Lord knows Daisy wasn't happy at all when we saddled up and took to the road again. I can't say that I blame her. In fact, I did everything I could to coax her into a better mood, but the poor gal just wasn't having it. I got her to moving, though—don't get me wrong, she just didn't like it nary one bit.

We were all tired. Lord knows my arm felt like it was ready to fall off from all the digging we did for the grave. And the lieutenant wouldn't take no for an answer, as he'd dug just as much as I had, considering the shape he was in.

"Jonathan's death sure complicates matters when it comes to the watch," Collins said, staring ahead as we rode.

I reached for my plug of tobacco and remembered I'd already chewed the last of it. "At least with him, we knew who had the blasted thing, even if we didn't know where it was."

"Yes sir, it sure complicates things."

I nodded. "How do you want to proceed with York when we get there?"

"I have given this quite a bit of thought, and I am still trying to work things out in my head." He pressed a hand to where the bandaged wound was located. "We need to make sure we don't force him into hiding or fleeing."

"How well do you know York?" I asked, turning to him.

"I met him for the first time when I visited about the missing watch."

"The reason I ask is that he made some comments about you when I returned there for your shirt and bandaging. He got nervous and somehow knew I was with you because of the items I was collecting. I reckon he'd heard that the doctor was caring for an Army lieutenant's arrow wound. And I reckon the shirt and bandaging put him to that thinking."

Collins glanced toward me. "What did he say?"

"He told me not to trust you. Said it like he knew you well." I smiled. "I reckon I should have told him that I already didn't trust you."

Collins chuckled and turned back toward the road ahead. "Well, it does sound as though he knows me well, doesn't it?" He chuckled again and winced.

"I reckon it would probably be best if you went in to see him alone. He'd likely feel less threatened with just one of us, and I've already asked him about it." I shifted in the saddle. "While you're doing that, I can ask folks around town if they'd seen someone with Jonathan's description."

"I'm sure you'll be asking around in that German bakery."

"You better know it," I said with a smile. "I'd love to have me another one of those frilly things that I can't say the name of."

"Rider up ahead," Collins said in a low voice. "Coming this way."

Squinting, I sat higher in the saddle and craned my neck. "Seems to be alone as well."

"Appears so." Collins removed his rifle from the scabbard and cradled it across his wounded shoulder, his right hand at the trigger. "Just remember, that does *not* mean he is truly alone."

"Howdy!" The man's voice called from the short distance as he waved his arms.

"At least he's got enough sense to show us his hands." Collins glanced my way for just a moment. "But that could very well be a ruse to set us at ease, catching us off guard."

I placed my hand on my Colt when I recognized the Morgan. "I know exactly who this jackass is," I said, keeping my gaze fixed on Jarvis O'Sullivan as he drew near. "You need to know—"

"I do not mean to discontent you," the boy said, still waving his arms. "And I do not mean to cause alarm."

"That's close enough." Collins adjusted the rifle in such a manner that the barrel was aimed forward as an obvious warning. "And you'll do good by keeping those hands right where I can see them."

"I will not cause you any trouble," the boy said, shaking his head. "I make you this promise, Sergeant."

"Lieutenant." The word came from Collins as though it was painful in his mouth.

"Pardon me, Lieutenant." O'Sullivan's face pinkened. "I couldn't tell for sure with you not wearing your jacket with insignia. I was trying to go by your trousers."

"It's quite all right," Collins said in a flat tone. "We're going to move to the side of the road and let you go on about your business."

"I appreciate that, sir." O'Sullivan smiled before gesturing toward me. "But your prisoner there is me only business."

"You son of a—"

"Let me handle this, Thornhill," Collins said without moving his gaze from Jarvis.

O'Sullivan's smile widened.

"Are you a bailsman agent?" Collins turned to me before the boy could answer. "You failed to inform me that you are a wanted man." His hint of a smile told me he did not believe that to be true.

"I ain't no wanted man."

"Your prisoner there killed me father," O'Sullivan said, pointing, his smile completely gone now. "Then he killed me only brother."

"This ambushing dullard and his brother took me out into a heavily wooded area and tried to hang me!" It was all I could do to keep from shooting the bastard right there. "Your slack-jawed brother would be alive at this very moment if the two of you hadn't tried to murder me like that."

"Lieutenant, if you would just kindly turn over your prisoner to me, I'll see to it that you won't have to worry about taking him all the way to Fort Hays."

"For one thing," I said, gritting my teeth. "I ain't a—"

"I told you to let me handle this, Thornhill." Collins turned his gaze back to the boy. "What gives you the assumption that I am taking this man to Fort Hays?"

"That's where the sergeant who released him from jail was taking the murderous son of a bitch for a court-martial." O'Sullivan sneered at me as he spoke. "At least that's what the extradition orders said, according to the sheriff."

"I'm afraid I can't just let him go. After all, I am an officer of the United States Army, and it is my duty to see to it that this man stands trial for desertion."

O'Sullivan closed his eyes and lowered his head for a moment. "Lieutenant, that man killed me father and brother." He looked up with reddened eyes. "And you and I both know that whatever happens with his court-martial, he'll never pay for killing me kinfolk."

"I am truly sorry about the loss of your father and brother, son, but I have my orders, and I fully intend to see those orders through."

O'Sullivan's gaze moved to me and then back to Collins. "There is a reward, you know."

Glancing my way for but a moment, Collins smirked. "I thought you said you were *not* a wanted man?"

"I am not wanted. That boy is lying."

"I didn't say he was wanted." O'Sullivan pushed his hat back on his head with a grimy knuckle. "I just said there was a reward."

"I'll ask you one more time: are you a bailsman agent?"

"No sir," O'Sullivan said, shaking his head. "I'm but a grieving son, a grieving brother."

"Then who, pray tell, is offering a reward?"

O'Sullivan stared right into me. "Me family scraped up the money to make sure the murdering bastard pays for killing our loved ones."

A coldness entered my belly.

"Well now," Collins said with a smile. "How much is this reward you're talking about?"

O'Sullivan's smile revealed a smattering of discolored teeth in various states of decay. "Five hundred dollars."

The lieutenant gazed at me as his smile widened. "Five hundred dollars for this man?"

"I've got it with me." O'Sullivan gestured to a jacket pocket, as though asking permission to retrieve the money. "If you'd like to see it with your own eyes."

The lieutenant nodded.

"What are you doing?" I whispered to Collins.

"Give me your pistol," he said, holding his hand out to me.

"No, I ain't giving you my pistol. What are you trying to do?"

"Trust me," Collins said with a smile. "Hurry while he's distracted."

By the time the lieutenant tucked my Colt into his belt, O'Sullivan was revealing a fold of banknotes.

"Five hundred dollars," O'Sullivan said, holding the currency to where we could see it better. "And it will be all yours, Lieutenant, if you just hand T'ornhill over to me."

"That sounds awful tempting," Collins said with a nod. "It truly does. But I have to account for this man when I get back to Fort Hays."

"I would be more than willing to sign documents that testify that the prisoner attempted to escape and would have done so had it not been for your heroic efforts in gunning him down."

Collins smiled.

"And I would be willing to travel with you to Fort Hays and testify to the fact in person." O'Sullivan showed his jaundiced teeth again. "And you become five hundred dollars richer."

"Tell me something," Collins said, gesturing toward me. "Are you planning on shooting this man or hanging him?"

"Do we have a deal?"

"Now hold on just a—"

"Keep your mouth shut, Thornhill," Collins said. "This is none of your business."

"The hell it ain't! It's *my* life we're talking about here."

"Answer my question," Collins said to O'Sullivan.

The boy shrugged. "Does it matter?"

"It does to me," Collins said. "After all, I'll have to answer for his death."

"Do you have a preference?"

Collins slid his rifle into its scabbard. "If he's got bullets in him, then I have more explaining to do. But if he was hanged by a mob before I could get to him . . ." He paused, shrugged. "Well then, it's just a simple report."

"Then I'll hang the bastard like I wanted to do in the first place."

Chapter
Twenty-Five

Jarvis hummed the same dad-blasted tune over and over during the course of our half-hour ride. I never did recognize that melody, but it sure sounded Irish or Scottish, if you ask me.

All I could think about was how Lieutenant Collins duped me into handing over my Colt so the O'Sullivan boy could drag me off toward a lynching tree someplace.

All for five hundred dollars.

"Be sure to hang on with your legs," O'Sullivan said with a laugh. "Remember, I didn't tie your restraints to the saddle horn this time."

"Why don't you go straight to hell?"

"I tell you what I'll do, T'ornhill. I'll be sure to look you up when I get there. How's that sound?" He laughed again. "But since you'll be there before me, why don't you mark time for me just inside the gates?"

"I wouldn't want to do that and miss the opportunity of giving your regards to your pa and brother."

O'Sullivan stared into me, his reddening face contorted. "You . . ." Dismounting, he finally forced a chuckle that sounded more like a moan. "I'm certainly going to enjoy watching you hang, T'ornhill."

If I was to say I wasn't angry, you could bet your bottom dollar I was flat-out lying. But it had nothing to do with a single word Jarvis O'Sullivan said or did. I was furious with myself for trusting that damned lieutenant by handing over my Colt and leaving me defenseless.

"I tell you what let's do. I'm gonna let you choose which tree you'll swing from. How does that sound?" His left eye twitched as he smiled. "Go on now, choose one."

I gazed up into the branches and sighed. "I can tell you right now, none of these will do," I said, shaking my head. "Let's keep riding until we find one I like."

O'Sullivan let out another chuckle. "How about you make your choice between these two trees right here?" he said, gesturing toward a nearby pair with sizable limbs.

"I'm sorry, boy, but you're gonna have to do all the work yourself if you want to hang me." I leaned to the side to spit and remembered I didn't have a chaw in my mouth. "You choose the tree yourself."

"All right," he said, hobbling Daisy's front legs. "I just t'ought you'd like to choose your final view."

His gaze met mine, unblinking for what seemed like minutes.

"Tell me something, Jarvis. Where exactly did you run off to?"

His smile disappeared. "What are you talking about?"

"You know damn well what I'm talking about." I nodded as slowly as I could. "I'm talking about the day you and Liam tried to lynch me. The fool attacked me while I held his pistol under his chin."

Without a word, O'Sullivan limped toward his horse and took a rope from a saddlebag with a hangman's knot already tied.

"You remember, Liam and I fell to the ground while the poor fool was trying to take the gun from me. I ended up shooting him in the head."

Remaining silent, O'Sullivan moved his gaze back to mine.

"Then you and I got ourselves into a bit of an exchange with bullets before you got your leg shot and high-tailed it out of there like a scalded dog." I shrugged. "I'm just curious. Where exactly did you run off to?"

He cleared his throat as he began untangling the rope. "Me father always said to retreat when we had no other options so we could fight another day."

"It's too bad your pa didn't take his own advice, isn't it?"

Hurling the rope to the ground, O'Sullivan drew his pistol and glared at me, red-faced. "Shut your mouth!"

"If you're gonna hang me, then put your revolver away and get to it."

What must have been confusion changed his countenance. He slowly re-holstered his piece and smiled. "I see what you're doing."

"Do you?" I returned the smile. "The reason I ask the question, O'Sullivan, is because while you ran off like the yellow-bellied coward you are, I stayed right there and buried your brother." I noticed Jarvis's demeanor soften ever so slightly. "The poor boy didn't deserve to die that day—especially not like that. He didn't want to go after me in the first place, and you know it. He was just following his *brother,* who was hell-bent on revenge."

The boy dropped his gaze to the ground.

"And just when Liam didn't have a single Irish bastard looking out for him, I stepped up and buried his body so animals and such couldn't get to him."

O'Sullivan looked up. "T'ank you for that."

"And let me tell you something else," I said, shifting in the saddle. "Not long ago, you hobbled your Morgan by the roadside to relieve yourself. And you had no more buttoned up your trousers when you drew your pistol and shot a rabbit near a formation of rocks and hills."

O'Sullivan's mouth dropped open, giving the resemblance of his dead brother. "How . . . how could you know that?"

"Because I was right there hiding behind those rocks with a bead on your head the entire time." I did my best to unclench my teeth. "I could have easily blown your head off right then and there. But I didn't. I was just hoping you'd go home and move on with your life." I glanced at the crumpled rope on the ground. "Now it's plain to see that I should have killed you when I had the chance."

Picking up the rope, Jarvis limped closer. "I do t'ank you for putting Liam in the ground." He turned his face away, nodding. "And I t'ank you for the mercy you showed me when I didn't even know I was receiving it." He turned back to me. "But I will not be granting you the same mercy. I brought you here to hang you, and by God, that's exactly what I intend to do."

He tossed the rope over a branch and tied off its backend somewhere, leaving the hangman's knot swinging close to my head.

"Let's talk about this, O'Sullivan." A burning washed across my belly. "Let's just come to an agreement or something."

Jarvis mounted his horse with a grunt and sidled up next to my missing arm. "Hold still," he said, gripping a shock of my hair and cutting it away with a blade. "There we go." He held out the dangling lock and smiled.

"What the hell was that all about?"

"Something to remember this event by," he said, wrapping a braided twine tightly around the hair. "Whenever I grieve the loss of me father or brother, I'll put me hands to this and remember the justice I served for them."

He made a long loop with the twine, tied it off, and placed the whole thing over his head like a necklace.

I found myself offering that stupid grin again. "Well, I hope you never forget that I killed *two* of you O'Sullivan sons of bitches, and you only got to hang one of me."

"That's it, keep running your yap, T'ornhill," he said, placing the noose over my head and cinching it tightly around my neck. "By all means, keep your yappin'. The only t'ing I'll remember about today will be you emptying your bowels into your trousers when that donkey leaves you to swing alone."

A gunshot boomed behind us as blood spattered the side of my face.

"Jaysus! Me ear!" Jarvis held a bloodied hand to the side of his head as he kicked the sides of his Morgan and rode out of there like an Irish demon.

"Whoa, girl," I said, squeezing my legs against Daisy's sides, trying to keep her from running out from under me. "Steady now. Steady."

"What were you trying to do?" It was Lieutenant Collins's voice coming closer as he sidled up next to me, reaching for the hangman's knot. "Were you trying to *talk* that fella to death?"

He cut the restraints off me and smiled.

"I can't believe this. Did you plan this whole thing?" I rubbed the burning flesh of my neck. "And you couldn't have shot him *before* he put that noose around my neck?"

"Here," he said, handing me a leather purse.

"What the hell is this?"

"Your cut," he said, holding out my Colt. "You get half."

"Half? It was *my* neck on the line! And we never discussed *any* of this!" I holstered my pistol and immediately brought it back out, aiming directly at Collins's head. "You ever do something like that again, and I swear on a stack of Bibles I will blow your brains out."

"Not a problem for me," he said, kicking his horse to move. "Just don't be so gullible as to hand over your weapon next time."

Daisy and I roamed the town when we got to Tall Gap, just taking it all in. I stopped and asked a few folks if they'd seen a man of Jonathan's description over the past few days and if they'd noticed anything. And of course, as I would have reckoned it, no one could recall a thing.

Collins and I agreed to meet at the doctor's place when we were finished, and I was surprised that he agreed to get the old pill to check his bandaging to make sure we'd applied everything properly. But before I was going to head in that direction, I wanted to go back to that bakery.

Those big-boned German girls sure know how to treat a fella, I'll tell you that much. But for the life of me, I barely understood a word they said, so I pointed at what I wanted and showed them how many to get by the number of fingers I held up.

As I was paying for the goods, the door opened, and upon my honor to God, if it wasn't Jeremiah York stepping inside. He looked to the women and removed his hat.

"Well, I guess I shouldn't be surprised to see you," he said with a smirk. "Since your partner was just in my shop a few moments ago."

"York," I said with a nod before making my way outside.

He followed me there and closed the door behind him. "You know the watch was stolen, right?"

"Of course," I said, turning to him. "That's the reason we're looking for the damned thing."

He shook his head. "When I say the watch was stolen, I mean it was stolen from the commanding officer. Major Martin has owned that watch for a few years now. Someone stole it from him."

My gut felt like the knotted rope had returned. "What are you talking about?"

"The watch you're looking for," he said, stepping closer. "I helped the major purchase it three years ago. He told me what he wanted, and I ordered it special from New York for him. I had them engrave his name on the inside of the cover."

"So you're saying . . ."

"I'm not saying anything." He lifted his head and glanced around us. "But I'm telling you the watch that you thought was stolen was already stolen."

"Where's the lieutenant?"

"No idea. When he left my establishment, I decided to step out for a moment because I couldn't trust him to come back in when I wasn't paying attention and doing something deadly." He nodded toward the bakery. "As I was walking by, I noticed you inside. And I was pretty certain you weren't aware of the truth."

"I better get going." I studied his eyes as I moved to leave. "I'm a thanking you for the information. I've got a lot of studying to do on this."

"I told you before," York said with a nod. "And I'll tell you again, you best watch yourself with that lieutenant. He can't be trusted."

I almost walked away but lingered. "Do you know if the major is aware of what has been going on regarding his watch?"

He shrugged. "I wouldn't know. I haven't had contact with him for years."

I briefly dropped my gaze to the sidewalk before turning my attention back to him. "Again, I'm a thanking you."

The lieutenant's horse wasn't tied at the doctor's place, but I knocked at the door all the same. "Doc?" I knocked at the door again while I studied the front window.

"I'm coming," I heard his voice call from inside.

"I was beginning to worry you were gone." I smiled when he opened the door.

"Ah, you can't stay away from the German women, I see," he said, smiling at the goods in my hand. "Come inside."

"Where's the lieutenant?" I handed him one of the frilly pastries from the bakery and smiled.

"How should I know? You're the one who runs with him."

I glanced back at the door. "Are you saying he hasn't been here?"

He took a bite and nodded. "That's precisely what I'm telling you. Why would he be coming back here? Is his wound worsened?"

I stepped toward the door and gazed out. "We had some business in town and decided to meet here before we left." I turned back to the doctor. "I'd talked him into having you check the wound to make sure everything was fine and to get you to change the bandaging if needed."

"Maybe he hasn't finished his business and will be here directly." He gestured to a chair. "Sit down, and we'll have some whiskey until he gets here."

"He should have already made it here." Lord knows that knotted rope in my stomach was twisting. "I just spoke to the fella he'd met with."

"Sit down," he said, plopping the rest of the treat into his mouth. "I'm sure he'll be here directly." He brought a bottle of whiskey from another room. "Has he been complaining about the wound?"

"No sir," I said, taking out one of the pastries and taking a bite. "We just wanted to make sure it was healing well and all."

He poured for two glasses and handed me one. I had to put the sweet bread on my knee to take the drink. "I'm a thanking you." I drank the whole thing, and it just seemed to set that knotted rope on fire. "Let me ask you something," I said, wiping my mouth. "You wouldn't have heard of anyone getting shot with a scattergun, would you?"

"No one has come to see me with a wound of that nature." He drank his whiskey and poured again for both of us. "But someone mentioned they thought they'd heard a scattergun go off day before yesterday."

"Where did they say they heard it?"

A banging at the door damn near caused me to drop the glass.

"Doc!" a voice called from the porch. "You in there?"

He put down the bottle and made his way to the door. "I'm coming."

"You need to come quick," the man said 'fore the door was fully opened. "There's been a shooting at the trading post!"

The doctor started putting things into his bag. "Who is shot?"

"Didn't see," the man said. "But it was a shotgun."

Chapter Twenty-Six

I reckon I didn't know what to expect while I was running toward the trading post like a scalded dog searching for a creek. And I couldn't help but worry the whole way whether my stomach was about to let loose of that frilly pastry or not. And upon my honor to God, if there wasn't more than half a dozen people already milling about at the establishment's front door when we got there.

Doc came around, shoving folks as he made his way inside. "Move!"

I followed behind him, trying to keep up.

There was a few folks standing over what appeared to be somebody slumped over on the floor. I couldn't tell who it was until the crowd parted for the doctor.

"Have you been shot, Jeremiah?" The doctor knelt beside him, and that's when I noticed the blood.

"How did you guess?" York said with an addled smirk.

Doc shook his head. "Scattergun?"

York turned his gaze to me and coughed. "Come closer, Thornhill."

"Will you hold still?" The doctor pressed a towel against the wound. "You're bleeding like a stuck hog."

"He got it, Thornhill."

I knelt beside the doctor and leaned in. "The watch?"

He just stared at me.

"So you lied to me." I tilted my head to the side. "Told me you'd refused to take it from Jonathan."

"True." York's coughing wracked his body. "You were just going to give it to that lieutenant."

"And you're telling me that Collins left after talking to you and then came back?" I lifted my eyebrows. "And then shot you and took the watch?"

He coughed again and closed his eyes. "Not the lieutenant."

"I'm trying to save your life," Doc said through clenched teeth. "The least you could do is pay attention to what's going on."

"What do you mean, not the lieutenant?"

With his eyes still closed, York nodded. "Some younger soldier." He coughed again. "I think his rank was private."

"I don't follow." Leaning closer, I watched the breathing movements on his chest. "Are you saying this younger soldier took the watch? Or are you saying he shot you?"

York opened his eyes and sucked in a sudden gulp of air before releasing it slowly. "Both," he whispered.

"Stop making him talk," the doctor said without looking up. "He's having a hard enough time breathing as it is."

"What can I do to help, Doc?"

"Find some more towels," he said, nodding toward York's counter. "I'm having a hell of a time getting the bleeding to stop from all this buckshot."

York's cough sent speckles of blood onto the doctor and me as his face tensed up into some kind of twisted grimace, his mouth wide open.

"Go on," the doctor said to me. "Hurry yourself."

I scrambled to the counter, searching for towels, but couldn't find anything. And then it dawned on me that York wouldn't have them on his counter. So I ran to the shelving, searching as I went for towels or anything we could use to stop the bleeding.

The crowd was still milling about outside the windows, but I could have sworn I saw someone in a blue uniform riding by behind them.

"Can't you find the damn towels?" The doctor's voice brought me back to the task at hand.

"Here they are," I said, stuffing as many of the blasted things as I could into my arm. "Found them!"

York's eyes roamed the rafters as he groped at his chest.

"Hold that arm," the doctor said to me, nodding toward the one he wasn't holding down himself. "His thrashing around is going to keep me from stopping the bleeding."

"Calm down, York." I grabbed his wrist and held it to his side. "We're just trying to help you."

York grunted and growled, but I reckon it was more out of pain than an effort to free his arms. His face reddened, and those eyes were roaming the rafters like he'd lost something up there.

"Whoever did this must have been right up on Jeremiah, as close as he could get," Doc said with a strained voice.

"How do you figure?"

"The patterning of the scattershot is close." The doctor shook his head. "That means the shooter wasn't too far away at all." He pressed more towels to the wound. "It also means the scattershot has penetrated deeper."

York's breathing became ragged and rattled. His face was losing the redness from before, and his eyes no longer moved.

My stomach ached like something awful. "Is he . . ."

"He's still alive," Doc said, leaning closer. "But just barely."

I don't understand how in the world he was still alive. His chest had stopped moving, and he no longer struggled to free his arms or move his head or anything. "Are you sure, Doc?"

The doctor just stayed where he was. Didn't move, didn't respond, and didn't let on that anything else was around him. For a second there, I figured he was praying, but he just quietly rose to his feet and bowed his head. "Jeremiah was a decent man."

I reckon I didn't know what to do. I was still kneeling there, holding that one arm down like York was getting ready to start fighting again. "Yes sir," I said, finally rising to my feet.

"The two of you were talking about something," the doctor said, turning to me. "Something about someone taking a watch or something."

"He said that the same fella was the one who shot him."

The doctor picked up a few clean towels and started wiping the blood from his arms and hands. "You mentioned the lieutenant. Is he the one who did this?"

I shook my head and took a towel he was holding out to me. "I don't reckon so. He said it was a younger soldier who did it."

Scanning the room, the doctor released a heavy breath. "It doesn't appear as though the man took anything else. Just a watch?"

"It appears so."

"Do you know anything about this watch he mentioned?" The doctor dropped his towel next to York's body.

I nodded. "It's what the lieutenant and I were looking for. We suspected it was here in town."

"And where is the lieutenant?" He gave me a soured look. "You mentioned the two of you were in town together."

"That is a good question. We were supposed to meet at your place when we finished what we'd come for."

"Do you think the lieutenant killed Jeremiah?"

The burning in my stomach wasn't as bad as before, but it was sure still there. "I don't rightly know what to think, just to be honest." I held the towel against my leg as I rubbed my arm and hand against it. "York himself said it wasn't the lieutenant. And besides that, I know Collins didn't carry a scattergun." I dropped the towel atop the others. "But I ain't gonna lie about it, I can't help but think he sure had something to do with it."

The doctor turned back to York's body. "Jeremiah always seemed to keep himself one step away from legal dealings." He grinned. "But I guess we can all say we've been guilty of that from time to time." He turned back to me. "You probably should get yourself on the road, as the sheriff will be along shortly."

"You don't reckon the sheriff would accuse me of shooting York, do you?"

His face looked as though he was about to laugh. "Son, you were with me when it happened. I can testify to that." He intentionally stared at my empty sleeve. "Besides, how's a fella in your shape going to fire a scattergun anyway?"

I grabbed what was left of those German frilly pastries and got Daisy and myself to moving. I decided to travel in the direction of where I thought I saw the blue-uniformed fella going earlier. It was the road back toward Sanderson.

While we rode, I took out one of those pastries and started nibbling on it. There was still dried blood in the crevices of my fingers and under my fingernails. Daisy started sniffing around as though she was jealous of whatever it was I was eating. Lord knows she was worse than any hound I'd ever laid eyes on. I stopped long enough to feed her a couple of those sweets, and I reckon she was just as fond of those big-boned German women as well.

"I know," I said to her as I rubbed her neck. "We've been running back and forth far too much lately." I wiped my hand down my leg to get the stickiness off my fingers. "One of these days we're going to settle down and just take it easy."

Climbing back into the saddle, I thought I noticed rising smoke from a distant campfire ahead. "But for right now, we need to keep safe and find all the surprises we can find before getting surprised by any of them."

The more we rode, the less the campfire ahead appeared. It was dark at first, thick. But the closer we got to it, the thinner and lighter it became. Before long, I could smell the smoke, but it was more like smelling where a campfire had been. I reckoned whoever had the fire in the first place had already put it out for whatever reason. It put me to worrying some as I remembered when Charlie had us surprise a stagecoach driver once by setting a campfire close to the road. But most of us hid far back down the road from the fire so we could come up behind them in surprise, hoping the driver would focus on the actual campfire site. A perfect ambush.

I brought Daisy to a stop and just took in the surroundings, listening carefully. The last thing I needed was to have someone waiting for us to pass by and then jump us. I didn't say a word to Daisy—I just stroked at her neck the best I could. I didn't notice anything out of the ordinary around us and didn't hear anything either. I thought about turning back for a spell but decided to just sit there.

I tried to keep those bloody images of Jonathan and York out of my head, but they lingered no matter what I did to stop 'em. I couldn't help but reckon the same person was responsible for both killings. Both men were shot at close range in the chest. Whoever it was had them at ease before they commenced to shooting.

And if that somebody was wearing an Army uniform, then that could probably put either of them at ease. Especially a younger soldier like a private. They likely didn't see him as a serious threat—they probably just saw him as a kid.

I dismounted as quietly as I could and tied Daisy to the side of the road. Drawing my Colt, I silently made my way into the trees and brush. The noises were gone—the wildlife that should have been there when nothing or nobody was around. And I reckon that may have been because I was there, but the knotted rope in my stomach let on like it was something else.

I didn't do anything fast—I took my time with slow steps and movements, making sure I didn't make a noise. I couldn't help but remember doing the very thing when I was hiding from Pa when he'd get drunk and meaner than he normally was. I'd learned to not make a noise as I moved, and I was almost always barefoot while doing it. I remember him crashing through the trees and weeds like he was aiming to split my head open with whatever tree branch he'd bring with him. And the bad thing about it all was that was exactly what he was going to do if he caught me. And there were times I would move around a tree as he came by without making any noise at all.

That skill came in right handy when I started hunting later on. Some of my friends said I must have been part Indian or something, as they couldn't believe how I could sneak up on a deer and kill it 'fore the thing even knew what hit it.

But I reckon there are lots of things that fear can make us better at. Fear can make a fella pay close attention to even the smallest of details when there's a chance of getting thrashed in the head with a tree limb. Sometimes I don't reckon Pa was as drunk as he let on during those times, either. Sometimes I figure he used being drunk as an excuse for so much of what he did. Well, that son of a bitch is dead now, but I reckon the fear I had still lives in my feet.

I caught the scent of smoke again, but this time it wasn't from a campfire. This was tobacco smoke, but just a hint of it. The evening wasn't quite dark yet, but daylight was slowly fading. I studied the area around me, watching for an ember to glow with a quirly draw. But nothing. I maintained my position for a moment and kept watching for any movement or noise.

Then I saw a brief glow not too far from where I hid. Someone was there waiting. The scent of tobacco smoke was back, as I reckon I was downwind. Whoever it was obviously didn't know I'd stopped just down the road and came in behind them. I searched around to see if there were any others. The last thing I needed was to sneak around this fella only to get caught by one of his partners. After a while, I started making my way around to his backside, as I didn't see or hear anyone nearby.

I kept my focus on where my feet was going and on the figure slowly taking shape the closer I got to them. It didn't take long to see the blue uniform, but I was coming up on their back, so I couldn't see a face. The knotted rope twisted in my stomach something awful when I noticed a scattergun leaning against a nearby tree.

He was alone out here—I was pretty certain of that, but Lord knows I kept studying all around us just to make sure of it. He was quiet, but he'd been sitting there on the ground for a while, waiting. Sweat beaded my forehead, and I was worried it would start coming down into my eyes, but I wasn't about to wipe it. I just kept moving forward slowly and quietly, watching the man to make sure he wasn't spooked by a noise or movement of any kind. I kept the Colt down to my side but in my hand. I feared if I aimed it at him all this time, my arm wouldn't be worth a damn if I needed my aim to be sure.

He was just up a small embankment where he could look down not too far from the road, so I made my way up, which caused my legs to burn a mite with the extra effort. Thankfully, there were no dried leaves in this area like the forest I grew up in. The crunching on those damn things when you stepped on 'em was just about impossible to avoid.

I paused my advance when the fella began rummaging through a sack. I took the opportunity to continue moving forward again as his attention was distracted. That and because the noise he was making would hide any sound I made. He stopped his rummaging, and I could tell he was rolling another quirly. I tried to remember how long I'd been out here, but I quickly pushed that thought away as I couldn't afford the distraction.

The man didn't seem too big, but he sat mostly slumped forward. Every once in a while, he would peer toward the road, and I had to think he was watching and waiting just for me. I couldn't know that for sure since no one else passed by, but the knotted rope in my stomach sure did agree with me. All the while, I kept moving toward the soldier, little by little.

I stopped moving and lifted my Colt when the fella rose to his feet and stretched. He kept his gaze toward the road, just watching and waiting, but it didn't ease the knots or the burning. He started opening his trousers in an effort to make water, and I knew this was the best opportunity I would have. His back was still to me, but I waited until I heard the splashing on the tree.

I stepped forward and put the Colt's muzzle to the back of his head as I pulled back the hammer. "You can finish that later," I said in a low voice just in case there were others nearby. "Put it away and get your hands in the air where I can see 'em."

He did as I said without causing any problems.

"You do anything I don't like, and I promise you'll finish relieving yourself while you're dead." I pushed the muzzle against his head to make my point. "Do you understand me?"

"Yes sir."

"Put your hands on top of your head and get down on your knees."

He did so as quietly as I'd hoped while I kicked the scattergun away.

"Now I want you to cross one foot over the other at the ankle," I said in a whisper. "And then rest all the way back onto them."

He did so without hesitation or argument.

"Keep those hands on your head if you want to keep that head," I said, easing around to the front of him. "Do you understand?"

"Yes sir, Mr. Thornhill."

I was ready to make a little water myself when I recognized the boy's face. "Private Rogers," I said more to myself than to him. "Lord have mercy, boy."

Chapter Twenty-Seven

Aunt Alice had a whole batch of them cathead biscuits made 'fore I even got myself out of the bed. She also had bacon and eggs fried up and ready to eat. And I'll be dogged if everything didn't smell better than it looked. In fact, I reckon it was those beautiful smells that roused me out of my slumber as she let me sleep in on this day.

"I wanted to make sure you had a good breakfast in your belly before you took on out of here," she said with a smile that didn't look quite right. It was the very smile she wore when Ezra left.

"Why, if I didn't know any better, I'd reckon you was trying to convince me to stay instead of leaving today." I sat down at the table and waited for her to join me. That was something we'd worked on as well: manners. Apparently, I didn't have a lick of 'em when I got to her place, according to Aunt Alice.

"It's true, I don't want you to go, but I know why you have to do so," she said, taking her seat. "But that doesn't mean I'm about to send you off without feeding you well."

"I'm a thanking you, ma'am."

I reached for the pan of catheads, and she slapped my wrist. "You still have biscuits that you made yesterday," she said, pointing toward the bundle she'd set out on the table. "Eat those first."

I felt like a young'un that's just had his peppermint stick taken away. "But they're not as good as yours."

She gave me that don't-you-sass-me look. "You eat these first," she said, putting one on my plate. "Then you can take my batch on the road with you." She smiled. "Trust me, they will taste much better while you're away from home."

"Yes ma'am."

She held that smile the whole time she sat watching me fill my plate. "Do you have any idea where you're going?"

"I don't rightly know." I bit a piece of that bacon off and shook my head. "Thought I'd just ride for a while and see where I ended up when I got tired."

She smiled when I took another bite of the bacon, as I reckon I made some kind of happy face. "Do you have any plans as to what you will do?"

I stopped chewing. "About what, ma'am?"

"For a living," she said with a laugh. "What do you plan to do to make money and survive?"

I tore off a hunk of the biscuit and popped it into my mouth. "I reckon I'll find something. Somebody's always needing help with something."

"Don't act like you don't understand what I'm saying to you." She gave me a stony expression. "You know exactly what I mean."

I slowed my chewing and glanced at my plate. "Well, like I said—"

"I know about you and Ezra Dale," she said with sharpness. "I'm not a stupid woman."

"No ma'am," I said, shaking my head. "But I don't reckon I understand what you want me to say." I met her gaze and gave her a smile.

"You can ill afford to resort to the work you've done in the past," she said, leaning closer. "Without your partners."

"Yes ma'am, I understand that."

"I just don't want you to try to do anything on your own." Crossing her arms on the table, she placed her chin on them. "You have to have fellas who are watching your back, and you're watching theirs."

"Yes ma'am, I understand that." I put my fork down and leaned closer. "And I also know you can't trust just any gang either. You have to find the right fellas or it ain't safe."

She put a hand to my cheek and smiled. "That's all I want to hear." She leaned back and nodded toward my plate. "Now you go on and eat."

"If you was a fella in my position, what would your plan be?" I picked up my fork and started for the eggs. "Where would you go and start?"

"I guess your plan is as good as any," she said, lifting her eyebrows. "I just don't want you taking any unnecessary chances that could put you in harm's way."

"I understand, ma'am." I turned my gaze toward her pan of cathead biscuits.

"And those are still for you to take on the road," she said, rising from the table with the pan in hand. "I might as well wrap these up since they've cooled down enough."

"I do want to thank you for all you've done for me."

She started placing the biscuits onto an open towel. "Like I told you, you're one of mine now." She folded the corners of the towel over the heap of biscuits, tucking them inside one another. "And we take care of our own around here." She put the towel-wrapped biscuits into an old flour sack and wiped her hands on her apron. "And that reminds me of something," she said, leaving the room.

Sunlight came through the windows, stretching across the table and warming my insides just as much as my outsides. At least I wouldn't start traveling in the rain or worse.

"Here you go," Aunt Alice said, placing a coin purse in front of me before putting a hand on my shoulder. "To get you started."

"What's this?" I picked up the poke and found several silver and gold pieces inside.

"I want to make sure you're taken care of at the beginning of your beginning."

I pushed the purse toward her. "I appreciate it, ma'am, but I—"

"Pick it up and put it away," she said, shaking her head. "I did the same for Ezra Dale when he left." She nodded and lifted her eyebrows. "I'll do it for all my boys."

"But ma'am—"

"Don't sass me. Put it away and hush."

I stuffed it into my pocket and nodded. "I'm a thanking you, ma'am."

"That's what I want to see."

I took another bite of the biscuit and leaned back in the chair. "How come you ain't eating?"

She took her seat and touched my shoulder again. "I told you before, I'd rather see someone enjoy my cooking than taste it myself." She patted my shoulder and put her hands in her lap. "It sure does me good to see someone enjoying it."

"Would you be open for me to ask a question?" I dipped my head while keeping my gaze on her. "It being a personal question and all."

"I don't mind."

I nibbled at the bacon again. "Did you ever marry?"

Her smile was wide and seemed to be in relief. "I never married," she said, looking off toward the wall. "I guess that's why I have taken to you and Ezra Dale as I have—something inside me wants to mother you two boys, I guess." She laughed. "Whether you want it or not."

"I don't mind at all." I stared at the half-eaten biscuit. "My ma wasn't much to speak of anyways."

"Don't you get me wrong, it wasn't on account of nobody was calling for me," she said with a grin. "I turned down one suitor three times." She stared off toward the rafters and smiled, and I knew damned well that smile wasn't for me. "Floyd Davis." Lord, if that smile didn't stretch out even further.

"Why'd you turn him down? And you did it three times?"

"I had responsibilities here," she said as the smile faded. "My family needed me, and I wasn't about to abandon them."

I leaned closer. "But couldn't the two of you just built a place here?"

"Floyd wanted to start a newspaper somewhere back east." She just shook her head. "And I didn't want to hold him back from his dreams."

"So you just let him go?"

Nodding, she rose from the table and smiled. "That's something I hope you and Ezra Dale never have to do." She put her hand on my shoulder again. "I hope you boys never have to choose between your responsibilities and your dreams." She squeezed my shoulder. "Because responsibilities are no different from dreams sometimes. Sometimes they can both disappoint you something terrible."

"I'm sorry to hear that, ma'am."

"Just remember this," she said, making her way back to her chair. "When your dreams are to fulfill your responsibilities, you will never worry about your choice." She leaned close. "But when you find the woman you want to marry, you better make *her* your responsibility. And only then will she become the woman of your dreams."

"Yes ma'am."

"And don't you hesitate to call on the woman you love. You make your intentions known to her and to everyone else around you." She smiled. "When you make that woman your responsibility, she will make *you* her dream." She patted my hand. "I hope you understand what I'm saying. You do understand me, yes?"

"Yes ma'am."

I don't rightly know what I expected to find with that soldier, but I can sure tell you I didn't expect him to be Private Daniel Rogers.

"Are you alone?" I put my Colt's muzzle to his ear. "And you better think real good 'fore you answer that."

"It's just me."

His face was reddened, and I couldn't tell if it was from anger or embarrassment.

"You here waiting on me?"

"Yes sir," he said, letting his gaze drop to the ground.

"I reckon it was you who killed Meade and York." I nodded to my right. "With that scattergun right over yonder." The knotted rope was back in my belly. "And I reckon I was next."

Rogers just kept his gaze to the ground.

"I'll say this but one time, boy." I leaned closer to him. "The first reason you give me to blow your brains out, I will not hesitate. Do we have an understanding?"

He didn't move.

"I don't reckon I heard your answer."

Without looking up, Rogers nodded. "We have an understanding."

"Good. Because I'm fixing to step behind you." I held my gaze to his face. "And it'd be just as easy to blow your brains out from back there as it would be from right here."

Easing to the boy's back, I took in the surroundings when I knew he couldn't see me. I knelt next to the scattergun, quietly holstered my Colt, and kept my gaze on Rogers as I emptied both barrels of the scattergun. "You're doing fine," I said, dropping the shells into my pocket. "Just don't move." I left the scattergun on the ground, drew my Colt again, and rose to my feet.

I still had sweat on my face, although the cool of the evening was upon us. "Keeping your hands on your head," I said, kicking the private's feet. "I want you to get up and keep your back to me. We are going to walk back the way I'd just come up behind you and get my donkey." I put the Colt's muzzle to his back. "And then we're going to slowly make our way to your campfire."

I reckon that fella was just about ready to mess his britches the whole way we walked. And that was just fine and dandy with me, if you wanna know the truth about it. The more fear I could put in him, the less gumption I'd have to deal with. I had to make sure he knew he wasn't dealing with the Lawrence Thornhill he'd drunk bottles of whiskey with. I wanted him to think that this Lawrence Thornhill only wanted one thing: to end his life.

His camp was exactly what I suspected it to be. Nothing more than a distraction so he could get the jump on me. I couldn't help but wonder if the U.S. Army taught him that, and then I started to wonder if that's where Charlie had learned the trick. If it was, he'd never mentioned it.

The campfire was still smoldering when we got there, and I told the boy to rekindle the damned thing slow and quiet-like. The real darkness would be on us soon, and I wanted to make sure I could see everything before I made a move. The fire gave enough light to reveal that the private's horse was tied nearby, but that was about all there was to the whole setup.

"Come over here and get the rope I have in my saddlebag," I said, keeping my Colt aimed on him. "You'll find it near the side."

"Rope?" His eyes widened like I'd just stomped on his sore toes. "You can't hang me—I'm a soldier of the U.S. Army."

I fought back a smile. "I ain't got no plans of hanging you, Rogers. I've got better plans for you, my friend. And it ain't gonna be the two of us drinking whiskey all night and having a big-eyed time." I nodded toward Daisy. "Now get the rope, like I said."

He took it out and reached it toward me. "Please don't hang me, Thornhill. I'll tell you anything you want to know. I'll do whatever you tell me."

"I told you, I ain't got no plans to hang you." I shook my head. "All I want you to do is make a small hondo on one of the ends there," I said, nodding toward his hands. "And tie it off so the loop stays in place as sturdy as it can."

"How big of a loop do you want?" There was a quivering in his voice.

"I really don't give a damn," I said, shaking my head. "Make the loop big enough for the other end of the rope to go through like a lariat."

His fingers fumbled with the hemp as sweat beaded on his forehead.

"Where's the watch?" I asked, studying his reaction.

He stopped working the rope and gazed up at me. "Watch?"

Nodding toward his hands, I waved the Colt. "I didn't say nothing about stopping."

He started working a knot to hold the small loop in place. "Well? Where is it?"

"I don't have it." He didn't look up—just kept working the knot. "I'll ask one more time. Where's the watch?"

He gazed up at me and held out the looped end of the rope. "Lieutenant Collins has it."

I shook my head. "Thread the other end of the rope through the loop." When he started doing this, I stepped closer. "And where is Lieutenant Collins?"

Rogers shrugged.

"Boy, I ain't in no mood for this." I placed the muzzle against his head. "You best tell me what I ask."

"Sanderson." He reached out the rope to me. "He's heading to our camp in Sanderson."

"See there? That wasn't so hard, was it?" I shook my head. "Now get on your knees like before, with your legs crossed at the ankles, and sit back on your feet."

He did as I said without hesitation.

"Now get your hands together behind your back."

I put the sliding noose around his hands and pulled tightly before wrapping the rope around his wrists and feeding the rope between his hands and back to tie off the wraps. "There we go," I said, holstering my Colt and taking a seat near the fire. "Now tell me what the lieutenant is planning to do with the watch." I lifted an eyebrow. "And I know most of the story, so you best tell me the truth."

"Lieutenant Collins had me steal the company commander's watch while I was at Fort Hays so he could return it to the Major in hopes of gaining favor." Rogers kept his gaze to the ground. "He promised me that I would move up in rank when he was promoted. I stole the watch while the Major was asleep and sent it to Sanderson on a stagecoach at the lieutenant's orders so I wouldn't get caught with it." He shook his head. "But the stagecoach was robbed, and we've been tracking it ever since. Apparently, it went from your hands to Meade's to York's."

"And now the lieutenant has it." I rose to my feet and stretched. "So what is his plan? Just march the damned thing right back to the company commander like he's a hero for tracking it down? Killing the bastards who stole it?"

"That's what he said."

"And he left you to do the dirty work," I said. "Your job was to get rid of all the people who knows the truth. You're supposed to get rid of anyone who could tell the Major what really happened. Does that about sum it up?"

He just stared at the ground.

"Tell me, is the lieutenant planning on heading to Fort Hays to deliver the watch in person?"

Rogers nodded. "That's his plan."

I pushed another log into the fire and stared at the flames. "I reckon he wants to get it to the Major before the old man succumbs to his deathbed."

The private's face scrunched up.

"What was that look for?"

"How's that?"

"The look you just made when I mentioned the Major's illness." I leaned closer to him. "What was that look for?"

"Why would you think the Major was sick on his deathbed?" He gazed up at me. "He ain't sick at all."

"So that was a lie your lieutenant told me." I smiled. "I see now. He seems to be telling bits of truths and bits of lies to all of us to get what he wants."

"You saying he lied to me?"

"Son, I wouldn't be surprised if you are the next one to find himself dead." I laughed. "After all, you are just like the rest of us he wants dead. You know too much of the truth."

"But he and I had a deal."

I laughed a little too much at that. "Son, don't you see? We *all* had a deal with that devil."

Chapter Twenty-Eight

I made preparations for the two of us to hit the road 'fore sunrise. Rogers was awake and in a foul mood, constantly complaining about not getting a nod of sleep on account of being tied to that tree the whole time.

But having Rogers tied up like that made it possible for me to check his pockets for knives or other weapons, and I wouldn't have been able to do that and keep him in check at the same time with having just the one arm. It also gave me the chance to go back and get the scattergun we'd left.

I untied him long enough for him to relieve himself before we left, and then I bound his wrists in front of him and tied everything off to his saddle horn so he'd have a better balance. The last thing I needed was to have the son of a bitch falling off and breaking something.

"Are you going to make me ride like this all the way to Sanderson?" He was hunched forward a mite where I'd tied the rope so close.

"Well, do you wanna ride like that?"

"Of course not," he said, shaking his head.

I smiled. "Then I reckon the reason you're riding in that manner is because I am making you."

He turned his gaze forward as his face reddened.

"Besides," I said, taking his horse's lead. "We ain't going to Sanderson."

He sat up as far as the rope would allow. "Where are you taking me?"

I got Daisy started moving and let go of a deep breath. "We're going back to Tall Junction."

"Tall Junction?" He turned toward me. "Why are we going back there?"

"Well, for one thing, that's the last place where you murdered somebody." I shifted in the saddle. "And I reckon it's the safer thing for me to do, knowing I'm not turning you over to fellow soldiers who will more than likely take your side no matter what." I chuckled. "Especially when you have an officer giving you orders to do all manner of illegal activity that has nothing to do with the U.S. Army, including murder."

"I need a fair trial."

"And that's why we're going back to Tall Junction. At least I know you'll be safe there." I leaned toward him. "Because, like it or not, that lieutenant of yours will have a hard time killing you when you're in custody outside of his jurisdiction."

"Lieutenant Collins won't—"

"Son, if you think that fella's going to let you live with all the grime you have on him, you're dumber than I gave you credit for." I shook my head. "You don't mean nothing to him. And now that he don't need you anymore, you ain't nothing but a problem for him."

Rogers just stared ahead.

"Not to mention, your boys would probably hang me the moment we made it to your camp. Why they wouldn't listen to a word I had to say." I glanced at him again. "And you know that's the truth."

Rogers looked as though he'd just fought his way out of a deep lake after trying to stay afloat for hours. "He said he was going to promote me to take his place as the company lieutenant." He looked at me with hopeless eyes. "Said I would be his executive officer."

"He told me he would see to it that my friend would be released and exonerated." I lifted my eyebrows. "Instead of going to the gallows for horse thievery."

Rogers dropped his gaze to his tied hands. "So you're saying he just told us what we wanted to hear so we would do whatever he wanted us to do?"

"I reckon that about sums it up."

A crowd started gathering as we rode through Tall Junction. They walked along and followed us as we went. And I reckon somebody ran ahead to get the sheriff and others before we even made it to the jail, as they were waiting on us there. Sheriff Walters and Doc Stevens came toward us. Doc was moving his gaze from me to the bound private. "Is this the fella who killed Jeremiah?"

"It is," I said, stretching my back. "Also killed a fella named Jonathan Meade."

The sheriff stepped closer. "Where'd you find him?"

I dismounted and rubbed Daisy's neck. "He was waiting for me not far from here." I glanced up at Rogers. "I reckon he was trying to surprise me and do to me what he'd done to them others."

"I'll be damned," the sheriff said, untying the rope to get Rogers down from his horse.

"But this boy was only following orders, Sheriff." I met the private's gaze. "And to be right honest with you, this fella was probably going to be the next one murdered after me."

"Lieutenant Collins," the doctor said.

"That's right." I nodded at him. "Apparently Collins has some big scheme he's trying to work so he can get back into the good graces of his commanding officer by heroically returning the major's gold watch that had been stolen." I couldn't help but smile. "Stolen by this very private under the orders of Lieutenant Collins himself."

The doctor shook his head. "I'll be damned."

"Sheriff, I'd like to leave this boy in your custody, as I fear he would be in mortal danger if I was to take him straight back to Sanderson."

"He killed York, so we have every right to jail him here until we see what the judge has to say." He helped Rogers down and started leading him toward the jail. "I assure you he will be safe here."

"I need to get Daisy fed and watered so she and I can get back on the road as soon as possible," I said, walking behind them. "I'm going after Collins to make sure the commanding officer and his troops know what he's done."

"Let's get this fella locked up first," the sheriff said over his shoulder. "Then we'll get someone to take care of your critter."

While they was caring for Daisy, I decided to go visit them big-boned German women again at the bakery. Lord have mercy if I didn't have a hankering for those frilly pastries. The doctor laughed at me as he tagged along.

"The bread here is quite addictive," he said with a smile.

"You better know it." I went inside and inhaled that scent. "I reckon a fella could founder himself on these pastries."

"That is true," the doctor said, laughing. "And now you know why I settled in Tall Junction."

"Is that a fact?"

"In my profession, I could settle down anywhere and make a decent living," he said, pointing at a loaf of pumpernickel for one of the women to fetch. "So why not reside where your simple pleasures are within reach?"

"I like the way you think, Doc."

"After all, life is short and doesn't make too much sense as it is." He handed the woman a few coins and smiled at her. "Tall Junction has great whiskey, poker games where I can help men too proud to ask for help, and of course the finest bakery you'll ever find."

"Lord have mercy, Doc. You've near talked me into moving here myself." I pointed at the rack of frilly pastries. "I want 'em all, ma'am," I said to her.

The doctor laughed at my purchase. "That's right, stock up until you can come back next time."

We walked outside, and I nodded for the doctor to help himself to one of the pastries. "You ever been married, Doc?"

He took a bite and shook his head. "Not that I am aware of." He chewed for a moment and smiled. "How about you?"

"No sir. I reckon I have met a girl I'd like to call on, though."

He took another bite. "Is she a pretty girl?"

I was a mite surprised when the heat moved into my face. "I sure think so." I'll be dogged if I couldn't see her face in my mind right then and realized I was grinning. "I reckon she's about the only person who makes me feel whole, if that makes any sense at all."

The doctor gazed at me with a smile in his eyes.

"I don't mean that because of my arm and all," I said before he could speak. "What I mean to say is she makes me feel like I'm normal or a good man." I laughed. "And we both know I ain't neither of those things." The heat in my cheeks spread into my ears. "Anyway, to answer your question, yes sir, I think she's a right pretty girl."

The doctor stopped and turned to me. "Well, Mr. Thornhill, it sure sounds to me like you've already found your Tall Junction."

I stopped at Warren's Gap for a number of reasons. First of all, it would have been an awfully long trip if I'd chosen to just keep riding, so it only made sense to stop and get Daisy fed, watered, and rested some before moving on. But the real reason, I suppose, is I don't reckon I was willing to pass up a chance to see Rose and declare my intentions if I'm right honest.

Everything seemed to be a lot quieter than normal in town, and I'll be dogged if the mud wasn't damn near dried with the skies showing nary a cloud out front. There was a sign in the eatery window stating it would be closed until the cleanup was finished. I don't reckon anybody wants to eat pancakes with blood splattered all over the place.

I put Daisy in her stall and removed the saddle. The old gal seemed happier than a colt in clover when I put out fresh water and feed. "Get you some rest, girl," I said, rubbing her side. "I'm real sorry, but we ain't gonna be here but a spell."

I heard the back door of the house slam shut and footfalls running toward the stable. 'Fore I could even turn toward that direction, Rose nearly knocked me right off my feet in a sudden embrace. "You're alive!" she said as tears flowed.

"Lawrence? Is that really you?" Mrs. Appleton's voice wavered as she came up behind us.

"Lord have mercy," I said, pulling back a mite. "The two of you are going on like it was me that was just buried and not Jonathan."

"We heard you were dead," Rose said, placing her hands on my face.

Mrs. Appleton moved forward. "By a scattergun, just the same as Jonathan."

"Where did you hear something like that?"

"Lieutenant Collins," Rose said, wiping her tears.

A coldness washed through me, making it a struggle to catch my breath. "Collins is here?" I drew my Colt and stepped to the doorway. "Is he inside the board house?"

"No," Mrs. Appleton said, wringing her hands. "He stopped by yesterday to water his horse before continuing on toward his camp in Sanderson."

Moving in front of me, Rose looked as though I'd pulled the gun on her. "What's going on, Lawrence? I'm scared."

I holstered the Colt and reached for her shoulder. "Lord have mercy. I don't know what I would have done if he'd hurt either of you."

"Are we in danger?" Appleton said, gazing up at me.

That coldness was now a spreading burn in my chest. "I reckon if he was aiming to do something here, he would have done it yesterday."

Rose shook her head. "Are you speaking of Lieutenant Collins?"

I licked my lips and took in a deep breath. "He fooled me," I said, trying not to grit my teeth. "He had Jonathan and a Tall Junction proprietor killed. Both by scattergun." I dropped my gaze to the floor. "And I reckon, had I not been as vigilant on the road here, I'd a been the third one killed."

"Oh my." Rose dabbed at her eyes with a handkerchief. "He told us you had been killed."

"I reckon he was putting a lot of faith in that assailant of his." I grinned, hoping to make her smile. "But I promise you I ain't dead."

She laughed and dabbed her eyes again.

"I captured the assailant and turned him over to the sheriff in Tall Junction before I started back this way."

Rose closed her eyes. "Thank goodness."

"Mrs. Appleton, would you please allow me to speak to Rose privately, ma'am?"

"Of course," she said, moving her gaze from my face to Rose's. "I shall get back to the kitchen and check on dinner." She put a hand on mine. "I am so thankful that our Heavenly Father has protected you, Lawrence."

"So am I, ma'am."

I waited until Appleton was inside the house before I made my way to the saddlebag. "I have something for you." I retrieved the sack and came back to her. "There's a German bakery in Tall Junction," I said, handing her one of the frilly pastries. "And upon my honor to God, if these ain't the best things I've tasted."

She took a small bite, and her whole face came alive. "Oh my, this is delicious. What is it called?"

"They told me, but I ain't got a clue how to say the danged word."

She laughed. "Mm, I taste cinnamon." She took another bite. "I love cinnamon."

I gazed at the floor for a moment. "I'm sure you recollect the evening I handed you your silver beetle," I said, looking up and gesturing to the brooch on her lapel.

Her hand went to the beetle as she smiled. "I do. Thank you for finding it."

I cleared my throat. "Yes ma'am," I said, dropping my gaze again to the floor. "About that." The burning in my stomach was still there and felt as though it had spread to my legs. "I want you to know that I hold you in high regard."

She smiled. "Well, Lawrence Thornhill, I hold you in high regard as well."

The burning was now in my chest and neck. "I reckon what I'm trying to say is that I would like to call on you if you would be accepting of that."

Her smile widened.

"But before you give your answer, I need to be right honest about a few things."

Her eyes narrowed as her smile faded.

"I have to admit to doing some terrible things in my past." I couldn't look her in the eye at first. "I reckon, if truth be known, not all those terrible things were done in my past either."

She just stared at me.

"I ran with a gang for a number of years." I nodded at my empty sleeve. "That's how I lost my arm. During a gunfight during a bank robbery."

She put her hands over her mouth.

"But the gang broke up a long time ago." I dropped my gaze to the floor again. "Truth is they're all dead, I expect. That is except for me and the fella who saved my life when I got shot."

"Lawrence, what is in your past should remain in your past." She shook her head. "Besides, I know the man you are today."

"That's just it, Rose. What is in my past *hasn't* remained there."

"What do you mean?"

I cleared my throat and tugged at the collar riding up my neck. "That brooch," I said, gesturing toward the silver beetle on her lapel. "How do you reckon I was able to find it?"

She covered her mouth again with both hands. "Are you saying you were a member of the road agents who robbed the stagecoach?" She removed her hands as her mouth remained open. "You were there?"

Lord have mercy if the burning wasn't now in my ears. "The truth is, there were no road agents."

"I was there," she said, lifting her eyebrows. "They robbed me along with all the other passengers."

"It's true, you was all robbed." I tried to smile. "But there was no road agents. Just one fella who did the whole thing. You only saw one fella." This time I smiled. "And that one fella was me."

Rose started laughing. "Don't be ridiculous, Lawrence. The man I saw had two arms."

"I stuck old rifle barrels out of the brush to make the driver think there was a whole gang of men aiming on him." I shook my head. "And I stuffed the right sleeve of a thousand-mile shirt with tall grass and tied a burned revolver and gauntlet to the end." I nodded. "Didn't you see the suspenders I used as a sling to hold the whole thing up?"

Her face went blank as her eyes searched memories. "Oh my . . ."

"But the friend who saved my life is about to be extradited to Fort Hays and hung for horse thievery." I shook my head. "And I've been trying to find a way to save his hide. I can't just let him die."

She just stared at me, which made the burning worse.

"But you made me feel like I was complete. You made me realize I didn't have to prove nothing to nobody. That I could be a normal fella, living a normal life." I smiled again. "As long as I had you, I didn't have to be what I'd been."

"You've given me an awful lot to think about," she said, staring off into nothing. "I assure you, I did not expect any of this."

"Yes ma'am. I understand." I wiped sweat from my forehead. "And I'm not expecting you to give me an answer now. But I wanted to make sure I told you everything before you made any decisions."

"I appreciate that, Lawrence." Her smile wasn't the same one I was used to. "Like I said, you've given me an awful lot to think about."

Chapter Twenty-Nine

The worst part about Sanderson was knowing I was in the same town as Ezra and couldn't do a thing to help him, or even get a chance to speak with the bastard for that matter. And to be right honest, Sanderson was no longer a safe place for me because of everything that happened the last time I was there. Not to mention, now that Lieutenant Collins believed me to be dead, it was that much more dangerous if I was caught walking around otherwise.

The saloon was a problem, as I surely wouldn't be able to go unnoticed, as that's where all my troubles started for the most part. So many of the soldiers in there would have questions of me and could very well throw me back into that damned tumbleweed wagon . . . or worse. But there again, the saloon would probably offer my best chance at getting the information I needed.

Tying Daisy out front, I hid my face when a few young soldiers came out the front door and headed down the street. I figured staying away from the tables and holding close to the bar would be my best chance of getting the answers I needed while not getting caught.

"Well, there's a face I'd never expected to see in here again," the barkeep said to me in a soft voice. "What can I get you?"

"How about we do this?" I leaned closer. "Give me a whiskey, and I'll pay you for a bottle." I smiled and slid coins across the bar top. "That is, if you'd be willing to answer a few questions."

He briefly glanced at the door. "As long as those questions don't put me in poor standing with the boys in blue."

I took a drink and realized it'd been a few days since I'd had one. "Has the lieutenant made it back to town?"

"Got back yesterday, as I understand." He set to cleaning a few glasses. "He'd come back with an arrow wound."

I finished the whiskey. "Anybody with him?"

"Not sure," he said, cleaning the same glasses again. "But he left out of here early today for Fort Hays." He put one of the glasses under the bar. "You didn't seem too surprised that he'd showed up with that savage wound."

Shrugging, I cocked my head. "I was with him when it happened. Damned fool couldn't keep his mouth shut long enough for the Kiowas to leave us be."

His shoulders shook with laughter. "Sounds about right."

"How many men traveled with him to Fort Hays?"

"I wouldn't know." He nodded toward a table where an older soldier sat. "But I'd hazard a guess that Lee Murray would have the answer to that."

I glanced in the direction and quickly turned back. "Under the circumstances, I reckon revealing myself to one of the lieutenant's men would be a very dangerous action."

"For one thing, there's nothing that goes on in that camp that Corporal Murray doesn't know about." He leaned closer and lowered his voice. "But more importantly, the man *hates* the lieutenant with a passion."

"Is that a fact?" I said, stealing another glance at the corporal. "Why is that?"

"Murray doesn't talk about it in front of the men, but from what he's told me, Collins can't be trusted." He lifted his eyebrows. "Said the company commander doesn't trust him either."

"Care to introduce us?"

He put the glass under the bar top and nodded. "Give me but a moment," he said as he made his way toward the corporal's table.

My stomach rumbled as I watched the barkeep lean close to the man. He glanced back toward me during the conversation, but the corporal never turned my way. He just rose to his feet and walked out the door as the bartender made his way back to his station. *Well, that does it. He's going to fetch men to come arrest me.*

"He said to wait a few minutes and then meet him toward the side of the building." He nodded. "Said he'd feel more comfortable with fewer eyes on the two of you."

I stared at him for a moment. "Why do I get the feeling I'm about to be put in fetters?"

"You can trust Murray."

I followed the tobacco smoke and found Corporal Murray leaning against the building, puffing on a pipe. "I apologize for taking you away from your whiskey," he said in a low manner. "But we can ill afford to be seen together."

The light from the window next to him wasn't bright, but it was enough that I was able to recognize the man as the one who'd taken Ezra back to the jail when he'd busted out. I nodded. "Understood."

"I suppose you are aware of the fact that Lieutenant Collins is as crooked as a dog's hind leg."

"I am well aware of that now."

He drew from his pipe and blew smoke upwards. "He told that you were killed on the road back from Tall Junction."

"He had a young private waiting for me in ambush, but I didn't fall for it." I cleared my throat. "The same fella had already killed two other men under the lieutenant's orders."

Murray took another draw on his pipe. "Who is the soldier?"

"Private Daniel Rogers."

"Figures."

"I captured the boy and turned him over to the sheriff at Tall Junction." I rubbed the back of my neck. "I feared bringing him here would have been to my detriment."

"Smart thinking."

"Collins had Rogers steal your company commander's gold watch so he could return it like a hero to get himself into better graces with the major. Rogers apparently put the watch on a stagecoach to be delivered to Collins." I grinned. "Problem is the watch was stolen during a robbery."

Murray offered a smile. "So that's where you come in."

"You would be correct." I shrugged. "In the end, Rogers killed two different men to get the watch back, and apparently he'd given it to Collins, who, by my estimation, is on his way to hand-deliver it to your company commander at Fort Hays."

"With Indian wounds," the corporal said. "Of which he'll no doubt testify he suffered while retrieving the watch from supposed thieving savages."

I nodded. "I hadn't studied that into it, but that will no doubt be his story."

"I knew he was crooked, but I never would have figured Collins for a murderer."

"I'm going after him." I cleared my throat again. "Can you tell me how many men are with him?"

"None," Murray said. "He had a fresh horse saddled, got himself a bite to eat, rested a few hours, and then took off by himself."

"He wants all the glory for returning the company commander's watch. He's trying to get himself into a position where he can get promoted to captain and somehow become the company commander."

Murray came off the wall with a disturbed look on his face. "Dear God," he said, probably more to himself than to me.

"What is it?"

"Don't you see? He's planning to get the major to recommend him for promotion."

"I reckon that's what I said."

"What's to stop him from killing the major once the paperwork is done?" He shook his head. "No different than what he's done in killing the others."

"Lord have mercy." I couldn't help but think of Jonathon. "He wanted one of the men he'd killed to falsify some documents for himself."

"I'm going with you," Murray said, cleaning the residue from his pipe's bowl. "You can't do this alone. Besides, it's my duty to protect the company commander."

The burning returned in my stomach. "I don't mind you coming," I said, lifting my chin. "But you need to understand, I don't trust any of your other soldiers. It's hard to say how many of those men are following orders that are not legal or not benefiting the U.S. Army."

"I agree. These men were trained to follow orders and to never question those orders from a commissioned officer." I saw disgust on his face. "And until Collins is apprehended, I think it is best we keep things to just the two of us."

"I need to get my donkey fed and watered," I said with a nod. "I need to get myself fed and watered as well. Both of us should rest for a spell, and then we can leave."

"I don't think we have to rush." He put his pipe into a pocket and retrieved a plug of tobacco. "The lieutenant's injury is going to slow him down considerably." He cut a piece off for himself, put it in his mouth, and offered what little remained. "But the sooner we leave, the faster we can catch up to him."

"Sounds as good of a plan as any."

I reckon the ride to Fort Hays weighed heavily on my mind during the trip. Now don't get me wrong, there was a great deal of comfort in knowing I wasn't riding alone. But there was just as much concern in the fact that I wasn't riding alone either.

There was no denying that Corporal Murray wore his honor on his sleeve, but I'll be damned if bitterness wasn't right there on his other sleeve like a stripe of rank. He was a by-the-books kind of fella, and he expected everyone else who took the oath of service to have the same constitution.

"I recognize the motives behind the lieutenant's actions," Murray said. "I'm not saying I agree with those motives, mind you. And I certainly do not condone them, but there's one thing I cannot seem to work out in all my estimations."

I just gazed at him, waiting for his words to continue.

"I cannot seem to recognize *your* motives in this whole thing, Mr. Thornhill." He shook his head. "After all, the thief of a thief gains no reward, as they say."

I smiled. "Do you remember the day we first met?"

"It was when we captured that escaped prisoner."

"Ezra Tackett," I said, nodding. "The closest friend I've ever had. If it wasn't for him, I woulda surely lost my life when I lost my arm." I did everything I could to smile. "He's fixing to hang for horse thievery, and all I want to do is find a way to save him from the gallows."

"And you figure if you deliver that gold watch to the major, he'll grant your request to pardon your friend."

I brushed at something on the saddle horn. "I don't rightly know what I figure anymore, but all I want is for my friend to live."

He stared at me for a moment before nodding. "So it is true—there is honor among thieves."

"I wouldn't go that far," I said with a laugh. "But I reckon we care for our friends as much as anybody else."

He nodded. "Maybe more than most."

"Would you know when they plan to extradite Ezra?"

Shaking his head, the corporal adjusted his jacket. "I'm afraid not. I have been removed from jail duties." He lifted his chin as though taking great pride in his position. "That's what happens when you question the lieutenant's decisions about things, and he knows damn well he's in the wrong."

"Do you know if Ezra has been extradited already?"

"I cannot say for certain, but it is my understanding that your friend is still waiting in the Sanderson jail."

"Well then," I said, staring into his eyes. "There's still a chance, isn't there?"

Murray gave me what seemed to be his first genuine smile since we'd met. "Not to change the conversation," he said, moving his gaze forward. "But I'm not sure you're aware of a rider in the far distance ahead."

"Where?" I studied the vast openness in front of us. "I can't see anybody."

He retrieved the spyglass he'd been using, lengthened it, and peered into the eyepiece. "He's pretty far away, but you can just make out the lieutenant's shape."

I took the spyglass when he held it out to me and searched the landscape. "How do you know that moving shape is Collins?"

"It may not be him."

"To be honest," I said, peering through the lens, "it very well could be someone hellbent on seeing me hang. But we must proceed as though it is Collins."

It didn't take long before the road cut through hills and rocks, causing us to lose sight of the traveler ahead of us. We stopped to let the critters drink from a small brook and took the opportunity to stretch our legs and take relief.

"That fella is traveling at too good of a pace for someone with a shoulder injury like the lieutenant's," I said, rubbing Daisy's neck.

"I'm not sure pace has anything to do with it."

I moved toward the brook to fill my bladder and turned back to him. "What do you mean?"

A gunshot rang out from somewhere among the hilltops, and within seconds, something struck my upper arm, sending what felt like a raging fire down the whole thing. "Get down," I said as I dropped to the ground. My arm hurt like a son of a bitch when I drew my Colt and scanned the hillocks.

Murray pulled a rifle from its scabbard and found cover near a rock. "Do you see anything?"

"I do not," I said, studying the higher ground.

"Are you hit?"

"I am indeed." I turned my head to get a better view. "I'm not sure how bad."

"Hold still and I'll come check."

"Keep your position," I said as Murray rose to move.

Another gunshot rang out, and this time I spotted the smoke plume from the ridge and returned fire in that direction.

"Shit!" Murray fell to the ground, holding his stomach.

"Don't move," I said, squeezing off a couple more rounds into the same area, even one into the dirt. I just wanted the shooter to understand I knew right where he was.

A quiet settled over everything as I kept my focus on that spot and the areas immediately around it. "How bad is it?"

"Got me in the gut," Murray said. "Damn it, he's been there waiting for us."

"You reckon he saw us and took to the high ground?"

The corporal moved to sit up and grunted as his reddened face sneered. "It appears so." He lifted his hand to inspect his wound and pressed it again. "Did you get him?"

"Not sure," I said, checking my wound again. "Hard to judge when I'm shooting a revolver with an arm that is burning something awful." I shook my head. "And I'm fairly certain he's out of range for my Colt. There's no doubt that fella is using a rifle."

Nodding, Murray finally sat up. "The lieutenant took his with him when he left."

I holstered my weapon, glanced at the ridge one more time, and rose to my feet. "Let me take a look at that wound."

"Let's get yours patched up first," he said, struggling to stand.

"I'm fine. Yours is in the gut."

"No, we need to deal with yours first." He slid his rifle into its scabbard while still holding his stomach. "You've only got the one arm as it is. We can ill afford for you to lose that one."

"I have bandaging in my saddlebag," I said, making my way to Daisy, who surprisingly hadn't moved at all during the gunfire. The corporal's horse, on the other hand, took to running at the first shot. "Probably enough bandaging for the both of us."

The bullet was still lodged in the meat of my upper arm, and it hurt like hell when Murray was feeling around for it. "I fear I'm going to cause more pain if I try to remove it," he said, wrapping my arm. "It looks like you will be fine, and you can have the bullet removed when we get to Fort Hays."

No matter how bad the damned thing hurt, I couldn't help but move it as much as possible. I reckon deep down I was terrified of letting the arm rest a moment and never being able to use it again. Terrified that I'd have to go through the process of having this one sawed off, and then what? So I knew the pain was a good sign if I could still move the arm.

"Lie back and open your jacket. I'll take a look at yours now," I said, wincing as I reached for him.

He didn't move. He just stared upward. "I'm cold, Lawrence."

"I'll build us a fire right away, but let me get you patched up first."

His fingers fumbled with the buttons, so I moved his hands out of the way to do it myself, and that's when I noticed the whole front of his jacket was sopping with blood. "Jesus," I said before I could stop myself.

"That bad?" His voice was thin and soft.

I got his jacket opened and then his shirt. "I'm not gonna lie to you, Murray. You've lost a lot of blood." I cleaned the area to find the wound, and he didn't even flinch. "How are you feeling?" I asked, glancing at his face.

"I'm cold."

The wound was now barely seeping blood. "I understand," I said, gazing at his face again to find his eyes fixed on the sky, unmoving. "Murray?"

I felt for his heart and knew before I did so that he was gone. "You knew, didn't you?" Coldness washed through my stomach before quickly warming. "That's why you wanted to get my arm patched up first, wasn't it? You knew I wouldn't have been able to do the bandaging myself." I glanced toward the ridgeline and twisted my mouth to hold back what I knew was coming. "Well, I'll make you this promise." I realized I was gritting my teeth, more to hold back the tears than out of anger, but the anger was there. "I will make sure that son of a bitch pays for this." I nodded. "I'll make sure the son of a bitch pays for all that he's done."

Chapter Thirty

All I could do was keep moving in the direction we'd been riding and hope Murray had actually known where the hell he was going. My arm burned from the gunshot wound and ached from the exertion of burying the corporal, but through it all, I was right thankful to be able to just move the damned thing.

I rubbed Daisy's neck and smiled at her twitching ear. "I know, girl. It can't be much further."

The midday sun put me a mite heavy in the saddle, keeping me sodden with sweat. And by the time its setting commenced, we was already out of the hills and rocky areas.

I couldn't find hide nor hair of that runaway horse. I was more interested in keeping the corporal's rifle out of the shooter's hands, but I reckoned getting caught with an army horse would have been a mite worse.

Daisy bobbed her head and slowed her pace. I quickly brought her to a halt and scanned the landscape in front of us. "What is it, girl?"

We were losing daylight, but I couldn't allow that to rush us into a dangerous situation. An emptiness filled my stomach, and I was fairly certain if I had hackles, they'd been raised at that very moment. There wasn't any campfire smoke or fresh tracks of any kind to speak of, but I trusted Daisy's sense of alarm as much as I did my very own.

I dismounted and moved us to the side of the road, where I tied Daisy to a small sapling and silently entered the sparsely wooded area. I studied everything in front of me, searching for movement or anything that would stand out, but nothing seemed out of the way or a danger.

A rustling came from just ahead and to the right of me. It wasn't sudden or threatening, but it reminded me of friends who tried to be silent in the forests back in Kentucky yet still managed to make more noise than a ground squirrel playing in dried leaves.

Focusing on that area, I waited to move just to make sure I didn't give away my position. And that's when the gunshot rang out, striking a nearby tree. I dropped to the ground as quietly as possible and drew my Colt.

My ears rang from the rifle's report, but I sat motionless, still scanning the area.

"Is that you, Thornhill?" It was the lieutenant's voice.

I just sat behind a tree without moving.

"I was a little surprised to see you back there with the corporal." The voice came from the same direction I'd heard the noises, but I still couldn't see him. "I'd heard you had been killed on your way back from Tall Junction."

All he was doing was trying to get me to reply so he could get a better read on my position.

"I guess the corporal was too scared and decided to go back."

I placed the Colt in my lap and picked up a small stone.

"Left you out here all alone, I guess."

Making sure to not strike anything close to me on the launch, I tossed the stone as far back behind the location I speculated him to be in so it would create a distraction.

Gunfire rang out again, this time targeting the area where I had thrown the stone.

"Are you sneaking up behind me, Thornhill?"

And this time the rustling revealed Collins was moving out of his cover, focusing his attention and rifle aim on the area I'd distracted him with. He had the butt of the rifle against the same shoulder as the arrow wound, and I noticed blood on his forearm. *I must have hit him in the exchange after all.*

"Let's just talk this over, Thornhill. Together we can get what we both want."

Retrieving the Colt from my lap, I knew cocking the hammer would surely give away my position, so I waited for an opportunity before making a move. Since he was addressing his words loudly, I decided to cock the hammer the next time he spoke, hoping it would be hidden in his words.

"I guarantee your friend will be fully exonerated and freed from jail."

I studied his face to see if he'd even noticed my action.

"What do you say, Thornhill? Let's do this together."

As slowly as I could manage, I lifted my Colt and took aim, simply waiting for him to speak again.

"After all, you and—"

The recoil and report of my Colt came as quickly as his crashing into the foliage. I brought the Colt back in front of me and waited as ringing filled my ears.

Other than a few more instances of rustling about, Collins was quiet. And I feared that was as much of a ploy as his talking was in order to draw me out. I just sat there as quietly as I could, waiting for something—anything.

I put the Colt back into my lap and picked up another small stone. I could ill afford a mistake that he was more than likely hoping for, so in the same manner, I tossed the stone into the area I'd thrown the last time. It crashed without a response. Silence.

Retrieving the Colt again, I held my focus to the area where I'd fired. A coldness came on me, and this time I knew it was because of the approaching darkness. I couldn't wait any longer.

I rose as quietly as possible and made my way forward, keeping my gaze and aim on the spot where I suspected he'd fallen. There was no movement and no noises, but I made sure this did not comfort me in the least.

I noticed the rifle 'fore I saw him. It was a few feet away, and he was just staring right at me. His forearm was bloodied with a bullet wound, but it looked to have been from earlier in the day during the exchange. His shirt was slick with blood, and I reckoned that's where I'd just shot him.

"You're a tough son of a bitch to get," he said, coughing.

His hand was close to his sidearm, but he didn't seem to realize it.

"You got my arm," I said, nodding toward the bandaged wound.

"I thought I got you, but I wasn't sure." He coughed again. "I was pretty sure I got the corporal as well."

"You got him in the gut." I pulled back the Colt's hammer as I held my aim on him. "He didn't make it."

"What about Rogers?" He coughed so hard I thought he was going to strangle himself. "Did you kill him?"

"This ain't no competition, Collins," I said, lifting my eyebrows. "You know that, right?"

"I just want to make sure you remember that you are no better than me."

"I reckon I understand that completely." I smiled. "But I didn't kill Rogers. I caught him and took him to a jail away from the Army, where he's confessed to everything the two of you have done."

Collins let into another coughing fit, turned his head, and spat blood. "You can't save your friend without me."

"And you can't save yourself without me. So don't give me nary a fearful bargaining."

He smiled and coughed again. "Just help me up, Lawrence, and we can help each other."

"Tell me something, Collins—"

"I am *Lieutenant* Collins! I am a commissioned officer in the United States Army." He coughed again and squinted. "You will address me with the respect I have earned."

"You ain't nothing but a piece of shit."

He reached for his revolver, and I squeezed the trigger, shooting him in the forehead. It happened so fast he wasn't even able to get the piece completely out of the holster.

"A dead piece of shit," I said, kicking the revolver away from his hand.

His eyes was blank, just staring up toward the heavens.

All I wanted to do was just sit down and relax. I realized the building tension had the muscles in my stomach cramped up. But with darkness coming, I had to move.

I holstered my Colt and started checking his pockets. The watch wasn't on him. A coldness washed through my gut and moved into my chest. "What the hell?"

I checked the area and found his horse hobbled nearby, where I discovered the gold watch inside his saddlebag. I put it in my pocket, retrieved a rope, and led the critter back to the lieutenant's body.

Laying the man over the back of the horse would have been hard enough as a one-armed fella, but when the one-armed fella has a gunshot wound in his only good arm, it made it damn near impossible. But I was able to manage with the rope, a tree branch, and Daisy pulling him up. I secured him as best as I could and ponied the dead man's horse behind us as we made our way to Fort Hays. Lord knows I was going to have a lot of explaining to do when we got there.

Chapter Thirty-One

I don't rightly know what I was expecting, but Fort Hays was certainly not what I envisioned. There was no wall around the damned place, for one thing, and it appeared to be nothing more than a number of settlement structures that just so happened to include a blockhouse.

My first thought was to just keep riding, as this was obviously a small town before getting to the actual fort. And I reckon that's exactly what I would have done, too, had I not noticed the soldiers standing guard at several posts.

The two soldiers at the fort's entrance stepped into the road as we approached. "Halt," one of the men said, raising his rifle without taking aim.

Bringing Daisy to a stop, I lifted my hand.

"Both hands, mister," the same soldier said, stepping closer.

"I would if I could," I said with a bigger smile than usual. "But I ain't got but the one."

"What do you have on the horse back there?" the second fella said, moving behind me.

"Dead man," I said, watching for the first fella's reaction. "Your executive officer, Lieutenant Collins."

"The lieutenant is dead?" The first soldier's face wilted, and then, with a sudden sense of urgency, he met my gaze. "Get down from the donkey!"

"Not a problem," I said, dismounting with my arm still raised. "I'm here to see Major Martin."

'Fore I knowed it, I was standing in front of a wiry sergeant whose disposition certainly explained his crooked nose. They'd already took my Colt and checked me for other weapons. And Lord knows I didn't have an idea where they took Daisy, Lieutenant Collins, or the horse he was tied to.

"You want to explain how you just showed up out of nowhere with a dead officer?" His left eye twitched a few times as his face reddened. "And not just *any* officer, mind you, we're talking about our executive officer, Lieutenant Collins."

Well, that's all it took for the knotted rope to find its way back into my stomach. "I understand how this must look and all," I said, nodding. "But it's a right long story, to be honest, and I reckon it's one the major will want to hear, seeing how it's about him and his stolen watch."

"How do you know about the watch?" The sergeant seemed to grow angrier the closer he stepped toward me. "Are you the no-good son of a bitch who stole it?"

"No sir," I said as a trickle of sweat made its way down my back. "But I know who did the thieving and who set it all up." I cleared my throat. "And I reckon I would like to tell all that directly to the major."

"I suppose so," he said, clenching his teeth. "And you can sure as hell hope to live long enough to do just that. But right now, you have to answer to me."

The knotted rope was now twisting in my gut. "I ain't trying to rile you none," I said, locking my gaze to his. "But I've been deceived far too many times during this whole mess." I shook my head. "And more than once by fellas wearing the same uniform you wear."

Well, this didn't take well at all with the sergeant, as you might imagine. His reddened face darkened even more somehow. "We've checked you and your donkey. You don't have the watch."

"Never said I had it." I smiled, letting him know I wasn't a feared of him, although I was damn near ready to mess my britches. "But you can guaran-damn-tee I know where it's at."

"Listen to—"

"And I am the *only* person who knows where it is." I lifted my eyebrows. "Now, what was it you were going to say?"

"I bet I can make you talk," he said, grabbing my lapels.

"There was a few fellas who said that to me a long time ago." I forced another smile. "One of them worked his way up my arm, cutting parts off it here and there as he went." I chuckled at the lie. "But that arm was all them sons of bitches got."

"I don't mind making your sleeves match."

"If that's what you reckon will do the job," I said in a low voice. "It's all fine by me. But I already told you that I am willing to explain every detail to the major." I smiled again and shook my head. "But because of recent dealings, I'm right sorry to say I don't trust nary a one of the rest of you."

The sergeant held his gaze to mine. No movement. Not a hint of what he was thinking. "Go tell the major the situation," he said to one of the soldiers without turning away. "Let him know I will do whatever he wants."

"I'm a thanking you," I said with a nod. "And just so you know, I respect you fellas. But a few of the crooked ones has made me distrustful in this whole situation."

"You keep saying that." He walked to a table and poured a coffee. "Just who, exactly, are you accusing of crookedness?"

"See, that's the problem. If I tell you, and you're in cahoots with 'em, then you're gonna do everything you can to make me out as a liar."

He sat down at the table and gestured to the seat across from him. "The major has already been made aware of the situation.

It's out of my hands now. So you might as well let me know who you're talking about."

I took the seat and made sure my hand rested on the tabletop within his eyesight. "See, here's the problem I'm dealing with," I said, nodding toward the door. "How do I know those fellas have actually gone off to inform the major at all?" I shrugged. "Hell, the man may not even be here at the fort right now, I don't know. But you saying what you said to them could have been nothing but a way to get me to tell you what I know."

He grinned and leaned forward. "You're smarter than I'd given you credit for. But a suspicioning mind is usually a conniving mind."

"Now that is something we can agree on." I glanced at my hand and noticed the reddening grime of blood. "I ain't saying I'm not guilty of any lawlessness, but I can tell you this: I've learned from mistakes . . . mine as well as many others'."

"Just so you know, those soldiers have gone to inform the major." He pushed the coffee toward me. "And the reason I want to know who it was you say dishonored their uniform is I want to make sure we get every one of those sons of bitches."

"Do you know Corporal Murray?"

A sneer crossed his face as he leaned back in his chair. "You're a damned liar. Murray is one of the best men to wear the uniform."

"There's another place where you and I will agree." I stared at my hand, rubbing my thumb and forefinger. "He came this way with me to help the major," I said, nodding. "Murray was a true man of honor." I gazed up at the sergeant's face. "He deserves a far better resting place than he's got right now."

The sergeant stared at the table. "Just tell me who did it. Just tell me where I can find the worthless son of a bitch who killed him."

"Well," I said as soft as I could muster. "I don't rightly know where your men took him when we came in here."

His face twisted up as he squinted. "Are you saying . . ."

"I'm afraid so. In fact, Lieutenant Collins is behind every bit of it."

He just sat there, staring at me without moving or speaking.

"I reckon now you see why I was a mite troubled to even talk about it." I shook my head. "Put yourself in my position. Would you want to carry a dead lieutenant to a fort where he's the executive officer and tell his men that he was guilty of being a thief and a murderer?"

He leaned forward again. "Do you have proof of any of this?"

"I caught one of his men and have the fella being held in a jail cell far away from here." I shook my head. "The boy admits to killing two fellas and attempting to do the same to me under the direct orders of your executive officer, Lieutenant Collins."

"My God." The sergeant closed his eyes and shook his head.

"Collins tried to cover his tracks, though. That's why the other two men were killed." I smiled and lifted my eyebrows. "And why he tried to kill me."

"And it was all for the major's gold watch."

"No sir, I believe the major's watch was a small part of a bigger plan."

I just about messed myself when the door banged open, and a husky older fella stepped inside like he was ready to strangle us all.

"Atten-hut!" the sergeant yelled as he rose to attention with the other soldiers in the room.

Chapter Thirty-Two

Major J. B. Martin moved toward the center of the room with fists planted firmly on his belt. "At ease," he said to the room and stared right into me.

I realized I was standing as well. I must have done so when the others got up.

"Is this him?"

"Yes sir," the sergeant said without moving his head.

"What's your name, boy?" His voice sounded like he'd been chewing broken glass and burnt shavings for years.

"Lawrence Thornhill."

"Thornhill?" His face wrinkled as he looked toward the rafters. "Are you any relation to Colonel Thornhill in Colorado?"

I shook my head. "I doubt it, sir." I gave him a nervous smile and wondered how awful it must have looked. "I'm from Kentucky."

"Sergeant, I'd like everyone but you and Mr. Thornhill to wait outside." The major sat himself at the end of the table and continued to stare at me.

"You heard the major," the sergeant said in a raised voice. "Everyone outside."

After all had exited and the door closed, Major Martin leaned forward. "They tell me you know where my watch is."

"I do, sir. I reckon I know the whole story."

The major leaned back at this and crossed his arms over his barrel of a chest. "And that's precisely what I want. The entire story."

He and the sergeant sat quietly as I told them everything from Jonathan breaking me out of jail dressed as an Army sergeant to the murderous actions and eventual ending of Lieutenant Collins. Lord have mercy, the knotted rope in my stomach felt like it was coming up my throat, trying to choke me to death the whole time.

"I never trusted Collins," the major said, shaking his head. "That's the reason I sent him to Sanderson in the first place." He glanced at the sergeant and then back to me. "The lying bastard even wanted to call on my daughter."

"I reckon he'd pulled the wool over all our eyes at some point." I leaned in a mite. "But that boy that's being held for those murders only did what he did because he was following the lieutenant's orders."

"He conspired to move up in the ranks because of his actions as well." The major rose to his feet, leaned forward, and placed his hands on the table. "One thing you failed to mention, Thornhill, is the location of the watch."

"Well, sir," I said and cleared my throat. "I wanted to make sure that Corporal Murray's body would be moved to a better location." I glanced again at the bloodstains on my hand. "That man deserves a place of honor in my estimation." I met the major's gaze. "So after the altercation with Collins, I tracked back to the corporal's grave and buried the watch with him. I didn't know you or any of your men, but I knew you would take the time to care for the corporal if you knew the watch was there."

A smile stretched across the old man's face. "Sergeant, I want you to take this man to the post surgeon and get that bullet removed." He turned to me. "Once Thornhill is up to it, you will take a buckboard with several men to the location he instructs you. You will retrieve Corporal Murray and bring him back here to have a proper burial. And you will bring the watch to me."

"I'd like to go ahead and get the corporal first, sir," I said, rising to my feet. "That is if you don't mind. My arm can wait, and I'd rather get that man where he belongs as soon as possible."

The major's smile broadened. "I appreciate the honor you give the corporal, son. But that arm is going to get treatment first." He turned to the sergeant. "And it will give your men adequate time to get everything together and planned."

"Yes sir," the sergeant said, rising to his feet.

The major removed his hands from the table and straightened his belt. "After all is said and done, Thornhill, you will come to my office for a more private talk."

My arm was sore from getting the bullet removed, but the new bandaging, although cumbersome, seemed a mite more comfortable somehow. We hadn't been back from collecting the corporal's body but minutes when the sergeant took me to see the major.

"I'd like to thank you for caring for Corporal Murray the way you did," the sergeant said before we entered the office. "You didn't have to do that, but I'm very thankful you did."

"Come in," the major's voice came from the other side of the door before I could reply.

The sergeant handed the major the gold watch and pointed to where I was to stand.

"Thank you, Sergeant," he said, inspecting the timepiece. "I assume everything went well with the corporal's retrieval?"

"As well as could be expected, sir."

"Good," the major said, looking up. "That will be all for now." He placed the watch to the side. "As for you, Mr. Thornhill, have a seat."

"Yes sir."

He made his way around his desk and sat against its edge in the front. "So how much of a reward are you expecting?"

"I don't want no reward, sir." I shook my head. "With all the grief it's caused, I'm just glad to be rid of the damned thing . . . all due respect, sir."

"Of course," he said with a smile.

"However, there is something I would ask of you."

He lifted his eyebrows and waited for me to continue.

"You're holding my friend at the Sanderson jail for stealing horses." I tried to remain calm and not get ahead of myself. "I would like to ask you to consider dropping those charges and letting him go before he is brought here to be hanged."

"I see," he said, moving back to the chair behind his desk. "And what is this man's name?"

"Ezra Tackett." I leaned closer. "He saved my life when I lost my arm . . . more than once. I just want to do everything I can to return the favor."

The major started going through papers on his desk without a word.

I couldn't help but continue talking in the silence. "It's my understanding the horses were all returned, and I'm sure he's learned his lesson."

"Ah, I thought the name was familiar for some reason," he finally said, gazing up from a document, his face turning dour. "It is with much regret that I must inform you that your friend, Ezra Tackett, has died." He handed me the letter. "Apparently, Mr. Tackett made yet another escape attempt, stealing a revolver from one of the guards and shooting the man before being mortally wounded by another guard."

"Jesus," I said as the coldness came over me. "I can't believe he's dead."

"If it is any consolation at all, Mr. Thornhill, I want you to know I would have most certainly granted your request." His gaze went to the letter in my hand. "But not because of the watch. I would have granted your request solely because of the respect and honor you have given Corporal Murray."

The coldness burned and festered in my gut. "I'm a thanking you, sir."

The major took out a cigar and lit it. "The watch was a gift from my father," he said with a smile that obviously wasn't meant for me. "He was a lawyer back east and was as proud as he could be when I received my commission." He took a draw and blew smoke upward.

"He and I would run hounds when I was younger." He chuckled to himself. "It was about the only time he ever took with me, I guess."

The only thing going through my thinking was how I was going to tell Aunt Alice the news. "It's a right handsome watch, sir."

"I'm sorry about your friend, Thornhill." He nodded slowly. "Let's revisit our talks of a reward, shall we?"

"I appreciate you thinking of me, sir. But like I said, I didn't come here for no reward." Lord knows I fought back those tears with everything in me. "I came here for one thing, and I reckon I'm a mite too late."

"I understand that, but . . ." His eyes held a sadness he didn't seem to know what to do with.

"I reckon a reward would feel like I'd betrayed Ezra somehow." I shook my head and chuckled. "As queer as that may sound, I just wouldn't feel right by taking any money with all that's gone on." I gazed into his eyes. "But I sure do appreciate your willingness."

"Well, you get yourself rested and healed," he said, rising to his feet. "Stay as long as you need before thinking about getting back on the trail."

"I'm a thanking you, sir." I stood, not knowing what to do next.

"And when you are ready to ride, I'm sending a few men to escort you safely to wherever it is you're going."

I nodded as I willed the sobs back. "I'm a thanking you, sir."

Chapter
Thirty-Three

Iwanted to be sure I was ready for the long haul back to Warren's Gap with the limitations of an injured arm. For most folks, that wouldn't present much of a problem, but when you're nursing a gunshot wound in your only arm, it could be a mite cumbersome for the simplest tasks, such as getting in and out of the saddle or just trying to stay in the danged thing at all.

I didn't think I was ever going to talk them bluecoats into letting me ride out on my own for a few hours, but they finally consented to it. Lord knows I didn't want nary a one of them fellas around if I happened to fall off Daisy or if I started moaning or yelping from too much pain.

I couldn't help but wonder how a single bullet wound in the arm was able to stiffen and ache nearly every part of my carcass at one time or another. The fort's doctor said the rest of my body was compensating for the arm's inability to function properly and was complaining about it.

I told him if that was the case, my entire body was telling that arm to go straight to hell.

Daisy seemed to recognize that I wasn't feeling my best and made her movements a little slower and less jarring. At least that's what it felt like to me.

"You're a good one to have around, girl," I said with a smile. "I declare, if you don't look after me better than my own brother."

About an hour into the ride, all my worries were relieved just knowing I'd have no more of an issue on the upcoming trip than any other rider. Don't get me wrong, I knew it wasn't going to be easy, but I was convinced I would be able to push through the pain and stiffness.

Turning to head back toward the fort, a blur of movement just to the right caught my attention as something struck me in the chest, knocking me to the ground with such a force I lost all my breath. I tried sitting up, struggling like a fish out of water, only I was desperately trying to get air down inside me instead of water.

"T'ought you'd seen the last o' me, didn't ya, T'ornhill." Jarvis O'Sullivan stood by the roadside holding the tapered end of a black walking stick with a bulbous knob at its other end.

I reached for my Colt but found the holster empty. "Shit," I said, holding my chest, thankful my air was back.

"Packs quite a wallop, doesn't it?" O'Sullivan held up the shiny stick. "I t'ought it'd be appropriate to finish you off with me father's shillelagh."

"One thing about it," I said, rubbing the ache in my chest as I climbed to my feet, "you're much better with that thing than you are with lynching."

O'Sullivan limped my way, ready to swing again. "It's in me blood." The knotty end of the wood just missed my head as I barely ducked away.

Upon my honor to God, if it wasn't a downright chore trying to keep from getting my brains bashed in while my body was already stiff and sore—all while searching for my missing Colt.

Daisy began foraging by the side of the road as though nothing was going on around her to cause alarm or excitement.

"I t'ink it will do me father's honor good knowing it was his blackthorn that avenged his death." O'Sullivan swung the stick again, striking the ground as I moved.

I caught the glint of gunmetal not too far away as the boy was winding up for another swing. "Let's talk about this, Jarvis," I said, moving closer to the Colt.

"There's nothing left to talk about, T'ornhill." He swung again, causing me to duck to the ground just in time to scoop up the pistol. But by the time I got it aimed, the bastard struck the damn thing right out of my grip.

Pain engulfed my hand and wrist like I was reaching into a raging fire. I knew I didn't have time to retrieve the Colt because another blow was coming my way. As O'Sullivan swung overhead and brought the stick downward, I lunged into him, sending him stumbling backward before slamming into Daisy's rear end, where the old gal kicked him so hard he hit the ground with a force I'd never witnessed before.

"Jaysus!" He used the stick to pull himself to his feet before dropping immediately as his leg wasn't cooperating. "Jaysus, Joseph, and Mary."

Snatching up my Colt, I rushed toward the boy and placed a boot on the stick. "That's enough, O'Sullivan."

"Me leg's broke," he said with a trembling voice. "I can't even stand on the damned t'ing."

His revolvers were still holstered, but they seemed to be the last thing on his mind.

"Help me, T'ornhill," he said, gazing up like a trapped fawn. "We'll call it even, you and me. Just help me, and I swear you'll never see my face again."

I knelt next to the boy and placed the muzzle of my Colt against his forehead. "Toss your revolvers as far away as you can." My voice sounded hoarse in my ears, deeper than normal. "One at a time. Nice and slow."

His gaze never left mine as he eased the first pistol out and tossed it to the side. "There be the first one," he whispered. I'm not sure he even blinked as he did the same with the second. "There we go."

I stared quietly without moving. "Now I want you to remove that lock of hair from around your neck and hold it out to me."

There was something in his eyes at that moment that wasn't there just seconds earlier—recognition, pain, or regret—possibly all three at the same time. "Not a problem," he said, easing the twine necklace from his head and holding it out toward me. "I hope you'll forgive me. I'm sorry."

Using the barrel of the Colt to pull the necklace from his fingertips, I nodded. "I'm sure you are, O'Sullivan."

"If you can just help me back in the saddle, this will be the last that you'll ever see of me." He offered a smile that didn't seem to even convince himself. "I swear to you."

I stood and glanced back toward the fort. "If I were to do that, I'd be watching over my shoulder for the rest of my days."

"I swear to you—"

"No, I reckon the best thing I can do is just go ahead and reunite you with your pa and brother." I shrugged. "Then you can all three meet me at the gates of hell when I eventually get there."

"If you want me to beg—"

"It won't make a difference, O'Sullivan. I will not make the same mistake again." I aimed the Colt toward his chest. "And I will not risk you hurting those closest to me."

He stared at me without movement. "If you t'ink you can just kill me point-blank like this while I am unarmed, then you just go right on ahead and do it."

"You need to understand one thing, boy," I said with a grin. "You're looking into the eyes of a wolf. I ain't no damn farm dog."

The Colt's report echoed across the valley as smoke drizzled from the barrel. The boy's eyes were frozen in that same defiant glare as blood darkened his unmoving chest.

I holstered my piece and kicked the big stick away. "You won't be needing this thing any longer."

I heard riders in the distance and moved toward Daisy, still foraging as though nothing had happened. "I'm a thanking you, girl." I rubbed her side as she continued eating. "You sure got me out of a real mess."

I could see several soldiers riding toward us in the distance, obviously checking on the gunshot they'd heard. I studied the lock of hair in my hand before placing the twine necklace around my head. "I'll see to it these fellas bury you somewhere safe, O'Sullivan." I shook my head. "Lord knows I'm too sore and stiff to even think about it."

Chapter Thirty-Four

Imay have been riding back to Warren's Gap with four of the major's men, but I don't reckon I'd ever felt so alone in all my live-long days. I was empty—just a husk of a man. And if I'm being right honest, I reckon the hardest part was the fact that I never doubted for one moment that I was going to get Ezra freed. I was so sure I was taking him back home to Aunt Alice, where we'd all set out whiskey for the Indians and eat cat-head biscuits until our bellies were full.

And now he was gone.

I don't reckon I'd ever been so angry either. I was downright furious with Ezra for stealing horses and getting himself caught like he did, and for making things even worse by trying to escape. And then I'd get just as angry at myself for blaming him or for not being able to help like I wanted.

The soldiers rode on to Sanderson when I turned in toward the board house. One of them handed me a purse and said it was from the major. 'Fore I could argue or decline, they ignored my calls and hurried on down the way. The purse held more than several gold and silver coins. I didn't bother to count it—I just put it away and headed on toward the stable.

I was getting Daisy into her stall and removing the saddle when I heard the back door of the house close. My stomach growled, and I realized I hadn't eaten in a spell.

"Lawrence?" Mrs. Appleton's voice was soft and hopeful. "Is that you?"

Upon my honor to God, when I turned and saw the compassion in that woman's face, it was all I could do to keep myself together.

Her gaze went to my bandaged arm, and she ran to me. "Are you all right?"

"Yes ma'am."

She hugged into me with her head on my chest. "We have prayed for the Good Lord to keep you safe every day you've been gone."

"I'm a thanking you, ma'am."

She placed her hands on my face and stared up at me. "Let me look at you," she said, near tears. "I am so thankful the Lord has answered our prayers."

"Lawrence!" Rose's voice carried from somewhere outside as I could hear her running toward the stable. She stopped at the door just long enough to stare for a moment. "It *is* you!"

Mrs. Appleton barely got out of her way when Rose clung to me in tears. "I've been worried sick about you." She quickly pulled back when she noticed the bandaging. "What happened?"

"I got myself shot," I said, trying to smile so they wouldn't get upset none. "But I'm fine."

"Come inside when you're ready," Mrs. Appleton said. "I'm going to get you something to eat."

Rose stared up at me with reddened eyes.

"I know you've had—"

I'm here to tell you that girl put both hands to the sides of my head and pulled me in to kiss me right square on the mouth. Now don't get me wrong, I wasn't angered by it nary a bit, but I sure was surprised.

"Rose," I said, catching my breath. "I know I gave you a lot to ponder while I was gone, but—"

"I've done a lot of thinking, Lawrence . . . a lot of praying as well." She smiled. "And, well, I don't care what you've done in your past. Or even things you've done more recently."

Warmth tingled in my cheeks.

"I *know* the man you are," she said, nodding. "In fact, I look at you and see the man I know you want to be."

I just smiled at her.

"What's this?" she asked, touching the lock of hair around my neck.

Well, I reckon it didn't take long for that emptiness I was feeling to get filled up. "Nothing," I said, pulling the dad-blasted thing off and tossing it aside. "Nothing at all."

She gave me a curious smile.

"I want you to go with me somewhere." I shook my head. "Not today, but when me and Daisy can rest up a bit."

"All right."

"I have something I need to get done, and I sure would be happy knowing you were there with me when I did it."

It's right peculiar how just a few days of eating good and resting peaceful-like is all it takes to get a gunshot wound on the mend. Although I have to admit, Rose and Mrs. Appleton tried their darndest to get me to wait a week or more before making the trip.

I borrowed Parnell's buckboard so Rose could ride on the bench next to me. I also borrowed his donkey so Daisy wouldn't have to do so much of the pulling. Lord knows I was happy to learn his donkey was a female, as I didn't want to have to intervene or separate the two when staked.

"You remember me talking about my friend who just passed?" I said to Rose as we rode through terrain so rough I thought it was going to jar our guts right out from under us.

"I do," she said with a sweet smile. "Ezra."

I nodded. "Well, Ezra apparently robbed a bank somewhere and hid the money before getting caught. Nobody was ever able to find it. That's how Jonathan and I met. Ezra knew he was about to be hanged for horse thievery and told Jonathan where he buried the money." I smiled. "But Ezra didn't tell him where that location was—he just told him that I would know the location when he revealed it to me, and then Jonathan and I could split the money."

"I see. So Ezra was looking out for you."

"That's exactly right, but the thing is, Jonathan never got around to telling me the location. You see, I didn't trust him, and he didn't trust me." I grinned. "But I know exactly where Ezra buried the money."

She laughed. "So that's where we're going?"

I laughed along with her. "Yes ma'am. And I'm looking forward to introducing you to Aunt Alice as well." I shook my head. "I reckon she's about as close to kin as I've got. In fact, she is the only kin I've got now."

I started digging and could tell right away the dirt had been disturbed not too long back. "Ezra told Jonathan there was right close to ten thousand dollars buried here."

"Are you sure this is the spot?"

"Ain't a doubt in my mind," I said, continuing to dig.

"Ten thousand dollars," she said, shaking her head. "Are you planning to give that money back to the bank?"

I looked up at her. "No ma'am. If I was to do that, then you and I would be suspects, and they'd probably put the two of us in jail to be hanged." I commenced to digging more. "I reckon the best we can do is keep the money and not tell a soul."

That seemed to satisfy her for the moment. "How are you so sure this is the right spot?"

"Hold on," I said, moving more dirt out. "I think I've hit something."

I reached into the hole and tugged at a heavy sack matted with dirt. "I gotta make it bigger."

"Did you find the money?"

"It appears so," I said, continuing to dig. "It sure feels like it."

I tried again and managed to drag the damned thing out. "Lord have mercy," I said, sitting back to catch my breath. "I knew it would be here."

She knelt beside me as I fumbled to open the sack. "How?"

"Well," I said, pausing. "This is the one place that only Ezra and I knew about." I smiled and gazed toward the hole. "A mite deeper there, and we'd find my arm."

She put her hands to her mouth. "Oh my."

"Don't worry," I said, opening the sack. "I don't want to see that thing any more than you do." The strings pulled away on the sack. "There we go."

I ain't gonna lie about it none. I'm here to tell you I don't reckon I've ever seen so much gold in all my life put together. "If that ain't enough money to burn a wet mule," I said.

"My goodness," Rose whispered, finally moving her hands away from her lips.

"Help me get this to the buckboard," I said, closing the sack. "The last thing we need is for someone to see this."

"And then what?"

I smiled. "I reckon we'll stop somewhere and get a few sacks of flour, sugar, and coffee to put around it so it don't stand out none." I pulled her close to me. "And then we'll head on to Aunt Alice's place. She'll be happy to meet you for sure." My stomach soured a mite. "But Lord knows all the news I have for her ain't gonna be good."

Acknowledgements

I've been privileged to work with some of the most talented people in the publishing industry, and if there's one thing I've learned over the years, it's that it takes a village to build a home in any genre. There are far too many to name who have offered advice, lent a hand, or even stuck their neck out for me along the way. But I do want to acknowledge a few who played a part in bringing this book to life.

First and foremost, my thanks to Tony Acree and everyone at Lawless Trails Press, an imprint of Hydra Publications. I'm also deeply grateful to Heather Graham, Johnny D. Boggs, Michael Zimmer, Cherry Weiner, Lee Murray, Ben Henry Bailey, Jeffrey J. Mariotte, Vonn McKee, Bobbi Jean Bell, and Matthew Pizzolato for their steadfast support and friendship.

MICHAEL KNOST is a two-time Bram Stoker Award®-winner and has written in various genres and helmed dozens of anthologies. Michael received the Horror Writers Association's Silver Hammer Award in 2015 for his work as the organization's mentorship chair and was recognized as the 2021 Mentor of the Year from the organization. He also received the prestigious J.U.G. (Just Uncommonly Good) Award from West Virginia Writer's Inc. and was recently inducted into the inaugural class of the Imagination Hall of Fame in July of 2025. His novel *Return of the Mothman* has been filmed as a movie adaptation, and he has taught writing classes and workshops at several colleges, conventions, online, and currently resides in Chapmanville, WV with his wife and daughter.